CONFESSIONS OF
A BADD WIFE

A NOVEL BY
ZEE. W

www.zbookpublishing.com

ZBook Publishing, LLC
P.O. Box 2085
Stone Mountain, GA 30087
www.zbookpublishing.com

Confessions of A Badd Wife
First Edition

ZBook Publishing, LLC

ISBN-13: 9781941689011

ISBN-10: 1941689019

LCCN: 2018910821

Book Cover Design by Marion Designs

www.mariondesigns.com

TABLE OF CONTENTS

DEDICATION

This book is dedicated to my biggest supporter in life, my mother (Emah), Chris Ann Lewis. You support all of my accomplishments, big and small. Not only are you an amazing mother, but you are also an amazing human being. Words cannot express how much I love and appreciate you. You do so much for me and my siblings and are our biggest fan club. You listened to every story I told when I was younger; you read every short story and novel I've written. You have seen my work in its rawest form (just as a paper manuscript) because you refused to wait for the book to be published before reading it. You always give me positive feedback and make me feel like my talent is supernatural. If it wasn't for your constant love, encouragement, and celebration of my gift, I would not have the courage to be where I am today. You are beyond a blessing to me. Thanks for everything you do… *This book will always be for you.* I love you, Mommy.

— Zee. W

ACKNOWLEDGMENTS

Thanks to everyone who read my first published title, *Badd Wives*. Your feedback, Facebook shares, emails, and reviews is confirmation that my *Gifts Have Made Room for Me*.

Thanks to all my sisters. Getting through life is so much sweeter because of the four of you (Chyah, Hahnah, YaMemah, Deborah). You guys love me without fault and celebrate me every chance you get. Most people are blessed just to encounter one soulmate, I'm blessed because I have four (my sisters). Thanks to my brother Matthew Zadok who always makes me feel like a genius and whose wisdom has guided me in my journey.

And as always, thanks again to Katura Tucker (FYI: you're always going to make this page...always ☺) You were there from book one and I know you will be there for the last. It means a lot to me.

Thanks to Betty Celestian, a person who celebrates me and loves me just like family. You always have a way of making me feel like I'm the perfect pretty, the perfect smart, and the perfect creative. (I borrowed Vinci's name for this book, lol)

And to the little loves of my life, my nieces and nephews, Kaylah, Jyah, Eleazar, Alyjah, Roniyah, Maliyah, Levi, Tolu, and the beautiful little bundle that's still cooking... I can't wait to meet you...

Thanks, Jide...all the opportunities that you gave me helped finance my dreams. You truly are family.

And last but not least, thanks to my daughter just for being my daughter; bold, beautiful, courageous, and unique, Abri Gabrielle. You are so rare; there is no one on this planet like you!!

— Zee. W

PROLOGUE

DALLA BADD

Ace told me he was going to kill me. At first, I didn't believe him. I even laughed at the threat. I didn't think he could; it wasn't supposed to be possible. After all, I was a Badd and untouchable to everyone, including him. But, after years of planning, tonight he's finally going to get what he's been waiting for. When I hear a baby let out a gut-wrenching scream sounding as if someone pinched him or he just woke from a horrible nightmare, I know he's going to die too. Ace is sick enough to kill a baby. I hear the baby scream and I want to run to him, but I can't. I want to save them all, but I can't. What have I done? Lord, what have I done?

Blood is everywhere. Badd blood has finally been spilled. It's streaming, pouring, and dripping everywhere they lay. All I can do now is watch it pour from the bodies that once contained it. I watch the blood change forms. It can go from thin to thick in a matter of seconds. When it's fresh, it's a beautiful bright red but that changes after a while. Then, there's nothing beautiful about it. Especially when it's being coughed up in large clumps or flowing from places you didn't know can bleed. It's no neat mess like the movies either. This is a grotesque sight and I have front row seats to witness all the horror. Ace wanted a blood bath and he got it. It looks like he is finally winning his war against the Badds and he has me to thank for it.

"*Kneel*," Ace says to Taffy calmly. Ace has Taffy sitting on both knees at the edge of his pool. Just before he brought her out, he had one of his men fearfully lead two of his gators into the water. Ace considers the gators to be pets but really, they're killers and he planned to feed them Taffy tonight. They're swarming in the water in circles; they're anxious and hungry.

I didn't expect it to end this way. When I met with Bobby a few months ago, I was desperate and running out of time. I spent the last year planting moles at the Ranch and spying as much as I could, but it was all pointless until Bobby showed up with Lera. It was my first break since I fled the Ranch. Lera was my link to Bobby. And Bobby was my way out of this mess; At least I thought he was.

Bobby was a hard nut to crack. He didn't want to believe me when I told him the truth about how his mother died, but I had the proof; the real autopsy report revealing that his mother's death wasn't a suicide but a murder. So, he had to believe me. Brock, the oldest Badd brother, killed their mother to protect the secret that's keeping him in control of the Badd Ranch. Being a Badd and running the Ranch is Brock's entire existence. He'd do anything to protect his position, including kill his own. If the truth got out, he stood to lose everything.

The secret is that Brock isn't a real Badd but the product of an affair with the Badd's only rival, Carlo Lucky. The Lucky family is now run by Ace Lucky. When Brock's mother confessed the truth to him, he killed her thinking that the secret would die with her, but he was wrong.

Ace is petting Taffy on top of her head like she's a dog. It's almost as if he has compassion for her trembling body but he doesn't. Taffy doesn't try to fight anymore. She just does what he says. I warned her about trying to resist Ace but at first, she didn't listen. That's why her left eye is swollen shut and she has thick red welts around her neck. Taffy endured days of savage beatings and assaults by Ace. But now, she finally believes that he is going to kill her. She didn't know that Ace was as sadistic as he was. She didn't know that in his house, her Badd necklace could not protect her. It was the one place in this city that wasn't welcome.

Taffy has been a Badd so long that she did believe that she was invincible. Everybody did and they used to be right, but tonight Ace Lucky is going to prove them all wrong. Ace motions with his hand and one of his men throws him a thick rope he kneels on one knee behind Taffy and starts to tie her hands behind her back. Taffy begins to sob. "Don't cry," Ace says softly to her. "You're about to be a part of history." He kisses her on the cheek and ties another knot in the rope; Taffy squinches.

My plan was for Bobby to help me free Billy. Thanks to my informant, I knew exactly where he was. In Brock's prison on the Ranch and the last I heard, he was still alive. I told Bobby the truth about his mother to get him on my side. I told him that Billy would be next if he didn't do something. I caught his attention then. Brock had Bobby and the others thinking that me and Billy stole from the family safe and fled but that wasn't true.

The night Billy and I supposedly stole from the family safe and fled, I planted a bug in Brock's ear and it's still driving him mad to this day. I took Brock's dirt and used it against him. I told him that Billy killed their father to vindicate his mother's death. Brock was so focused on finding Billy that he gave me enough time to escape. It's how I got away; just as I planned. As strange as it sounds, I lied to protect us both. At the time, I figured Billy was safer with Brock than he was with Ace who had a bounty on his head. If Ace got to him first, he would've killed him right away, but Brock needed him alive. At least long enough to find me. I'm the last person that knows his secret besides, Ace.

Brock's not like Ace. He's no murderer. Although he killed his mother, he considered her a causality of war. I knew it wouldn't be that easy for him to kill Billy. He had to be sure that I wasn't lying first and that meant he was going to take a lot of time investigating and contemplating, just as he's been doing. I spent the entire year sending Brock on dummy missions just to delay Billy's death. I've kept myself busy sending Brock one fake lead after another. Including fake leads of my whereabouts.

Brock wanted me dead more than he did Billy. I knew too much and during his investigations, I'm sure he linked me to a lot of other shit that made him even more nervous like my marriage to Ace. But, without Billy, Brock knew he would never find me. That's one reason Billy is still alive. Once Brock found me, he planned on killing us both and then his secret would be dead forever. Or at least that's what he thought. I knew Bobby would do anything to get Billy back. He loved his brother. He even loved Brock, but he had to do what was right. Bobby had one hell of a conscience. I know that because I played off every bit of it to get to where I was going. That's when I came up with the plan for him to fake his death. I figured he could move around better presumed dead than alive. I was surprised when he agreed with me. He thought it was a great idea and it was. Of all the days to do it, he chose his wedding day. It was perfect timing. If there was anything real about Bobby, it was his love for Lera. No one would've expected him to do anything fishy on the day he was to say I do to Lera and receive his inheritance check; we pulled it off but now everything has backfired.

Ace pulls a red bandana out of his jacket pocket and places it over Taffy's eyes to blindfold her. Before Ace covers her eyes, Taffy gives me a horrified look but there's nothing I can do. Out of everybody, I feel like I owe her the most but I'm helpless. Taffy trusted me once. Even loved me but that's all over now. Taffy bites down hard on her bottom lip and takes a brave deep breath and sucks up her last tear. The girl is tough. Ace is so amused by her bravery, that he chuckles. Then he gets mad. He wants her to plead for her life. He wants her to beg him but Taffy isn't going to give him the pleasure.

Ace yanks her up to her feet and shakes her a bit. He whispers something in her ear that causes Taffy to shudder then screams, "Lights, camera…. action," sporting an evil smirk. Within a matter of minutes, I hear a loud thump and bright lights beam out in every direction from the ceiling. Then, out walks three men with cameras. Ace plans on broadcasting Taffy's death live so that everybody connected to the Badds can see. He wants to ruin their reputation. If the tape of Taffy's death gets out, The Badds will be considered weak. It looks like the set of a movie but unfortunately, it's all real. I hear the baby crying again and it gets even more real. I have to do something but I'm helpless. I'm all plotted out; there's nothing left in me.

My initial plan was just to free Billy but that evolved over time. Once Billy was free, I didn't care what happened to the rest of them. I was going to reunite with my family and flee. But all of that has changed. I'm too involved now. It would have all worked out if Bobby would have just trusted me a little more. He started to ask too many damn questions. Questions I couldn't answer. At that point I'd lied so much, I didn't know fact from fiction. I avoided his questions the best I could, but they just kept coming. He interrogated me about his father's death and his mother's death. He wanted to know who I really was and how I knew so much about his family. I told him the same stories over and over again but that wasn't enough for him. Bobby was trying to find loop holes. He was too suspicious, and he had good reason to be. It was obvious what was going on though; somebody was talking in his ear and turning him against me by telling him things I didn't need him to know and in turn, fucking up my plan. I needed Bobby just as much as he needed me, but he didn't trust me the way I trusted him. That complicated things and in the end, led to the disaster I'm witnessing now.

What can I do to stop this or at least delay the time before the others get here? If they come at all. Ace is pushing Taffy closer and closer to the edge of the pool. The gators are getting anxious, gliding around the pool, lurking at Taffy with their heads just above the water. They can smell the blood and the fear on her. I hear Ace ask Taffy if she's ready to die. He has his hand out ready to shove her in the water. Taffy responds to him. She screams, "fuck you." Not what Ace was expecting to hear. He's stunned by her reaction and offended. Ace hates being disrespected, especially by women. At that point, I know it's over. When Ace places his boot on her back to kick her in the pool, I close my eyes and pray. There's nothing else I can do.

1

DALLA LUCKY

Three Years Earlier

I want out. I've punished myself enough. Even Hitler doesn't deserve the shit I put myself through with Ace. No one does, yet here I am. Ace Lucky or to some, Lucky Ace. He never loses, but I'm not that lucky. I snort another line of coke and lean back. My body is getting numb and my thoughts are light. I got to quit this shit. It used to feel like an escape, but now it just feels like a trap. I feel like a living corpse; the undead.

I hear footsteps tapping evenly down the hall. By the sound of thick soles echoing against the marble floor, I know it's Ace. He's wearing his party shoes. A pair of custom-made alligator boots. I can make his footsteps out from miles away. He walks like's he counting. Timing every movement like it means something. Hearing his footsteps reminds me of the theme music that plays during the climax scenes of horror movies. My heart races just the same, wandering what's going to happen when the footsteps finally stop and I'm face to face with him; the monster with the face of a man.

The heels of his shoes sound like iron and feel like it too. I know this because yesterday while trying them on for the first time, he slid off his boot and knocked me in the face with it. Then he laughed and kissed the puff that swelled instantly under my eye. He told me he hit me because he wanted to see if I would jump. I didn't. I didn't cry either. Instead of being hurt, I was relieved. I was dazed and eventually passed out a few minutes after which was a good thing because that meant I didn't have to see him or his crazy mother and sister for hours. His family is beyond fucked up. I wish I never woke up, but I did. Now, he's coming to my room to see how close I am to being ready for his party. I hate his parties. He throws one every night of the week. His parties are his entire existence, and they are just like him; over the top and sick.

I snort harder. I need to be numb by the time he walks through the door. The clicks get even closer, and I cringe. I finish my last line and even though I've been doing this shit all day, I don't feel numb enough. I take a swallow of Gin straight from the bottle and dab against the bruises on my face with foundation. It's not working. My foundation is no match to the reddish blue welt resting under my left eye. This is going to piss him off.

Without seeing him, I know he's wearing one of his flamboyant, loud-colored silk dress suits with a polka dot bow tie and matching hat, looking like a cartoon version of a pimp. He's wearing a shit load of cologne. He probably just had his glam squad put the finishing touches on his manicure and is freshly shaved. The man the v in vain. Every morning, he spends hours with his hired staff, getting ready like a celebrity does before a show. He changes his outfit three times a day. He buries his low self-esteem in clothing and expensive colognes.

He has his morning wear, usually more casual. Never jeans though. Always perfectly pressed slacks an expensive polo shirt and nonprescription eyeglasses. If I look at him through squinted eyes, he could almost pass for a professor. Then for the afternoon, he's a little more free-flowing and artsy; he's going through his rock star phase. He's probably wearing suspenders with a collared shirt and cut-off shorts with loose threads dusting over his calves and boots that never seem to match but somehow, he pulls them off and of course, his staple sunglasses. I call them his male Marylin Monroe's. And, at night, he's always in his pimp suits and hats.

I really do hate him. He's an anal, sadistic, sociopath but he's also my husband. So, what does that make me? I bend down ready to sniff another line, but nothing is there.is I open the drawer to my vanity and notice that I'm fresh out of coke. No worries though. It's like Ace grows the shit on trees and it'll be mountains of it at his party tonight. I settle for another swig of Gin and continue to cake my face with makeup. I look like a fucking vampire, and I don't care. Ace will. He's just as much into my appearance as he is his own. It's like I'm the Barbie doll he plays dress up with. He picks out all my clothes and instructs the stylist on how to do my hair. When he sees me barely dressed and looking like a coked-out zombie, he's going to have a fit. Maybe he'll hit me with his boot again. At least if I'm lucky. That way, I'll be excused from his weekly, Wednesday night sex party. I hate his fucking orgy parties. They are full of circus freaks just like him.

I have to pretend to be amused by all the shenanigans going on and sometimes I am. It's a lot to see at his parties. At the party, he has a woman fucking a donkey, men-on-men action, and a whole bunch of other shit you won't see in the most grotesque porno. But the coke is being passed around like sugar in a candy store and the drinks are bottomless.

You'll be surprised at how many sophisticated, supposedly elite freaks are into this stuff. Black, White, Chinese; all kinds of people attend Aces' secret society-like parties and they are all filthy rich. It's great networking for Ace. It's how he gets and gives favors, without having to work, and keeps him in the inner circle of the elites. They're just as fucked up as he is. A pretentious group of insatiable rich maniacs. With all the fucking going on around them, nobody acts like they're looking but they are. They are getting turned on but don't dare show it. They chat among each other like the sounds of the woman moaning and coming to a fucking donkey's dick in her ass is no different than somebody playing the violin or cello; it's music to their perverse ears. They sip their champagne, snort their coke, and chit-chat among each other like they're at the Masonic ball.

Among the guests are Lady L and Angelo. His mother and sister. Lady L glides around the party, playing the social butterfly, greeting everybody by last name while holding her champagne flute in one hand and her designer bag in the other. She's flaunting her money and her latest plastic surgery. If you spot her with her back turned, her ten-foot wavy weave and perfectly petite tight body would have you think she's in her early twenties then she turns around and you want to scream. Lady L has to be at least sixty-five and if you look at the wrinkled lumps of hanging flesh in her neck, you can tell that she hides them with expensive scarves or turtleneck shirts. She thinks she's beautiful, but she looks like a plastic surgery nightmare.

The Botox has her face looking like a distorted blow fish and all the nose and lip jobs she's had affects her mouth. She can barely spread her lips when she speaks but that doesn't stop her from talking. She's a very chatty woman and in some kind of way, she's mastered a phony French accent. All she talks about is money and her riches. She wears a diamond ring on every finger and both arms are covered with dozens of diamond-crusted bangles. It's obvious she puts a lot of effort into trying to look rich. When she's not talking about money or cursing Ace out about giving her more money to blow, she's fucking young boys. They don't look older than 21. She takes them everywhere she goes; they're her entourage and she treats them like accessories by the way their outfits correlate with hers. Most of them are gay but she doesn't care. Ace gets his evil wit from her. The woman is a walking nightmare and although she's tiny, she's as viscous as a snake.

Angelo, formerly known as Angela, is always in the corner looking like a street thug. I didn't know Angelo when she was Angela, but I saw a picture of her and she used to be pretty. But now, she looks a hot mess. Angelo stays in a black wife beater and baggy pants that expose her boxers which she complements with matching tennis shoes. She wears a baseball cap turned backward and always has a cigar behind her ear. She's in the transition for a sex change. Her vagina is still in tack, but she had her breast cut off. Her hair is cut low and she's got a mustache and little peach fuzz popping out around her cheeks. Even with all the hormones, she still has to fake a deep voice. I guess she's supposed to be the muscle. She's just as tiny as her mother but what she lacks in strength, she makes up in knives. The girl or guy or whatever she is, is obsessed with knives and knows how to use them. I close my eyes really tight every time Ace gives her a chance to cut a person. She can make a human bleed like a stuffed pig.

Angelo is violent and tough as nails, but she has it more together than Ace and her mom. Glued to her hip is who she calls her wife, Flo; tranny who is transitioning into becoming a full woman. They are the strangest couple I've ever seen, and I mean *Guinness Book of World Records* kind of strange. Flo wears a weave ponytail that dusts the crack of her ass. Her makeup is always perfect but there is no mistaking that she is a man. There is no way around her big masculine features. Flo towers over Angelo but Angelo is very vocal about who wears the pants in the relationship; no pun intended. Flo is six feet tall and with a size thirteen foot. I don't know how Flo did it, but she has an ass that will put Beyoncé's to shame. It's wide and round and looks as hard as bricks. Angelo is always grabbing and slapping it like it's her prize position.

At the parties Ace is sitting on a custom-built throne, watching over the party like a gate keeper with his legs crossed and his chin resting on his hand. He has perfect posture, and he is silent most of the night. He always has a serious look on his face and the two oversized white tigers he owned since cubs are sitting behind him, looking evil and hungry. He has this obsession with exotic animals. He owns a zebra, monkeys, snakes, and the ones I hate the most, the gators. I watched him feed his gators a man before. It was during one of his sickly-themed parties. He had Angelo abduct a crazy, cracked-out homeless man off the streets just for feeding. So many people came to watch. Ace watched intensely with a wicked smile curving up at the corner of his lips and his dick swelling in his pants. He loved every bit of it and so did his psychotic guest. He told me that if I'd ever crossed him, he'd make me gator food. That's why when I think about leaving, I have to make sure I'm ready to die.

At parties, I'm always sitting in the thrown next to him, but I'm not treated like a queen. More like a showpiece. I'm coked out my mind, but I'm there. At least until Ace steps down from his 'thrown' and starts his networking. By that time, I'm doing my last line of coke and slowly making my way back to the mansion, hoping to slip away from the party unnoticed. Sometimes Lady L catches me and slaps me across the face, cursing and threatening me not to poison her son's mind against her and beckoning me to ask him for more money on her behalf.

When Angelo sees this, she always runs to my rescue, not because she loves me but because she hates her mother, and her mother hates her or at least what she's become. She's embarrassed by Angelo. Angelo shoves her mother, and she falls to the ground and makes a big dramatic scene. Now, she's embarrassed. I never stay long enough to see what follows. I just disappear into the night and prepare myself to get more coked up before passing out on the corner of my bed. Sometimes I wake up and Ace is on top of me. I just close my eyes and fall back to sleep. I don't fight him anymore. I'm too tired.

The family is more fucked up than anybody you'll ever see on the Jerry Springer show and I'm a part of them, so just by affiliation alone, I'm just as fucked up too. They burn through money like it grows on trees and they're all selfish as shit. They don't love each other the way they love money and if either one of them got the chance, they'd stab the other in the back and take it all. They don't trust each other, and all have their motives and possible secret plots to stay on top. They'll do anything for a dollar, but who am I to judge because I will too?

Their image means more to them than their own lives. Ace throws these parties every day as a passive-aggressive way to say, they're still on top but the truth is they're going broke. Daddy's money is finally running out and they're shitting on the last bits of it. Now, they're bickering more than ever. The name Badd gets thrown around a lot during their fights. They hate them with a passion, especially Ace. He's always talking about feeding them to his gators. I used to hate them too, right after they killed Keno but then I got over it. After all, it was a dirty game Keno and I were playing.

Ace has a plan though. He's been strategically plotting it for years. Something about a setup that would bring them in millions. Or something about taking back the money and land that was stolen from his father. Then he mentions that name Badd again. Then blah, blah, blah. I barely listen to him when he talks, and he doesn't need me to. As long as I nod my head and agree with him. Ace may look like a clown but he's a fucking evil genius. He's a master manipulator and the mastermind behind why the Lucky name is still thriving although it's only nominal, carrying no real weight.

Ace has a PhD in Human Psychology. He's good at reading people. It's how he snagged me. Ace gets in your head, and stays there, planting seeds and pulling up roots. He can play you like a puppet when he gets in your head. His scheming and backstabbing is the reason their dollar has stretched this far over the years and Lady L and Angelo know this. They're at his mercy whether they like it or not. Whatever plan he has, I'm sure it's going to work, and I know it probably involves something gritty and grimy. But, I need my own plan. I have to get away from these people. They're killing me slowly.

Ace finally walks into the bedroom. I don't bother to look up at him. "What the hell is wrong with you? You look worse than Lady L," he yanks my chin towards him so hard, my neck pops. I smile at him, hinting that I don't give a fuck and he takes his thumb and wipes what I assume to be red lipstick off my teeth. He sees the backless sequence dress he picked out for me still lying across the bed and grunts. "You coked up again?" he asked rhetorically, raising his hand to slap me and when I don't flinch, he seems taken back. Instead of slapping me, he grabs me by my hair and throws me to the floor. I just lay there idle. I'm too high to care or move or get dressed for this freak show party and for some reason, I can't stop laughing. Ace hates it when people laugh around him and he doesn't know for sure what they're laughing at. He always assumes they're laughing at him, and he can't handle it. Being ridiculed or chastised is his weakness. He kicks me in the side, and I gag. Undigested Gin rolls out the corner of my mouth. I scream less and less when he attacks me now. I know he's getting bored with me. "You want out?" he asked me calmly.

I look up at him confused. Maybe I was hearing things or maybe it was a trick question, but I answered anyway. I shake my head yes. "You might just have a chance…if you don't fuck up. It's time for me to upgrade you anyway," he kneels beside me on one knee, and I see the tip of his alligator boots as he gently strokes the side of my face, "all your bells have stopped ringing baby and I need to hear that magic tune again," he kisses me softly on the cheek and jumps up. I bury my face in the carpet, and it feels like cotton soothing my burning nose. I hear footsteps clicking away in a timely rhythm. Ace is gone. I don't bother to get up.

I lay on the floor all night until after the party when Ace returns. He lifts me and throws me on the bed, then hikes up my robe before unzipping his pants. Out of all the women at the party, he could have fucked tonight, he chooses me because he knows I don't want him, and that thrills him. I don't think about how much I hate him on top of me. Not tonight. I just think about the chance he's going to give me to *get out*. I'll do anything to get out. Anything.

2

Ace canceled his ritual Sunday night séance party. It's the first party he canceled in years. Something's up.

Sundays are reserved for what I call his sacrilegious safari parties. He lets all his animals roam around free. Monkey shit is everywhere. Men are walking on stilts, and some are playing with fire, juggling it, eating it, dancing with it. He has a bootleg witch doctor looking like he's dressed for Halloween, dancing and chanting something he probably made up the night before. There's even a fortune teller. Some bullshit Creole woman that Lady L swears by. Last Sunday, she told Ace that he would succeed in his journey to conquer if he acted fast. Whatever the fuck that means. After that, he went quiet. Or at least more quiet than usual. Now, he's canceling parties and calling family meetings. He even summoned me to the nightmare in the making. I want nothing to do with it unless it's the way out he promised. Then, I'm all ears.

Ace has his arm possessively draped around my shoulders, squeezing them tight every time Angelo does or says something to piss him off. I try to break away from his tight grip, but he yanks me back into his armpit.

"Where the fuck is that bitch?" Angelo hisses, looking over her shoulder and down the hall towards the front door. She was talking about Lady L. She's late to the meeting but I don't know why Angelo is so upset, Lady L is purposely late to everything. She loves making what she assumes to be a grand entrance. I think Angelo is just anxious to see what Ace has up his sleeve. We all are.

I break free to go fix myself a drink. Ace reaches out to grab my elbow but gets the hem of my sleeve instead. He gives me an evil eye and lets me go free.

"Calm down, baby," Flo says and pats Angelo on the shoulder with her large hand. Angelo slaps her hand away. Flo rolls her eyes but doesn't say anything, swings her long ponytail from one side of her shoulder to the next, and smacks her lips. "Baby, you need a drink."

"No, I need that bitch to be here. I got shit to do. Ace, I'm giving her five more minutes and I'm out," Angelo gestures with her hand then takes a seat on a tufted red leather chair and sticks her hand in the waist of her pants like she's grabbing her imaginary crotch. Flo shimmy's over her way and sits on her lap. Angelo slaps Flo on the ass and she squeals.

Ace is sitting on the leather chair in front of them, looking poised and calm. Although he canceled the party, he's still wearing his party clothes. A navy chevron patterned suit with yellow and red polka dot bow tie. I'm still wearing my long silk night robe. I return to my seat and take a sip of Gin. After two sips, Ace snatches the glass away from me and downs the rest with one swallow. He gives me back the empty glass and I get up to fix another cocktail, but he pulls me back down and gives me his *-stay-put eye*. I don't argue with him.

We're in what he calls the coffee room although he never drinks coffee. I can tell he's getting annoyed by Angelo and her fidgeting and complaining. Flo is probably getting under his skin too. The two of them make him sick to his stomach. Somehow, he looks at their relationship as a mockery to him; everything is always about him. Ace clears his throat, and everybody goes silent. He loves all the attention and power he has within the family. He straightens out his shoulders and rolls the kinks out of his neck. Then, he fixes his eyes on Angelo and Flo. Angelo stares back at him like she's not intimated by her big brother, but she is. She just has an image to uphold and is saving face in front of Flo.

"You can give her five more minutes and leave if you want. That's fine. But, once you leave, you're out," he slices through the air.

"What the hell you mean I'm out?" Angelo pushes Flo off her lap and she takes a seat on the chair next to her, giving Ace a nervous look.

Ace chuckles and for some reason looks at me like he wants me to elaborate for him. I say nothing; I don't even satisfy Angelo's rage with a look back at her. "What I mean, Angela," he taunts her with her birth name.

"My fucking name is Angelo!" Angelo jumps up and Flo grabs her arm gently, trying to calm her down. "I got to keep telling you that shit?" Ace still doesn't budge. He's just as poise as he was before.

"No. But if you want to keep getting your undeserved allowance every month, you gon' sit down, put up, and shut up," Ace says seriously.

Angelo starts shaking her head. She looks down at Flo like she's at a loss for words then she looks at the door like she's debating on rather to leave or not. She decides quickly to stay and sit down after a few seconds. She gives Ace an evil stare before pulling out one of her pocketknives. She plays with the blade as if she is warning him. Ace is amused by her. He winks and then smiles at her in a taunting way. This pisses Angelo off even more. She starts squirming around in her seat like she's resisting the urge to hit something, but she doesn't say anything. She just keeps staring at Ace like she's imagining cutting him.

Ace stops smiling and starts beaming in on Flo. Flo looks scared and turns to face Angelo like she's her knight and shining armor. "Come here," Angelo says to Flo, patting her lap. Flo hops up and sits back down on Angelo's lap and she whispers something in Flo's ear to ease her mind.

"Your special friend can stay until Lady L gets here but when the meeting starts, he got to go!" Ace says sternly.

"Now you've gone too far, Ace!" Angelo screams over Flo's broad shoulders. "You don't have no fucking respect. This is my wife. If your wife can stay," she gives me an evil grimace, "So can mine!"

Ace laughs. "That dude's got to go!" he mocks.

"Fuck you, Ace," Angelo yells and throws a knife toward his head, but it lands in the wall. Ace didn't flinch. Angelo wasn't aiming for his head. She could have got him if she wanted to. The girl knows how to throw a knife but she ain't crazy. She just wanted to shake him up a bit but it didn't work. Flo screamed, fearing Ace's wrath.

"Baby, calm down. I'll leave. I'll wait for you back at the house. It ain't no problem."

"Hell, no. You go when I say you go." Angelo pounds against her bare chest.

Amid the confusion, Lady L waltzes through the door with her entourage of gay lovers; two on each side of her. They're all shimmering with different color sequence shirts and tight-fitting white pants.

"Have you all started the party without me?" She twirls around teasing them as her entourage escorts her to her seat. "Knives in the wall and clutched fist already, shoot…I'm missing all the fun," she whines playfully.

"It's about time you got here. Your fucking watch broke?"

"No darling, mommy was getting fucked by men that know what to do with their dicks," she looks at Flo and smirks. "If you wanted to know the truth," she adds matter-of-factly.

Angelo hops up and storms towards her mother, but her boy toys barricade themselves around her, protecting her. I jump up and away from the crossfire. I stand a few feet away from the couch and watch the madness.

"That's enough!" Ace screams. Now he's standing up and looking at me like he wants me to sit back down. I fix myself another cocktail before I do.

"Ooh…" Lady L purrs playfully. "So demanding," she banters him with a chuckle.

"Lady L, your dudes got to go and so does yours, Angelo."

Lady L shrugs like she doesn't care. "No problem." She claps her hands two times, and they get up to leave. Flo leaves too. Angelo looks hesitant but she lets her go.

"So, why is everybody so serious?" Lady L says looking at everyone's expressions. She scoots back into her chair and slowly crosses her legs before daintily placing her hand on top of her bony knee. She toys with the surgically implanted mole she had placed just above her lip and looks at me and laughs like I'm pathetic. I just roll my eyes because to me, she's the pathetic one; I'll be it a fucking joke. I take a long sip of Gin.

Ace paces around the room with his arms behind his back for a few seconds like he's deep in thought. Angelo looks pissed off and Lady L seems amused. When he stops walking, he speaks.

"Things are about to change around here."

"In what way?" Angelo asks defensively.

"Parties two times a day instead of one? That'll be nice," Lady L says half joking half serious.

"No more parties," Ace says quickly and slices through the air with his hand.

"What?" Lady L and Angelo say in unison. They give each other confused stares.

"We got to cut back," he looks at them to see if they're getting his point. "A lot. So that means your monthly allowances are getting reduced drastically."

"You can't do that!" Lady L starts to rage. No more fun and jokes anymore. Ace is hitting her where it hurts in her wallet.

"Yes, I can, and I will," Ace says calmly.

"Reduced by how much?" Angelo asks levelheaded.

"Sixty maybe -seventy-five percent," He replies.

"Who the fuck do you think you are?" Lady L says in her real accent and jumps up so quickly, that her six-inch heels cave in, and she falls back down. Her wig shifts to the left side of her head. She quickly adjusts it and gets back up, waving her bony arm and clutching her fist in the air. "I brought your weak ass into this world! Me," she points her finger viscously at Ace, "Not the other way around. You don't tell me how much of my husband's money I can have."

"Calm down, Mother," Ace says sarcastically. "And let's be honest, your husband's money hasn't paid a bill around here in years."

"It always will be his money. He planted the first seed and I have the legal right to my fair share, you bastard!"

"I'm the new man of this empire and if you think you can fill my shoes better, then go ahead but until then…I decide what's fair and right now that's eighty percent less than what you're getting."

"Eighty!" you just said sixty to seventy-five? What the fuck, Ace?" Angelo whines.

"Well, your dear mother just pissed me off and quite frankly, I'm tired of paying for Botox and boob jobs and hormone pills and fake dicks and all the other shit you two blow my money on. At the end of the day, it's my ass that's on the line."

They both were speechless. Angelo and Lady L did spend money recklessly.

"Why are you doing this?" Angelo asks.

"Because I have to invest money into something that's going to bring us a huge rate of return. Money ain't flowing like it used to and we need a boost. A major boost to keep us on our feet. If you guys are patient your allowance will increase just as drastically as it decreased. Then, Angelo, you can buy enough hormones to turn into Superman and your wife Flo can get enough plastic surgery that he looks like Dianna Ross. Oh, and, Lady L, you can buy a new face for every day of the weak if you want. I don't give a fuck, but we have to make sacrifices. I'm doing it too. Think of it as an investment toward your future. This shit I'm planning is going to cost us. We need an army and we have to pay for bribes. It's a whole lot of money that got to be thrown around for us to succeed."

Lady L relaxed the tension out her shoulders and Angelo scooted closer to the edge of her seat. They were all ears now.

"How?" Lady L asked calmly. Her fake accent was back.

"We're taking down the Badds. It's time we finally launch our attack."

Lady L and Angelo looked at each other stunned and Ace looked at me to read my reaction. I kept a straight face. Then, Lady L almost fell over with laughter. Angelo just shook her head and pushed back in her seat like she'd been duped.

"What the fuck is so funny?" Ace demanded to know.

Ace starts walking towards his mother. She continues to laugh hysterically, and Ace is getting so angry, that his yellow complexion is turning red. He stops in front of her. I know the look he's giving her. He's going to hit her. He hates to be laughed at. I've never seen Ace strike his mother, but I wouldn't put it past him. Just like his mother said, he's weak.

"If you put your hands on me…. I'll slit your throat while you're sleeping," his mother finally leans up and looks him dead in the eyes. Ace knows she's telling the truth and backs down. "You're a fucking idiot, son. Do you think you're a match for the Badds? Even your father wasn't a match for them and you're not even half the man he was. You have but a crumb of your father's heart…just a crumb." She starts to chuckle again. "You're not cutting my allowance for this disaster in the making. This fucking suicide attempt you have for yourself is yours alone. Leave me and your sister out of it!"

Ace pushes his lips in his mouth and walks away from his mother. He starts pacing around the room again like he's regrouping his thoughts. He takes a deep breath and turns back to face us.

"I'm moving forward with my plans. It's already started and when I do succeed," He looked at Lady L, "I'll have something special in store for you just for your candid humor." He smiled wickedly at her, and she shrugged off his cruel intentions like it didn't faze her.

"Watch yourself, son. Their strengths are the epitome of your weaknesses," Lady L's phony French accent intensified the coldness of her criticism; Ace shuddered like he knew what his mother was saying was true. "They have structure, order, and a whole army of muscle. They're too strong, Ace. They've always been."

"Not if we weaken them," he said quickly like he had everything figured out.

"How do we plan on doing this?" Angelo asked hyper. "Are we gon' just roll up on them gangster style or what?" She flicked open her knife, tossed it in the air, caught it by the handle, and made a stabbing gesture.

"No. That'll never work. *That* mother, would be suicide," he looked at Lady L. "They'll expect an ambush like that. It's what they're prepared for. When we come, they not gon' see us. We gon' be like a ghost, and take this slow and sneaky," he clasped his hands together anxiously. "One by one…all them motherfuckers gon' die starting with that old nigga they call Papa Badd; he the motor of that Cadillac. Then we went to take it all. Everything green goes."

"They got more money than we can carry," Lady L said.

"Who said we were going to have to carry the money out? I can spend it right there on their Ranch. The Lucky Ranch. That sounds good. It's got more of a ring to it than the Badd Ranch."

"You know that Ranch belonged to your father? He lost it in a silly bet. They stole everything from us. Our land, or money and or honor. That weak bitch even stole my husband. When she started fucking with his head, he went numb. He got weak," Lady L ground her teeth so hard, saw dust fall from her mouth. "I want them dead! Fucking, bloody, dead. Can you really kill them?" Lady L asked desperate. Her nostrils flared like a bloodhound.

"Yes," Ace assured his mother with a brief but serious head nod. "Then, we gon' be on top. Just like it should've been."

Lady L breathed in deeply like she was taking it all in. "All that money," she said lustfully.

"I'm gon' buy Flo a L necklace. A big phat ass diamond-crusted L necklace to flaunt around the streets." Angelo chimed in.

"We all gone have one," Ace said excitedly.

"Hmm," Lady L said like she was finally considering her son's plan.

"So, what you need me to do?" Angelo asked, letting Ace know she's game.

"I'll let everybody know their task in due time," Ace said, looking directly at me. "But in the meantime, your patience and sacrifice are essential."

It was the first time that they all agreed with each other.

3

For the first night in years, I didn't snort that shit up my nose. I need a clear mind, so I can fantasize about *the way-out* Ace promised to give me. It's my second chance not to fuck up.

The first time he tried to use me to get to the Badds, I fucked up. But, this time is going to be different. I don't care what I have to do, I'm setting myself free. I just hope he's not fucking with my head again. He's good at doing that. It's how he got me in the first place; by mind fucking me. If I knew then, what I know now, I would have taken my chances out on the streets. There are far more dangers in between the walls of this house than on the streets but back then, I didn't see it that way. I was afraid, and Ace was the only person that I thought could protect me. Now that I know I'm wrong, it's too late. I wish I would have just ran that day. My life would be so different.

————— ··●·· —————

Three Years Earlier (Before Ace)

Keno told me to wait for him in the parking lot of some old run-down country bar out in the middle of nowhere. I'm pretty sure no one will know us here. The cracked asphalt parking lot is in desperate need of repaving and the bar looks more like a barn, but you can't tell the patrons that. By the way they were partying, you would think they were at the swankiest of nightclubs. The lot isn't packed, but it's got enough people crowding it.

I'm parked on the other side of the lot, looking at my watch and waiting for Keno and Tony. They should have been here over an hour ago. I'm starting to get nervous because something is wrong. Normally, we meet at this cabin way out in the woods somewhere. It's our safe house. It's where Keno and Tony hide out to count their crooked earnings and clean the guns, they swear they don't use. It's just where I wait for them so that I can pick up my money and go but today, they wanted me at this parking lot a few miles from where we normally meet. I don't care, as long as I get paid.

I've been working with Keno and his brother for two months now. It's the easiest money I've ever made. They came into the club one night and scouted me right off the pole. I was no stranger to conning people. It's how I earned my living when I was living back in Florida. I stepped into the career when I was fourteen. I had no other choice. After my father killed my mother in a drunken rage, I had to fend for myself, and I wasn't about to get caught up in no system. So, I conned people for money, food, room and board, and whatever else I needed.

Tony wasn't too keen on his brother taking up a third partner, but it didn't matter. Keno ran the show and what he said went. The job was easy money; risky but easy. They give me a picture and the name of some low-level criminal. It's never the main guy; just the flunky or groupie of the clique. The one that keeps his hands dirty with someone else's filth. He keeps drugs and the money in between drop-offs. He's the best candidate for Keno and Tony because it ain't his money and at the end of the day, he ain't gon' watch it as hard.

Once I get the picture Keno sets up a place for me to meet the guy. Then, I become whatever they need me to be to get the money. A private dancer, a working girl, or just a pretty face that just so happened to run into him on the street. After that, I'm at his house or hotel; sometimes even in his car, and then, so are Keno and Tony.

I never stay long enough to see just how Keno and Tony take the money. Keno said they're not murderers. All they do is rob them blind; literally. I always have to make sure I get the blindfold over their eyes. That's the most difficult part of my job, but I succeed every time. The guys we rob stay paranoid because there is always someone out to get them in this business but somehow, they never see me coming. All that tension seems to melt when they got a sexy woman straddling their lap, holding their dicks in her hand. After Keno takes the money, we meet up at our safe house and I get paid. Then, he gives me another name and face that I have to con. It's just that simple.

I see the headlights of a car dipping in and out of potholes coming my way. It doesn't look like Keno's champagne-colored Yukon but who else could it be? I jump out the car. My hand is itching from the eight grand he promised me. The closer the car gets I notice that it's not Keno's Yukon but a nickel-silver Mercedes. It's a little too flashy for Keno's taste but with those two you never know. I use my hand as a visor, shielding out the bright lights of the car and trying my best to squint and see past the tinted windows. The car pulls up alongside my car and turns the engine off, but no one gets out. For some reason, I'm starting to get nervous. I don't move. I just watch the car and wait. I got a strange feeling, this ain't Keno or Tony.

After what seems like several minutes, the driver's door opens slowly, and out walks a tall, average-built man, dressed just as flashy as his Mercedes. As a matter of fact, he is dressed as his Mercedes. He's wearing a steel-colored suit, almost the replica of the color of the car and to match the black tinted windows is his button-up silk dress shirt, peeking out under his vest. He is wearing a matching hat and shoes so black and shiny, that I can see the reflection of the moon bouncing off them. Who the fuck is this?

By the way, he's looking at me, I can tell he means no harm, but I know that look. I've been in this business long enough to know when somebody wants something from me. He's about to proposition me.

"Keisha? Or is it Rhonda? Or should I say Dalla?"

I went by a lot of different names, but few knew my real name, Dalla. Everybody else who thought they knew my real name called me Sari. He had my attention.

"Who wants to know?" I say and study his face hard. I'm trying to remember if I ever seen him out before.

"Ace Lucky," he holds out his hand for me to shake. This guy is real smooth but I ain't trying to get caught up in all his smoothness. I don't shake his hand.

What kind of name is Ace Lucky anyway? Probably an alias. Everybody has an alias in this business.

"What do you want?"

"Straight to business, huh? I like that." He says seriously and smooths down his unwrinkled suit.

"Let me guess…it was your money my partner took. You want it back? You gon'gon' give me a certain amount of days to hand it over to you or else I'm dead right?" I jump to conclusions.

Ace chuckled like I was amusing him. "Wrong. No one takes anything from me unless I give it to them. Just like I want to give you something."

He fidgets with his pocket and then his trunk pops open. He pulls out the leather briefcase, just like the ones you see in the movies. When he opens it, I already know what's inside. Neatly stacked crisp $100-dollar bills with an intense new money smell. Lots of them. The wind blows, and I get a good whiff of the new money smell straight up my nose. Now I'm high off it.

"It's $20,000. You want it or not?"

"That depends," I lied. I wanted that money. I didn't give a fuck what I had to do to get it. That $20,000 made up a month's worth of work with Keno and Tony. I wanted that money alright, but I couldn't let Mr. Ace Lucky know I was that easy.

Ace laughed like he seen right past my bullshit; almost like he knew me.

"I don't work with strangers," I told him.

"Yes, you do. You don't know shit about them two other dudes that got you doing all the work and ain't paying you half of what you're worth. That's a real shame." Ace shook his head and closed the suitcase before neatly placing it back in the trunk. As soon as he closed the trunk, I missed the money already and he knew it. I stared at the trunk of the car.

"What do you know?" I asked.

"I know enough. My eyes see little, my ears hear a lot," he smiled at me. There was something evil behind his smile that I couldn't put my finger on.

"How do you know me?" I asked.

"I don't know you. I've been watching you. I thought now would be as good as ever to meet you before your boys come to bring you that chump change. Tell me," he toyed with the tip of his Fedora and looked at me, "why you sell yourself so cheap?"

I don't know how he was doing it, but he got me thinking. "A sexy ass woman like you is worth more than what they giving you. Why don't you know your worth? He grabbed a lock of my curly hair and twirled it around his finger. I jerked away from his touch. "What is it? Somebody fuck you against your will when you were little? Daddy put his hand where they wasn't supposed to go. Mama put you out and told you wasn't good enough? Not pretty enough. Not smart enough."

"Fuck you!" He hit a real nerve.

"I'm getting closer, huh?" he chuckled. "Who lied to you, Dalla? Who told you to sell yourself so cheap?"

"I don't have time for this shit!" I turned to get back in my car.

"Come on now," he grabbed my arm and squeezed it a little too hard. "Where you going so mad? I'm just here to help you. I want to tell you the truth. Put a smile back on that pretty face." He stroked my cheek.

"What do you want from me? You some kind of pimp?" He sure dressed the part.

"I look that ignorant to you?" He seemed offended. "If it was your ass I wanted to sell, it would be sold easy." He said sharply.

"What the fuck do you want then?"

Ace smiled. "I want your business and after that…who knows," he stroked my face with his long finger. He was giving me an evil stare that was so intense; that I shied away from his gaze.

"What's the business?"

"Pretty much the same grimy shit you doing now."

"Who's the guy?" I held my hand expecting a picture. It's how Keno did it but he looked at my hand like I was holding shit.

"I look like a low-budget thief to you?" He was right. He was on another level than Keno and Tony, but he still needed my help. "There ain't no picture. All I need you to do is make a phone call."

"What?"

"A phone call," he repeated annoyed.

"Who am I calling and why?"

"You calling me," he answered quickly. "And it ain't your fucking business why. Your partners gon' be here in about twenty minutes. They gon' hand you a picture of the next fool they gon' hit up. All I want you to do is call me before you call them. All I need is the address."

"Fuck no!" I hissed. "I'm not setting them up for you. What I look like? A fucking dummy?"

"Yeah, you do," he rushed towards me like he was going to grab me, but he didn't. I flinched and stepped away from him. He took a deep breath. I can tell a man like him was used to getting his way and he threw a hissy fit when he didn't. "Right about now you look like a real dummy," he said harshly. "I'm not setting up your boys. They just bait. An appetizer to my fucking entrée," an evil grin spread across his face. "It ain't them I want," his smile faded, and his face went rock hard. "Your partners are like honey. They just there to attract the bees."

Ace popped the trunk open again. My eyes landed right on the suitcase of money. He pulled out a crisp white linen business card from the pocket of his suit jacket. All that was on it was a phone number in bold lettering. Nothing else.

"I'll be waiting." He winked at me before cracking another evil grin, then sped off.

I could still smell the money long after he drove away. I looked down at his card and debated how bad I wanted to smell the money again. I needed that money. The money I made with Keno was quick but saving it wasn't easy. Little by little, I put away five grand at a time. I only had ten grand saved. I need about fifty to be comfortable. I had plans. I can't make a career out of helping Keno and Tony rob niggas for the rest of my life. After a while, my face would be a little too familiar and there would be a bounty on my head. I stuffed the card in my pocket. What would making one phone call hurt?

⎯⎯ ••●•• ⎯⎯

Just like Ace said, twenty minutes later, I spot Keno's Yukon coming towards me. He pulls right into the same spot Ace had parked earlier. They had to pass each other on the way in. I try to keep a straight face and an open mind but the more I think about it, the more Ace's proposition sounds good to me. After all, it's not like he was in it to hurt Keno and Tony.

I get out the car and Keno waves me to the front seat of his car. I've been working with Keno and Tony for months now and I've never been inside his car before. They kept their shit private, and I kept mine private. I got in the car and locked it. I don't know why. Just out of instinct. Tony, who never really liked me anyway, gave me a weird look. I started to get nervous. Tony never trusted me and I'm not sure Keno did either, but the fact was I made their jobs easier. Aside from today, I gave Tony no reason not to trust me, but he was smart for following his first instincts. In this business you don't need to trust anybody, you just need to know how to play your cards right.

"I'm sorry I'm late," Keno says. He looks like he has a lot on his mind. Tony sat in the back seat, counting stacks of money. I looked up at him expecting an apology as well, but he didn't say anything. He just frowned at me.

"Did everything go ok?" I asked curious about the two-hour delay.

"It went as planned," Keno answered me short.

"Next time don't take so fucking long. We were lingering around that man's house for way too long," Tony complained. I just ignored him. He was always complaining.

"So, what you got for me?" I was ready to take my money and go. For some reason, I felt devious being in the car with them knowing the conversation I had only a few minutes ago with Ace.

Keno turns to the back seat where Tony is and holds out his hand. Tony throws a stack of bills at him, and he catches it and gives it to me. I don't waste my time counting the money. It's always right.

"You not gon' count it?" Keno asked me for the first time.

"Do I need to?"

"That's up to you. You trust us like that?"

"I ain't got no reason not to," I answer nervously. "You trust me?"

"Do we have reason not to?" Tony says from the backseat.

"You tell me?" I say back, keeping my eyes on the money. Keno is watching me so hard; I start squirming in my seat.

"You good," Keno said. "Chill out, Tony."

The tension is getting thick and I start to sweat. I put my hand on the handle to get out the car but Keno stops me.

"Hold up. Don't you want your next picture?" He leans up and pulls out his wallet.

I hear Tony sigh and suck his teeth in disapproval.

"Keno, what the fuck you doing, man?" Tony complains like this is something they discussed already.

"Making us some fucking money!" He yells at Tony like it's the second time he's told him that today.

"I don't trust that shit. We never needed anybody to give us any leads. Why are we taking them now?"

"Because of the payout. I told you if we do this shit long enough, it's gonna get real easy. Niggas starting to come to us. That's not a bad thing and they are paying us a fee plus what we take from the house. This might be something good."

I kept quiet. Instantly, I think about Ace. I can't help but wonder if he paid them a little visit before me.

"I still say no," Tony says and shakes his head in opposition. He loses track of the money he's counting and throws it back in the bag, cursing under his breath.

"It's all good little brother. It's all good," Keno says to Tony, and he shrugs.

Keno opens up his wallet to give me the picture of the new guy he wants me to attract, and a wallet-sized picture of a pretty girl falls onto my lap. She looks like she's barely in her twenties. Too old to be his daughter and too young to be his girlfriend.

"Who is this?" I ask, holding up the picture.

"Nobody," Keno says and snatches the picture out of my hand like he'd just made a mistake.

"Scrappy can do a better job than she can. Why don't we start training her?" Tony says referring to the girl in the picture.

"We keeping Taffy the fuck out of this," Keno lets the girl in the picture's name slip. I told you that shit already! What's wrong with you?"

"At least we know for sure we can trust Taffy."

I put two and two together and figured that Taffy, the girl in the picture, was their younger sister.

"This is your sister huh?" I ask smiling at the idea that Keno keeps a picture of his sister in his wallet. Little by little, I'm learning a little more about Keno. He has a sweet side.

"Never mind this picture," he stuffs the photo back in his wallet. "This is the one you need to be focused on." He slides me the picture of my next job.

I frown at the picture. The man looks like he weighs at least 300 pounds. Then I remember it's not a date I'm on but a job.

"What's his deal?" I ask.

"His name is Leon. There ain't nothing special about his fat ass. He the same as any," he says talking more to Tony than to me. "Let him take you on about two dates before you go to the house and seal the deal. I need you to learn a little more about him *before we make our move. Once you get my go-ahead, get in, blindfold him, and call us."*

"My fee is going up," I say.

"Why!" Tony shouts at me.

"Because this is a three-day job. My time is money."

"That's cool, Sari. I got you." Keno interjects like it ain't no problem.

"I still think this is fucked up," Tony sighs and starts to recount the money.

"It's all good bro. It's all good," Keno says nodding his head.

I stuff the picture in my bra, the money in my purse, and get out the car.

"I'm on it," I assure Keno before getting in my car.

———— ··●·· ————

It took me forever to handcuff this gorilla of a man, but I managed. I got him cuffed and blindfolded, but I didn't call Keno yet. I've been walking around in circles debating who to call first, Ace or Keno. Leon, the fat fuck, was cursing and threatening me so much he was messing with my train of thought. I had to gag his ass with a towel just to shut him up. It's been half an hour. I know Keno is wondering what the fuck is up. I pick up the phone and let my instincts choose for me and low and behold, I call Ace. He answers on the first ring like he's been waiting at the edge of his seat for my call.

"You in?" He asks without saying hello.

"That depends. What you paying again?"

"20. You know the deal."

"That's your deal. I want forty."

"I'm being more than generous giving you twenty gees' for practically nothing."

"Well fuck it then," I say like I'm going to hang up.

"Wait," he says anxiously. "I'll give you a little extra but it ain't gon' be nowhere near forty fucking grands." I guess that's still more than what he offered, I think to myself. "Where are you?"

"I'm in."

"Where!" Ace is getting impatient. "I told you I need an address."

I give him the address but he has another request right after.

"You gon' have some other visitor so don't go too far. As a matter of fact. You need to hide out in the house. As soon as they get there call me back. You don't have to wait for me to answer either. Just ring my phone once. Got it?"

"Wait a minute. That wasn't part of the deal. "

"Neither was the extra money I'm throwing your way." He says and hangs up the phone.

I instantly get a chill. What visitor is Ace talking about? I don't like the way it sounds. I got dressed and immediately decided not to call Keno and Tony. I'm going to text them that it's a bust and not to come. But, before I can get one leg in my pants, I hear the door crash open. Shit! I dive into the linen closet of the hallway not far from the bedroom. "Sari," I hear Keno's voice. They came anyway. I hear both their footsteps running up the stairs. Just when I was about to jump out of the closet, I heard another crash. Without guessing, I know it's the visitor Ace was talking about.

"You heard that?" Tony says to Keno. I didn't hear Keno respond.

That's when I jump out of the closet, startling them so much they both point their guns at me.

"Keno, something ain't right," I say in one breath.

"You damn right something ain't right," Tony whispers loudly. "This is a fucking set up and this bitch is in on it," Tony looks like he wants to shoot me.

"Shh," Keno silences us both. "Get back in the closet and don't move," Keno says to me. I follow his orders and dive back into the closet. "Tony, you go around the back and cover me."

Tony does exactly what his brother says without question. My heart is racing in the closet. I can see Keno and Tony's bodies crossing ways in the hallway from the crack in the door. I feel like I can't breathe. Then I hear a voice.

"Surrender motherfuckers! This shit is over. We got the house surrounded. You fucked with the wrong ones this time. All things come to an end eventually, right?" The voice yells and clicks his gun. I jump and close my eyes tight. What the fuck have I gotten us into?

Keno and Tony are nowhere in sight. I don't even hear them. I start to feel alone. I hear footsteps rushing up the stairs and different bodies passing by the closet entering every room they see, toting guns. Then the voice talks again.

"Allow me to introduce myself. I'm Brip Badd. Does that ring a bell to you mutha-

fuckas? I've been called here to bring you in for treason. You see…this shit y'all been running amuck doing got an order to it. And y'all niggas all out of order in this bitch. Y'all fucking with our affiliates. We take that shit very personally!" Brip clicks his gun and I jump again, praying no one finds me in the closet. "So, come on mutha-fuckas, come show Mr. Badd what you got!" I hear gunfire. It's so loud my eardrums pop. Then I hear the man who calls himself Brip Badd laughing like he's having the time of his life. "Come on now! Don't be shy!" Another round goes off.

I see Keno's boots run by. Not much longer after that, I hear gunfire, and somebody gags and falls. I see Keno's boots again and hear more gunfire and more gagging and falling noises. I see Keno's boots head down the stairs towards Mr. Brip Badd. I hear more shots. This time from three different guns. It sounds like the Wild Wild West. The gunfire stops and all I hear is laughter. "That's one," I hear Brip say. "I got one more to go. Come on now. Don't be shy." Brip clicks his gun again and more shots roar out.

My heart stops. Did Keno get shot? Not much longer after that thought, I see Tony's boots running down the stairs. He's screaming and shooting his gun like he's Rambo. I hear Brip's gun again followed by a loud thud. Then I don't hear anything else.

"That's all folks," Brip says laughing. "Soldiers, grab the wounded, leave the dead and let's get the fuck up out here. We got some more people to visit."

"What about the big dude tied to the bed upstairs?" I hear a voice say.

"That ain't got shit to do with me. I ain't come for him. Let his people handle him." Brip shoots his gun one last time. "It's bad luck to leave one bullet in your gun after a war. All you motherfuckers, that's down to one get rid of it." Brip demanded.

I hear a round of shots and then the voices trail off. Laughing and heckling each other like they didn't just kill two men. They're finally gone. I wait at least fifteen minutes before I cower out of the closet. I run straight downstairs. I'm sure somebody has called the police by now and I can't get caught up in this mess. On my way down, I stumble over Tony's twitching body. Blood is oozing from his head, and he looks like he's having a seizure. I gag at the sight of him. I get to the end of the stairs and not too much further from Tony is Keno, lying on his back with three bullets in his chest and one in his head. His eyes are open. I try my best not to look at him. I run right past him and away from the nightmare I put myself in. I'm not even wearing shoes. I run across the street to my car but before I could get inside, I spot Ace's Mercedes speeding up behind me. He jumps out of the car and grabs me, throwing me in the back seat before speeding off.

———— ··•·· ————

I can't stop screaming. No matter how many times Ace slaps me, I can't stop. Maybe I'm having a nervous breakdown. Ace is slapping me and shaking me to get a grip, but I can't. He pushes me off his lap and I fall to the floor. I'm still screaming. All I see is Keno's blank stare and blood oozing from Tony's head.

I finally stop screaming when Ace throws a bucket of cold water on me. I look up at him and for the first time, I notice I'm at his house. When and how did I get here?

"Shut the fuck up?" Ace yells at me. He has no sympathy for me.

I wipe the water from my face. Then, Ace throws the remaining water from the bucket on my back. "You better be done!" Ace says before throwing the empty bucket against his marble floor. The clanking sound of the metal bucket hitting the floor brings my mind back to all the gunfire and triggers another episode. I get ready to scream again but Ace yanks me off the ground and wraps his hand around my mouth.

"That's enough! You fucked up my plan you simple bitch. Now I got to hear you yell about it. I should be the one screaming in this bitch. You know how long I waited for this shit? How long I wanted to kill that mutha-fucker and your ass fucks it up!" He covers my mouth like he's trying to suffocate me and then he pushes me to the ground.

"Shit!" I Ace screams. He kicks the bucket with his boot, and it hits the legs of a coffee table. He's dangerously pissed.

I stagger to my feet and try and regain my composure. When Ace sees me get up, he charges towards me, pulling me into his chest. "You owe me big! Real big!" He says, squeezing my arms and shaking me. "Your job was simple. All you had to do was let me know when he got there. Just let me know when that fuck up Brip Badd showed up, but you couldn't even do that. You know how fucking incompetent you make me look to my associates? You fucked up my business and cost me money."

Ace pushed me again. My body flew down to the cold marble floor. He started to pace again. Then he stopped pacing and gave me a considerate look.

"I should just throw you out to the wolves. You know they are looking for you right?"

"No!" I screamed. It was the first word I was able to speak.

Ace leaned over me and yanked me off the floor with one hand. He hastily pushed me towards his patio door, swung it open, and threw me outside. He closed and locked the door behind him. "No! Please," I banged on the door. "They're going to kill me," I pleaded hysterically. After witnessing what happened to Keno and Tony, I couldn't imagine being next, but I was. They had to be looking for me and there was no one to protect me anymore.

No one but, Ace.

Ace watched me begging from the other side of the glass door. He had an emotionless blank stare on his face. I couldn't tell what he was thinking. Would he protect me or draw back his drapes and forget about me? I continued to plead with him. I sobbed so hard, I lost my voice. Then I got weak in the knees. My body slid down the glass door and collapsed onto the concrete. That's when Ace opened the door. He had me right where he wanted me.

He pulled me up and wiped my wet cheeks with the tip of his tie.

"I'll protect you." He said to me with an even tone.

———— ··●·· ————

I was unaware that I was falling into his trap. That I would be the prisoner I became for him. He played with my mind so much, threatening me with brutal scenarios of the murder that the Badds had plotted against me that he got me to agree to marry him. Why he wanted me to marry him, I would never know. Maybe it helped his business associates take him more seriously to have a wife; it made him look sane and reliable. Or maybe he just really wanted to own a modern-day slave. And what good is a slave without the deed of sale that Ace calls our marriage license?

4

It's crazy the things you can hope for with a clear mind but then again, it's also crazy the things you can fear with a clear mind. I stopped snorting coke a few weeks ago. I haven't had a drink in a few days either. I just want to prove to Ace that I can pull off whatever tasks he has for me. Then, I can be free just like he promised.

I never knew there was so much time in a day and how boring and time-consuming it is to lay around and do nothing. I'm more active now. I go to the gym Ace has in the housein the morning and the evening I jog around the property. Every time I jog past that gate and see the doors open and close, I fantasize about the day I get to walk away from this horror house a free woman. I never leave Ace's gated residence; not unless I'm with him. Ace says I don't need to leave because everything I need is here; he's wrong. My identity isn't here, and neither is my self-worth. But all that is going to change real soon.

It's been weeks since Ace hosted a party. The house feels different without a bunch of strangers lingering around, leaving their corrupt energy to haunt the house once they leave. Ace has been pretty busy plotting whatever it is he's plotting. I know it has something to do with what we discussed at the meeting a few months ago. He really is taking this revenge against the Badds seriously. I don't mind because I barely see him these days. As a matter of fact, I haven't seen Ace in three days. But all that is going to end today because one of the housekeepers just came up and told me that Ace wants to see me in the basement. I've been summoned.

I washed my face and threw on a clean T-shirt and a pair of jeans before I headed to the basement. I want to look fresh for Ace. Since I've stopped snorting coke, I can see my beauty again. My eyes are sparkling, and my brownish-red hair is shining. I'm starting to feel like the old me. As I walk down the long hallway on my way to the basement, I look down over the catwalk railing into the ballroom and see people inside setting up chairs and tables. Once I make my way down the large spiraling staircase, I stop to look and see what's going on. Ace's hired staff is laying out a bright white rug that's big enough to cover the entire marble floor in the room. They're also dressing chairs and tables with silk white coverings. The guy who maintains the house is applying white wallpaper on the walls.

What the hell does Ace have going on now? One of the servers looks at me and smiles uneasy like she's praying that I don't ask her any questions. I guess Ace threatened her not to clue me in on what's going on. I continue down the hallway. After I pass the kitchen, I smell the chef preparing something that smells exotic. If I didn't know any better, Ace is planning a party and not just any outrageous crazy party but an elegant one. He has never hosted parties in the ballroom before. Who did he have attending this party? The President?

I get to the basement stairway and stop to take a deep breath. Ace hadn't said as much as two words to me since the family meeting. I smooth any loose hair I may have back into my bun and adjust my clothing. I'm nervous as hell. I've only been to his basement suite once and that was enough.

Ace pretty much lives in his basement. He only comes up to my room to bother me when he wants to fuck or when he is bored and agitated and needs someone to hit. His basement is huge. It's just as big as the top of the house. He has a full kitchen, living quarters, an office…everything. And for his 24-hour entertainment pleasure, is his human aquarium of strippers and peep shows.

As soon as you step foot in the basement, there is a wide hallway. But, instead of drywall, Ace has thick floor-to-ceiling double-pained glass on each wall. Behind the glass to the left of the wall, you'll see his strippers, dancing nude and sliding on poles, and to the right is his peep show; women fucking each other and sometimes their fucking men. He has a live porn show, and they are there all day; different women working exclusively for him in three shifts. He has a pretty diverse mix of females when it comes to race. When I first saw it, I was stunned. Even in Hugh Heffner's wildest imagination, he couldn't think of anything this perverse; a human aquarium of naked women fucking each other.

When I get down to the bottom steps and walk into the basement, I notice Ace right away. He's casually dressed in a polo shirt and khaki pants. His cologne fills up the room. He's leaning one shoulder against the glass, tapping on the wall, and flirting with a woman who is trying to entice him with her seductive movements. These women do try every night to retire early by stealing Ace's heart but if they knew what I knew, they'd leave that tarnished piece of loveless muscle just where it is.

Ace looks up at me like he doesn't recognize me. He almost does a double-take. Then he smiled as I amused him. Maybe he thinks I'm trying to flatter him.

"What have you been doing to yourself, Dalla? You almost look like I remember you looking," he smirks evil at me and grabs me behind my neck, pulling my face into his. "...almost," he whispers in my ear before forcing me into a tongue kiss.

The woman he was flirting with behind the glass, rolls her eyes at me and hisses playfully at Ace. He smiles, flattered by her jealous gesture. Ace loves attention more than money. One of her friends joins her and they start to kiss too while rubbing against each other's body parts. There trying to hold Ace's attention, but it doesn't work. He's too interested in me and what I'm thinking. He's staring at me like he's trying to read my mind. His evil smirk fades into a dour grimace.

"What you been up to Dalla?" Ace questions me.

"What do you mean?" I don't clue him in that I've been working out or that I've stopped snorting coke. Ace doesn't want me doing anything productive because he knows that once I get my head on straight, I might think my way out of his prison.

Ace continues to stare at me. Then he leans in and sniffs my hair. "Smells good," he says through an exhale. He uses the tips of his fingers to trace against my face. He starts at my forehead and lands at my nose. "You in need of a refill? I haven't heard anything from you in a while." He's referring to the coke.

"I have enough," I answer quickly. "You wanted to see me?" I try to change the subject before the conversation takes a turn for the worse.

Ace looks at me briefly before answering. "Yeah, I did. I guess by now you notice what's going on in the ballroom," he says then turns his attention back to the women behind the glass.

"It looks like you planning a party."

"Something like that," Ace says without looking at me. He is still watching the women rub on each other.

"You need me to do anything?"

"Something like that," he says again.

"Ok," I say even toned. I try not to show how excited I am. Ace giving me something to do is big.

"Remember what we discussed at the family meeting?" he says and gestures to another woman behind the glass to join the other two.

"Of course," I say through a cracked voice. My heart is racing with anticipation.

"You think you ready?"

"If you need me to be," I say confidently.

Ace stops watching the woman and gives me a serious stare.

"But you fucked up last time. Remember that?" I shook my head yes. "How I know you ain't gon' fuck up again?" I shrugged my shoulders. I didn't know how to answer his question because I wasn't sure I wasn't going to fuck up myself.

Ace is watching me so hard, I start to fidget. I avoided eye contact with him and in the process my eyes landed on the whorish women riding on top of one another, licking and rubbing. My eyes quickly dropped away from the freak show and down at Ace's leather loafers. I could still feel him staring at me.

"I don't think you're going to fuck up," Ace said to me confidently. I looked up at him and he gave me the evilest stare he could muster. "You know why?" I shook my head yes. I knew why. "Tell me why, baby." He used his index finger to lift my chin so that I was eye-to-eyewith him.

"Because you'll kill me."

Ace smiled like he'd just won a prize. "You're a smart girl, Dalla. But don't be so smart that you're dumb." He turned around to walk away but I stood in place. "Come take a walk with me," he yelled over his shoulder. I followed.

I followed him to the end of the long hallway and then we made a left. When the smell of chlorine filled my nose, I knew we were going to his indoor pool. "You didn't happen to bring your swimsuit, did you?" Ace asked me randomly. I was confused.

"No," I said and shook my head.

"I could call one of the housekeepers and ask them to bring it down if you feel like swimming."

"I don't feel like swimming," I said again.

"Are you sure you don't feel like swimming, Dalla?"

He was confusing me. I didn't respond to his question because I had a strange feeling it was rhetorical. He opened the double doors and we stepped into the pool area. Light from the huge skylights in the ceiling reflected off the water and made the Olympic-sized swimming pool sparkle. Ace walked on top of the grayish-blue slate tiles until he got to the edge of the pool and then stopped. I followed him. He kneeled and ran his fingers through the water. "Water feels good." He looked at me like he was still waiting for my answer.

"Go over to that table and bring me that bag," I watched his finger as he pointed in the direction of a chestnut-colored wicker and glass patio table. A plastic grocery bag sat on the table. It was tied in a knot, so I couldn't see what was inside. I grabbed the bag and it felt heavy, but I carried it back to Ace as quick as I could. I didn't want to annoy him. I handed the bag to Ace and he dropped it by his feet. He continued to look at me. I bit down on my bottom lip and looked up at the rays of the sun shooting inside the pool. Ace smiled.

"You look so beautiful when you're tense," he said. "So, I'm having a dinner party tonight. An all-white party. It's going to be really elegant and sexy. I want to show my guests that Luckys are pure and incapable of being blemished. You understand?" I didn't understand what he was saying but I shook my head yes anyway. "White is also the color of honesty," Ace said thoughtfully. "Did you know that some studies show that when a person is wearing white they are presumed to be trustworthy? You can get people to believe your lies. Crazy, isn't it? White's going to be everywhere tonight. All over."

I shrugged my shoulders and nodded my head at the same time. He was going off into one of his deep psychology tangents and I didn't want to tick him off.

"So, everybody wears white tonight, including you. I already got your dress picked out. All you got to do is put it on."

"Is that all?"

"Not quite. We're having a very special guest tonight. Very special," Ace repeated. Then he was quiet for a few seconds like he was trying to think something out. "Lady L and Angelo are not invited to this party. I don't want them making a fool of us. As a matter of fact, this party is going to be very small. That way, I can get more one-on-one time with my special guest without any distractions. I got to talk to him. I got to get him to listen to me. It's my only chance," Ace said more to himself than me.

"You will," I said to Ace and patted him on the arm. When I touched him, he jumped like I stuck him with a needle. Ace wasn't used to anyone showing him any kind of affection. I wanted to know more about my role tonight and hoped that the pat of assurance would help.

He looked at me like I said something that pissed him off. "I know I will!" he said defensively. Ace leaned over and picked up the plastic bag. He watched me closely as he commenced to untie the knot. "I need your old mask tonight."

"Mask?" I didn't get where this was going.

"You know the mask I'm talking about. The same one you used to wear when you blindfolded them nigga's and robbed they ass. That mask!"

I knew just the mask he was referring to.

"Who's the guy?"

"Billy Badd," Ace said quick.

Billy Badd, I thought to myself. How in the hell was I going to blindfold and fool him? He was too connected, and I never will forget the evil heckle of one of his brothers named Brip the night they shot Keno and Tony. I thought Ace was serious about giving me a way out but instead, he was delivering me into the hands of the enemy. I didn't think I could pull this off.

Ace must have noticed the hesitant, uneasy look on my face. He got agitated and grabbed me by the arm real tight and shook me. His tight grip felt like a blood pressure cuff.

"You gonna fuck this up, ain't you?"

"I said I will help you. Not commit suicide."

"What the fuck you talking about?"

"You want me to get up close and personal then con a Badd? No! I won't do it!"

He squeezed me even tighter, pulling me into his chest. "You will do it!"

"If they find out who I am, they're going to kill me. You told me yourself they had a bounty on my head. Why the hell do you think I'm here with you anyway!"

Ace dropped the plastic bag and slapped me across the face. Before I could compose myself, he had his hands around my throat, swinging me around his pool like a rag dog. "Fuck you bitch! You gon' do this shit or your ass is dead you hear me?" he squeezed my neck tight enough to scare me but not tight enough to kill me. He let go of my neck and punched the air with his fist. Ace sure was good at throwing hissy fits when he didn't get what he wanted.

He picked up the bag dug his hand deep inside and grabbed something. He was breathing in and out really hard like he was having a minor asthma attack. That meant he was real pissed off.

"What about the bounty? They're looking for me," I said trying to catch my breath.

"There is no bounty you dumb bitch," he said and threw what looked like chunks of meat into the water.

"What?" I said exasperated.

"You heard me! You think nigga's like that got time to be remembering bitches like you? Y'all come a dime a dozen. You silly." He said through a wicked chuckle.

I felt like I wanted to faint. I spent years in this prison with Ace thinking he was protecting me but it was all a lie. Yet, another mind game. Ace smiled at me, but anger was still in his eyes. He dug his hand in the bag again and pulled out a handful of meat and threw it in the pool.

"Now I'm gon ask you one more time. Do you feel like swimming today?" he dropped the remainder of the bag in the water and started rushing towards me. He grabbed my arm and dragged me to the edge of the pool. When I looked inside the water, I seen both of his alligators swarming around, eagerly swallowing the little bits of meat. "You think that little meat is enough to hold them? That's just a tease. So, answer the question. You feel like swimming today?" he put his hand on the back of my neck and lowered it toward the water like he was going to push me in.

"No," I yelled between screams.

Ace pushed me away from the pool and I fell onto the slate tiles, scrapping the right side of my arm. I started to cry not because I was afraid but angry.

"I didn't think so," he said calmly and walked away.

5

y hate for Ace evolved to a new level. All these years he had me fearing for my life when the only person I should've been fearing was him. I was sleeping with the enemy, but he had me thinking he was protecting me. And somehow, I found a warped sense of comfort being with him. I thought I was better off with him than on the streets where I could be spotted and killed by one of the Badd crews. I have to get out of here. I have to do as he said and not fuck up. He thinks tonight is his only chance but tonight is my only chance to make it out of here alive.

The party started almost an hour ago. I'm sitting at my vanity in my bra and panties staring at myself in the mirror. My hair and makeup have already been done by Ace's glam squad. Once I stopped snorting, I didn't go through withdrawal. Because of that, I convinced myself that I wasn't addicted to the powder but tonight, I've proved myself wrong. I don't know if it's my nerves or the tremendous anger I'm feeling toward Ace and myself for being a willing prisoner for so long, but my body is craving a few lines. I try to shake the feeling by nursing a glass of Jack Daniels but it's not working fast enough. Ace is probably getting more upset every second he doesn't see me downstairs, but I don't give a shit. Today I've realized that Ace needs me and because of that, the balls in my court; so, fuck him. If he wants this shit done it's going to be done my way.

I hear the music downstairs. It's the soft kind of instrumental tune you hear in elevators at fancy hotels. It's such bullshit. Ace is pulling out every card he has to try and impress Billy Badd. The white dress Ace picks out for me is lying across the bed inside a plastic covering. I hadn't put it on yet. I just can't bring myself to do it. Everything about it represents Ace and I cringe at the sight of it. I grabbed my cocktail stood over the dress and frowned just as if it were Ace himself. I manage to unzip the plastic covering with one hand and yank out the dress. Without giving it a second thought, I pour the remaining Jack Daniels in my glass on the white dress. A stain saturates it immediately. There's no way I'm wearing this dress.

Before I walk to my closet, I pour myself another glass of Jack and take a long sip. I start to sift through my clothes. Almost every piece of clothing in my closet was picked for me by Ace. I get upset again and throw my entire glass at a rack. Then my eyes land on this silk red dress. It's been untouched by my cocktail. The dress is long and elegant and will fit nicely over my hourglass silhouette. It's strapless, open-backed, and has a slit in it that starts at the hem and ends at my thigh. It looks like it came right off Jessica Rabbit's back. The dress is one of the few I picked out for myself, but I never got a chance to wear it. Ace hated the dress but only because he didn't pick it. I grab it and carefully walk out of the closet, holding it above my head so that it doesn't dust the floor. I lay the dress on the bed and smile. I think I'm ready for the party now.

———— ··•·· ————

It's been a while since I felt this confident and independent. I'm standing on the balcony looking down at the party. The ballroom is so bright with crisp whites my eyes are hurting look down at it. It's not many people but a large enough crowd to get lost in. Everyone is looking chic in their all-white attire. They're chatting in small groups sipping on champagne and white wine of course. Servers are serving white appetizers in their white tuxedoes. This is the most pretentious party Ace has thrown yet.

Just when I was about to stroll downstairs and make my appearance in my cherry red dress, my eyes landed on a commotion at the front door. It's Lady L. Not a surprise. Ace can't keep her from a party. She's dressed in all white from her white wig to the white mink she has draped around her sagging shoulders. Her entourage of gay lovers is with her dressed in the same fashion; hair and all.

Ace must have gave security strict orders not to let her in because they are blocking her way. One of them is grabbing her arm. She's hitting them with her purse and cursing. I know she's embarrassed. I chuckle at the spectacle she's making of herself. Out of nowhere Ace appears and whispers something to security and they let her go and clear the way. She adjusts her wig and pets her mink fur before gracefully walking into the ballroom with a big smile on her face like she's dignified. She doesn't make it two steps in the door before Ace grabs her and pulls her out of the ballroom and into the den away from the party. I know he's giving her an earful about showing up after he asked her not to. It's turning out to be a typical Lucky part after all. All this white only brings out how dirty his family is.

Once the show is over, I start to walk towards the stairway, but I get stopped in my tracks at the sight of a man who cut through security like butter, gliding into the ballroom unimpressed almost as if he owned the place. He's not wearing all white either. Instead, he's handsomely dressed in a stylish light grey suit jacket with a bright red silk shirt underneath it; his shirt matches my dress exactly. He's wearing blue jeans and tennis shoes. He doesn't look like any of the guests I've ever seen Ace have before. I don't know why but for some reason, I'm instantly intrigued by this man. He is the picture poster for swag.

He's looking around the place like he's casing it. The other guests look at him but are careful not to stare. It's almost as if they're afraid. He scratches his neatly trimmed goat-tee, pulls a cigarette from behind his ear, opens his jacket, and pulls out one of those old-fashioned lighters that you have to flick open and lights his cigarette. Out of all the things Ace allows to go on at his parties, smoking isn't one of them. He hates the smell of cigarette smoke and forbids it anywhere near his house. This guy must not have gotten the memo because he's smoking that cigarette like he's at a bar and he looks damn sexy doing it.

He scratches his neck and starts to move through the crowd, searching every angle of the house. I can watch him walk for hours. He walks to a rhythm. A beat that only he can hear; I can almost hear it too. He takes another drag of the cigarette and uses Ace's white rug as an ashtray, flicking the black ashes onto the carpet. People are starting to whisper while sneaking glances at the man. He's quickly becoming the star of the party.

One of the waiters hesitantly walks up behind him and taps him on the shoulder. The man jumps and grabs his hand so quick it's like he never touched him at all. He gives him a kick-ass look to say *how dare you touch me* while twisting his wrist back. The waiter grimaces with pain. I can't make out everything they're saying, but I see the waiter point at the cigarette with his free hand. The guy lets him go, takes a long drag of the cigarette, and blows the smoke in the waiter's face. He puts the cigarette out on the white carpet. The server looks bewildered. He knows that he's going to feel Ace's wrath because of the stain on the rug. He immediately drops to his knees and dabs at the ash stain with a handkerchief from his jacket pocket but there is no use. That stain isn't going anywhere. The guy walks off.

He finds another spot to stand and starts observing the people in the crowd like he's looking for somebody. I wonder if he's looking for Ace. He flaps his suit jacket open again and pulls out a black flask. He opens the top and takes a few swigs. I can't help but wonder what he's sipping on. I began to stare at this man so hard, that I fell into a trance of curiosity and fantasy. So much so that I didn't notice when he looked up at me. Once our eyes locked, I couldn't look away. That's when I decided to go downstairs to join the party.

I sashay down the stairs as sexy as possible. He's watching my every move but I'm not nervous. Instead, I thrive off of it, putting an extra twirl in my hips. We're still watching each other. He knows I'm coming for him. I'm feeling bold and beautiful tonight. Fearful thoughts of Ace aren't weighing me down. I'm in the mood to take a risk regardless of the consequences.

When I get to the bottom of the steps, he is still looking at me. By the look he is giving me, I know he thinks I am sexy in my red dress, but he has no idea how much more sexy I can get. Unlike everyone else in the room, I boldly walked up to him. Within a matter of seconds, I was face to face with this mystery man. By now he's found himself a comfortable corner of the room to watch patrons of the party. He is leaning back with his foot pressed against the wall. He seems comfortable even though he is in a strange place. He is even more handsome up close than from afar; his face is chiseled to perfection. Masculine features stand out subtly underneath his smooth maple-toned skin. He plays with his sexy full lips a lot, unconsciously pushing them in and out of his mouth like they're coated in candy. He had another cigarette behind his ear and in the pocket of his suit jacket was a deck of cards. That's kind of weird; yet interesting.

"Are you at the wrong party?" I was sarcastic.

"Maybe I am," his voice was so deep.

I smiled at his quick comeback. He didn't. "You don't play by the rules do you?" I asked him, staring back at his attire.

"No, I don't play by the rules. I make them." He matter-of-factly answered me. "What about you?" he looked me up and down, slowly. "I like your red dress. It looks good on you but, how does it look off of you?" He gave me a serious look, staring at me as if he were waiting for me to answer his question.

I was stunned. I didn't expect him to come at me this hard with the flirting. I was at a loss for words. He smiled at my scattered reaction to his lude but sexy comment.

"I don't know. Why don't you go to sleep tonight and let me know after you wake up from that sweet dream you have."

He laughed without smiling. "What's your name?" he asked.

"I'll tell you mine if you tell me yours?"

"My name," he repeated then looked into the crowd, "just call me Mr. Unpredictable."

"Mr. Unpredictable huh? Is there a story behind that name?"

"Why? You want me to tell you a story?"

"Maybe," I shrugged.

"A bedtime story?" he flirted again then finally smiled. His teeth were big and bright.

"Maybe," I repeated taking it up a notch.

"Well, when I come up with an ending to this story, I'll tell it to you," he said and walked away.

I watched him walk into the crowd, rudely cutting through groups of chatting patrons like they weren't even there; he even knocked some over. I overheard one of the guests whispering, pointing her finger in his direction,like she knew him. Then she said a name; Billy Badd. My heart stopped for a second and I gasped. I had no idea I was flirting with Ace's special guest.

6

Billy Badd is nothing like I expected. Actually, I'm not sure what I expected but it wasn't him. He caught me off guard. I spent years fearing his family but that all may have been in vain. I didn't feel threatened by Billy at all. I know a man that has it in him to hurt a woman when I see him. But, that's not him. Billy's not that man.

I have to keep focused but now, I fear that I fucked up my only opportunity to make it out of here because, for some reason, I feel some kind of way about this stranger. How if he finds out that I'm Ace's wife? Maybe he won't. Especially being that I'm Ace's best-kept secret. Our marriage is anything but public. The rare moments that we are out in public, I'm just the girl at his side, not his wife.

Ace wasn't clear on what he needed me to do. All he said was to pull out my old mask and back then that meant concealing my identity and tricking my victim before I set him up to get robbed. But, I'm sure he's not trying to rob, Billy. An hour has passed since I was last face-to-face with Billy. I've been trying my best to avoid him and the entire party altogether. I've been hiding out on the balcony off the kitchen. Now that he knows who I am, I don't want to run into him again. At least not until I get my game face on and a plan together.

My nerves are getting bad and that anxious feeling from earlier is starting to revisit me. I'm craving coke. My weak substitute, the bottle of Jack Daniels, is upstairs in my bedroom. Ace isn't serving brown drinks tonight, so I have to settle for a glass of champagne. I motion for one of the servers to come outside. "Champagne," I demand, and he scurries off to get it. He comes back a few seconds later and hands me a cold glass and the remaining bottle. Smart man. I swallow everything in the crystal flute in one big sip. I pour myself another glass and swallow it all down.

I haven't seen Ace since he left the ballroom with Lady L. Come to think of it, I haven't seen Lady L either. Maybe it's time I stop hiding out and go back to the party. I can't stand around and wait for Ace to give me instructions. I need my own plan. I pour myself one more glass of champagne before I go inside. I drink it down so fast, it drips from my lips and sprinkles onto my dress. I wipe my mouth and walk back in the kitchen. When I slide the balcony door open, I spot the server that gave me the champagne motioning me his way. He's standing in the pantry but it looks more like he's hiding. His eyes are darting all over the kitchen, making sure no one sees him. I don't want any more champagne so what does he want? I walk over to him.

"Mam," he says through a shaky voice and looks over my shoulder. I turn around but no one is there.

"What is it?"

I'm just now recognizing how afraid he is.

"Someone needs you in the study."

I instantly thought about Billy.

"Who?" I asked trying to mask my excitement.

"Lady L, mam. It seems Mr. Lucky has locked her inside the study and she wants you to get her out. I can't do it," he said through a nervous huff.

Like I have time for this bullshit. I shake my head and walk out of the kitchen past the ballroom and toward the study. On my way out, I give the large room a quick once over to see if I spot Billy, but I don't. I begin to wonder if he's still here.

I arrive at the double wood doors that lead to the study. The door is closed and has a rope tied across the knobs. I can hear Lady L banging on the door, screaming for someone to let her out.

"Lady L," I say in between the slight crack in the door.

"Let me out of here you worthless bitch! You put him up to it didn't you?" She pulls on the door, but it doesn't open all the way. Ace has the rope tied to the knob too tight.

"I had nothing to do with this, okay. But I will still try to get you out. It's best you leave the party though."

"You don't tell me what's best for me. Do you even know what your husband is up to? He has that lying, murderous thief in this house! Did you know that?" She was referring to Billy. "I can't believe him. That stupid son of mine is messing with fire." She banged on the door.

"Where are they?" I whisper into the door. It seemed like she knew more about what was going on than me.

"They're on the other side of the house in the bar room. He's telling him everything he knows that fool!" She said referring to Ace.

"I'm going to get a knife to let you out," I lied.

"Hurry up," she banged on the door. "I'm going to suffocate in here," she said dramatically.

I ran down the hall on my way to the bar room. It's the area of the house where Ace took guests to discuss business. What business did he have with Billy besides wanting him and the rest of his family dead? There's no telling what kind of bullshit Ace is feeding Billy, but Billy doesn't look like the type that buys into bullshit. I turn the corner and stick my head down the hall. Ace's bar room is secluded from the rest of the rooms at the end of the hallway. It's right above my bedroom closet. I remember being in my closet and hearing everything he discussed with his guest through my vent just as clear as day. Once I heard voices, confirming that Ace and Billy were actually in the bar room, I made my way back to my bedroom and went straight for the closet.

I'm lying down flat on my stomach with my ear glued to my floor vent. Cigar smoke is lingering in the air, making its way through the vent. I quit my thoughts to try and focus on what they're saying. I hear Ace's voice first. His voice is so calm and even that Billy might be convinced by him. If anybody knows how to play mind games, it's Ace. He's a certified mind fucker and has the degree to back it up.

"I know what I'm risking by telling you this. You can have me killed. My mom, and my sister by midnight if you want. You can even take my wife and she's all I got," Ace paused to let what he was saying sink in. "I don't doubt how powerful your family is. Hell, you strong-armed my dad out of the business years ago," he said playfully. "I know that you carry real weight Billy and I'm not challenging that."

"You damn right!" Billy yelled. "I should have your ass killed before the clock strikes midnight. How dare you bring this bullshit to me!"

"I just put it out there Billy, but you came to me. You're in my house tonight."

"You know what I came for," Billy replied. "I don't know what this bullshit party is about. I want the letters you claim to have. If my mother confesses all this shit in some secret letter then let me have them."

Ace is silent for a while. "All of this is just hospitality man. Somewhat of a peace offering. And, I have some of what you came for as promised but not the letters. I told you that my mom has them locked away." Ace and Billy were both silent again. "I have the other thing you want but first I need your word. Remember this is a give and take situation. Billy didn't respond right away.

"I got to be sure before I give you any money."

"I need more than the money for the trade. I need the connection. That'll last me longer. I need to get in the group. I got a wife man," he said like he actually cared for me. "A mother. A sister. They all are depending on me. I'm just trying to keep my head above water."

"Don't look like that to me," Billy said referring to Ace's lavish mansion and party.

"Well, I want more."

Ace was so convincing I almost believed him. At that moment, I understood why he married me. It was all part of his plan. I was merely a small fragment of his big plan.

"Look man, I just want the same connections you giving everybody else. I need protection and reliable networking like every other hustler out there. I don't mind paying taxes either."

"Man, ain't nobody trying to do business with you."

"I know your father and brother Brock won't allow it. That's the chain of command, right? First your father, then Brock. I know y'all Badd's believe in order." Billy didn't say anything. "I told you what I told you tonight because I got a strange feeling you gon' be next in command and that'll allow me to be in the inner circle. It's selfish of me but I got to get in the door regardless of how it opens," Ace went quiet like he was trying to give Billy time to consider what he was saying. "I know it's hard to hear Billy, but your mother was murdered," he said in a soft voice. "Brock did it. He killed her because he didn't want to break the chain of command. Your brother killed her Billy. Our brother." He interjected.

I tried to wrap my mind around what Ace was saying. I was confused. Billy still wasn't saying a word. I know that meant he was believing Ace.

"Don't hold what I'm about to say against me but if it were me, I would do the same thing. I wouldn't let anything jeopardize my inheritance. I mean Brock is next in line to inherit the entire Badd Ranch and manage all the finances. Who would want to lose all of that power? Your dad seems real hardcore. If he finds out that your mother fucked my father and made Brock, I'm sure he'd throw his ass out on the streets. Wouldn't he?"

Billy didn't say anything. "I have what I promised you. You don't have to pay me right away. I'm sure you gon'" want to do your research and I'm cool with that. I mean why should you believe me anyway? But, this autopsy report doesn't lie. It's the real one. The other shit is fake; a cover-up to a crime. My mother talked about the affair my father was having with a Badd wife for years. She still talks about it. It's true. Everybody seems to know about the shit but y'all but then again, I guess some things you don't want to know. But, know this," Ace paused, "Your half-brother, murdered your mother. You're really the next in line to take over the Ranch and if you are smart, you'd act on it. Here," he said. I assume he was handing him something. "Don't worry. I promise I will get the letters for you. You need to read what I read. With this autopsy report and the letters, you will have all the proof you need to avenge the crime against your mother"

"How you come across this shit again?"

"I got connections just like you. Maybe not as many but a few out there that tell my ears lucrative secrets. It's how I survive. I know somebody that knows some of the doctors you employ on the Ranch including the one that did this autopsy report on your mother. You guys been using him for what...

about five years now? You don't think it's weird the report that read your mother committed suicide came from a different doctor? That was awkward timing to switch things up don't you think?"

Billy didn't respond. "The report that your half-brother Brock has, is a fake. Some nigga name Tyler Jones forged it."

"Tyler Jones?" Billy repeated like the name rang a bell. He knew the name.

"He came to me afraid. Brock confessed what he did to your mother before he forced him to forge a new report. He told him he would kill him if he didn't do it." It went silent again. Then Ace cleared his throat. "She died of asphyxiation. Not suicide." I heard one of them sigh hard. "You go ahead and think about it. Then you can get back to me with my money and maybe we can talk business."

"Get me Tyler and the letters and then we can talk."

Ace chuckled, uneasy. I knew that fake laugh. "You think a man that did something like that gon' stick around? He will be hard to find."

"Do I look like I give a fuck? You get me Tyler, I may consider what you asking. But if anything smells fishy with this, you gon' be swimming with the fishes. Bet that nigga. Bet!"

"Hey, I already know all that. I ain't stupid and I don't got a death wish. I'm just a businessman trying to make connections the best I can. That's all." They were silent again. "Before you leave, I want you to meet my wife."

My heart started to race. Ace's plan was falling into place but not like I imagined.

"Why?" Billy replied suspiciously.

"Like I said, I'm big on hospitality and it's rude to invite you in my home and not introduce you to the lady of the house. Besides, I wouldn't let you meet my wife if I was doing something devious. I wouldn't want nothing to happen to her and your meeting her proves I have nothing to hide."

I didn't stay to hear Billy's response. I jumped off the floor, smoothed down my dress, and rushed to the mirror to touch up my makeup just in case. My hair wasn't out of place, but I smoothed it back anyway. I had it pulled up in a bun so tight, I gave myself a facelift. I rushed back down the stairs and disappeared into the crowd like I was there all along.

I was in the crowd all of five minutes when I turned and saw Ace. When he saw my red dress, he looked like he wanted to kill me. He motioned with his finger for me to come to him and I did. Once I got close enough, he yanked me out of the ballroom and away from the crowd.

"What in the fuck are you wearing?" he shook me, and I pulled away from his grip.

"Why do you care?" I said boldly. Ace needed me now more than ever. I could say and do what I wanted.

Ace bit down on his bottom lip. He knew he couldn't hit me. At least not tonight. "Somebody wants to meet you in the bar room."

"Who?" I played dumb.

"Billy Badd," Ace gave me a telling look as if to say gear up because it's game on.

I swallowed hard and followed behind him.

——— ·•●•· ———

I was face to face with Billy again. He looked like he was surprised to see that I was the wife Ace wanted him to meet. Nevertheless, that didn't stop him from looking at me with the same lustful eye as he did when we met earlier. I watched him back. Right in front of Ace and it felt good. "This is my wife, Dalla," Ace said, guiding me closer to Billy with a push on the back.

I held out my hand and Billy shook it but didn't let go. He continued to stare at me. I felt awkward and looked away. I could feel Ace fuming. Beneath his calm composure, he was raging at everything that was going on. Even though he set it up this way.

"So, this is the lady of the house, huh?" Billy was still holding my hand.

Ace wrapped a possessive arm around my shoulder and pulled me away from Billy. He was pretending to care about the flirtatious stares Billy was giving me. Or at least I thought he was pretending. Who knew?

"Nice to meet you," I said to Billy.

Ace looked at both of us like we were keeping a secret from him. He didn't know about our chance meeting in the ballroom earlier.

"I know you got to go," Ace said to Billy and squeezed my shoulders, "and I don't mean to hold you up. I'm sure you got a lot of business to tend to, but I just got to ask you about those cards in your pocket." Ace was just as curious about the cards as I was. Or maybe this was one of his mind games. "They lucky are something?" Ace looked at me and smiled like he was trying to amuse me. Like he gave a fuck about what I thought.

"No, I don't believe in anything, lucky. That's bullshit." Billy said looking directly at Ace.

Ace swallowed hard and squeezed my shoulders even tighter as he tried to contain his anger. "I got a little time before I go," Billy said looking at me. "You wanna play a little game?"

"I don't mix business with pleasure man. Not my style," Ace replied. I knew he was lying.

"Just one game. We'll make it interesting."

"Oh, yeah."

"Yeah," Billy said and looked at me.

"How so?"

"We can play for something. Winner takes all." Billy pulled the cards out of his pocket and started to shuffle them in his hands. It was then that I noticed they were all mismatched. Some were blue, some were red, some black; it was a makeshift deck.

"Not with that deck," Ace said jokingly.

"Why? They're all here. I'll spread them out for you." Billy walked over to the bar and started placing the cards on top of the granite top. "See, I have nothing to hide." He gave Ace a sarcastic look.

"Okay, well what are we playing for?" Ace asked the question strategically. He already knew how Billy was going to respond. He was just that good at being manipulative.

"A weekend?" Billy said looking up at me.

"We are betting on a vacation?" Ace played dumb.

"Something like that. But different. If I win, I get to spend a weekend with your wife. If you win, you get to spend a weekend with her."

Ace cleared his throat. I know he didn't plan on Billy being this bold. He was getting upset. I shifted my weight uncomfortably especially when both Ace and Billy looked my way. I started to feel cheap. But then I remembered that freedom wasn't cheap, and neither was I. I allowed myself to feel excited. Hopeful even. Also, I was very flattered by Mr. Billy Badd's proposition.

"No," Ace said, surprisingly.

"You sure?" Billy said gathering up the cards. Ace didn't respond. He turned his head away from, Billy. He didn't want Billy to see him getting upset. "You afraid of losing?"

"I never lose."

"You sure?" Billy challenged him.

"As sure as my name is Ace Lucky."

"Well let's play," Billy started dealing the cards.

They played one game of Poker and if I wasn't mistaken, Ace looked as if he were trying to win. I got so anxious that I couldn't watch the game. I walked around the room in circles, watching bits and pieces of the game. Whenever Billy would slap a card on the table, Ace cringed. Billy was trash-talking him the whole time making Ace even more uneasy. At the end of the game, Billy won and got to take home the prize; me.

"Well…" Billy paused, "I guess I win the grand prize." He looked directly at me.

Ace sat at the bar and watched Billy gather up the cards. He grabbed my arm and yanked me by his side. "Come on now. Don't be a sore loser. Hand over my prize!" Billy taunted Ace and held out his hand.

"A deal is a deal, right?" Ace said. "Just give me a minute with my wife."

"That's cool with me but don't be too long. We got shit to do," he winked at Ace just to piss him off. "I'll be waiting for you out front."

Once he was gone and the coast was clear, I thought Ace was going to slap me but instead, a smile stretched across his face so wide, I got startled. I had never seen him smile so big. It was like he hit the lottery.

"That fucking idiot. I had that nigga eating right out my hand," Ace raved as he walked back and forth feeling excited and accomplished. "Them fucking cards. Everybody knows that nigga likes to gamble. That nigga will gamble away his name if the stakes were high enough. He is convinced that I give a fuck about you," Ace looked at me and smiled. "I know his type. Always wants what he can't have. Ha, ha," Ace laughed. "A conquering mutha-fucka. He likes to take what doesn't belong to him just like his fucking daddy. The shit is in his genes," Ace continued to laugh. "That's one mother-fucka down if you don't fuck up," he turned to me and said.

"What do you want me to do?"

"What you do best," Ace stroked my cheek, "play pretend."

"Then what? I'm gone after that right?"

Ace yanked me into his chest. "You gone when I say you gone. You getting to be pretty damn useful and I ain't done with you yet, but soon. If I'm reading this nigga right, after this weekend, Billy is going to want to see you again. He gonna need a shoulder to cry on. Someone to vent to; bitch ass nigga," Ace said disgustedly. "He's the picture poster for a captain save whore, mama's boy; a typical." He shook his head. "You gon be that shoulder I guarantee it. You gon' be able to hear and see shit that I can't. After I get enough information, I'll break you off a little change and send you on your way. I promise I won't come after you if you pull this off for me."

Trusting Ace was a risk I was willing to take. I had no other options. I could leave the normal way but I'm sure he wouldn't rest until he hunted me down and killed me just for spiting him. I've already wasted two years of my life in hiding and wasn't going down that road again. I had no choice but to trust him.

"How are you so sure he's going to want to see me again?"

Ace was good at reading people. It's almost as if he was physic but he was just manipulative and evil and used his education to aid him in his devious ways. However, I didn't know if he was good enough to predict that Billy would initiate an ongoing affair with me.

"Oh, he will. It's in his genes. He wants what he can't have." Ace said confident.

7

When I walked out the front door, I felt free. A gush of cool wind caressed my skin and danced its way up my dress while the night sky greeted me with a smiling half-moon. But, Billy was nowhere in sight.

I stood on the stone paved steps in front of the courtyard, accompanied by security, with nothing but the red dress on my back and my clutch purse under my arm. All I had in my purse was the cell phone that Ace gave me, a tube of M.A.C. red lipstick, and my I.D. I didn't think to pack a bag and I didn't want to waste another second being in that house. For all I know, Ace could change his mind at any moment; he's a fickle man.

I knew why Ace wanted me with Billy but what did Billy want from me? Maybe just to fuck. I was up for that. Although Ace forced himself on me most nights, being with him made me feel re-virginized. It's been way too long since I had sex merely because I wanted it. And make no mistakes, I wanted Billy Badd.

Looking around the courtyard, I started to get anxious wondering about Billy's whereabouts. Had he changed his mind? People were still coming and going. White limos, Mercedes, and other luxury vehicles crowded the circular driveway. Every time a car pulled up, my heart raced with anticipation. But, it wasn't Billy.

When the hairs on my neck started to rise, I knew Ace was watching me. If he wasn't watching me from a window, then his camera system. This made me even more uneasy. Ace was impatient. If Billy didn't pull his car up the driveway within the next few seconds, Ace could potentially pull me back in the house and call the whole thing off; then regroup. But, I would stay out here until the sun rose if I had to.

I wasn't wearing a watch, but I knew at least ten minutes had gone by although it felt like half an hour. I pulled a piece of my hair out of my bun and twirled it around my finger to curb my nerves. I took a deep breath and looked up at the moon again. It was no longer smiling at me and in fact, it vanished somewhere behind the clouds. The wind didn't feel soft and caressing anymore either but cold.

Then, I lowered my eyes back down to earth and that's when I saw the headlights of a white Sedan coming our way. I smoothed my hair back and straightened my posture. Everything in me told me that it was Billy. It had to be. The car pulled up in front of us and I rushed down the steps. The Valet walked around to open the door but was quickly stopped in his tracks by the roar of a motorcycle that cut through the grass and zoomed onto the pavement only inches away from running him over. The driver was carelessly popping willies around parked cars, making a huge, loud scene.

Some kind of way, he made his way onto the driveway and really made a grand entrance by doing a trick on his bike where he stood up on the left pedal with both legs. He was reckless and wild, and he didn't have to take off his helmet for me to know it was Billy Badd, and this time I knew I was right. I smiled and walked up to the bike. He waited for me, balancing the bike in between his legs with his feet firm on the ground. He pulled off the black helmet with a red B emblem on it. Underneath the helmet was a black bandana. He looked rugged and sexy.

"What took you so long?" I asked.

"I should be asking you that question."

"Excuse me?" I was confused.

"And I've been waiting since you came down from that balcony." I was flattered. I tried my best to hide that I was blushing, but I couldn't. "You ready to ride?" He asked flirtatiously and handed me a helmet. I didn't answer, I just hopped on the bike with my dress and heels. I was more than ready.

————— ··●·· —————

We've been cutting through wind on the highway for almost an hour now. The sound of the wind rushing in my ear put me in a zone and relaxed my mind; it's an exhilarating experience. Out of all the shit I've done, riding on a bike isn't one of them. The aggressive ribbing of the engine was too intimidating of a sound for me and turned me off completely from bikes. But, tonight I was turned on. I loved having a reason to wrap my arms around Billy's chest and resting my chin on his shoulder. I had no idea where I was going and didn't care either. It's ironic how the same man I feared so much that I kept myself in bondage with Ace for years could turn around and make me feel so comfortable without doing a thing. What is it about this man?

We pulled off the exit and the wind slowed down. I could hear my surroundings again. Billy drove about four minutes off the exit and pulled up to a country-ass, backyard-looking liquor store. Where in the hell were we at? He hopped off the bike like it was nothing, but it wasn't that easy for me wearing this dress. He watched me struggle trying to balance being sexy and safe at the same time like it was comical to him. He didn't try to assist me either.

"You cool?" He smiled at me. "You kinda was digging your nails in my jacket pretty tight out there."

"I felt like I was flying!" I said in an adrenaline-filled breath. He smiled at me like he agreed with me. My eyes were wide with excitement. "When you curved the bike, it felt like I was falling but in a good way," I said fast.

"Yeah, she can fly." He said looking down at his black and chrome bike in admiration. "That's why I call her, Eagle."

"I always wanted to ride an Eagle" I flirted a bit. Billy laughed and then turned around and started towards the store, gesturing for me to follow him with a wave of his hand.

Once we got inside, I followed Billy around like I was afraid he was going to lose me. I hope it didn't creep him out how close I was on his heels. I didn't care though. The redneck-looking cashier wearing a cowboy hat and a confederate flag shirt watched us like a hawk, frowning at us the entire time. It must have bothered me more than Billy because Billy didn't look up at him once and I couldn't take my eyes off the man giving us bold stares.

"So, what's your poison?" Billy asked, looking through the bottles of liquor. Before I could answer his question, he said, "Wait, I might know." Then he leaned down. Naturally, I leaned away from him but stopped myself. His mouth was coming towards mine and I didn't want to stop it. Billy kissed me so hard it was like he sucked the taste buds off my tongue. He caught me off guard. It wasn't the best first kiss but from him, I'll take what I can get. "Un-huh…just what I suspected," he said and reached for a bottle so casually I started to wonder if he ever kissed me at all or if I just imagined the entire moment.

He grabbed a bottle of Jack Daniels whisky. He was right on point. He knew his liquor. I followed him to the cash register. He placed the bottle on top of the counter and opened up his jacket to pull out his pack of cigarettes. Only one was left in the box.

"Aye, let me get a pack of Newport's too." He pulled out his lighter and flicked it above his cigarette to light it.

"There ain't no smoking in here," The cashier said in such a southern twain it was almost like he wasn't speaking English.

Billy ignored him and took a long drag of the cigarette anyway. "Get my fucking Newport's man," he demanded and pointed over his shoulder at the cigarettes. The cashier got the cigarettes and slammed them on the countertop. I guess he didn't want any trouble. "Get me two Black and Mild and a pack of grape cigarillos," he demanded again. "You want anything?" he turned to me and asked. I shook my head no. "Let me get a plastic cup too."

Before getting the cup, the man turned to the register started ringing up the items, and gave Billy the total.

"Pack the shit up," Billy said, and the man did just what he told him. Once he put all the items in the bag, Billy snatched it from the register. "Appreciate, ya," he said to the cashier. "Oh, here. I almost forgot" he said like he was about to pay him but instead, he flicked his lit cigarette on him and said, "Put this out. There's no smoking in here," mimicking the guy's country accent. He laughed, and then he walked out the door just as slowly and casually as if he paid for the items.

"Where you going? You got to pay for that!" The man said, coming from behind the counter. Billy didn't even turn around to give him a second look, so I didn't either.

The cashier started cursing and threatening to call the police, but all Billy did was put the bag in a cart in the back of his bike and put on his helmet. "Fuck you," he said and ribbed up the engine. I jumped on the bike before he left me standing there and I gave the man my middle finger. We speed off.

———— ··●·· ————

Ten minutes later, we were pulling up to a place that looked like a large abandoned barn. It sat in the middle of nowhere and was surrounded by towering trees and thick bushes. The foundation sagged, the wood was rotting, and the building structure leaned to the side like it was about to topple over, yet several cars were parked outside on the gravel road. Loud music thumped from the speakers and I could hear voices laughing and cursing from inside.

"Where are we?" I asked.

"We at the spot," he answered like I knew what that meant.

I followed him inside. Billy walked about three steps ahead of me. I wonder if that was because he didn't want any females inside to think I was his date. But really, I wasn't his date but merely his prize for the night. The inside of the place didn't look too different from the outside. Some people sat at wooden tables with broken chairs drinking and smoking while others played cards. When they noticed Billy, it was like everybody stopped what they were doing to greet him as if he were a King. But, Billy was humble. He shooed off their attention by giving them daps and making naughty jokes. A real heavy-set woman wearing a tight dress that made her look like an overstuffed burrito blushed at Billy. He made her day when he wrapped his arms around her and squeezed her before kissing her on the neck.

"Big sexy ass," he flirted with her and she all but melted. He slapped her on the ass before walking over to a table and taking a seat. "Y'all ready to lose tonight?" Billy teased the crowd.

"We ain't playing for no money tonight?"

"So, what we playing for?" Billy asked.

That's when the guy pulled out a bag of weed. I looked around and noticed it on all the tables where men were gambling. Instead of money, these fools were gambling for weed. I guess the meaning of green was all the same to them.

"Hell, yeah!" Billy yelled. "Let's get to it." Billy handed me the bag of liquor that he stole from the store. "Make yourself comfortable," was all he said to me. This wasn't what I had in mind tonight but what could I say?

I sipped on Jack Daniels and watched him smoke cigarettes, take shots, and gamble like he was playing for money. I balanced myself on a chair with three legs for almost two hours. No one looked at me or spoke to me; not even Billy. It's almost like I wasn't there. That liquor went straight through me and I had to pee. When I asked the girl next to me where the bathroom was, she trembled like she was afraid as he pointed me in the right direction. I know I looked out of place wearing this red dress, but did I look scary or something? I got up to walk to the bathroom and that's when I finally caught Billy's eye. He gave me a funny look that he thought I didn't notice but I saw it. Did he think I was going to leave? Could I even leave or was I his hostage as well as his prize? I would never no because he never said anything. He just continued to play cards like my movements didn't faze him. I knew better though.

The bathroom might as well have been a hole in the floor. It was disgusting. The toilet leaked, and the raw sewage smell was overwhelmingly funky. I had to drip dry because there was no tissue and when I went to wash my hands, the sink didn't work. This night definitely wasn't going the way I planned. When I walked back out of the bathroom, Billy looked at me again but only for a split second. A Black and Mild dangled out the corner of his mouth while he laughed real hard and grabbed a stack of weed, pushing it towards the high pile in front of him; I guess that meant he was winning. He didn't seem like the man I heard talking with Ace earlier. Then he was tense and angry. With all that shit Ace told him about his mother being murdered, it seem like he'd be somewhere burying his sorrows in liquor, but he wasn't. He was here but maybe this was how he buried his sorrows.

Another 30 minutes passed, and I got up to stretch my legs I think Billy got the point because I heard him say, *I'm out and* slam cards on the table; finally. I made a pretty big dent in the fifth of Jack he bought me. Drinking it on an empty stomach started to make my head spin. The blasting radio and the smell of cigar smoke didn't help. Billy collected his winnings, stuffing all the weed in a brown paper bag, and snugly placed it in his jacket. He teased the men and gave them all dabs as he prepared to leave.

Billy walked towards me, catching me in an exhausted stretch. "You still here?" he said playfully waving his hand in my face to see if I was coherent.

"I'm here but that bottle of Jack might not be," I teased.

Billy picked up the bottle and held it in the air, analyzing what was left of the liquor.

"Damn, girl! You might be able to hang after all."

Did this mean I had his approval? I smiled at him.

"You look like you won big," I said looking at the bag of weed that was hanging out of his pocket.

"I always win big," he said pridefully. "I won you didn't, I?" Billy smiled at me then reached his hand behind my right ear and pulled out one of his playing cards just like the magicians did at carnivals.

"How did you do that?" I was amazed by his magical illusions. He answered by winking at me, gesturing for me to keep his secret by placing his index finger against my nose. His finger smelled like the cigar he'd been smoking. He reached again and pulled another two cards from behind my left ear.

Did Billy really cheat Ace in the card game that granted me this weekend of freedom? The thought of it alone made me want to grab his neck and kiss him. Ace thinks he's the tricky one, but apparently, he's wrong. I couldn't stop smiling at what he was revealing to me. Where does someone pick up a trick like that and more importantly, how many more tricks did he have up his sleeve? Billy stared at me like he was seeing me for the first time. It was awkward because he wasn't saying anything, and I didn't know what to say.

"Dance with me," Billy insisted. "I never danced with a lady in a red dress before." The speaker switched tunes and old school jam by Zapp & Roger's, *I Wanna Be Your Man*, hummed through the speakers. Billy pulled me into his chest and I wrapped my arms around his neck and we danced right where we stood in perfect harmony. He held me gently like he thought I was fragile, and I was. I never danced with a man before. Surely, not Ace. I rested my head on his chest and closed my eyes. The things I begin to imagine swaying to the beat while in his arms, caused my insides to tingle. It started in my stomach then shot up my chest and finally landed at its final destination, my underwear. It was at that moment that I realized that my mission was going to be impossible from here on out. I was fucking up big time. Something I promised myself and Ace I wasn't going to do. I was falling for the man I was supposed to con.

8

Twenty minutes after we were back on the road, we were pulling off another exit. Where to now? This was getting too exciting and I had to stay focused. After all, this was a job for me. For Billy, this weekend may just mean a rump in the bed with a rival's wife; a personal conquest but for me, it meant my life.

Out of all the guys I deceived, I never had this issue before. I don't know if I was just starved for affection being with a man like Ace, but I couldn't understand the feelings I was having for Billy so soon. It made no logical sense; It couldn't be real.

We stopped at a red light. "You hungry?" Billy asked. I was starving so I told him, yes. We drove a few miles down the road and swerved into a Krystal's parking lot so fast, I thought I fell off the bike. He came to a screeching halt.

"I know you use to filet mignon and caviar, but tonight, you gon' have to settle for a greasy ass burger."

He was right. Living with Ace had some benefits. Like a personal Chef on call 24hrs. I hadn't eaten fast food since I married him but then again, I hadn't eaten at all. I was always too stressed or too high to eat. "Hey, I grew up with a plastic spoon in my mouth. I know I'm wearing a fancy dress and met you in a fancy house but I'm not that girl you think I am." I said defensively. Billy brushed off my comment with an unconvinced head bob and turned to walk in the restaurant. I followed behind him. On our way inside the restaurant, an older lady was coming out. I stepped aside as Billy held the door open for her and patiently waited as she slowly made her way out the door. I thought that was very charming and respectful of him.

When we got inside, Billy ordered a sack full of Krystal burgers with cheese, fries, and two cokes without ever asking me what I wanted. When they gave him the food, once again, he snatched the bag without paying and walked out the restaurant. The young cashier was so shocked, she was at a loss for words. She let us walk right out without calling her manager or threatening to call the police. I think she was afraid.

"You know that girl is going to have to pay for this food, right?" I was beginning to think that Billy was a petty thief.

"How'd you figure that?" He said digging in the bag and pulling out a handful of fries.

"Because I use to work in a shit hole like this. My dad used to think that because I was the cashier, he could treat the place like a free all you can eat buffet. My check got docked every time my register came up short until they finally fired me."

Billy took a moment to consider what I was saying, then dug deep in his pocket and pulled out a crumbled fifty-dollar bill. "Here, go give her this. Let her keep the change, too" he said and took a long sip of his coke. For some reason, his kind gesture warmed my heart, but I shook it off. *This is just a job*, I reminded myself.

A few minutes after we ate, we were back on the road. This time we were pulling into what looked like a gravel road. The bike kicked up a cloud of dust that hovered behind us. With all the sticks and rocks and bumps in the road, you'd think Billy would have slowed down but he didn't. Every time we dipped into a small ditch, I squeezed him tighter, gently clawing him with my nails. He must have been turned on by my fear because it seemed like the more I squeezed him the faster he went. When we finally stopped, he parked the bike on a patch of dirt in front of a huge lake that was surrounded by towering trees. The croaks of crickets and frogs serenaded us as the moonlight lit up the dark sky. Its reflection bounced off the subtle ripples of water; I couldn't believe it when I saw stars sparkling in the sky. I couldn't remember the last time I saw a star. I almost thought they didn't exist anymore; like they'd gone extinct but, not out here. This place felt peaceful.

"Where are we?"

"We at my secret paradise," Billy said in a calm voice. The place did feel like a paradise. There was a certain stillness in the air that perpetuated a calmness. It felt like we were on another planet. "Come on," he said doing that head gesturing thing he did when he wanted me to follow him.

I loved Billy's secret paradise, but I wasn't dressed for the occasion. My dress was so tight, I couldn't move my legs good enough to step over the rocks and sticks and the spikes of my heels kept getting stuck in the mud. Billy didn't take what I was wearing into consideration. He was way ahead of me before he turned and noticed I wasn't right behind him. He stopped, laughed, and came to my aid. "Hurry up, grandma," he teased me.

"These heels aren't made for walking, nevertheless, hiking."

"Take them off then?"

"Then I'll be barefoot."

"So," Billy acted like he didn't understand me.

"I'll manage," I said and took a step forward only to get stuck in a wade of mud. "Shit," I whined.

"Let me help me help you," Billy offered.

Billy leaned over and grabbed my waist before lifting me off the ground. He picked me up so swiftly he yanked my shoe right off my foot. It was still in the mud. "Wait, my shoe," I tapped him on the back, but he didn't stop.

"I'll get it later," he told me.

I felt awkward with him carrying me in my evening dress and only wearing one shoe. He only carried me a few feet before we stopped in front of an old canoe. I hoped he wasn't about to do what I thought he was going to do. I couldn't swim and getting in that canoe didn't seem safe.

"What is this?"

"Our chariot for the night," he said, picking up a rope out of the mud and pulling the canoe toward us. He jumped in the canoe and then held out his hand to help me in. I hesitated. "What are you waiting on? A rescue boat?"

"I can't swim."

"Well we ain't going swimming," he extended his hand even closer and I grabbed it.

The boat swayed from side to side like it was going to flip over. That made me anxious but when I finally got settled, it stabilized. It was bigger and deeper inside than it looked. Billy started to push the paddles in the water and before I knew it, we were in the middle of the lake. We were directly underneath the moonlight and in clear view of the stars. It was beautiful.

"How often do you come here?" I pried. My question confused me. I didn't know if I asked it to make a note for Ace or if I was curious. Maybe it was a little of both.

"Whenever I can," he answered and opened his jacket and pulled out a bag of weed and a pack of cigarillos.

"You don't strike me as the type of guy that will be into shit like this."

"Oh, yeah," he said as he broke down the cigarillo. "You surprise me too."

"How so?"

"You don't seem like the type of chick that will marry a reject." He said referring to Ace. I was relieved he noticed that Ace and I weren't equally yoked. "What are, y'all? Swingers or something?"

I was embarrassed and offended by the comment he phrased as a question.

"No!" I responded quickly. He didn't seem to care that he offended me.

"You in it for the money then, huh?"

"Why do you care?"

"I don't really care. I just find it odd."

"You find what odd?" I asked.

"If another man ever propositioned me for my wife, I would break his fucking face in half." He said, giving me an intense look. I got turned on by the possibility of a man loving me so much he was willing to fight for me.

"Even if that proposition was coming from a man like you? A Badd." I challenged him.

Billy just looked at me with a half-smile. He never answered my question. After sealing the blunt with his tongue, he lit the cigar and took a puff.

"So how do you know Ace anyway?" I pretended not to know.

"The question is how that nigga know me?"

He took another puff and handed it to me. I didn't take it. At least not right away. For some reason, I didn't want Billy to see me in a negative light.

"It's alright. I know you like to party." He winked at me and brushed the bridge of my nose, hinting to me that he knew about the coke I used to snort. How did he know that? Was I stained by it? Did I look a certain way to him? "I won't judge you, I promise. It's not my style, Dalla."

I grabbed the blunt from him and took a puff. Billy leaned back and looked up at the stars. He stared hard at them. He was deep in thought. I wonder if he was thinking about all the shit Ace told him?

"You see that star right there?" he pointed at one of the thousands of stars in the sky. I just said yes although I didn't know the particular one he was referring to. They all looked the same to me. "I'm gon buy that star one day."

"How do you know it's for sale?"

Billy leaned up looked me directly in the eyes and replied, "Everything's for sale," he said like he was referring to me. I looked away from his gaze and took another puff of the blunt before handing it back to him.

"So, what's your story, Dalla Lucky?" Billy asked me in between puffs.

"You don't want to hear my story. You just want to fuck me. Right?"

"I'm not sure what I want to do with you yet but it ain't gon' be nothing you don't want to do. Forcing women ain't my style and I have no need to do it." He answered honestly.

I didn't know how to take his response. I watched Billy watch me. He took his hand and dipped it in the water. It got so quiet between us, that I started to get nervous. I had to say something. I needed to continue to pull him in. Get him to trust me so I decided to be honest with him. I told him my sad story. "I killed my mother and my father." I blurted. Maybe he could relate to my story being that both our mothers were murdered. Billy stared at me without blinking. He didn't say a word. He looked at me with a blank expression, but I knew a million thoughts must have been going through his head. So, I explained myself.

"I grew up in Miami. My mother was an aspiring singer. I get my talent from her," I smiled remembering my mother. "My father was a drunk," I said in a low voice. "I get my bad habits from him. I paused for a moment then took a deep breath. "We were dirt poor and had no extended family to lean on. They both were foster children and I was their only child. The biggest surprise slash mistake of both their lives. My father was possessive, he didn't want my mother to work because he was scared that somebody would discover her talent and she would leave him, so he never let her leave the house. The little money he did bring home doing odd jobs and gambling he drank up, so I had to do what I had to do to take care of my mother and I.

I stole food, clothes, money, jewelry…. Anything I could get my hands on. I stole from my favorite teacher. The only person to show me compassion. I stole from my best friend who used to let me sneak in her window and sleep on her floor when my dad would go on his whoop-ass rampages. I even stole out of a church offering before. The same church that fed me and my mother from their soup lines. I stole from my job even though I begged him to hire me and he took a risk hiring me being that I wasn't of legal working age yet. I got so good at taking things that didn't belong to me, it became second nature. It almost didn't feel like stealing anymore but just a way to get by. It was surviving.

One day I stole a few dollars from my father. He blamed my mother for it although he knew it was me. He just wanted a reason to beat her ass. Like he ever needed one anyway. He was drunk that night," my voice dropped as I relived the horrible memory. When I looked up at Billy, he was still staring at me, but this time I saw compassion behind his eyes. "He was always drunk, but this night was different. He was so angry," I took a deep breath.

"He wrapped his hands around my mother's throat and held her until she passed out. Usually, he would squeeze, then release, then squeeze and release again. That's why I didn't do anything at first. But, he didn't let go. He didn't give her time to catch her breath. He held her throat until her eyes rolled back in her head and her face turned blue. I remember how her arms fell limp by her side and her head fell back. I watched her die. Everything was happening so fast yet her last moments played out in slow motion. I was in a state of shock but by the time I snapped back into reality and accepted what was going on, my mother was dead. And even then, he was still holding her throat, and cursing her. So, I grabbed a kitchen knife and charged at him. I didn't realize what I was doing until I saw the blood. Then, I just ran and never looked back until now. I've been on my own since I was fourteen years old. And I'm still trying to survive."

Strangely enough, I told this story to break the ice between us and possibly manipulate Billy a little, but it only made it thicker. Neither one of us said a word. I stared at the reflection of the moon in the water. I felt Billy looking at me, but I didn't look up at him. I never told anyway that story before. Ever. I felt so raw and exposed that I just wanted to disappear. I wonder what he thought of me now? I'm the picture poster for damaged goods and it's better he finds this out now than later. Maybe it'll help him understand me when I do what I have to do for Ace. Or, maybe not.

I didn't notice I was crying until Billy leaned over and caught a falling tear from the corner of my eye. Then he kissed me on the forehead so softly, another tear fell from my eye. I still couldn't look at him. He grabbed my hand and squeezed it. He offered no words of wisdom or encouragement, but he didn't have to. I felt it in his touch.

Billy pulled his jacket over his head and took off his tennis shoes. The canoe begins to rock. I held on to the edges tight and watched him as he unzipped his jeans and pulled them off. What the fuck was he doing now? Then he stood up. The canoe shook even more. I started to get dizzy and nervous. "What are you doing?" I asked squeezing the edge of the boat.

"I'm going to get your shoe," he said and dived into the lake.

"Don't leave me here?" I started to panic. How did I know for sure that he would come back?

Billy either ignored my plea for him to stay or didn't hear me because he kept on swimming. The lake was big and we're almost in the middle of it. Could he really swim that far? I watched his arms dip in and out of the water, reaching above his head in long strokes until I didn't see him anymore. Shit, I fucked up now. If he didn't come back, what the fuck was I going to do? I squinted my eyes and tried to see past the fog and trees, but I couldn't. I thought about screaming his name, but I was afraid I would wake something out here that needed to stay sleep. For some reason, I started to think about Ace's alligators. Did alligators live in lakes? I sure hope I didn't find out tonight.

A few minutes passed by and I continued to torture myself with all the things that could happen if Billy didn't come back. Before I knew it, I was sobbing quietly to myself. When I lifted my hand to wipe my tears, I poked myself in the eye because the canoe started rocking again. I saw a hand grabbing the edge and before I could blink, Billy pulled himself back inside the boat and tossed me my wet shoe. I was relieved. Then I felt stupid for crying. I wiped my eyes quickly.

"You alright?" He said wiping lake water from his face. He gave me a strange look. I had a feeling he knew I was crying.

"You're so fucking weird!" I blurted out of frustration and he laughed.

"Let's go," he said and started to steer us further into the lake.

"What are you doing now? We came from that way," I pointed behind me, 'didn't we?'"

"Yep, but now we are going this way," he raised his chin. It was so dark and gloomy, I couldn't see past the fog, but I didn't say anything else. I just went with the flow.

9

We paddled deep into the lake for about twenty minutes. The sounds of the crickets got louder, and the surrounding bushes got thicker. I spotted a light shining out from the darkness. Billy steered in the direction of the light. The closer we got to it, the more I could see. We were coming up on a dock. The dock connected to a wooden bridge that led to a small house. The light I saw was the porch light. I would have never guessed in a million years there was a cabin hidden behind this lake. Crossing the lake was the only way in and out.

When we got to the dock, Billy jumped out of the canoe and tied it to a hook. There was a motorboat floating in the water beside it. Hopefully, it was the boat we were going back on. He extended his hand for me to grab and helped me up the dock. I took my other shoe off and Billy smiled. He was still down to his boxer shorts. He scooped his clothing out of the boat and started walking down the short bridge. The closer I got to the house, the more amazed I was. It was beautiful. I'd never seen anything like it. The cabin was mixed with a contemporary and a country style. Floor-to-ceiling stationary glass windows enclosed the timber wood cabin. I bet you could get a good view of the lake from any room in the cabin. The country porch wrapped around the house as well; it was made complete with a few rocking chairs and swinging benches. I smelled sawdust. It sprinkled in between the wood floor planks. A cutting saw was sitting at the side of the door. It was still plugged into an outlet in the wall.

Billy opened the door and I was hit with the smell of cedar and burnt wood. Polished oak floors stretched across the entire cabin. The walls were made of cabin wood and the ceilings were high with exposed wood beams. The home was beautiful. The bedroom, kitchen, and living area weren't divided by walls but makeshift furniture. Like the half-finished oak kitchen table with fresh lumber sitting on top of it and what looked like an old ceramic claw foot tub he painted and cut into a couch; a box guitar lay on across the cushion. It was cute in its own way and very different. This cabin showed me the parts of him that he was hiding.

"This is where you live?" I said looking around, trying to take the place in.

"No," he answered and dumped his clothes on top of the mattress on the floor.

He walked back into the only room that had a door attached to it. I assumed it was the bathroom.

"You renting this place?"

"Why?" he walked out the bathroom and asked, giving me a strange look like I was inquiring too much. He had a towel around his neck.

"I just never seen anything like this before," I said still looking around. "I just think it's amazing that's all."

"I built and designed this place myself," he said modestly.

"What?" This house alone made Billy Badd that much more interesting.

"It ain't nothing. Just a little cabin, off the map, out in the middle of the nowhere." He walked over to an old chest and pulled out a white t-shirt.

"But, it's so more than that," I said in awe.

Billy gave me a look that told me he thought I was trying too hard but I wasn't. I was amazed by this place; a creation from his unique mind. This cabin gave me an idea of who he was; humble, complex, diverse, fun, and mysterious. I liked him even more.

"So, you just woke up one day and decided you wanted to build a cabin? How does that work," I continued to walk around.

"Something like that. I went to school for architecture."

"What?" I said quickly. I didn't mean to sound so surprised. But what was up with criminals and college degrees? It just didn't make sense to me. "You're not the average Joe, Billy."

"Are you the average, Jane?"

"I try to be," I responded softly, and he nodded his head like he understood what I meant.

Then there was that awkward silence again. But this time, Billy broke the ice by dropping his boxer shorts and revealing the six-pack that seemed to not have an ending point and his thick dick that was pointing right at me, beckoning me to come to him. I tried not to look but I failed. Billy is comfortable in his own skin. He had no reason not to be, but his confidence wasn't cocky or conceited like most men with a body like his; his confidence had a natural and relaxed way about it. Even more of a turn-on for me.

"I'm going to take a shower. I got to get this lake water off me. Make yourself comfortable. There is another shower for you to use down the hall", he pointed. I needed to freshen up and cool my flesh from the hot flashes Billy was giving me. I didn't want to come off as desperate. "I pulled out a t-shirt for you to throw on. Unless you want to sleep in that dress. It don't seem comfortable to me."

"The T-shirt is fine," I said bashful. It was hard to have a normal conversation with him being naked.

Billy turned around to walk to the bathroom and I got a glimpse of his ass. Damn, how many squats does a man have to do to get an ass like that? This shit is getting real hard.

I took a quick shower put on Billy's oversized t-shirt and made myself comfortable on his mattress; the shirt smelled like him. I felt weird sniffing it every second, taking in as much of his scent as I could but I like his smell. The mattress was soft and expensive feeling. I wonder how he got it out here? I pulled one of Billy's cigars out of his jacket pocket and rolled myself another blunt. I hope he didn't mind me smoking in his bed. He did tell me to make myself comfortable. I leaned my head back against the wall Billy used as a headboard and stared outside. The glass was so wide and clear, it was just like I was sitting on the front porch. I saw everything. The stars, the lake, the trees, and that beautiful half-moon smiling at us. I began to love the sound of the crickets chirping; they and whatever else was outside making a beautiful noise. It sounded like a nature symphony.

Billy sure could take a long shower. Almost fifteen minutes went by before he walked out the bathroom with a towel tied around his waist. Steam rushed out the door and lingered in the air before dissolving. I had already caught a buzz and was trying to make it stronger by taking heavier puffs and holding them in longer. He sat down on the bed pulled an incense out of his nightstand and lit it using the lighter on my lap. Maybe he didn't want me smoking in here after all.

"You cool?" he asked me, and I nodded my head yes. I was cooler than I'd been in a long, long time. Truth be told, I didn't want to leave this cabin. Billy took the blunt from my hand but instead of taking a puff like I assumed he was going to do, he put it out. I sat up on the bed with my knees against my chest and Billy walked around the other side of the mattress and sat down beside me. He gently grabbed my hand and lifted my arm. He looked down at the mark Ace left when he pushed me down. He ran his hand over the bruises like his soft touch could erase them.

"You got to be a real weak ass man to hit a female," he replied to himself, turning my face and observing the red welts on my neck. I started to feel pathetic. Like a victim. That couldn't have been attractive. "I used to think my daddy was a hero. A regular Superman. But then one day I saw him slap the shit out of my mama. Blood gushed out of her nose like a fountain and then he cursed at her for getting blood on his white shirt. He wasn't no hero anymore after that. Just a weak ass nigga slowly killing the only woman I ever loved."

Billy continued to rub my arm up and down like he was in a trance. His brow lowered into a scour and he squinted his eyes like he was trying to fight off a bad memory. "I wasn't bold as you thought." He looked up at me. "But maybe it ain't too late," he said like he was talking to himself." Billy gave me a look that I recognized. He could relate to my situation. We had more in common than he thought. "Why you let him do this to you?" I didn't respond. I felt embarrassed and just as weak as Ace for allowing him to hit me. It's not like I could tell him the truth. The real reason why I was forced to stay with him. "Your husband is one bitch ass nigga. You know that?"

I shook my head yes. I knew better than anybody. "I don't love him," I replied quickly. It was my only defense.

"You loving something about the situation," he said and continued massaging my arm. "Does it hurt?" he asked further looking at my bruise. His touch was so gentle.

"Not the way you think it does."

Billy gave me a considerate stare then leaned down and planted small kisses on my arm. He kissed all around the bruise. My body tingled. I closed my eyes and leaned my head back. His kisses made their way up my neck and stopped at the bottom of my ear. It was the first kiss I had in years. I felt like a schoolgirl. He brushed against my cheeks and lips with the tip of his nose and then kissed my chin. Lowering his hand under my shirt, he gently massaged his way up to my breasts and caressed them so softly, I almost cried. I've never been touched this way before. He lowered me to my back and my heart started to race. The anxiety I was feeling coupled with mixed emotions caused me to tense up. Everything was happening so fast and I wasn't in control of the situation like I usually was. "Just relax," he whispered in my ear before kissing his way south of my belly button, stopping right where I hoped he would. I needed this. I wanted this.

I gasped at his touch, arching my back and gripping the sheets. My legs began to shake uncontrollably, and my entire body quivered. I was ready to explode but I held it in. I never felt this way before. Never. Billy lifted his head and unwrapped the towel from his waist. He carefully pulled the t-shirt over my head. When he leaned down close to my face, I leaned up for a kiss on the lips, but he turned away from me. What was that about? He'd kissed me earlier. Or did he not consider that to be a kiss? When he started to suck on my neck and massage my midsection with two fingers, I didn't care anymore. I just let him do his thing.

I was getting so wet, I almost felt ashamed but that didn't stop Billy from making upward circular motions with his fingers, enticing my river to run even deeper. I lifted my hips from the mattress to move in closer to his touch, twirling my hips to the same pattern of his touch. When my insides started boiling over, I knew I was ready for him. Then, he finally made his way inside of me. The man's rhythm was on point and his timing was perfect. When he moved fast it felt slow and when he moved slow, it felt fast. He knew the exact moment of when to kiss the tips of my nipples. He knew when to squeeze my ass and pull me in deeper. And best of all, he knew when to let his fingers rub against my clit, heightening the experience.

Billy grabbed my waist and anchored me on top of him. I didn't have to do any work though. He used my body to his advantage. He squeezed my waist, bouncing me up and down on top of him. I just moved with his movements and after a while, we became in sync. My body was being touched in places no one had ever touched, and my mind stayed in the moment. The ecstasy I was feeling confused me. Just as I sucked in air, tighten my thighs, and prepared to climax, I had an epiphany. I realized what was going on; for the first time in my life, I was making love to a man. Although I fucked several men, making love to Billy felt like my virginity had finally been broken.

After we made love my body felt like putty. I could barely blink, nevertheless move, but I still wanted to hold Billy. It just felt right but he grabbed a cigarette and smoked instead. He got up from the bed and walked over to his makeshift couch and picked up the box guitar. He toyed with the strings and a tranquil melody echoed and bounced off the walls of the cabin. I guess he was done touching me for the night. He barely nudged me with his elbow when he rolled off the bed. I longed for his touch to the point where I felt pathetic. I told myself that there was no way a man could make love to a woman the way Billy made love to me without feeling something afterward. If he wanted to lie to himself about what was taking place between us then that was his issue but I wasn't playing myself; I knew what was happening.

As strange of a feeling as it was, I knew just what was going on in my heart. I was in love with Billy Badd. The love thing was new territory for me, but I was prepared to navigate my way through this unknown territory without a map or rules. Two seconds after I came to this conclusion, a flash Ace ran through my mind and I remembered what I was trying to forget. I couldn't fall in love with a man I was out to betray. Could I?

10

I can't believe it's Sunday already. The day that I have to return to Ace. I can't think of anything worse than going back to him. Especially after spending all this time with a man like Billy Badd. We just checked out of the Day's Inn hotel and now we're having breakfast at a waffle house. For someone to be as rich as Ace claimed him to be, Billy sure was cheap with his money but I didn't care about his money. His character was what attracted me.

This has been an adventurous weekend. I don't think I will ever have this much fun again. Billy took me to the dog races and I won him five hundred dollars that we gambled away at an underground casino. A stranger mistook me to be his wife, commenting that we were a beautiful couple. That was the best thing anyone said to me that day. Billy took that and ran with it. Everywhere we went we became different people with different names. I watched Billy pickpocket strangers just for fun and trick random people into gambling with his magical deck of cards. He won chains, watches, and rings but he didn't keep any of it. He gave it all to the homeless people. He was like a black Robin Hood.

We ate greasy food and drank hard liquor; Of course, Billy didn't pay for a thing. We fucked like teenagers twice a day and treated his bike like it was jet on the highway. He stole me a pair of jeans, a tank top, and some sneakers from a local department store. He joked with me, saying I looked like a biker chick in my clothing. Everything we did was random. But, now it was all coming to an end.

"Why you not eating your waffle?" Billy asked stuffing food in his mouth.

"Why does it matter to you? You're not going to pay for it."

Billy shrugged. "That's true," he said and stuffed a piece of bacon in his mouth. He continued to look at me like he was trying to read my mind although I knew he already knew what I was thinking.

When Billy made love to me last night, I savored every moment of it because I didn't know when I would be able to touch him again. For all I know, Ace was setting him up to be killed. That didn't sit well with me. Saturday night, I started to get burdened heavily thinking about Ace's plot against, Billy. I didn't know exactly what he planned on doing to Billy once it was all over, but I knew he wanted me to deceive a man I was in love with and that was bothersome.

I thought about spilling everything to Billy. After I told the story about what happened to my parents, I felt like I could tell him anything, but this was too risky. Chances are if I told him the truth, he'd never trust me, and I ran the risk of never seeing him again. But, if I followed Ace's plan, maybe that would give me more time with Billy. With all that time, maybe he could see that he could love me the way I loved him.

"Why did you ask Ace for me? You think I was some kind of whore?"

"I don't entertain whores anymore. I learned my lesson with that shit," Billy said and took a sip of orange juice. He shook his head like he was remembering a bad story.

"Then why?"

"You look like you needed a break and although I won that card game, that nigga was in no position to tell me no. I just took advantage of the situation is all."

"Is that it?"

Billy shrugged and responded *yep* like this weekend was no big deal to him. "You homesick or something?"

"The exact opposite I'm sick of home if I can call it that."

"Then leave."

"It's more complicated than that."

"How so?" Billy gave me a serious look.

"It's a long story. Let's just say if I leave, I'll spend the rest of my life in hiding. He'll hunt me for the rest of my life. What you think you know about Ace is all bullshit. His ego is viscous!"

"What don't I know about him?" Billy looked me directly in the eye and waited for me to respond. I got nervous, so I looked away. I don't know why I expected Billy to save me. I guess because he was the only one who could. "I told him I would bring you back. And I'm a man of my word."

"Bullshit!" I yelled.

"Calm down," Billy whispered loudly before wiping syrup off his mouth. "What the fuck you want me to do? The mess y'all got going on ain't got shit to do with me. It's a lot of shit going on right now in my life. I hate to fucking say it but...I might need that mutha-fucka."

"Need him for what? I've heard of you and your family."

"What the fuck you know about my family?" Billy was defensive.

"Your family runs the entire city. You have connections and resources. Why do you need Ace?"

"It's personal not business. There's a big difference between the two when it comes to connections and resources." Billy said rough. He threw his napkin on the table and got up to walk out the door. I rushed behind him before the waitress beckoned me for money I didn't have.

Billy jumped on his bike almost like I wasn't there. If I hadn't got on as soon as I did I wonder if he would have left me? He sped a few blocks down the road and stopped at a gas station. I got off the bike while he put gas in it.

"I'm taking you home," Billy said to me like that was his final answer.

I took a deep breath. "When?" I prepared myself to hear the worst.

"Now," he said without looking at me.

We got back on the bike and headed back towards the city. The party was over.

When we pulled up the driveway, Ace was waiting for us outside. I guess security tipped him off when we arrived. When I saw him standing on the steps, wearing a pair of dress pants and a button-up shirt, my stomach turned. I almost wanted to break down and cry.

Ace watched me from head to toe. I bet he was judging my attire. He would have never approved of this outfit. Then he gave me a strange look, almost like he didn't know me anymore. He seen the change in me but I'm sure he didn't have a problem with beating me back into submission. Billy stood by my side and watched Ace watch me. I looked at Billy and he looked at me. He didn't seem like he had peace with his decision to bring me back.

"Did you have a good weekend with my wife?" Ace asked Billy but stared at me.

"We had a ball," Billy said and looked at me. Ace started to get uncomfortable.

"So now it's back to business, right?" Ace asked Billy, letting him know that playtime was over. Billy didn't respond. "Dalla," Ace beckoned me to come to him. I hesitated and gave Billy one last look, hoping he seen the desperation in my eyes. "Dalla," Ace said again, this time warning me. He started to bite down on his bottom lip. He was getting angry.

I took a hesitant step forward only to be pulled back by Billy.

"I came to tell you that she ain't coming back with you! Y'all done! Understand me?" Billy threatened Ace. Ace smiled evil at both of us. Billy grabbed my hand to comfort me and I squeezed it to thank him. I was so relieved, I began to cry.

"You don't mean that," Ace said calmly to Billy through a chuckle.

"Fuck you! In the words of my brother, Bobby Badd, *I mean what I say, and I only say it once.*"

"What about all the shit we discussed? You gon' let my dope head, tramp of wife come between our business, man? I thought you were smarter than that, Billy?"

"I ain't got no business with you, nigga. You gave me what I asked for, I considered it and now we're done. You don't fuck with my family man. You keep fucking around, your ass gon' end up dead. You feel me?"

Ace got really quiet. He looked like he was holding his breath but really, he was containing his anger. Ace didn't like to be caught off guard or not to get his way. He needed to be in control of the situation, but he couldn't be; Billy was the boss now. He looked like he wanted to hit Billy. Striking me was one thing, but striking Billy Badd was suicide. There was nothing he could do.

"You're making a mistake, Billy. A big mistake. If he did that to your mother, what do you think he gon' do to you?"

Billy let go of my hand and charged toward Ace. Ace, feeling protected by his bodyguards didn't flinch, but when Billy got close enough, the bodyguards got out of his way, allowing Billy to grab Ace by the throat and slam him against the front door. Those bodyguards knew not to fuck with Billy Badd. Ace didn't bother to try and fight back either. He just stood still and let Billy choke him and laughed but I knew he was fuming inside.

"I'll kill you right here, nigga! You don't know shit about my family and don't you ever mention my mother again. Ever!" he said before letting him go. Ace slid down the door. Billy turned to walk away but turned back around just to cold sock Ace in the jaw. Ace fell to the ground but quickly jumped back up. He was so angry he was twitching.

"You not the man I thought you were, Billy. That's a shame. It's a real shame."

"Fuck you, bitch" Billy said, storming back to his bike. I grabbed the helmet, ready to get the hell on.

"So long, Dalla," Ace called out to me. I looked at him and he was holding his jaw, giving me an evil look. "Who knows…maybe I'll run into you again and we'll go swimming," Ace winked at me. I knew he was threatening me and so did, Billy.

"You stay the fuck away from her, too! Come tomorrow, y'all divorced. It's over!"

"Hey, whatever you say, Mr. Billy Badd. It's your world. I'm just passing through." Ace said, giving me a stare so evil, I shuddered. I took the phone that he gave me out my purse and flung it at him then I waited on the bike for Billy to gear up. I looked up at Ace one last time and he mouthed the words, *you fucked up*, to me. Then I begin to wonder if he was right.

11

Billy pulled into a gas station and drove around back near the dumpsters. It smelled awful but that didn't stop me from trying to read Billy's mind. He jumped off the bike and began to pace back and forth. If I didn't know any better, he was looking as if he'd made a mistake and was having second thoughts.

I got off the bike and stepped over crushed glass and cigarette butts to get to him. He stopped pacing and looked at me. I was so grateful for what he did I extended my arms and hugged him to say thank you, but he didn't hug me back. I leaned my head up for a kiss on the lips and he gently pushed me away like I was crossing the line. Was there really a line between us? Where did that come from all of a sudden?

"Thank you," I said to him.

"For what?" He played dumb but sounded serious.

"You know what you did for me."

"I did it for me," he replied curtly. Billy stared at me for a reaction, but I didn't have one because I didn't know what he meant. "Tomorrow, I'm going to get you divorced from that nigga. Then, the next day after that…" he hesitated for a few seconds, "I'm gon' marry you."

I thought I was hearing things. Were my fantasies becoming verbal hallucinations? "What?" I had to be sure I was hearing right.

"I'm gon' marry you," he said it again like it was all settled.

I exhaled a great breath of relief, smiled bigger than I ever had, and rushed to him again with open arms and an open heart. He did love me after all. But, before I can wrap my arms around his neck and say *I do*, to his non-traditional proposal, Billy grabbed my hands and placed them back on his side like he was trying to restrain a crazy person.

"It ain't that type of party, Dalla," Billy said cold. He looked at me strange. I felt so stupid that I just wanted to disappear. I uncomfortably looked away from his gaze. "I figure I did you a favor getting you away from that bitch ass husband of yours and now you can return the favor by marrying me."

"What type of fucked up favor is that?" I was pissed off. I felt misled but then again, who was I fooling. This man didn't love me. He just needed something from me like every other nigga in my life.

I opened myself up to Billy wider than I ever have for anyone and he just rejects me like I'm nothing. I married Ace for protection and in turn, signed away my life. My body was in bondage to him. Now Billy wants me to turn around and do the same thing. Only this time, it's my heart that will be in bondage. My life has been full of beguiling propositions, deceit, and loneliness. Is that all I'm worth to people? I know I've done a lot of fucked up shit and maybe attracting fucked up people is my karma.

"I'll make it worth your while?"

"Fuck you!" I said and turned to walk away.

I wasn't going down that road again. Co-dependency and fear nearly killed me. It's only now that I'm finding myself again. I never needed anyone before. I could handle shit myself. I need to get back to that. But, how? It's been so long. Billy grabbed my arm and pulled me back.

"Why are you getting so pissed? You didn't believe I was proposing to you did you?" Billy asked me like I was silly.

"No," I lied to defend my pride. "I'm just..." I tried to find the right words to make me look less foolish and vulnerable, "I'm confused and tired and..."

Billy cut me off. "Well, you can rest now." Billy stroked the side of my face. Why did he have to touch me? If he doesn't want me that way, why bother touching me so softly? "I know you been through a lot but when it's all over, I'm gon' help you get on your feet. Then you can go anywhere you want to go and you ain't got to hide and steal to survive either. All that shit is over, Dalla."

"Okay," I said and took two steps away from him, separating myself from his touch.

I took a deep breath. He had my attention now. I was back in my right mind. Maybe Billy was the final link that led to my independence. After all, I've been so starved for affection that I really can't trust my feelings when it comes to Billy or anyone else for that matter. This whole thing started off as a job for me and that's just how I intend on finishing it.

"Why marriage? And what's in it for me?" I got down to business.

Billy took a deep breath and looked up at the sky and down at the cracked asphalt before meeting my eyes.

"Money is the answer to both your questions."

"Well…money talks," I said to him, hinting for him to tell me more.

"When I marry you, I'm going to inherit twenty million dollars and a bunch of other bullshit that I don't want or need. I just want the cash. Once I get that cash, I'm gon' break you off five million and split."

"Why do you have to marry me to get your inheritance?" It didn't make sense to me.

"Because that's how the shit works," Billy said frustrated more with the rules that dictated his inheritance than my question. "It ain't gon' be that easy though. They ain't seen me in a while and because of that, I'm sure my brother gon' convince my father not to be so quick to pay me. We gon' need to be married at least a year. Maybe even two before I get the money."

If I could survive two years with Ace and his fucked-up family then this two years should be a walk in the park.

"How long has it been since they seen you?" I asked Billy.

"Almost two months," he said. "I left a few weeks after my mother died."

"Why?" I pried.

"I needed time to breathe. Clear my head. Think. Research and plan." Billy looked up at the sky again. I guess he realized that the answer to his problem wasn't in the sky. So, he looked back at me. The answer to his problem.

"Two years, huh?" I said, giving it more thought. "What do I have to do as your wife?" I wanted to know the terms. The good, the bad, and the freaky.

"Nothing you don't want to do," Billy said respectful.

I folded my arms against my chest and paced back and forth. Billy followed me with his eyes. Just like when I married Ace, I had no other options. I could do a lot with five million dollars. That's a whole lot of money. Maybe I could go somewhere and buy a blue pill that made me forget all this shit ever happened or maybe the money was the blue pill. What's the worst thing that can happen? Billy was no Ace. He wouldn't slap me around, threaten to kill me, or cause me any physical harm but the chances of him breaking my heart every day was a real threat.

"When do I get the money?" I tried to act cold just like him.

"As soon as we're in the clear."

"How do I know you'll really pay me and that this isn't another one of your card tricks?"

"You don't know. You'll have to trust me."

"Trust you…" I said like that was hard to do.

"In this situation, yes. Can I trust you?" He asked me, and my heart stopped.

Maybe now would be a good time to come clean about everything I knew about Ace's plans of war against his family. It was at the tip of my tongue to tell him. So much so that the truth had to show in my eyes. I turned my back to Billy to save face. I wasn't ready to tell him the truth, yet. Besides, what if there was a chance that Billy really did love me and in the two years we spent together he realized it? I couldn't tell him. Not now. If I did, I bared the risk of losing it all. Including the possibility of true love. I turned back around to face him.

"In this situation, yes," I repeated what he told me.

"So, we have a deal?" Billy said holding out his hand for me to grab.

I looked down at his hand before grabbing it. "Yes," I replied, and Billy kissed my hand. I felt that fluttering filling rush through my body when his soft lips, touched my skin. I reminded myself that the kiss meant nothing to him. It was just his way of sealing the deal.

"Good. Now, I got some things to explain to you."

Billy gave me the low down about his family. He told me about the private Ranch he lived on that sounded more like Gotham City and the B-Necklace that I would have to wear and what it would do for me. Then he told me a little bit about his three brothers, Brock, Bobby, and Brip. They all worked for the family business which was an empire for criminals.

I wasn't surprised when he told me his job was to develop the Ranch, so it brought in revenue. He also bought land in the family name and developed it, then leased it out as profitable havens for criminals to do their dirt unbothered by the police or their enemies. He called them mini Ranches. They basically were ghetto royalty and by default, I would be too. They did own the city. He promised me that as his wife, I would never have to worry about Ace or anyone else coming after me. I was just as protected as the First Lady of the United States if not more. It was so much to take in.

He barely mentioned his father. By the sour look that crossed his face when he spoke of him, I could tell they were at odds. He talked about his mother a lot. He smiled when he mentioned her. He didn't mention anything about how she died. He didn't have to though. I heard it all when I eased dropped on his and Ace's conversation. He just said she died four months ago.

I had a week to prepare to meet the rest of his family. We stayed in a hotel where Billy drilled me every day about the story of how we met. In short, I was a realtor who sold him land in L.A. We dated for two months before getting married in Vegas. We've been spending the last few weeks on our honeymoon in Sedona, Arizona. It was a simple story that I embellished in my mind, adding my wishful spin to it. I even tried to pick Billy's brain by asking him scenario-phased questions about our honeymoon just to get an idea of how it would be if it were all true. The thought of honeymooning with Billy in a city with red mountains and orange sunsets was too good to be true because it wasn't true.

He gave me random pop quizzes. It was getting intense, especially when I messed up on simple things like where we had our first date or what restaurants in Arizona we dined at. It would have been easier if he'd just taken me to Arizona. But, was his family going to drill me that hard? He warned me about Mona, his oldest brother's wife. He said she would be the primary one asking the questions and to watch what I said around her because she would be looking for flaws. Apparently, I was going to be seeing a lot of her being that I had to live on the Ranch with her. Billy had a house on the Ranch. It was a part of his inheritance.

At first, I was getting nervous. Especially when I thought about meeting his brother Brip face to face. Although Brip didn't know I was there the day he shot Keno and Tony, I still felt uneasy about it. I had nightmares about his evil heckle for months after that. I asked Billy about the chances of the family doing some research and finding out that I was married to Ace Lucky. He told me not to worry. Apparently, I was Ace's best-kept secret. He said that if he never linked me to Ace then they wouldn't, and that Ace Lucky wasn't a concern of his family, so I didn't have to worry. Ace Lucky was *a nobody* to the Badds; he didn't pose a threat, so they left him alone. I didn't say it, but I was thinking that maybe they should reconsider that. Your biggest enemy is always the one you don't see coming.

Billy did his footwork too. He set me up with a new I.D. that read Dalla Smith instead of Dalla Davis which was my real name. I never changed my I.D. when I married Ace. He got rid of my marriage records too so there was nothing to link me back to Ace. I hoped. Billy also hooked me up with an L.A. realtor's license, a fake degree in finance from UCLA, and bills in my name from a place I supposedly leased before we married. He even had fake phone and bank records. I was clear just in case they decided to double-check our story. After the week was over, I was ready. Billy was more nervous than me. He kept commenting that I wasn't taking it seriously whenever I would laugh off one of his last-minute quizzes but he just didn't understand. After living with the Lucky family, living with the Badds on a luxurious Ranch was going to be like a vacation. At least I assumed it would be. Knowing my luck, you never know.

12

We were pulling into the Ranch. The moment the armed guards opened the big black gates, I began to get nervous. Billy explained the Ranch to me but seeing it was a different story. The place was like its own city. I watched the gates shut behind us from the rear-view mirror and for some reason, I started to feel caged. Does it take all of this to be a Badd? And more importantly, do I have what it takes to pull this off? I guess I was about to find out.

Billy was quiet during most of the ride. I had never seen him this way. He didn't even try to sneak in a last-minute pop quiz on me. It was like something in the air out here transformed him into a different person. He had a bothered look on his face and was deep in thought. He knew there was a ghost that lived on this Ranch. It haunted him. His nerves were starting to get to me. If he was nervous about seeing his own family, then maybe I should be too. I started to hear Brip's heckle again and then sweat popped up in beads on my forehead before rolling down the sides of my face. I took deep breaths to calm down.

Looking out the window, there was so much to see. There were several buildings under construction and neatly cut-out dirt paths that I'm sure were being formed as roads. How did this place exist? Was it even on the map? As we got deeper into the Ranch, I saw peaks of rooftops that I assumed were the houses Billy told me about.

"You designed all of this?" I tried to get Billy to talk. Maybe a casual conversation lighten the tension.

"Not all of it. Some of it was here before I was born," he said short.

"You sure you want to leave all of this?" I said looking around his corrupt kingdom.

"Yep," he answered short.

"Where are you going to go, Billy?"

"Some place where the eagles don't fly."

"What does that mean?"

"It means I'm going to a place where nobody knows my name. Somewhere I can walk the streets like a ghost, seeing and hearing shit without being noticed. Away from the hype… bullshit… the pretending. That way I can always know what's real and what's fake. People can say what they think about me without fearing what will happen. They can say hello or goodbye or shoot me a bird on the highway for cutting them off. Hell, if a stranger walks up to me and says, *Billy, you real fucked up*, I might just say thank you." Billy went on an unexpected rant.

I understood what he meant. He was born and raised with people kissing his ass and he had enough of it. Naturally, it just wasn't who he was. Billy went quiet again. I guess he was fantasizing about the mysterious place he'd just told me about. I did wonder if a place like that existed for him. I could see in his eyes he needed it to exist.

"Billy," I said, and he turned and faced me, "you're real fucked up," I joked

"Thank you," he turned to me and grabbed my hand before smiling.

———— ··●·· ————

We pulled into a circular driveway of a really big white house. Before we could get off the bike, a woman with a low haircut and red tights was standing outside with her hands defensively folded against her chest. She almost broke her neck, dipping and turning her head to see who I was. When Billy has saw her, his face went sour.

Billy grabbed my hand to help me off the bike. Once I was off, he didn't let go. I guess that meant it was showtime. We walked towards the woman who seemed to not be able to take her eyes off me. She opened her mouth to say something but was cut off before she began by the man who just walked out the door. The man had a stern look on his face. The thick welt that went from his chin and curved around his jawbone, stopping right at his eye, made him look intimidating. He put his arm around the woman.

"Is it you, brother?" The man asked Billy.

"Live and direct," Billy replied dryly.

The man walked down the steps and extended his arms to hug, Billy. Billy hugged him back, but I could tell it was a phony hug.

"Welcome home, brother."

"Thanks, Brock," Billy replied. After hearing the name, I knew that it was his older brother and the woman grimacing on the steps had to be his wife, Mona.

Mona walked down the steps and hugged Billy then gave him a tiny peck on the cheek.

"We were worried about you, Billy," she said still looking at me.

"Y'all didn't have to do that. I'm always good."

"Yeah, but what about your responsibilities on the Ranch? Your Job? Pops?" Brock went in hard on Billy. "He been worried sick about you man. You know he ain't got over momma yet and here you go running off without a trace. The casino construction don'came to a stop. We are losing money with that and we lost two clients waiting on you to finish up that other project. They ready to pay us big money and sign a two-year lease for that land you supposed to be developing but you bullshitting by running off like a little boy cause you ain't get your way," Brock argued.

Mona placed her hand on top of Brock's shoulders and he calmed down. "Not now," she said, looking at me like he was saying too much. Then Brock finally looked at me like he was just noticing I was there.

"Who is this?" he said pointing at me like I was an object.

"My wife, Dalla," Billy said with his chest out.

Mona gasped, and Brock just stared at Billy in disbelief. I swallowed hard and held out my hand for Brock to shake. He just looked at me like I was crazy.

"Why so formal?" Brock asked me. "We family, now right?" He said like he wasn't sure.

I laughed uneasily and extended my arms to hug Brock. He didn't squeeze me back. He just patted me on the back and gently but rudely pushed me off of him like I had fleas. I turned to hug Mona and she held out her hand for me to shake instead.

"Wow. Your wife?" Brock said like he couldn't believe what he was hearing. "So, you ran off and got married and ain't tell nobody nothing," Brock seemed offended.

"And where her ring at?" Mona said looking at my hand.

"The ring is being made with the necklace," Billy snapped at Mona. "You of all people should know how the shit works. And, I'm grown as hell, man," Billy said to Brock. "What the fuck I need to tell you for? I don't need your damn permission, Brock."

"You don't but you kinda do," Brock replied cocky. "And it's just a common courtesy. You know how this family operates. You just married her to get back at me. Didn't you?"

"Everything ain't about you, Brock," Billy said shaking his head like he was exhausted with his brother. "Look, I ain't trying to have a bunch long chat with you. I just came so y'all can meet my wife, then I'm gon' take my stuff, and we gon' split for a few months." Billy tried to put an end to the bickering.

"Split? So, you gone again, huh?"

"Dalla got business in LA to finish."

"You mean to close out," Mona interjected. "You know all them ties got to be cut. She ain't no different than me, Billy. From here on out, her business is Badd business."

Billy sucked his teeth. He didn't respond to Mona's comment. I guess Mona was trying to remind him that once anyone married into the family, they had to leave everything else behind.

"She's right, Billy. Besides, you can't leave yet. You got a job to finish."

"I'll finish the job when you stop withholding my pay!"

"I'll pay you when you stop fucking up."

"Yeah, but what about that freeze you got on my account? There was no reason for that. That's my fucking money! I worked for it," Billy pounded against his chest. He was getting heated. "When you gon' lift that freeze so I can have access to my damn money. You stole my stash. What type of shit is that?"

"Billy," Brock said calmly like he was ready to reason with him for his madness, "I ain't want to have to do none of that shit but you left me no choice when you ran out here and ain't tell nobody where you were going. You weren't in your right mind; you were talking some real crazy shit. I had to do what I had to do to protect the Ranch and the family. You know that. But, now that you back with your beautiful wife," he looked at me out of the corner of his eye, "we can talk about getting things back on track man," Brock gave Billy a look like he was trying to make peace. He gently patted him on the shoulder. "Everybody was surprised and hurt by Momma's death, but life goes on. We got a legacy to continue."

Brock seemed like he had Billy until he made the comment about their mother. Billy clutched down on his jaw and his chest filled with air. He stared at his brother like he was about to sucker punch him, but he didn't. Brock just stared back at Billy with an evil smirk on his face like he was daring him to hit him.

"I'm gon' get my money, Brock. All of it. This bullshit ends today. Where Pops at?" Billy said, going straight to the source.

Mona was blocking the front door. Billy grabbed my hand and pulled me with him as he tried to move past Mona, but she didn't budge. He elongated his neck to try to see past her, peering into the house for his father.

"Watch out," he said to Mona, but she ignored him. She waited for Brock to give her, her cue.

"Pops is in the study working. He ain't been feeling good man and now ain't the time to bring some bullshit his way. We can't work this out like two grown men? You ain't got to run and tell Pops on me like we ten years old again," Brock chuckled.

"Nigga you don't tell me when I can speak with my own father!" Billy said and squeezed my hand tight. I guess he was trying to release the tension he was feeling. I gave him a gentle squeeze back just to try and calm him down."

"He's my father too and you know the fucking rules man. Anybody wanna speak to the big man they gotta go through me. The shit ain't changed since you left, Billy."

"Oh, you have no idea how much has fucking changed," Billy said to Brock giving him an incredulous look. He pushed his way past Mona, pulling me along the way. Brock reached to grab Billy and I ducked but Mona stopped him, grabbing his hand to hold him back.

"Brock don't do this. Just let him go."

They both watched us as we walked across the foyer and turned down a long hallway. Billy was still squeezing my hand, cursing words I couldn't comprehend under his breath. I didn't know a guy as cool and easygoing as Billy could get so mad. I thought that this was going to be a breeze, but I wasn't sure anymore. The intense stares they were giving me, gave me an eerie feeling. I don't know why but I just didn't feel as safe as Billy said I would. Brock looked like a felon and Mona was the picture poster for a hood rat on steroids. Ace and his family were insane in there on right but full of bullshit; they were all bark with no real bite, but I knew right off the back that this wasn't the case with these people. Bullshitting wasn't in their blood.

13

Billy knocked on the huge double mahogany wood doors and waited. He was still holding my hand. He was breathing hard like he'd just got finished running a marathon. He tried to turn the huge bronze knobs to open the door, but it was locked. He took a deep breath and began to shake his head like he was about to lose it. I never seen him like this before.

"Are you alright?" I asked and tried to wipe the sweat from his brow, but he slapped my hand away like I was crazy for trying to touch him.

"I'm cool," he said quickly. "I'm just gon' get my money and get the fuck out of here," Billy said more to himself than me.

Billy wanted his money. Now I think I understand why he stole all those things. He was broke. Billy knocked on the door again but this time, harder than the first. Then finally, a deep, husky voice, called out from behind it.

"What is it, Brock?" he seemed annoyed that he was getting disturbed.

"Pops this ain't, Brock. It's Billy."

There was silence for a while. Then we heard a loud click and the knob turned. A few seconds later, a skinny woman in a short skirt, leather halter top, and smeared lipstick slipped out the door. The girl looked like she was younger than me. She adjusted her backward skirt and gave Billy a flirtatious look as she walked by him. I could have slapped that bitch for flirting with my fake husband. Billy watched the girl like she looked and smelled like shit. Then he let go of my hand and pushed the heavy door open wide enough for both of us to walk in.

"Who the fuck is that whore Pops? Ma ain't been in the grave but a few months and you still disrespecting her house."

"Watch your tone, boy!" The man said sternly, standing up from behind his desk and zipping up his pants.

Surprisingly, Billy humbled himself. He lowered his head to his father. "Yes, sir," he said under his breath.

His father was a few inches taller than him and had broad shoulders. He had very masculine facial features; a strong jaw bone, bushy eyebrows, thick lips, and a wide nose. He was a very handsome older man, but I didn't see Billy in him. Other than their height, they looked nothing alike. He was dressed like the CEO of a Fortune five hundred company. Everything about him screamed old money. His office smelled like expensive cigars and new money. Billy's father looked good for his age but there was something off about his handsomeness. He seemed mean. Just like Ace. He walked from behind his desk.

"Who do you have with you, son?" He gave me a strict look.

"My wife," Billy said in a voice so low I almost didn't hear him. Long gone was the aggression he shared with Brock.

"Excuse me? Speak up, son!" His father said like a drill sergeant although he heard every word Billy said.

"This is my wife, sir," Billy finally looked up at his father. "Her name is Dalla."

Now, I was squeezing Billy's hand. I couldn't look this man in the eye, but I had to. I finally got the nerve to look at him and he was smiling at me, his gold cap, sparkling.

"Dalla," he repeated my name like he was fond of it. "I'm very pleased with your choice son. Marriage is just what you need to keep you straight. I'm proud of you," He patted Billy on the back and although our marriage wasn't real, Billy seemed thrilled that his father was proud of him. "Come here, Dalla."

He pulled me into a hug. His cologne had a mature smell. It was perfect for a man of his age and caliber. It smelled expensive and masculine; just like him. His body felt solid like he still worked out.

"It's very nice to meet you, Dalla." He told me. His baritone voice made me tremble.

"Thank you, sir," I said bashful.

"Just call me Papa Badd," he gave me a warm smile then grabbed my hand and kissed it like a gentleman.

He was wearing a diamond ring on his pinky finger that was so big and sparkly that his hand felt cold to touch. The matching diamond-crusted Rolex was a nice compliment to it.

"Could you give my son and me a minute to talk in private?" His face went stern again.

"Sure," I said and was about to turn to walk away but something told me to kiss Billy on the cheek. So, I did and Poppa Badd smiled.

I walked out into the hallway and was met by the dynamic duo, Brock and Mona. I hope they didn't start integrating me. I wasn't ready. I walked right passed them like I knew my way around their mansion.

"Hold up, Dolly," Mona said my name wrong intentionally.

"It's Dalla," I said sternly. "D.A.L.L.A. Dalla," I made sure she didn't make that mistake again.

"I don't give a fuck if it's Mary Poppins. Where do you think you're going?" She and Brock both were looking at me like I was a hired assassin but ironically, a few weeks ago, I kind of was.

"Out front to wait on my husband," I said snidely. She was starting to get on my fucking nerves. "He and his father are speaking, privately." I gave a look that hinted to them to mind their own fucking business for a change. Mona turned her nose up at me so far, I thought it was going to fall off her face. She seemed shocked by my tone of voice, but I didn't give a fuck. This bitch was nothing special. I grew up defending myself against women like her. After taking a few ass beatings, I perfected the craft of fighting back. I could take Mona if I had to.

"Well, we don't need you walking around this place like a tourist. Security may mistake you for an intruder. If they are mistaking at all," she added snidely. "Follow me, I'll show you where you can sit and wait on, Billy."

"I'm going to make sure he doesn't get Pops all stressed with his bullshit," Brock said anxiously.

"Okay, baby. Handle it." Mona kissed Brock on the lips and gave him a look that said, behave and he rushed off to interrupt Billy and his father's private conversation. What an asshole.

I followed Mona to a living room across the hall. A woman holding a tray was standing in the doorway.

"Get us two waters," Mona ordered for me.

I decided right then and there that if I wasn't going to let Mona run all over me I had to do something about it now otherwise, I was going to be her fucking bitch and I was no one's bitch; not anymore.

"Actually, I'll have a glass of red wine." Mona looked at me like I was crazy and I gave her the same look. "How long do you think my husband will be? We've been on the road for hours and I just want to relax. I'm anxious to see my new house, too."

"*Your* new house," Mona said sarcastically.

"Well, our new house. Isn't that the way it goes?"

"So, he told you about the house, huh?"

"Of course. I am his wife."

"Hm," she said like that was up for discussion. "What else did he tell you about our family?"

"Enough. He told me a lot about you though," I said condescending.

"I don't care what he told you," Mona got up to stand her ground. "You still don't know shit about me, but I'm gon' teach you. You gon' learn all about me real fast."

"I guess we gon' have to teach each other. So, we both gon' be learning," I snapped back.

Mona sat back down and stared hard at me. The server came back with our drinks and I sipped on the glass of wine, watching her just as stern. She didn't intimidate me in the least. I wasn't here for her. If she pushed me the wrong way I didn't mind socking her big ass.

"So, where did y'all meet?" Mona leaned in close to me and studied my movements like a body language expert. She waited for me to respond.

"Out in L.A. He was inquiring about a piece of land I had listed for sale."

"He does a lot of land buying for the family. So, that means sometimes he might be gone for weeks out on business without you. That ain't gon' be no problem, is it?"

"I don't have a problem with my husband handling his business. As long as he's getting paid," I added piggybacking on the conversation Billy had with Brock out front.

"Excuse me," Mona stood up offended like she was ready to fight. "What the fuck are you trying to say? Billy been talking shit about my husband and you got the nerve to stare me in the face and repeat it."

"Calm down," I waved my hand at her, gesturing for her to sit back down. "I'm not here to fight with you. I'm just sipping my wine and waiting on my husband."

"Bitch don't talk about shit you don't know. That won't get you far in this family."

Did she just call me a bitch? Fuck her. I don't have time to argue with this buff broad. Mona sat back down, grimacing at me like she was ready to throw blows.

"Next to Papa Badd, my husband is the second in command around here. He cuts the checks and oversees everything. If he sees fit to withhold a *worker's* pay, then so be it. So, get used to it, bitch."

There she go with that bitch word again. I wonder what she would do if I called her a bitch? She probably would be happy then she would have a reason to fight me, but I'm not gon' give her what she wants. If I and this big broad gets to scrappin', it's gon' fuck up Billy's plan and in turn, my money. So, for now, I'll be that bitch for her.

"Whatever you say, captain," I teased. Mona got annoyed.

"You real silly, bitch. You caught Billy at the right time. Right when his mother died. Out of all the bitches that's been throwing themselves at him offering their condolences he brings home your simple ass. Billy may be at odds with the family but he's still one of us and I'm gon' do just like I promised Mama Badd and look out for him. I ain't gon' let you fuck with his head."

"That's so sweet," I said sarcastically and smiled before sipping my wine totally unmoved by her ranting.

The front door crashed open and somebody excitedly screamed Billy's name. Mona rolled her eyes and jumped up. I was relieved to have a moment away from her.

"Brip, he in a meeting with Papa Badd. Quiet down." She walked out of the living room and yelled down the hall.

Brip, I thought to myself. I felt myself start to panic. I was about to be face to face with the man I had nightmares about. I wasn't ready for this. I felt sweat beads start to pop up on my forehead. I quickly wiped them while Mona was still distracted. I didn't want her to catch on to my weird behavior. Brip rushed in the living room. I kept my eyes on the floor. My leg was shaking.

"When he gets back?" He said excitedly not noticing me right away. "Who dis?" He referred to me. I didn't look up.

"Billy's wife, Dalla."

"Wife," he roared.

I finally got the nerve to look up and then I was eye to eye with Brip and he wasn't what I expected. In my dreams, I saw him as a monster but in reality, he was a young man with a big mischievous smile and cartoon-like eyes. He was really hyper too.

"Dalla? What the fuck did Billy get himself into?" Brip said and clapped his hands. "Get up, sis. Let me look at you."

Before I could stand up good enough, Brip was lifting me off the ground and spinning me all over the living room.

"Put the damn girl down before you break something in here. Damn, Brip." Mona ordered. Brip did just what she demanded.

"Wait till Bobby hears this shit. I can't believe this. Man, I'm gon' have to settle down, now." Brip looked at me from head to toe. "Damn, Billy didn't do too bad."

"When is Bobby getting here?" Mona asked.

"Soon," Brip looked away from Mona. "He's in traffic," Brip said like he was covering for Bobby.

Mona sighed and rolled her eyes, like she saw right through Brip. "Is he still with that damn bitch?"

"Which bitch?" Brip played dumb.

"Brip, don't fuck with me. Is he?"

"I don't know Mona," Brip shrugged as he walked over to the glass table and finished off my last bit of wine.

"We got enough issues. We don't need more bullshit adding to the piss pot. I'll be glad when he leaves that damn Tara girl alone. That shit is bad for business. How many times have we got to tell him that? Mona put her hands on her wide hips and shook her head like she was exhausted.

"He been knowing Tara forever. Hell, since he was what…10 years old. We all have. That's even before you, Mona," Brip teased an annoyed Mona. "Why don't everybody just get over it, so we can all be happy?"

After a deep sigh, she replied, "Because that ain't the way shit work. You don't know that by now. Papa Badd don't want him around her. All that bullshit her dad was out there doing fucked up any chances of them ever having a relationship, so he might as well leave it alone for good. I'm gon' remind him again tonight too." She waved her finger in the air. "When did you tell him that Billy was back?"

"Billy told him his self. He called Bobby after he talked to me."

"Well, he ain't call Brock or Papa Badd."

Brip gave Mona a funny look. "Why wouldn't he? You think he still upset about…"

"Watch your mouth," Mona said looking at me like he was saying too much.

Brip sighed hard and rubbed the side of his face like he was getting stressed out. "I thought this bullshit was over. He cleared his head now let's get back to business as usual. I'm tired of all this fucking fighting man!" Brip punched the air. "It's making me fucking angry, man. Brock and Billy need to squash whatever bullshit they got going on right now. It's affecting all of us."

"Brock ain't the problem. It's Billy. You know why he mad. He been gone for months and now he comes home with her." She said like I wasn't in the room.

Brip looked at me with his brow lowered like he was trying to put Mona's insinuations together. Then he shook off her suggestive comment.

"Man, that's why he been gone for so long. If I get me a wife as sexy as her, I might not come back for a while either," he winked at me and smiled. "Come on, Dalla. Let me show you around the Ranch." Brip said excitedly and waved his hand for me to follow him.

I sighed in relief. I never thought I'd actually be excited about being alone with Brip Badd. I jumped up to follow him, but Mona stopped us.

"Um…let me handle this. You just get yourself ready for dinner and get on the phone with Bobby. Nobody got all day to wait on him and he better not have the nerve to show up with that bitch, Tara. Papa Badd is under enough stress. He don't need all this shit tonight."

"Aw…you know Bobby and Tara. They are off and on. He'll be done with her by the end of the month."

"Long as he doesn't walk through the door and say he married now, too…I don't give a fuck."

"I'll be ready in time, Mona," Brip whined like he was talking to his mother. "Let me spend a little one-on-one with my sister."

"Yeah. We can catch up later, Mona," I said getting up to follow Brip. Mona rolled her eyes and watched me as I grabbed Brip's hand. He pulled me all the way down the hallway until we got to the front door.

14

I've been touring the Ranch on foot with Brip for almost an hour now. Surprisingly, he's a real sweet guy. I couldn't imagine that he would be capable of killing someone but then again, that innocent sparkle in his eye could change in a moment. Someone was driving too close to us on the road and I'm sure they couldn't see us because we weren't in a well-lit area but Brip picked up a rock and flung it at the car anyway. What a temper he has but he treats me like I'm delicate. He held my hand as I stepped over dirt and construction debris. He pulled off his jacket and draped it around my shoulders when I shuddered from the cool night's breeze and he called me mam. I didn't like that as much. I wasn't that much older than him.

"Yeah, my brother designed all of this," he said pointing at various infrastructures. Brip walked me around showing me everything Billy designed on the Ranch. Billy was talented. "I can't wait for him to get done with that casino. I don't think he's ever gon' leave." Brip joked. "Billy's got real talent. He's an artist. Did he draw you yet?"

"Not yet," I tried not to act so surprised. I didn't know he was an artist too.

"Yeah, he's real funny about his work. I begged him to draw me for years, but he wouldn't do it. The only person he ever drew was Mama. I know he must have serenaded the hell out of you with that guitar though," Brip put his hand over his mouth and chuckled. "The boy can play an instrument," Brip said like he was proud of his brother.

"Yes, he did," I answered bashfully, remembering our first night together at his lake house. But, he was doing more serenading at me than to me. I'll take what I can get though.

"Come on," Brip held out his hand. "I want to introduce you to somebody else."

I wondered if he was talking about his brother, Bobby. He was the only brother I hadn't met yet. Then I remembered him saying Bobby was stuck in traffic. I didn't know who Brip was taking me to meet. I just followed behind him.

I don't know where Brip was leading me but the further we walked, the darker it got. We were getting deeper into the underdeveloped parts of the Ranch. Paved roads turned to gravel and noise from the Ranch died out. I got an eerie feeling. I don't know why I was getting so nervous. Brip was still holding my hand. He must have felt the sweat on my palms and got the hint that I was feeling uneasy.

"You, okay?" Brip asked me with a chuckle. "I know it's kind of scary out here. Me and my brothers used to play out here when we were little. Especially, during Halloween. I remember one year when I was about seven years old, them nigga's left me out here by myself." He laughed at the memories. "I still have nightmares about that shit."

"Where are we going?"

"To the family cemetery," he said casually.

Now I was really freaked out. This place had a cemetery on it too? That was weird as shit and creepy as hell. Putting two and two together, I figured the person we were going to meet was his mother.

"Actually, up until a few months ago, this place still spooked me out. But, not anymore." Brip's voice dropped. "I come here as often as I can now. Now that she's here. I just don't want her to feel alone."

"Who," I asked although I knew who he was talking about."

"Mama."

"You really miss her, huh?"

"Man, I didn't know it was possible to miss somebody so much. You think people you love gon' live forever until they surprise you and die. This shit hit the whole family hard but we're pushing through it. We're strong. Billy took it the hardest though. He was a serious mama's boy. Mama was his heart and he was hers."

"Is that why he left?" I pried.

"Yeah, that and some other shit. Nobody wants to believe that their mother killed herself," Brip blurted out not knowing he was giving me the information I didn't know. So that was the cover-up story. "That's hard for all of us to swallow. But what can we do? It happened and we need to move on. That's what Mama would have wanted. Billy just won't accept it. He will soon though. We just got to be patient with him. Give him more time."

"Who found her?"

Brip turned and looked at me like he assumed I already knew the story. "Billy didn't tell you? He found her. She had been lying in her bed for two days. That made it even worse. He was out in the city doing business and didn't check in with her like he usually did. Billy would call Mama every night just to talk with her. When he left the Ranch, he would always come back with flowers and chocolates for her. He had flowers the night he found her dead. If I had known that she was hurting so much that she had to kill herself, I would have spent more time with her. I would have brought her gifts and called her every night too." Brip was hurting.

"Every relationship is different, Brip. I'm sure your mom loved you just the same."

"Yeah, but I should have paid more attention to her. Out of everybody, Billy should be the most at peace because of all this shit he did for her. But, he ain't. He didn't call her those two days she was lying there dead and now he blames himself for what happened; he blames everybody. I guess it makes it easier for him to cope to think that this shit wasn't a suicide. He doesn't wanna believe that Mama was that unhappy, but she was."

"Why was she so unhappy? She had a whole paradise at her fingertips."

"She had everything she wanted but love. At least the type of love that could keep her living. She had a lot of heartaches over the years too.

Heartaches we just all ignored. We pretended that Mama wasn't in pain because of her lifestyle but truth be told, she was lonely as hell."

Brip stopped talking for a while. He sniffed as the cold wind hit our faces. We continued to crush small rocks under our feet as we got closer to the cemetery. Thankfully, it was well-lit. I noticed the huge white marble headstone from where I stood. I big statue that looked like an angel stood out the most to me. It was beautiful in an eerie kind of way. The cemetery was enclosed with a huge iron gate. Brip walked up to the gate and tugged on it. It made a scary creaking sound as it opened. He let me walk in first.

"I come here and talk to her as often as I can. Sometimes I feel silly. Like, I'm talking to myself but then sometimes I feel like she hears me too," he looked at me for confirmation.

"I believe she hears you."

Brip smiled at me. I followed behind him as he walked towards the huge statue. When we got close enough, I could read the scribe on the stones. It was his mother's grave. I stared at it and began to feel so guilty that I almost vomited. I took deep breaths to keep my composure. Could Ace be telling the truth? Was this woman really murdered? I felt like the truth was going to cry out from the grave. I was so uncomfortable I wanted to leave. Brip took a step forward and sat down on his knees. I took a few steps back. I shouldn't be here. Not knowing what I know. It just didn't feel right.

"Don't be afraid," Brip held out his hand for me to grab. I hesitated at first but I had to play cool. I took a deep breath and grabbed his hand. I knelt down beside him. My heart raced. I wondered if she knew that I knew the truth. What if her ghost was screaming for me to vindicate her death; to expose her murderer? I saw enough scary movies to know how this shit works. I started to feel haunted. I don't know if I could stay on this Ranch after this.

Brip started to cry silently to himself. I only knew he was crying when I saw him quickly wipe a tear from the side of his face. Then he smiled. He stared at the statue like it was his mother.

"Papa Badd had this designed by some French artist. It took him two months and a few hundred grand to finish it. I look at this angel and see my mother."

"It's beautiful," I said and tried not to look up at the statue.

"Mama, I got somebody I want you to meet. Her name is, Dalla. She's Billy's wife. Can you believe he got married? He took your advice. You always told him you wanted him to settle down with a nice girl and he did it. She's pretty too ain't she?"

I started to feel uncomfortable and extremely awkward. I hope he didn't expect me to say anything. What could I say to a dead woman that I never met before? I'm sorry about how you really died, and I'm not really married to your son the way you think. I was actually hired to set him and your family up, but I fell in love, and then he offered me a job to be his fake wife and I took it. I felt like a devil sitting underneath the angel headstone. I hope Brip isn't planning on staying here long.

"Don't worry about it, Billy. I got a feeling he gon' be okay now. You know how stubborn he can get. And that imagination of his is bigger than this universe. He was still just upset and is struggling to accept what happened but he coming to his senses now. He finally came home! I told you he would be back. He, Daddy, and Brock gon' work everything out when we gon' get back to normal. I love you, mama. I'll be back to see you again in the morning. I just wanted to bring your daughter-in-law to meet you."

Brip kissed his hand, then touched the headstone. Then he pulled himself off the ground and dusted the loose grass off his pant legs. He helped me up. I was so relieved it was over I almost ran out of the cemetery. "Slow, down," Brip said. I kept a good pace until we were outside of the gate. Once out, I felt like I could breathe but I still was haunted.

"I meant everything I told my mama. I know Billy is going to be okay because he got you now. You came right in time Dalla cause it was getting really bad between us. We were starting to divide. My brother really needs you right now and I thank you so much for being there for him. You saving this whole family and don't even know it."

My guilt tripled. I smiled uneasily at Brip as he pulled me into a big thank-you hug. Damn, I'm one devious bitch.

15

We are having dinner in a room so grand it looks like something right out of a Disney storybook. The thick carved, mahogany wood dining room table seems to stretch on for miles and the dinette chairs are velvety and soft and look like thrones. I feel royal sitting at this table but the true king of the castle, Papa Badd, is sitting at the end of the table.

He has his elbows anchored on the table with both hands clasped together. His chin is resting in the cups of both thumbs. He's moving the rest of his fingers up and down like he's stretching them, but I can tell he's just thinking. He's looking over all of us. I can't tell what he's thinking. Brock, who is sitting the closest to him is studying his every movement like he's trying to learn something new from his dad. Mona is right beside Brock, waiting on his beacon call and giving me the evil eye whenever she has a moment to spare.

Billy has his arm draped around my shoulders. It's all for show though. There is nothing intimate about his touch right now. I feel the tension coming out of his presumably soft squeezes. I almost want to pull away from him, but I can't. Not with all these suspecting eyes watching. Brip is sitting right next to me. He's playing the role of a nice distraction. Every so often he playfully taps me on the knee or beacons one of the servers to tap my glass of wine when it gets too low. Thank God for Brip tonight. Bobby is sitting across from us. A few chairs down from Mona and Brock. Aside from him excitedly greeting Billy, he hadn't said two words since he got there. There is something mysteriously sexy about, Bobby. Not to mention that dimple in his chin. I try not to stare at him too hard.

Mona starts to stare me down again. Then she whispers something in Brock's ear and he starts to gawk at me but not for too long. Something tells me that Brock isn't too concerned with me; at least not as much as, Mona. I lean over and kiss Billy on the cheek. I must have caught him off guard because he jumped just as if I bit him. That's when Mona starts to stare us both down suspiciously and he has no choice but to kiss me back. Then he gives me a look that only I can read. I know it says *don't pull that shit again.* My pride is hurt but I don't show it. I look up and make eye contact with Bobby. I bashfully stare away from his gaze but when I look back up, Bobby is still watching me. What's that about? I lift my wine glass to take a sip but Brip pulls it out of my hand and starts drumming a fork against it. He stands up. He's about to give a toast. I just pray he doesn't put me on the spot. I don't need any attention right now.

"Listen up, Badd's. I would like to propose a toast," Brip says and looks at his dad, waiting for the okay to continue to speak. Papa Badd nods. "We've been through a lot these past months, but we're all here and we're all together. Just the way Mama would want it. So, I dedicate this toast to old family," he looks at Billy, "new family," he smiles at me, "and most importantly, who's looking down at us right now and smiling."

"To family," Papa Badd repeats with authority and everyone holds up their glass, be it water, wine, or scotch, and toasts; everyone except, Billy.

Papa Badd takes a sip of his scotch and swallows it hard. He's staring at Billy like he's getting annoyed. Brock leans over and whispers something in his ear and it ticks him off even more. Mona almost broke her neck trying to hear what Brock was saying to Papa Badd. Billy is staring Brock down. Brock is looking back at Billy with a smirk on his face like his little brother isn't intimidating him. Brip's fidgeting with his straw like his spirit is broken by the sudden shift in moods and Bobby is silent and solid as a rock; I'm stuck in the middle of it all.

When Papa Badd clears his throat and leans in closer to the table, everyone prepares themselves to listenn. Even Bobby is tuned in. The amount of respect they have for this man is unreal. It's almost god-like.

"Son," he looks at Billy. "Do you have anything you want to get off your chest?" Papa Badd asks Billy with an even tone. "Because we are all here and now is the time to speak out."

"Yeah, Billy. Speak now or forever hold your peace" Brock says in a harsh way.

Billy finally removes his arm from around my shoulder and I feel like I can breathe better. He looks at everybody at the table except me. Everybody is watching him and waiting. "I want to apologize to everyone for leaving the way I did. I know that's not how we do things and that I got a responsibility as a Badd to do things differently and an obligation to this Ranch." Brock seemed a little relieved. He nods his head like he agrees with his brother. "But," Brock gets uneasy again, "If I didn't leave when I did, things would have gotten worse."

"Why do you say that, son?" Papa Badd asks.

"Because I felt like we weren't looking out for each other the way you taught us to do."

"In what way?" Papa Badd asked.

"We have an obligation to each other in this family. So much so that we sacrifice having normal lives, but it's worth it because we're doing it for each other. For the honor in the name. For the love we are supposed to have for each other, but I just don't feel that love anymore. It ain't there."

"I love you, man," Brip said sympathetically.

"I hope you do, Brip. I hope you love me as much in life as you do in death."

"What you talking about, man!" Brip was getting stressed. "Ain't nobody else gon' die!"

"Calm down," Papa Badd warned, Brip. "Let your brother finish."

"He needs to get to the point, Dad," Brock said annoyed.

"The point is this. Someone murdered our mother and we sitting here eating dinner like ain't shit happened." Billy said and looked directly at Brock.

Papa Badd slammed his fist against the table so hard, the silverware shook. "Enough!" he yelled, and I jumped. "Enough of this nonsense, Billy! You had plenty of time to get over it. You left here, and I gave you your space. You need to accept reality boy. Your mother murdered herself!"

"That's bullshit! Why now? After all these years, why now?"

"Because she was sick," Brock interjected. "She was sick man. Can't you understand that?"

"I don't buy that shit and we won't know the truth unless we dig up her body and redo the autopsy."

"I told you, Dad. He's losing his mind," Brock said.

Brip had his face buried in his hands like he couldn't take any more of the stress. Bobby was listening to Billy and Brock, remaining neutral.

"What do you think, Bobby?" Billy asked.

Bobby thought about what he was about to say before he said anything. "I think that it's hard to accept, but if it bothers you so much, we should just do it and put this shit to rest."

"Really, Bobby?" Brock said. "You want to dig up your mother and go through all that bullshit just to appease this simple mutha-fucka!" He pointed at Billy.

"I just want peace," Bobby replied.

"That ain't gon' cause peace. It's gon' cause turmoil. Who wanna see Mama's moth-eaten skeleton right now? That's sick!" Brock yells.

On that note, Brip picked up a glass and threw it against the wall before storming out of the dining room. Bobby got up and chased behind him.

"See what you done?" You happy now?" Brock asked Billy.

"This family is falling apart," Mona said teary-eyed.

I looked at Billy and he sighed heavily like all the drama had him ready to throw in the towel.

"Billy, if we dig your mother up and do that autopsy you may get peace but what about the rest of us? I frankly don't want to see my wife that way. I want to remember her just as she was. I want her to rest in peace. I'm hurt by her absences just as much as you but I know your mother better than you and she's always been weak and she was weak enough to take her own life." Billy clutched his jaw at his father's harsh words.

"You have to let her go. We have to move on even stronger because there are a lot of people out there who love to see us weak. They want to see us fall apart so they can step in and take what we worked so hard for. I'm not gon' let that shit happen. You understand me!" He was looking directly at Billy, but Billy had his head down. "Trust your family, Billy. Don't listen to all the bullshit you hear out there. It ain't true. Ain't nobody killed our mother. It wouldn't have been done the way it was done if it was a murder. It would have been a lot more evil and bold. If someone killed our mother, they would have left us a message to let us know they did. You know how this shit works and if you don't you need to learn 'cause I ain't gon' be here forever to teach to you!" he yelled. "Your mother took her own life," Papa Badd said stern. "Just accept it," his voice softened.

Billy seemed to be considering what his father was saying. He finally looked up at him and nodded. A single tear fell from his eye and my heart broke. I wanted to wipe away his pain but I didn't dare touch him. Billy took a deep breath stood up from the table and walked towards his father. "I'm sorry," he said with a deep voice. Papa Badd stood up to hug Billy. Then Billy made his way to Brock and repeated the same cycle of apologies and hugs.

"Now, that's the man I raised you to be," His father seemed proud.

"Yes, sir," Billy said sternly.

"You have a beautiful wife and a new life ahead of you. Let's get back on track."

"Yes, sir" Billy repeated. "What about my money, sir?"

"We decided to hold off on that," Brock answered for Papa Badd.

Billy shot Brock a look that could kill. "Why?"

"Because it's the best thing to do for right now," Papa Badd responded. "Don't worry. You'll get your money as promised. It's just not going to be today. In the meantime, I've told Brock to lift the freeze off your accounts and hand over the keys to your mansion. Your wife must be anxious to see her beautiful new home."

Papa Badd smiled at me and I nodded. Billy looked defeated, but he went along with it. "Yeah, she should be. I designed it just for her." He smiled at me uneasy and then looked up at Brock, grimacing at him with a phony smile on his face. Brock smiled vindicated.

"Welcome home, brother," Brock said.

16

One Year Later

I can't believe someone agreed to marry that maniac, Brip. He's sweet though. He's trying his best to model his life after his big brother, Billy. He's following in his footsteps by getting married so soon, but he's only following a lie. I wonder how that makes Billy feel? He knows Brip looks up to him. Then again, everyone admires our lie; even strangers. They see things between us that aren't there. But, who can blame them? So, do I.

When Brip walked through the door with his fiancé, Taffy, I recognized her right away. She was Keno and Tony's little sister and she looked just like she did in the picture. I gasped within myself when I first saw her. I thought my buried guilty conscience had risen to the surface and was playing mind tricks on me. Then I started getting paranoid and thought the whole thing was a setup. Maybe she was looking for revenge. Or maybe Mona and Brock had finally dug up dirt on me and was ready to throw it around. Or worse, maybe it was Ace; in the world I live in, you can't be too sure. But, it was merely irony.

At first, my guilt wouldn't allow me to make consistent eye contact with her. But when she flashed me that innocent smile and wrapped her arms around me like I was her long-lost sister, I knew she needed me and just like that, the guilt was gone. Her presence alone made me feel normal and in some sick way, I felt responsible for her. It was my one way to show my respect for Keno and Tony and my second chance at redemption. It allowed me to finally forgive myself for having some part in their deaths. I needed that; I needed her.

We're having dinner at our new condo, downtown. We finally moved off the Ranch. We paid our dues by serving our one-year sentence. Thank God it's over. I couldn't take two more seconds of Mona. As a going-away present, I socked that bitch in the nose. Yep. I hit the raging bull. Before she could retaliate, Papa Badd stepped in and she backed down. Hitting her felt like therapy; physical therapy. I don't know what got into me. Maybe it was all the *bitches* she called me or maybe it was her rubbing in my face that she didn't think Billy loved me. That was my sore spot and maybe she was right but, either way, the bitch got hit. Billy laughed after I hit her. I think he kind of got turned on by me socking that fat whore because after that he pulled me up back into our mansion and fucked the hell out of me before the movers came. That was my best memory in that tortuous place.

I wanted to do something special for Brip and Taffy. I thought a nice intimate dinner at the house would be better than a noisy restaurant. After all, this girl needs to be eased into this family as gently as possible. Hiring a caterer and decorating the table was a nice distraction from how quiet Billy's been lately. He's up to something and I have a feeling it involves Ace and those rumors I thought he was over. I try not to think about any of it though. Especially, Ace. I just want to pretend like that part of my life never existed but that's hard to do when that part of my life is the reason for this part of my life. And, there is a really thin line between my past and my future. At a moment's notice, everything could change and it all will be over.

It's been a year since our fake marriage. I'm still madly in love with Billy although I never tell him. I don't care about the money. I just want him. Being with him is the most normal my life has ever been, and I never felt safer. I can lie down and sleep. I can sleep for hours without waking up in a paranoid frantic because I hear a creak in the floorboard warning me that Ace is coming. I know all of this is fake, but I tell myself it's real. Why not? I might as well enjoy it while it lasts because when it's over, I'll never have it again.

Billy sends me mixed messages. I might as well pluck flower petals and chant, *he loves me…. he loves me not* to get an answer to how he truly feels about me. On the days when we're lying in bed and my head is resting on his chest and he's massaging my scalp with the tips of his fingers it feels real. When he randomly scoops me up and carries me off to our bedroom to make love to me, it feels real then. Especially when he kisses me on the bridge of my nose and tells me that I'm beautiful. But then there are days when I don't see him for weeks or he's not speaking to me. When I lean in to kiss him, he darts away, giving me a confused stare like he doesn't understand what I'm doing.

His ever-rising and falling emotions could be a mystery to me but I know where it stemmed from. He doesn't trust me. Since his mother died, he doesn't trust anyone. To gain his trust, I have to start coming clean about a lot of shit. But, that's so risky. Playing pretend seems so much easier but I've been pretending my entire life and I'm tired of it. I'm ready for something real. When I see the way Brip looks at Taffy, I know the love between them is real. I envy her for that but after all she's been through she truly deserves it.

Our dining room overlooks the city. At night, the view is mesmerizing. I sit there and have dinner all the time by myself. I wouldn't dare ask Billy to join me. I avoid rejection from him any chance I get but tonight feels special. It's the first candlelight dinner I had with Billy even though we're not alone.

"Everything looks so good, sis," Brip is so excited. He kisses Taffy and gives her reassuring hugs every minute. To my surprise, Brip seems more level-headed around Taffy. Long gone is the anxious jumping or the continuous sudden movements. Taffy isn't saying much but she does seem impressed by my spread.

I designed the table just the way I saw it in a magazine. I have a contemporary mixture of metallic placemats and dinnerware. The solid wood table is adorned with huge vases and beautiful earth-toned colored candles with flickering flames. Billy didn't say anything, but I know he likes the setting too.

"Anything for you, brother," I smile at Brip and Taffy.

Brip comes around a lot. I've gotten closer to him over the last year. He truly has a place as a little brother in my heart. I don't see Bobby as much but when he does come around, he's always with a different woman and they all look like supermodels.

"Three weeks, huh?" Billy said to Brip. He doesn't seem too excited that his brother was getting married so soon. Maybe he didn't trust it. Billy is too paranoid.

"Yep," Brip looked at Taffy and smiled.

"Why you rushing? Is something going on? We need to talk?" Billy said all in one breath.

Taffy's face dropped like her feelings were hurt. Brip looked at her and then at his brother like he was trying to figure out what he meant. Brip was only looking for a pat on the back and I'm sure he wasn't going to get that from Mona or Brock. So, I gave it to him.

"I think that's great. When you find the right person, you shouldn't waste any time. Life is too short."

When Taffy perked up, Brip perked up. Billy watched me out of the corner of his eye like he wanted me to shut up.

"I hope you ready, Brip. Don't do anything because I did it. This is serious," Billy said in a stiff tone.

"I ain't never been more serious about anything, man" Brip wrapped his arms around Taffy and pulled her into a hug, ending it with a sultry kiss. I melted from envy.

"What about you, Taffy? You ready to be a Badd wife?" Billy asked.

"I'm just ready to be Brip's wife. I'll take whatever comes with that," She looked at Brip and smiled. "Billy, I promise I love your brother," Taffy said in a sweet voice. She was looking Billy directly in the eyes. "I don't care about the money, the fame, or any of that. I fell in love with him before I knew he had all of that. I know I'm young but I'm going to be a good wife to him. The best," she assured Billy and flashed him an innocent smile.

The outpouring of a young girl's heart softened Billy up. The tension fell from his shoulders and he finally smiled at his brother and his soon-to-be young wife. He looked genuinely happy for them both.

"I wish both of you the best and welcome you to our family," Billy got up and hugged Taffy for the first time. Brip looked like he hit the lottery. He was beaming with pride.

"Thank you, brother. I'm just trying to be like y'all. I love to see y'all together," Brip said with enthusiasm. He started to shake his head getting as emotional as he could. "Seeing y'all two together does something to me," Brip said referring to us. I shot Billy a guilty look but he purposely avoided eye contact with me. "Billy remember when you told me that being with Dalla made you feel normal."

Billy's eyes widened bigger than mine at Brip revealing this secret confession. Billy didn't respond. He still avoided eye contact with me. "I understand what you mean now. We live our lives so different from everyone else. At the end of the day, I need that balance. It's what I've been missing all this time, man. Shit!" Brip slapped the table, jumped up, and pulled Taffy out of her chair and into another hug. Taffy just chuckled like his randomness was cute.

"I feel you," Billy nodded, smiling at his brother's sudden outburst. Then, he looked at me and I got butterflies. I'm so thirsty for his love that I could be hallucinating but there was a tender truth behind his look. Almost as if he was learning something from his little brother; almost as if he was ready for love, too. Real love.

"Pops loves her too man. He said she reminds him of Mama. Can you believe that? I know I got his blessing for sure. He was bout ready to give me my money right then and there but I told him to hold off. I ain't ready for that kind of money yet. I rather just get mine in small spurts, you know. What you do with yours?"

Billy went quiet. His eyes narrowed into a scour and he started to look tortured. "I ain't got it yet."

"What? How is that?" Brip seemed confused. When he saw the tensions start to build up in his brother's neck and shoulders he put two and two together and backed down, trying his best to try and smooth things over. "Well...you know...a lot of things changed," Brip stuttered over his words. I knew he didn't want any family problems. Especially now. "I'm probably gon' have to wait too actually."

"It's okay," Billy said dry and swallowed a sip of water like it was a shot of whisky.

It was my turn to clear the air. I didn't want anything messing up Billy's mood for the night. I wanted to get behind the look he gave me.

"So where are you from?" I asked Taffy.

Taffy thought about it for a second. Almost as if she was remembering what she told Mona when she was integrated. "Chicago."

"Wow," I said. "You have any family?"

"It's just me and my mom. I have a brother but he's back in Chicago."

"Just one brother," I said wondering who she was speaking about.

"Yeah, Tony" She said his name like he was a sad case.

My heart dropped to hear that Tony was still alive. How was that possible and more importantly, what did that mean for me? Was he going to be at the wedding? What would he do if he saw me? Shit! Now I'm feeling the tension. "My oldest brother died a few years ago," her voice dropped. Brip kissed her on the cheek. I'm assuming he knew the story. At least her version; the entire thing was starting to make me feel so sick I almost threw up. Brip couldn't possibly know that the two men he shot were her brothers. Could he?

"I'm sorry to hear that," I offered my condolences.

"That's okay, baby. Now you got three extra brothers and two sisters who gon' be ready to kill for you." Brip said to Taffy and squeezed her shoulders. Taffy nodded assured.

"Brip, have you met Tony yet?" I pried.

Brip shot me a look that told me I asked the wrong question. It was then that I realized that he did know. He pushed food around his plate, waiting off the awkwardness before replying.

"Only through a picture," Taffy answered for him quickly like she was hiding something too. "My brother keeps to himself a lot. It's been almost two years since I seen him. But, he's met momma. She adores him," Taffy emphasized changing the subject quick.

"You heard about the new rule, right?" Brip said to Billy. Now he was changing the subject.

"No. What's changed now?" Billy grabbed a piece of chicken from the platter with his bare hands and stuffed it in his mouth. He's not as engaged as he usually is. Brip's comment about the money was still bothering him.

"Taffy got to stay on the Ranch alone until we ready for the wedding. She got to be with Mona and then she got to be with Dalla."

"That's not a bad thing. Taffy can get used to the life being around them.

"I'm just happy Dalla's here. I think it will be good for, Taffy. Mona going in kind of hard on her."

"She's not so bad," Taffy said, coming to Mona's defense in an attempt to win brownie points but there were no brownies here for that bitch. "I passed the test and I think she liked how I did."

"What test?" Billy and I said in unison.

"Oh, that's some other bullshit y'all avoided. You don't even want to hear about it. I hate I had to put my baby through that shit," Brip leaned over and kissed Taffy on the forehead.

"What?" Billy was curious.

"Let's just say this past week I've been hog-tied, thrown in a trunk, and integrated by fake cops," Taffy laughed but behind her laughter was fear.

"What the fuck kind of shit is that!" Billy yelled so loud a piece of chicken flew out of his mouth. "Who's fucked up idea was that?"

"It's cool man. I see where Mona and Brock are going with this. We got to make sure that our wives can handle this shit, right?" Brip said like he wasn't sure himself.

"Mona and Brock," Billy said sarcastically. "Man, I wish they would try to pull some shit like that with my wife," Billy said angrily. It was the first time I heard him refer to me as his wife. "They running that place now or what?"

"He next in line for it so he might as well," Brip said in between chews of chicken. "Man, pops getting old. He bout to retire and leave everything to Brock. He don't care about much these days but his cigars, brandy, and his women," Brip said through a chuckle.

"Hm," was all Billy muttered, shaking his head. "Just don't let them push you around. You got your own mind. You're about to be married now. You got to man up, Brip!"

"It's cool man. Everything is good. The family is getting bigger and better," Brip said in a calm tone like he wanted peace. "We bout to be unstoppable. You just watch."

"I am watching..." Billy said under his breath with his brow lowered into a scour.

17

I'm rolling a blunt nice and neat; just the way Billy likes it. A blunt is just what we need to relax. I think Billy is trying to avoid me. After Brip and Taffy left, I cleared the table and walked upstairs to our bedroom to prepare for tonight. I need to get him to relax. If I had it my way, I would offer him a back massage, but I knew better than to do that. Billy didn't trust me enough to turn his back to me so a blunt was the next best thing.

He's been downstairs for almost twenty minutes. Last time I saw him, he was hunched over the refrigerator pulling the leftovers I packed out of the containers and stuffing them in his mouth, eating his bad nerves away. I know he's thinking about the conversation he had with Brip. The fact that Brip got offered his money so soon and there was still no word disturbed him. It proved that Brock was up to something and that alone was enough to allow Billy's curiosity to roam into dangerous places. That's the very thing I was trying to avoid. I could'nt care less about it all. The longer Brock delayed giving Billy his money, the more time we had together.

I sat the blunt down on his bedside table and then went to our closet to pull out some candles I bought. According to the sales lady, the chamomile and lavender aroma was supposed to help with relaxation. I guess we'll see tonight. Every time I purchased anything that could appear to Billy as romantic like body oils, lotions, incense, and candles, I always stashed it away in the closet. It was silly, but the possibility of rejection was too painful.

I sifted through all of Billy's unopened shoe boxes and neatly folded white t-shirts, all with the tags still on them, looking for the candles. I couldn't find them. I could have sworn I placed them behind one of his shoe boxes. I leaned in further and reached even deeper behind the high pile of shoe boxes only to mistakenly cause all of them to topple over and fall like dominoes. Shit. I better hurry up and clean this mess up before Billy came upstairs if he ever decided to come. He's such a neat freak and I don't need anything else setting him off tonight.

I began to pack the brand-new white tennis shoes, in different styles and brands, back in their boxes when I came across one that had no shoes in it but folded-up papers. I don't know why, but my heart started to race. I placed the box to the side jumped up from my knees peeked out the door, and over the catwalk at Billy. He was pouring himself a shot. I tip-toed back to the closet in a rush. Pulling all the papers out of the box, I gently placed them on the carpet.

I pulled out the first paper. By the way, it was folded, it looked like it was the size of a poster board. The paper had blue grids going across it. It looked like graphing paper, but I don't think it was. I smoothed out the wrinkles as I unfolded it to reveal what looked like a hand-drawn map. The map was very elaborate. I can't believe he drew something so detailed. It must have taken him years to finish this. There was so much going on, my eyes were landing everywhere. Some of the drawings were three-dimensional and certain pictures on the map were in color.

What stood out to me was a sketch of a blue car; then my eyes led to what looked like a red tent. Drawings of trees covered the entire page. His drawings showed how thick and tall the trees were and the unique way they curved and towered in the air. It was almost as if he drew each of them individually but more importantly, there was a road sketched threw the thick trees curving and crossing all over the paper. Some trees stood out, colored in red, like he marked them just for that purpose.

There were also notes on the sides of the map. I guess he used it as a legend. I didn't read all of them but from what I saw they looked like little hints. One read where Brip got lost and another note read where Bobby broke his arm. I smoothed out the wrinkles and took a closer look, but I only got more confused. There was too much to see. Where was this map leading to? When I flipped it over, in messy small print the words, *The Ranch* were written behind it. Why did he have a map of the Ranch hidden in his closet? It didn't look like the Ranch I've been on. I knew there couldn't be a second Ranch so that meant it had to be a second way in. That didn't concern me, so I carefully folded the map back up and reached into the box to unfold four more papers that were also maps but it didn't say where they led.

These maps were easier to understand with names of roads and landmarks sketched on them. He perfected McDonald's golden arches and the Circle K logo. I didn't spend much time looking over the other three maps but something on the fourth map stood out. It was a lake surrounded by woods with a canoe much like the one Billy and I used to get to his house. When I see the small sketch of the wooden house Billy and I made love in for the first time, I knew it was where the map led. I arranged the maps so that I could place them back in the box but there were two more papers folded inside. I'm pretty sure they were maps and I didn't need to see them. Besides, I was pushing it. Billy could show up any second now and he didn't need to see me snooping in his private things. He didn't need a new reason not to trust me. I was about to place the maps back in the box but felt compelled to dig out the last two papers. So, I did.

The next paper wasn't of a map but a sketch of a woman with eyes like Billy's. She was beautiful. It didn't take me long to realize that the woman in the picture was his mother. Attached to the drawing was a copy of his mother's autopsy report that Billy got from Ace. It broke my heart to see it. But, the second drawing shocked me. When I unfolded it, I had to catch my tears to keep them from falling on the paper and tarnishing the picture. It was unmistakably a portrait of me sleeping. Every detail was there down to the way my reddish-brown hair spiraled into soft, kinky curls. It was beautiful and revealed to me how Billy felt. This had to mean he loved me. Right? Tonight, I was going to make it my mission to find out. I was putting everything on the table. I put everything back in the shoe box. Before I placed it back on the shelf, I took a bobby pin from my hair and poked four holes in the side of the box so if I needed to, I could find it again.

———— ··●·· ————

Just as I was lighting the last candle, Billy came upstairs and flicked on the lights.

"What are you doing?" I asked him in an easy tone.

"What are you doing?" He repeated, looking around the bedroom like he was casing the place. "You know I don't like walking in dark rooms."

"You're not just in any dark room. You're in your dark bedroom that you share with your wife," I said boldly. Billy gave me a crazy look but didn't respond to me.

He walked straight over to his side of the bed picked up his pillow and began to sling it against the bed and punch it. That was his way of fluffing it. Then he lay down but not before he blew out the burning candle I placed at his bedside.

"It's something inside of it that's supposed to help you relax," I tried to cover how humiliated he was making me feel by smiling.

"That shit is giving me a headache," he complained but I had a feeling he was lying. He knew exactly what was going on.

I walked over to his side of the bed and he watched my every move with a raised, curious brow. When I leaned down towards his nightstand, he flinched. I smiled at him. "Take it easy Billy Badd," I said and handed him the blunt that was hiding behind the candle. "This won't give you a headache will it?" I winked at him and he took the blunt from my hand.

He leaned over to my side of the bed and snatched up a candle to light his blunt. Then he pulled an ashtray from his nightstand and placed it on his chest as he inhaled deep and exhaled slowly, blowing away the tension.

Before I lit the candles, I had time to take a quick shower and wrap my naked body in a short red satin robe. I hope that chamomile and lavender ereweren't giving him a headache because I rubbed the body oil all over my skin. I was shimmering and sexy. I sat down beside Billy. He tried to hand me the blunt, but I refused. Then he really looked at me like I was crazy.

He continued to take puffs of the cigar and I just watched him like a dummy. Suddenly, I didn't know what I was doing anymore. So, I broke the ice with small talk.

"Taffy seems nice," I said to him, but he didn't respond. "What do you think about her?"

"What does it matter? She ain't my wife."

"I know that. I'm your wife."

Billy looked at me like he knew this conversation was coming. He took one last drag of the blunt before putting it out. He leaned up and placed the ashtray on the nightstand.

"You're my business partner, playing the role of my wife," he said in a calm even tone like he was talking to a mental person.

"No. I'm your wife," I said through a cracked voice. I tried not to cry. "You love me Billy and I love you."

"I care for you," he responded. "I think you a real cool chick but..."

"You love me!" I screamed. "Why are you so afraid to admit it?" I tried not to raise my voice, but I couldn't help it. I knew Billy loved me and the picture I found in the closet was proof.

"Dalla please don't lose focus," Billy jumped up from the bed. "That's the last thing I need you to do. We had an agreement. When I get my money, you get a cut and we split ways. That's it Dalla."

"I don't care about that damn, money! I just want you!"

Billy laughed under his breath like he didn't believe me. Why didn't he believe me? Maybe he just didn't want to because then he would have to come to terms with his feelings.

"You don't care about the money because you haven't seen it yet. But, its coming. Stop wasting your time fantasying about silly shit and start thinking about what you gon' do once you get paid out because this Badd name ain't gon' be with you forever."

"Billy can't you just let all of this go and we live normal lives like everyone else?"

"I ain't never letting this go," Billy shot back. "Never!"

"Well let me leave with you when you go."

"Who said I'm going anywhere?" Billy replied in a matter-of-fact way. "I ain't the one that's going to be fucking leaving! You best believe that!" He yelled more to himself than me.

I didn't know what Billy meant by that, but I knew one thing for sure, I was living in a fantasy world thinking Billy was going to stay married to me. I felt so defeated, my shoulders slumped over until I fell in bed. Before I knew it, I was crying. I felt the other side of the bed move. It was Billy lying beside me. I could feel him staring at me, but he didn't touch me.

"You really think this is what you want, huh?" He said soft.

I turned around quickly and wiped my face. "I know what I want. I may have been a cokehead. A thief. A wife to a monster but I'm still sane enough to know what I want and it's you, Billy. We both could be happy if you would just let all this shit go. Ace has got you all fucked up in the head!" I declared. "Ace is a mind fucker. He fucked with my mind for years, I know how good he is at it. Don't let him fuck you out of a happy life because he's miserable as shit. Billy…he's lying!" I blurted out.

"Lying about what?" Billy gave me an incredulous look.

"Everything he told you that night. Everything he told you about your mother and your brother is a lie. I know it! He's plotting against you and your family and he has been for years. He wants all of you dead. All of you." I couldn't believe what I was saying but I was speaking the truth or at least what I knew to be the truth. A huge weight started to lift off my shoulders, but that weight fell onto Billy. His eyes widened as he realized that he might have been getting played this entire time.

Billy jumped up and rushed to my side of the bed and yanked me up. He squeezed both my arms as he shook me.

"What the fuck are you talking about?!"

"Ace is setting you up. He's playing off your emotions. His whole family is in on it. Now that he has you, he's sure he can win. That night you came to the house, we didn't meet by accident. He wanted me to get in deep with you and report back everything I knew but that changed when…"

"How did it change?" Billy cut me off, squeezing my arms harder. "You still talking to that nigga? You telling him about my family? About the Ranch?" Billy shook me.

"No!" I yelled and broke away from his grip. "That changed the day I left with you. I changed."

"How do I know that?"

"Because I'm telling you now, Billy. Shit! I never met anyone as paranoid as you before. It's killing and blinding you, Billy. It's really making you weak," my voice cracked, and I became emotional.

Billy turned his back to me and paced around the room. He was mumbling something under his breath.

"You can't trust him, Billy," I said in soft a tone. "Just cut all ties with him. Whatever you plotting with him is bullshit. Please, trust me. Just this once. Cut all ties," I encouraged him.

Billy stopped pacing and when he turned to face me, I saw tears in his eyes, but they never rolled down his cheeks. I know he was considering everything I was saying, and it was confusing him and throwing him off. Avenging his mother's death was all he thought about for the past year. Now, I was telling him to let it go. I knew he didn't know who to believe but I just prayed that he considered me to be more trustworthy than, Ace. I walked over to him slow and carefully extended my arms to wrap around him.

"Let's just start over, Billy," I felt him melting in my arms. He wanted to start over. He wanted to stop being tortured by the rumors of his mother's death, but he didn't know how. "We both can," I said in a soft voice. I squeezed him tight, but he didn't embrace me back. Ten seconds into the hug, he pushed me off of him like he couldn't trust me. "You don't trust me, do you?"

"No," he replied quickly.

"I told you everything I know. I don't know what else to do to prove to you that I'm not against you. What do I have to do?" Billy didn't respond. "I know Taffy," I blurted out, hoping that coming clean with him about everything would help me gain his trust. Billy looked at me like he was about to strangle me.

"What the fuck you mean you know her? Y'all plotting something against my brother?" He walked towards me and I ran from him.

"No! I never met her."

"You just said you knew her two seconds ago. Stop playing fucking games with me, Dalla!"

Billy tried to grab me, but I dodged him. "Hold on," I held out my hands, surrendering to him. "Let me explain," I said backing away from him until I hit a wall. He barricaded me with his hands.

"Explain," Billy demanded. We were nose to nose. I tried to push him away from me, but he wouldn't budge.

"I knew her brothers, Keno and Tony. I used to work with them. I was the bait that helped them trap niggas before they robbed them. I took a cut. That's how I met Ace. Some kind of way he fed Keno and Tony's name to Brip. The guy must have been a taxpayer. Ace new Brip would come. He was supposed to kill Brip that day, but I got cold feet. I didn't call. I stayed with him all those years because he told me that you guys were after me and that I had nowhere else to go," I began to sob. "I was his prisoner until you freed me."

Billy stopped looking at me so rough. His mood changed. I think he was finally believing me.

"How long ago was this?"

"Years ago," I admitted. "Every time one plot fails, he tries again. It's all he does. He's crazy and he hates all of you." Billy took a few steps away from me and gave me a considerate look. "I was just at the wrong place at the wrong time. I've been that way all my life up until I met you. I don't want to kill your family. I know I did some dirty shit in my life but that was the only way I knew to survive. The only way I knew how to stay safe Billy, but I don't have to do that anymore." I walked towards him. "Please believe me. And, trust me," I went on a rant. "I do love you, Billy. Truly."

Billy looked like he was fighting with himself about what to believe. I'm sure his paranoia was telling him not to believe me, but his heart was telling him that he could.

"Trust is a big thing with me, Dalla."

"I know and the only way to prove that I do love you and that I don't have any other motives or give a shit about your inheritance money is to leave."

"Leave?" Billy seemed nervous. "But we have a deal. You gon' break a contract?"

"Find someone else to be your fake wife. I'm sure there are plenty of women who would love to do it. But, I can't anymore. I love you too much to pretend. I'm leaving tonight, Billy," I said through tears. "Unless you agree to put an end to this madness and let me be your wife for real."

I looked up at Billy and waited for him to respond but he didn't. After what felt like hours of silence, he finally said, *do what you have to do*; he left the condo.

And, I did just that. I packed a bag and left before he came back.

———————— · · ● · · ————————

I felt like I was right back where I started years ago. Alone without a plan. I didn't go very far. I checked in at the Hyatt Regency hotel which was only a few blocks away from our loft. I cut through the crowds like butter. That's when I realized I was still wearing my Badd necklace. I should have remembered to leave it on the nightstand where I left my wedding ring. Billy probably thinks I stole it just for the perks. The perks were good but more so than that, it was what it stood for. I felt more connected to Billy and his family wearing the necklace than I did with my wedding ring. It made me feel like I was a part of something great.

Thank goodness I still had it on because I didn't have a dime to my name. This necklace could buy me anything I wanted. Even the penthouse suite at the Hyatt. When the concierge greeted me as Mrs. Badd, I almost burst into tears; if she only knew the truth. The penthouse was beautiful with a gorgeous panoramic view of the city, but it felt empty. Or maybe that was just the way I felt inside. I crashed onto the bed and didn't move for hours. I couldn't think either. I had no next steps to take. I was exhausted mentally and emotionally.

I was in too deep on both sides and leaving was something I needed to do to protect my heart and my life. But truthfully, I left to get Billy's attention. I've been here almost four hours now and still no sign of Billy so maybe he doesn't give a fuck. I went to the bathroom to splash water on my face. I've been crying so much, my face puffed up. The cool water helped to reduce the swelling. It also helped to keep me from going into shock. Not only did I walk away from my one chance at true love, I walked away from my money too.

Before going back to bed, I made my way to the mini bar and pulled out the closest bottle I could grab. I didn't know what I was twisting the top off of until I swallowed it. Vodka. If I wasn't mistaken it was Grey Goose. I grabbed a handful of the mini bottles of liquor, white and dark alike, and carried them back to my bed. Twisting the cap off the second bottle, I leaned over and called the concierge. I requested that he have someone bring me up a Tylenol p.m. I needed help sleeping and these bottles weren't going to do it for me.

Literally, seconds later, someone was tapping at the door with my sleeping pills just as if they were on standby for me. I grabbed the pills, threw them in my mouth, and washed them down with whatever I was drinking. I flopped back on the bed. I needed to figure out my next move, but I couldn't. Four miniature bottles of liquor later, the sleeping pills started to kick in. My eyes felt heavy and the room started to spin. I didn't fight it. I just let myself fall.

A few hours into my heavily sedated sleep, I began to have second thoughts. I don't know if I was regretting drinking the liquor or taking the pills but either way, the effect was giving me crazy dreams. I had a dream that Ace killed my mother. He strangled her the same way my dad had. Then I dreamed that I killed Ace. I felt myself tossing and turning and drooling all over the pillow case. My last dream was about Billy. It was so real. I was stuck in one of his maps and I couldn't find my way out. I heard him calling my name over and over again, but I couldn't find him. He sounded so close. He called my name repeatedly; *Dalla, Dalla, Dalla*. Billy! I yelled for him to come and find me. Then I felt someone slapping me on the face. It felt real because it was real. I opened my eyes and wiped away the sleep until the room stopped spinning. That's when I saw Billy.

"Billy?" I was confused. Maybe I was still dreaming. I rubbed my aching head and continued to wipe the daze out of my eyes. I squinted tight and stared at the man sitting at my bedside. He had my head in his lap. How long had he been here?

"You take something crazy?"

"Tylenol," I murmured. "Just Tylenol." I tried to lean up. Billy helped me.

"Be careful," He gently lifted me up and propped me against the headboard.

"Are you here to get your necklace back?" I said naively still heavily sedated.

"No, I'm here to get my wife back," Billy replied and scoped me off the bed and onto my feet. "Come on, we going home."

And just like that, we officially became husband and wife.

18

Another Year Later…

Whoever predicted that there would be a calm after the storm, must have known me personally. My calm is finally here.

The calm came the first day Billy started to hold my hand in public like he was proud I was his. It came when he decided to let go of all the paranoia and rumors surrounding the death of his mother; finding peace with his brother and father by deciding to work with them instead of against them. It came when he told me that I was the best card he ever bet on. It came when Taffy told me that this was the happiest she'd ever been in her life and that I was the sister she never had. And finally, it came last week when I told him that I was pregnant. He beamed with pride and instantly started referring to our family as an *us*. I liked being a part of *us*. It made me feel like I finally found my place in the world.

But, the thing about living a life where hurricane season is prone, there is always a chance that the storm will return. And who knows that the next time the storm comes, there will be a calm. I don't know if it's my ever-changing hormones or basic instinct but lately, I've been feeling paranoid. It could be that I just want so bad for everything to go right. But, I'm smarter than that and that's the problem.

When I'm out in public alone, I get this strange feeling that I'm being watched. Sometimes it's fleeting; it comes and goes. But, the worst case is when my hairs stand up on the back of my neck and goosebumps start to bead up around my shoulders and arms. Then, I start to pant excessively like I'm hyperventilating. Usually, three rib-stretching breaths and a few fist squeezes do the trick, knocking me back into reality but that doesn't seem to be working right now.

I'm out shopping for unisex baby clothes. It's my new hobby. Besides, I'm trying to rack up on all the baby stuff that I can before I move to the Ranch. When Billy found out that I was pregnant, he insisted that we move back to the Ranch so that he and his hired staff could keep a close eye on me, waiting on me hand and foot I suppose; ain't nothing wrong with that. He's been working at the Ranch a lot lately and some nights, he's not able to make it home. He said that he wants to keep *us* close. So, I'm moving back to our mansion this weekend. He assured me that it would only be until after the baby was born and promised me trips away every weekend. I didn't protest. Besides, that place is big enough for me to keep my distance from Mona and Taffy is there. She's good company.

We haven't told anyone about the baby yet. It's still very early and Billy suggested that we wait until I'm at least four months. I'm only a few weeks now. I don't know why he doesn't want to share our good news, but I don't care either way. Billy and our child are my only concern; *Us.*

I need to sit down. My breathing exercises aren't working, and my heart rate is starting to increase. I walk towards the corner of the store and take a seat on one of the benches near the cribs and baby beds. Seeing the tiny little beds seems to ease my nerves. I loosen up the grip of my fist and begin to slowly exhale through a smile. Everything in this store is so cute. Seeing the miniature clothes and shoes knocks me back into reality and my minor little panic attack is over. I never thought I'd be in love nevertheless a mother. I feel like I have a new purpose in my life. My eyes land on a green and yellow baby blanket; I get up from the bench and stroll right over.

I rub my hands across the soft plush fabric before leaning down to sniff it. It smells like baby powder and a Johnson and Johnson baby bath. Everything in this store smells like that. The aroma therapy in this place triggers something inside of me and my maternal instinct kicks in. I take the blanket off the shelf and carefully unfold it then cradle it in my arms like it's my unborn child. I close my eyes and pretend that our child is here. I'm rocking back in forth and have a sweet lullaby humming in my head. I almost forget where I am until I hear someone behind me call me by a name I no longer go by. *Dalla Lucky*; the masculine voice behind me calls out in a condescending way. I stop rocking and open my eyes only to stare off into a blank space. I can't move. My heart starts to pace, and the heavy panting is back. I take a deep breath, but I don't turn around. If I could disappear I would.

I almost didn't recognize you, the voice said to my back. I thought about just walking away without looking back but that wouldn't be wise. Anyone who knew me as Dalla Lucky was likely to stab me in the back. So, I had to confront this mystery man. It brought me some relief no right off the back that this wasn't Ace's voice. With that being said, it could have been anybody. It could have been one of Ace's sick associates who used to frequent his freak show parties. I turn around slowly with the blanket still cradled against my chest.

What, no, hug? The man standing in front of me extends his arms and I take a step back. I don't know this person. At least not right away. The man laughs and scratches the nap of his neck. He takes a step back to show that he's not trying to threaten me. I squint my eyes and study his face, trying to remember this person. He's a couple inches shorter than me and has really big arms and a small chest. His face is full of groomed facial hair and his black fedora covers his fade. He has sunglasses covering his eyes. He's dressed in a grey tailored suit and reeks of the kind of cologne you would smell on an older man but, this man is not old but young. Truth be told, he looks like a pimp. He has a toothpick sticking out of his mouth and is wearing a thick gold, diamond-crusted wedding ring. His hands and feet are small. When the man smiles again, I recognize the person right away. I know that smile. When he takes off his sunglasses and winks at me, I realize I know those eyes too. I gasp. It's Ace's sister, Angelo.

"Angelo," I say through a shaky voice and I instantly start to look over her shoulder.

"Don't worry. It's just me," she says with a smile. I stare at her for a while trying to digest everything. I don't know what to say. When she looks at my baby blanket, I hide it behind my back but it's too late. She saw it. "I thought you had a glow on you," Angelo smiles and takes the toothpick out of her mouth. "Happiness looks good on you Dalla. Damn! You almost look like a different woman," she says and starts to look at me up and down. Her eyes land on my Badd necklace. That's when I started to feel more confident.

"You following me?" I ask sternly.

"No. We just happen to be at the same place at the same time," she gave me a suspicious half-smile.

"Well, it was nice seeing you, Angelo," I say and start to walk away.

"Wait," Angelo gently grabs me by the elbow and I yank away from her. "My bad. My bad," she apologized right away. "I just thought maybe you wanted to catch up."

"We don't have shit to catch up on."

"Damn! What the hell did I ever do to you? It was my brother who tortured you. Not me!"

"Fuck you. Fuck him. Fuck your family," I snap and turn to walk away.

"Wait," she blurted out desperate and she tried to catch up to me. "I lied," she confessed. "I did follow you here. I've been following you for weeks."

I turned around slowly to face, Angelo. I sighed through a heavy breath and waited for her to speak. What the fuck now? Will this shit ever be over?

"What the fuck do you want from me?" I waited for her to respond. "All I have to do is make one phone call and that's it for you!" I warned.

"You don't think I know that?" Angelo said in a loud whisper. She looked over my shoulder and behind her back. She was getting paranoid. "I need your help," she said in another low and desperate voice.

I laughed like I was amused by her request as a way to remind her that I was in control. But, really, I didn't feel in control at all. If Angelo needed my help, that could only mean one thing. I needed her help as well.

"Me and you got a lot in common, Dalla," Angelo paused for a moment, giving me time to dwell on what she said. "My brother wants us both dead," she revealed.

I gave her a strange look. I didn't believe her. Why should I?

"The difference is, he can kill you but me, he can't touch," I held up my Badd necklace. "Angelo, I want no part of your family drama. I'm done with all that now. I have a new life."

"Not for long," Angelo said quick.

My heart stopped. It was the last thing I wanted to hear but I knew it was coming. "What the fuck are you talking about?"

"Your husband is going to die real soon. Ace is going to make sure of that."

"That's a lie!" I said in a low voice, looking around the store being sure not to cause a scene. "Billy is done with all that."

"It seemed that way at first but its bullshit. Ace is still fucking with his head. He told him that he has Tyler Jones."

"Who?" the name sounded familiar, but I couldn't recall who he was.

"The man that forged the autopsy on your mother-in-law," then I remembered the first conversation Ace and Billy had. Billy requested, Tyler. "Having a copy of the real report wasn't enough. Billy needed more proof and what better way to get it than from the man that faked the shit. It's what he's been waiting on all this time. It's his proof."

"What?" I said in a cracked voice. I was in a daze. It never was over.

"Ace been promising to deliver Tyler Jones to Billy for a year now, but he been having trouble finding him. When Billy gets Tyler, he plans on taking him to the Ranch and confronting both his father and Brock with the truth. At least that's what he think goina to happen," Angelo shook her head.

"What do you mean?" I said in a voice so low I barely heard myself.

"Ace told Billy he would have Tyler in his custody in a few weeks. That's when Billy is planning on getting him but what he doesn't know is that it's a scam. Ace can't touch Tyler. He is protected by your brother-in-law, Brock. I figured Billy would know that but Ace is really fucking with that niggas emotions.

Ace really is just planning on killing Billy right then and there. He's going to record it and distribute the video to all the Badd connects. While that's going on, he's sending someone to your father-in-law to hand-deliver the truth about who you are. He wants you dead too. He's going to make it look like you two were trying to set up the family from the beginning," she paused giving me a minute to take it all in, but I needed longer than that.

I took a few steps back trying to think my way out of this trap, but I couldn't.

"Ace don't care about the Badd family anymore. Just you and Billy. Once you two are dead, he's going to throw in the towel. Or at least that's what he says. This is personal now," Angelo revealed. "But I can help."

"Why do you suddenly want to help me?"

"Because if I save your life, you may be inclined to save mine," Angelo gave me a considerate look. She looked like she was trying to read my mind. "I don't fuck with my brother like that no more," Angelo said in a level voice. "That nigga put his hands on my wife. I promised I would kill him, and I mean it." She said to me in a serious tone. "And he promised me the same thing," Angelo went quiet. She inhaled deep like she was trying to hide her fear. "I believe him."

"I don't get it?" I was confused. I saw them fight before. They always bounced back. Fighting like enemies and making up was a big part of their dysfunction.

"You think that fool was crazy before, well you should see his ass now. After that last plot that he thought so sure would work blew up in his face, he went mad. He cut me off. Cut Mama off and had the nerve to break my wife's jaw," Angelo breathed in hard then let out hot air. "Flo couldn't eat solid foods for almost two months. That mother fucker," she said in one exasperated breath. Angelo punched the air.

Angelo tightened her jaw and clutched her fist like she was seeing red. "So, I got him with one of my knives," she smiled an evil smile. "I got him good too but not good enough. The knife stopped just inches away from his aortic valve. Had it not missed, he would have bled out right where his punk ass lay covered in blood. Squirming and crying like a bitch. But, I missed so here we are," she looked up at me disappointed. "He spent weeks in the hospital but once he got out, he started putting hits out on me and Flo." Angelo shook her head like she was surprised. "You know how Ace is. I know challenging him the way I did would lead to this, but I still didn't expect it until some nigga ran up on me and Flo."

"So now it's either kill or be killed. And I got shit to live for." Angelo stepped back and scratched the back of her neck. She looked down at the floor for a while almost like she had regrets about stabbing Ace. Then she looked back up, darting her eyes directly at me. "I need him dead." I see it in her eyes that she meant what she said but I wasn't sure I was the one to help her.

"I'm sorry to hear that, Angelo."

"Don't be," Angelo said quick. "Me and Flo don't got nothing but good things ahead of us. Separating from him was the best thing I did for my family. We gon' have us a baby real soon too," she looked back at me and smiled like she related to me. I'm not sure how her and Flo could manage getting a baby, but it wasn't my business. "My business is starting to boom. I'm running girls now. The baddest bitches in Atlanta." So, I was right. Angelo is a pimp. "Flo help me manage them. I'm getting paid. So, fuck him. My family is going to be taken care of regardless, but I have to live."

Angelo paused for a second then looked up at me concerned. "I'm happy you got away. That nigga would have killed you," she confessed.

"I know but then, I didn't care about dying," I confessed. But, I cared now. I had so much to live for. I have a family.

My heart started to race again. I knew Ace would never give up. Billy is so vulnerable that he rolled out the red carpet for Ace to do this shit. Billy just couldn't leave it alone. He so fucking stubborn. But, I can't blame him. It's not his fault; he was hurting. Displaced anger breeds chaos.

Ace's plan may work this time. Billy won't give up on proving that his mother was murdered and the idea of actually abducting Tyler Jones is not something I can talk him out of regardless. What about our baby? What about *us*? I can feel the tears filling my eyes, but I don't want Angelo to see me crying. I take a deep breath and push them back, saving the tears for later.

If Ace kills Billy and exposes me, there is nowhere I can run. And, Taffy? What is she going to think of me? This can't get out. It just can't. I'm not ready for this to end before it starts. My life is too good now. Angelo watched me deep in thought. She knows she's sold me on helping her before I even agree to it.

"This new dude Ace got on his payroll is just as determined to kill a Badd as he is," Angelo paused to see if she still had my attention. "Ace got him after me too. He's good, Dalla." It's like this nigga always staying two steps ahead of me," she shook her head. "Some dude that's on some black ninja-like shit... I don't know where Ace found this fool, but he seems to hate the Badds just as much as Ace do. Nigga walking around telling everybody they killed his brother. He said the same shit to me when he ran up on me."

"Who's the guy?" I asked Angelo, but I was scared to hear the truth. This bold black ninja shit sounded too familiar. There were only two people I knew in the city that could fit that description and one of them was dead.

"That nigga call himself Tony, but who knows what his real name is. He already been casing Billy. When Billy goes to meet Ace in a few weeks, he gon' grab him."

My heart melted. If a Badd was going to die, Tony would be just the one to do it. We were fucked.

"How do we do this?" I blurted out.

Angelo flipped open her jacket and pulled a linen business card out of her pocket. She looked around paranoid. "I got a plan. Call me at this number on a non-traceable phone and we can go from there but I'm going to need some cash to get around, make bribes, solicit favors..." She looked at me seriously.

I nodded my head, ok. There wasn't a dollar amount that I wouldn't pay to save my family.

19

I killed Papa Badd without ever touching him; it was easy. At least in a physical sense; mentally, I had trouble accepting what I had to do. But, I got over it.

After I met with Angelo, I didn't waste any time. She said she had a plan and I rolled with it with no questions asked. I was so desperate and in need of a quick solution that anything she told me to do would have made sense. I just wanted to protect my family. She convinced me that killing Papa Badd would not only stop Billy from meeting with Ace, but it would stop the messenger that he was sending to the Ranch to expose us.

The idea was that once Papa Badd was dead, Billy would be so distracted with making funeral arrangements he wouldn't have time to meet with Ace. That meant Ace would have to take time to regroup. While Billy and his family were planning for a funeral, I would be assisting Angelo in killing Ace; then it all would be over, but nothing works that easy in my life.

It happened eight days ago. Brock found him bent over the desk with his hands still clutching his cocktail glass. Shortly after that, some alarm went off. The sound was so piercing I jumped out the bed ready to run not knowing what for. It sounded like it was a warning that the end of the world was here, but it was just Brock putting the Ranch on lock down and alerting all the Badd men and hired staff that something major had happened.

Billy was lying next to me in the bed. *He's dead*, he said to himself like he'd just dreamed the exact moment before waking up. He almost sounded more relieved than grieved. There was a painful look in his eyes. If I know Billy as well as I think, I know he's remembering when his mother died. I wanted to console him, but I couldn't make myself do it. As a matter of fact, I stayed away from him. I was afraid that he would smell the betrayal on my skin.

When I asked him who he was talking about, playing innocent like I didn't know, he didn't respond. He just snatched a pair of jogging pants from a drawer and threw on a wife beater. He gargled some mouthwash and splashed three rounds of cold water on his face. Billy instructed me not to leave the house until he got back. When he spoke to me, he didn't look at me. That made it easier for me, but it also concerned me. What was going through his mind? Billy isn't an easy man to read.

The Brandy they found Papa Badd with after he died was tainted. I laced it with something that was so mild it was tasteless but lethal. It probably killed him after the first few sips. The dealer Angelo brought it from told her it would be quick and painless. He also said that after it sat in his glass a while with the air hitting it, it would become undetectable. That meant I didn't have to worry about anybody testing the Brandy and finding the poison. That was perfect because I know the first thing Brock would think to do is test the glass.

After I met with Angelo and greased her hands with cash, she gave me the bottle. I brought it home along with baby clothes and blankets. It seemed like I picked them all up while shopping in the city. I told Billy that I had a gift for his father and that I wanted him to give it to him for me. He told me to do it myself and I pretended to shy away from the idea.

I never spent a moment alone with Papa Badd and when we did speak, it was very brief and cordial. Billy seemed to avoid his father every chance he got so in the end, it was one of the housekeepers that delivered the poisonous gift. It took him almost a week to break open the bottle. The Brandy was around $4,000 and imported from Asia; It's called Tesseron. I was sure that he would drink it right away, but I guess it didn't impress him as much as I thought it would.

What I did didn't hit me until I heard Billy say he was dead but even my most guilty emotions are fleeting. I did what I had to do to save my family and I'm not through yet.

Taffy, who lived next door, called me in a panic after hearing the sirens from the alarm. I tried my best to calm her down. Brip must have given her the same routine that Billy gave me. She didn't know what was going on and I didn't offer her any hints. I just told her that it was probably nothing and not to worry. She asked if she was allowed to come over. We were only a mile away from each other, but I told her it was best for her to wait until Brip and Billy got back before we left the house. She agreed and sighed a heavy breath. Then she started going over all the scenarios of why the alarm was activated.

"Maybe we're being ambushed. Did you see how security ran into the big house with guns? What if someone is taking the Ranch? Oh, my lord. Brip! I hope he's okay."

"I highly doubt that. It could just be a drill. Regardless, I don't think we're in any danger."

"Did Mona call you?"

"You know me, and that bitch don't speak. I'm waiting to hear from my husband, not her. I suggest you do the same."

"Yeah, but it's weird. I tried to call her after Brip left but she didn't answer. Mona always answers. Always. Dalla, something major is going on."

"Did Brip say anything to you before he left? How did he act after the alarm went off?" I pried.

"It was weird. He seemed more spooked than anything else. Almost like he seen a ghost."

On that note, I knew Brip knew too. "When I asked him what the alarm was, he said formality. He said that it meant the family and the Ranch were in a state of emergency..."

"Make yourself a cocktail and relax." I cut her off.

"A cocktail? It's not even 7 O'clock yet."

"Who cares? Just try to calm your nerves so you can be cool when Brip gets back."

"You're right."

If it wasn't for the baby, I would be doing a lot more to curb my bad nerves, but I had to suffer through this cold turkey. After all, my baby is the reason for it all; and Billy of course.

Almost eight hours later and after a dozen phone calls from Taffy, Billy finally returned. He was still quiet. Quieter than I had ever seen him. But, as soon as he saw me, he kneeled to kiss my stomach and then embraced me. He needed me. I wanted to break away from his touch. I wasn't ready for it. The guilt was too overwhelming, but I toughed it out. I could feel a multitude of emotions behind his embrace. Almost as if he didn't know how to feel. It seemed like a huge weight was lifted off Billy's shoulders. Like this was his first breath of fresh air after spending months suffocating.

"I love you," he said and kissed me on the forehead. "I love both of you...things are going to get better for us. I promise. All that other bullshit I was on before, I'm ending that shit. I just got to tie a few loops and it's over."

My heart sank as I realized that my thoughtless plan was falling through. Billy still wanted Tyler Jones. With Papa Badd dead, now would be a better time than any for him to ambush Brock and Mona with the truth and take his rightful position as head of the Badd estate. He still was going to meet with Ace one last time expecting Tyler Jones, but it was a setup. He's going to get Tony instead. Billy is going to die if I don't do something.

I panicked. Angelo helped me do my part in killing Papa Badd now she needed my help to kill, Ace but I hadn't heard from her. After I killed him, I called to tell her he was dead, but I haven't been able to get in contact with her. It made me wonder if Tony didn't get to her first. I needed Angelo now more than ever. Without her, Ace was still alive and a threat. Killing Papa Badd was just one part of the plan. I needed Ace dead to end this.

"What do you mean?" I asked him.

"Don't worry about it," he grabbed my hand and led me to our leather chase and sat down. He pulled me into his lap. "My father's dead," he said with an even tone.

I tried my best to seem surprised. I really tried.

"What?" I said in a low, cracked voice. I needed some tears, so I channeled up all my fears of Billy meeting with Ace and Ace killing him and then the waterworks came in like a flood.

"What you crying for?" I think I was putting on a little too much because Billy was giving me a confused look almost questioning my sudden outburst of emotions. I barely knew his father; he made sure of that. I had to straighten up my act because he was obviously waiting for me to answer his rhetorical question.

Thinking quick, I responded, "For you," I told the truth and lied at the same time. "This is too much for you," I grabbed his hand and squeezed it. "How are you going to handle it all?"

I wiped my eyes and looked up at him. He was staring so hard at me, I almost melted. Damn, Billy. Still as paranoid as ever. For a split second, I thought I heard what he was thinking. I heard him questioning in his mind if I did it, but I knew it was only my guilty conscience causing me to hallucinate. At least I hope.

"I'm good. I'm gon' handle this shit like soldier; just like I handle everything else. I don't need you to worry about me or nothing else for that matter. It's not good for the baby," he said and massaged my stomach. "I guess this pregnancy got you real emotional, huh?" He asked the question like he needed confirmation more than a response.

I shrugged my shoulders. "I was just getting to know your father."

"Well, count yourself blessed."

"Billy, don't talk like that."

"It's the fucking truth. That nigga probably burning in hell right now, but still trying to conjure up an army of demons to have his back."

Billy chuckled a little bit then breathed in real hard like he was trying to push his emotions back. He stared off into blank space for a while, stroking my back, deep in thought.

"How did it happen?" I tried to break the ice and get information at the same time.

"It's got to be a heart attack. They found him in the study. There are no signs of foul play but Brock wants an autopsy done right away. It don't make sense to me but I feel him; I was in the same state he was in not too long ago."

"How's everybody doing?"

"That nigga going crazy. He ain't talking. Barley moving. Acting like he in a daze or something; like he stuck in a nightmare. He loved our father like a second skin. Always have. I told him I would handle all the arrangements until he get his mind right."

"The autopsy too?" I pried too quickly. Billy shot me a strange look.

When he didn't respond, I got nervous. The autopsy was going to be a gamble. There was going to be a 50/50 chance that the poison showed up in his system, but Angelo had a solution for that. She provided me with a fake autopsy to swap out with the real one. All of these fake autopsy reports confused me. It was a dirty way to betray someone, but I did it anyway. When I finally looked at the report, I noticed she forged Tyler Jones's name on it. At least I assumed it was a forged signature. I would have questioned her about it but like I said, I couldn't get in contact with her. Trusting her was all I had left so I let it go. I just figured there was a reason behind having him sign it. Maybe Brock wouldn't be so suspicious if he knew Billy was using one of his people.

"Anything I can do to help?" I said to try and take the attention away from me.

"I told you I don't want you worrying. I'm gon' be back in forth a lot, but I don't want you getting all worked up. Everything is cool."

"What's going to happen with the Ranch?"

"We gon' keep operating like it's business as usual. Brock is stepping up," Billy's voice dropped like the idea of Brock being the head concerned him.

"So, nothing changes?"

"Everything changes," Billy said in a low voice.

He gently scooted me off his lap and walked away.

———— ··●·· ————

Billy was right about being in and out. I barely saw him these past few days. Bobby's been on the Ranch since his father died. He's been by Billy's side helping him out as much as he could. I could tell he was burdened but he was too smooth to show it. Thankfully, Taffy hadn't been as glued to my hip as I thought she would. Brip isn't taking his father's death too well either. She's pretty much been by his side 24 hours. Mona's doing the same for Brock. I hadn't seen either of them. That was going to change today though. We are all going to meet as a family and enter the Chapel as a single unit. Then, there's going to be a family meeting.

Billy sped through making the funeral arrangements. I don't know why he wanted this process over as quick as possible. Maybe he was just ready to get back to life as normal. Papa Badd's autopsy happened a few days after he died. I wasn't expecting it to be so soon. I had to figure out how to swap the reports before Billy got wind of the real one, but I didn't have to do that. I assumed the poison didn't show up because I overheard Billy talking to Brock saying that the autopsy report confirmed that the cause of death was a heart attack.

Afterward, Billy gave me a weird look that I know I didn't imagine. He looked at me like he knew the truth. I looked away from his intimidating gaze for a moment, hoping that he would stop staring me down, but he didn't. A weird feeling swarmed over my entire body. Did he know I killed his father?

"Is everything ok?" I asked in a shaky voice. I tried to break the ice.

"I guess so," Billy said in a tone that I couldn't interpret.

I walked over to Billy wrapped my arms around his waist and squeezed him tight. I avoided eye contact with him. He wouldn't stop looking at me. Then he grabbed me and kissed me on the forehead. It almost felt like he was telling me thank you and goodbye. It was weird.

"Let's go," I said quick. I needed to get out of the hot seat.

I grabbed his hand, still avoiding eye contact with him, and walked out the door. It was time to face the rest of the family. I put on my poker face.

20

The Ranch is so quiet and calm. Except for the heavy rain, shooting down from the dark clouds and hitting the ground like tiny pellets, its eerily silent and still. It's almost noon but the dark gray clouds in the sky is giving the illusion of evening. I look over my shoulder and squint past the fog that's clouding my view and notice that cars are piling up. There's a long line wrapped all the way back towards the entrance gate. The road is full of every luxury vehicle you can imagine. And, they're all here to pay their respects to Papa Badd.

The hired parking staff is valet parking cars and directing people towards the Chapel. The funeral is strictly,invite-only. Everyone who got passed the gate went through a vigorous security check. No weapons are allowed on the Ranch. Neither are cell phones or cameras. There are no petty crooks here today but sophisticated criminals. The top-notch men; the real deal. I'm sure some of them are rivals with ongoing beef but not today; not here. Today is about honoring the life of a legend.

This funeral reminds me of the Pope dying. Papa Badd's pearl white casket is being carried away by beautiful, masculine black stallion horses with fur so shiny I can see my reflection. Everybody's dressed in black. I'm wearing a black veil. Covering my face makes it easy to hide the emotions that aren't there.

At first, I was nervous that my guilty conscience would get the best of me after seeing Papa Badd's dead body but surprisingly enough, I'm doing just fine. I barely feel the sting of guilt. It's more like a tingling that I can control with thoughts of me, Billy and the baby being okay. Although he's lying in the coffin because I killed him, I feel so far removed from it, it's almost as if I had nothing to do with it at all. Maybe being married to Ace all those years, really rubbed off on me; I could truly be heartless if provoked.

We are at the family cemetery waiting for Papa Badd's casket to be dropped in the dirt.

The rain went from a roaring pour to a drizzle and the sun was starting to peek out behind a silver cloud. Billy has one arm wrapped around me and the other covering our heads with a large black umbrella. He's rubbing my back like he's trying to ease my pain but really, he's trying to ease his own. Taffy's standing to the left of us. She's dressed funeral fashionable in her black peplum dress, black lace gloves, floppy hat, and shiny black red bottom shoes. Brip is wearing a black suit that Taffy probably picked out for him. She has her arm draped around his waist like she's holding him up. He's trying to stay strong in front of the crowd.

Bobby's to the right of me, looking like a soldier, standing with perfect form and posture. His all-black suit looks custom-made. Even under the suit and jacket, I can see the natural curves of his muscular body. Mona and Brock are standing in front of us. Mona looks toned down. I would venture to say she looks pretty but that may be going too far so, I'll just say she looks normal. She's wearing a long black dress that tones down her curves and a cute widow's hat that hides half of her face. Brock is dressed like a funeral director. His suit looks like he ironed it with way too much starch.

I have on a simple black dress that flares out and a matching hat. Billy is wearing a black suit with tennis shoes. When I saw him reach for the tennis shoes, I wanted to say something, but I didn't. Every one of us is wearing shades except for, Brock. His eyes look cold. Every chance he gets, he takes a disgusted look at Billy's shoes and then looks up at him with contempt. To Brock, Billy wearing tennis shoes to the funeral is a sign of disrespect. Other than that, we all look morbidly chic.

The service was beautiful. It was almost like a theatrical performance. White doves were released as woman dressed in all white played a harp. Another group of women danced a ballet in front of the casket. Aside from an older black woman singing gospel hems, and the Ranch's pastor reciting a few generic scriptures, the service was pretty short. A life size picture of Papa Badd was posted along side of the casket. There was no eulogy. And the pastor didn't say much about Papa Badd. With the family being as private as they are, I couldn't see it being any other way. We sat in the front rows of the pews. Brock, Mona and all their children almost occupied an entire pew. There oldest son, Vinchi, sat next to his father trying to look as strong as possible just as if he was warned not to show any emotion. Everyone else sat at least four rows behind us. Armed security was at every corner of the Chapel.

Towards the end of the service, people lined up to view the body. We were first of course. We all circled around the casket as a family. Brock stared down at his father like he was trying to raise him from the dead. Billy struggled with it. He looked down for a split second and then looked away, squeezing my hand. His hands started to sweat. I couldn't look at Papa Badd at all. Thankfully, I was wearing my shades. I just closed my eyes or kept them focused on everybody else. Mona leaned down and kissed him on the forehead. Brip followed her lead and kissed his father's hand like he was the Pope. Taffy tried not look at the body too long. She kept her attention on Brip who was struggling to keep it all together. I wandered if this funeral was conjuring up emotions about, Keno.

Bobby stared down at his father's body like he'd already accepted his death and was ready to move on. He gave Brock a reassuring nod as if he was telling him everything was cool. Then he looked at each of his siblings and consoled them with his eyes. Brock finally took his eyes off his father and fixed them on Billy. It was only for a moment, but I got the eeriest feeling from his look. Billy locked eyes with him, standing his ground. Brock only broke his gaze when Mona interjected, squeezing Brocks hand and leading him away. We all followed behind them.

The line to view the body was wrapped out the door. After we stepped aside, elaborately dressed criminals and politicians took their turns. It was a real sight to see. They all wore mink coats, fedora hats, custom suits and expensive jewelry. They carried gifts in their hands. Rolex watches. Diamond rings and wades of cash among other things. All the riches were placed in Papa Badd's casket to be buried with him. I wondered if their mother's funeral was like this? One sleazy dressed woman in a tight purple dress kneeled over the casket and started to scream. Her cleavage hung over Papa Badd's body. She kneeled to kiss him, smearing her red lipstick and leaving a lip mark on Papa Badd's cold cheek. Mona snapped her fingers at one of the guards and he yanked her out the chapel so quick it was like she was never there at all.

Once all the guest viewed the body, they turned around to honor us by offering their condolences. After they shook the men's hands, and kissed us wives on the cheeks, they dropped money at our feet just like it was rose petals. No one looked at the money, so I had to pretend it wasn't there, but it was hard. I had the mind to start scooping money under the pews with my feet, but I couldn't figure out how to do that without getting caught.

We all road to the family's cemetery together in a Bentley Limo. It only took us five minutes to get to the cemetery but, being in the car with everyone felt awkward. No one spoke a word. The silence said a lot. Brock continued to stare at Billy like he was trying to figure something out. Every now and again, his eyes would dart down at Billy tennis shoes. He would shake his head like he was disgusted. Brock stares didn't intimidate Billy in the least. Billy just stared back at him like he felt sorry for him. More so, like he understood him. He knew Brock was just trying to divert his pain by fishing for a distraction. Billy was at that place once; he may still be there. Bobby must have felt the tension building up, because he squeezed Brocks shoulders and Brock relaxed a bit. Brip's face looked as if it was frozen into one solid, emotionless gaze. Almost as if he spent the night before practicing it in the mirror. Whenever he shifted his weight or made any slight movement, Taffy grabbed his hand and squeezed it like she was reminding him to keep it together. She studied his face like she was waiting for him to crack.

Taffy looked concerned and nervous. I removed my shades and supported her with my eyes, giving her reassuring nods and, *the everything is going to be okay*, look. Whenever I locked eyes with her, she seemed relieved and was able to recharge her strength for Brip. To my surprise, Mona didn't look my way. I can tell she was struggling to keep it together. Not just for herself, but Brock. She worshipped Papa Badd the same way the guest did. If she could, I'm sure she would have dropped a luxurious gift in his coffin too. To her, he was a true hero. It almost made me laugh to see a woman like her so weak. I stared at her through my sunglasses. Although she couldn't see my eyes, I know she felt me looking at her, taunting her and beckoning for her to crack. I challenged the rock-hard woman she portrayed herself to be. I guess the big bitch has a soft spot after all.

Once they lowered the casket into the ground, Billy squeezed my hand tighter. He was killing my fingers. They cracked with every squeeze, but I took the pain. It was the least I could do being the person that caused this stress. I don't know why he fought so hard to act as if he didn't care about his father dying. I know it bothered him in more than one way.

We all carried a single white rose. Once the casket was in the ground, we each took turns throwing the rose on top. After we all had turns, we got back in the Limo and headed to the big house.

21

The house staff was waiting for us at the door. They stood in a semi-circle around the foyer entrance, taking our umbrellas, coats and asking what we would like to drink. I requested water and Billy ordered a beer. Brock gave him a funny look when he heard his request. Taffy asked for tea. Aside from us, no one else wanted anything.

Mona lead us to the formal dining room. We all took a seat at the long, conference room like wood table. Brock sat in the chair at the head of the table where Papa Badd used to sit. It looked more like he was claiming it to me. None of the brothers seemed to feel any kind of way about it. Honestly, I don't think they cared. Mona sat at the seat that was closes to Brock after going to the office and placing a legal pad and pen in front of him. Their oldest son, Vinchi, sat on the other side of Brock. Billy looked down at the pad and shot Brock and everyone else around the table confused stares, like he didn't know what was coming next. I squeezed Billy's knee to calm his nerves.

When the servants came with my water and Billy's beer, I took a small sip and offered it to him in lieu of the beer but he pushed my glass aside. I wanted Billy's head to be clear because we really didn't know what was coming and I didn't want him to be caught off guard. Billy didn't touch his beer. He was too focused on the legal pad sitting in front of Brock. Even though he squinted, there was no way he could read what was written on it. It was too far away. So, he just waited like the rest of us.

Brock took his time and to study each of our faces before he spoke. It was like he was trying to read our minds. Moments passed before he said a word. I can tell Billy was starting to get agitated by the way he shifted around in his seat, but he didn't say anything. Brock turned to Vinchi and demanded that he leave the table. But, Mona interjected.

"Brock, the boy is going to be 19 next month. Don't you think it's about time he learns how shit operates on the business end? Let him stay," Mona said in a careful tone.

"He don't need to be here right, now," Billy answered for him. Mona shot him a look that could kill. So, did Vinchi.

"Your uncle's right," Brock said to Vinchi who respectfully got up and left the meeting. Brock cleared his throat, then sighed like he was exhausted. "I guess we can go ahead and get started now." Mona nodded her head in agreement and looked over all of us. Brock picked up the pen and looked down at the paper like he was about to read a speech Mona prepared for him the night before. Then he pushed the pad aside and looked up. He stared at the wall a few seconds like he was lost in thought. Then he spoke.

"You all know how this shit works, so I really don't have to spend much time on it. With me being the oldest son, I'm taking Mr. Badd's seat. Nothing is going to change. At least not drastically. Billy," he looked at his brother. Billy perked up like he was in a class room and the teacher called his name. "You doing a real good job developing the Ranch and getting them contracts on the mini-ranches. I don't see no reason for nothing to change. You got a good vision for this place and I want you to keep doing what you have to do until you see us get there." Billy nodded his head. It was almost as if his big brothers pat on the back softened his heart.

"Bobby, keep the funding up. You brining in a lot of revenue on them loans. And, Brip," Brip straightened up his posture like his father was addressing him, "keep doing what you doing. You knocking in heads is keeping order and respect for us. I can't see that changing." Brip smiled for the first time all day. "We just got to remember we took a lost by losing Mr. Badd but not a hit. Niggas out there may look at Mr. Badd dying as us taking a hit. We got to be more united than ever now," Brock made his business to look directly at, Billy. "Nigga's waiting for us to fall and we can't let that happen." Mona nodded her head in agreement, watching me out the corner of her eye. "Mutha-fuckas might be suicidal enough to try us."

"You think so?" Bobby asked.

"Yes, Bobby. I do."

"Shit...," Brip said cocky. "Nigga's ain't crazy!"

"Yes, they are, Brip," Mona added. "And we weak if we too arrogant to consider that."

"Your right, baby." Brock patted Mona on the hand. "Right now, we untouchable but that shit ain't good enough anymore. It's time we take this shit to the next level and become invincible." Brock raised the pitch in his voice like he was preaching. Everybody at the table perked up except, Billy. Brock grabbed the notebook and pulled it back in front of him. Billy stared at Brocks mouth, waiting from him to speak. "We got shit to prove right now."

"You sure?" Billy cut him off before he went further. "We are who we are. What we got to prove?"

"That even with the King down, the princes shall continue to reign and even stronger than the King," Brock looked Billy directly in the eyes. "And what good is a teacher if his student doesn't out do him," Brock said referring to him and his father's business relationship. He flip the page on the legal pad. "First things first. Taxes are going up."

"What! We can't do that shit!" Billy said and searched the faces at the table for objections other than his own.

Bobby looked a little concern, but he didn't object. "How much?" he asked, staying neutral.

"I'm demanding a five percent increase."

"That's outrageous," Billy yelled. "Why we trying to piss people off? I can never see dad doing this shit."

"Dad ain't here," Brock answered. "I can give a fuck about who gets pissed off."

"What about retention. You sure it ain't too soon to be raising their fee? We don't want to lose anybody," Bobby said with a level head.

"Where they gon' go, Bobby?" Bobby didn't respond. "And I don't think it's too soon. It's perfect timing. Me raising the fee is making a statement on behalf of the entire Badd family."

"And what's that?" Billy asked sarcastic.

"That we can do what the fuck we want, and they have to put up or *be* shut up," Brock said in a matter-of-fact way. "We ain't raised taxes in almost a decade. That's got to change."

"It' how we kept them loyal to us," Billy responded. "It's why they respected dad so much." Bobby nodded his head like he agreed with what Billy was saying. "We don't need to lose that respect."

"Billy, you treat respect like it's an offering," Brock chuckled. "The way I see it, that shit can be taken." Brock stared at Billy. "Besides, it's not their respect we need. It's the boys in blue. Them niggas that wear the robes at the court house and all them dirty ass politicians and the law makers. Our fee goes up, they fee goes up. That extra money we greasing they dirty hands with is gon' buy us more respect than we can carry. Their respect keeps the shit we doing a monopoly. " Bobby was starting to agree with Brock. Hesitantly, Billy considered what his brother was saying. "That fifteen percent they paying us is priceless to them. It gives them peace of mind and free reign to get rich off dirt. No consequences. No questions asked. And, peace of mind appreciates in value over time just like fine art or real estate. They taxes are going up," Brock said like the decision was final. "I want all them niggas to learn that this shit ain't no fucking democracy, it's a dictatorship. Honor thy Badd country or be exiled."

Mona smiled at her husband's corrupt wit. Brip started to laugh full of pride and arrogance. "Brip," Brock said serious and Brip stopped laughing and tuned in to his brother. "Get with Bobby and get a list of everybody that is behind on their taxes. If they ten days behind, you pay them a little visit. You know what I mean?" He stared at Brip to see if he got the picture. Brip, shook his head yes. "If they 20 days behind, you break they fucking legs. And if they 30 days or more behind, you send them to me. These niggas gon' learn that we going harder than ever. Blood has to be shed. A few nigga's gon' have to go down to show we mean business."

"Hell, yeah!" Brip was getting excited. He slapped the table. His adrenaline was starting to race.

"I just want all of you to understand that we a family first. All of y'all know how Mr. Badd felt about family. This entire empire was motivated by family. Our blood is thick. We got to keep it that way. All these decisions I'm gon' be making are to help us stay strong and on top. You may not understand it sometimes," he looked at Billy. "You may not even respect my choices but just know, I am the final say around here," Brock said stern and the room went silent. "Respect that and we will go a long way."

Brock and Billy locked eyes. Mona sat up straight in her chair and held her head high in the air like she had just been crowned Queen of the Badds. She grabbed Brock's hand and looked at me and then the rest of the brothers. Brock shifted his gaze from Billy and stared at the rest of us to ensure he had *taken* our respect. No one challenged him. After all, this wasn't a democracy.

22

B rock is staring at me like he trying to turn me to stone. He doesn't try to hide that he doesn't like or trust me. Either way, I'm here with him in Papa Badd's old office, sitting behind the desk racking my brains on how to say what I was about to say.

It's been two weeks since the funeral and everyone has been busy keeping it all together and making sure we stayed on top. I still hadn't heard from Angelo. I feared that the worst may have happened. That meant, Ace was still alive, and Billy was still planning to meet with him. Billy hadn't left the Ranch since his father died but he told me last night that he had to make a run to the city. I knew exactly where he was going. When I asked if I could go with him, he told me no. Then I asked where he was going but he didn't respond. He just gave me a strange look that caused my body to shudder. I knew what that meant. He was walking into an ambush. I could tell him about the ambush, but I couldn't reveal that without revealing that I killed his father although I had my suspicions that he already knew what I did.

Ace was going to have Tony kill him. He had no other reason not to. That left me no choice but to do what I was about to do. I had to protect Billy. Meeting with Brock was the only way. I had to turn flips just to get Brock to meet with me alone without the presence of his overbearing wife,

Mona. She was sure to fuck up my plan with the evil eye she has towards me. She would be able to see right through my lies. I prayed Brock wasn't as intuitive as his wife. With Billy leaving the ranch in the next hour or so, I had to think fast. The sun was just starting to set, and I told Billy I was going out to take a walk. But really, I went looking for Brock exactly where I knew I could find him. At the shooting range with his son, Vinchi.

Every evening at 6 pm, the gun fire starts. Brock is training Vinchi like a real soldier. The size of the guns they shoot is like something Rambo would have. I don't see how all that fire power is necessary, but Brock and Mona thinks so. The closer I got to the gun range, the more my heart races. My ears popped at the loud noise. Two second in to it, I thought it was a bad idea. Brock was likely to shoot me right where I stood if he suspected anything out of the ordinary. When he seen me rushing towards him, covering my ears and looking dead serious, he signaled for Vinchi to lower his weapon. At first, Vinchi hesitated. Almost as if he was considering making me his next target but he followed his father's instructions. He stared at me like I was his prey. I guess hating me was a family effort.

"I have to talk to you?" I said quick. Brock squinted his eyes when he looked at me. I guess he was trying to see past the bullshit. "Now," I demanded. I didn't know how long I had before Billy left the Ranch. I'm sure he wouldn't leave without kissing me goodbye.

"Talk," he said and cocked his gun like he would fire it if he had too.

My heart began to race. "Alone," I said looking at Vinchi.

Brock turned to look at Vinchi. He was giving me a suspicious look then he looked back at me. He stared at me for a few seconds like he was trying to figure me out.

"Where's my brother?"

"On his way *off* the Ranch. He's going to the city," I said in a telling voice.

Brock looked back at Vinchi again. He didn't want him to witness anymore of what I had to say.

"Meet me at the office in the big house in ten minutes," he said to me.

"Sir, what about, mom?" Vinchi said to Brock like he was addressing a drill sergeant. "You want me to get her?" He suggested.

"No, son. I don't," He gave Vinchi a look that warned him not to say a word about this to his mother or anyone else. "You continue practice, I'll be back to finish up with you shortly."

Vinchi hesitated but had no other choice but to listen to his father. I could feel him watching us as we walked away.

Ten minutes later, here I am facing Brock with sweaty palms and a racing heart. I must have cleared my throat ten times. Brock stared at me without blinking. He didn't give me a moment to catch my breath. I looked behind Brock and at the bookshelves. That's when I spotted the liquor cabinet and the bottle I poisoned still sitting there. Brock followed the trail of my eyes and turned around to see what I was looking at.

"You want a drink?" He asked with a raised brow.

I swallowed hard and tried my best to keep a straight face. "No. I'm just amazed at your father's vintage collection of liquor and books," My voice shook. This made Brock even more leery.

Brock turned around and looked over all his father's things prideful. "Yeah, Mr. Badd had real class. All of his things down to the bottles have been archived. No one is to touch anything."

I felt relieved. At least no one would be drinking from the bottle that killed him. I'm pretty sure that Brandy was now haunted. Being in this office gave me an eerie feeling.

"What did you want to meet me for?" Brock face went stern. He cut straight to the point.

So, I didn't waste any time telling him. "Billy..." I tried to say it but I couldn't. Could I? I didn't even know what it would mean for Billy. Would Brock kill him right away? My hopes is that he would detain him for a few days or at least long enough to keep him off the streets at which point I would flee and link up with him later and explain everything with hopes of living happily ever after. My plan wasn't well thought out but it's all I had to work with.

"Billy, what?" Brock leaned in closer to me almost like he knew what I was going to say. Like it was something he needed to hear me say. I started to cry. When Brock seen my tears, he softened up a little bit but not enough.

"It's okay, Dalla" he said gently. "We're family," he looked at me for about half a second then yelled, "say what you have to say," his soft tone was long gone.

"He killed Papa Badd," I blurted out.

Brock pushed his self-back in his seat like my words blew him away. He twisted his face and lowered his brow like he was confused. Almost as if he thought he was hearing things. He didn't say a word, but I could hear him yelling at himself in his head; it showed in his facial expressions. He squinted his eyes and shook his head like he was cursing himself out. Then, he darted his head up like he'd been stung by a bee, forcing himself back into reality.

"What?" Brock whispered in a voice so low I could barely hear him. He pushed back from his seat and tried to get up but didn't move. "What did you say?" he asked again.

"He killed your father," I looked him directly in the eyes and lied. That look sealed the deal. "He poisoned him with that bottle of Brandy," I said pointing a shaking finger in the direction of the Brandy.

Brock turned around and yanked the bottle of the shelf like it was a ticking time bomb. He placed it on the desk like it was hot, then stared at it; deep in thought. Just as if he were trying to see the poison floating around inside. He fell back in his chair; then his eyes darted up at me.

"What the fuck did you just say?" he hissed at me. I saw him squeeze his fist and naturally my body flinched. The hate in his voice felt just as intense as the sting of a slap. "You bold enough to come to me with this shit? Who are you really, Dalla?"

Brock didn't believe me. He didn't want to because that meant he was weak enough to let it happen right under his nose. He was going to make this hard for me.

"He did it, Brock. He confessed to me the other night. He's hurt by it. He knows he made a mistake, but he was convinced to do it by someone. Ever since his mother died, he hasn't been right in the head. Your father's death only makes things worse. Please forgive him, Brock!"

Brock used the desk to support his weight and leaned up from the chair. He took a deep breath, then straightened up his posture. "He wouldn't do this," Brock said more to himself than me.

"He hired someone to fake the autopsy report. Tyler something..." I blurted out and push the forged report that Angelo gave me in front of him. The forged report came out to be useful after all. I knew dropping that name would seal the deal. Brock's jaw dropped so low, I could see his tonsils. I knew Tyler Jones had nothing to do with this, but it was the only way Brock would believe me. I'd just killed two men with one stone. The first one was Papa Badd and the second Tyler Jones; both casualties of war. But, I had a third. If Angelo couldn't help me kill Ace, then I know Brock could.

"It's not his fault Brock. He didn't plan this." I tried to soften my voice. In part, I was telling the truth. I needed for Brock to feel so sorry for Billy that way he felt conflicted; if that was possible. That way, he wouldn't kill him. At least not so easy. "It was another man. He set the whole thing up. He calls himself Lucky...Spade or," I pretended not to know the name of the man that ruled my life for so many years. I snuck a glance at Brock and I knew that I didn't have to say anything else because he already knew.

"Ace Lucky," he said under his breath.

"Yes," I said like I was just remembering. "Ace Lucky. He set the whole thing up. Billy followed through until the end then he tried to get out of it, but it was too late. He didn't want to kill your father. He was just confused."

Brock carefully sat back down like his knees were about to give out. He was silent. He looked right past me and at the door like he was trying to plan his next move.

"I'm telling you this because I know you were going to find out anyway and I wanted you to know the truth. Billy did this but he's innocent, Brock. Please have mercy on him. Please..."

"Where is Billy? Where is my brother!"

"At the Casino finishing up some work," I lied. Billy was at home, packing. This would give me time to explain myself to Billy before Brock found him.

Brock looked me directly in the eye, giving me a look that I couldn't read. I'm not sure if he was considering what I was saying or not, but the look was so intense, my entire body shook. Then, he jumped to his feet like he was preparing himself to march off into war. He grabbed the bottle of Brandy and rushed passed me, leaving me alone in the office. That's when I took it upon myself to flee.

———— ··●·· ————

I ran all the way home. I got there just as Billy was walking out the door. He was startled by my reaction. He ran to me and I fell in his arms. I knew I didn't have long.

"Where are your keys, Billy? I need the keys to your bike."

"What's going?" Billy went into protective mode. He looked over my shoulder.

"Somebody hurt you? Is the baby, okay?"

I pushed myself out of his embrace and ran into the house to retrieve the keys Billy usually left in a drawer in the kitchen. "What the hell is going on, Dalla?"

"I did it for us, Billy. I promise, I did it for us. He was going to set you up. Have you killed. Ace never had Tyler Jones. It was a set up. There's a bounty on both our heads."

"What the hell are you, talking about?" Billy grabbed my shoulders. I struggled to break away from him. "What did you do, Dalla?" he began to shake me like he was trying to get the truth to fall out of me, but he knew what I did. Now, I hope he would understand why.

"Brock is coming for you. I told him you did it to protect you. Your safer here than out there," I jumbled my words together and spoke in one exaggerated breath. Billy seemed like he broke into a million pieces right in front of me. My heart broke.

"What did you do?" he repeated, although I already confessed what I done without saying a word. He still wanted me to say it. But, I couldn't.

"Please don't hate me," I said and kissed him hard. He pulled me off him and I kissed him again. I knew it was going to be the last kiss I got from him in a while. "I'm coming back for you. I promise." I ran towards the front door.

Billy grabbed my arm and pulled me back into the house before I could touch the knob.

"What about our baby?" He looked at me like he didn't believe there was a baby.

My heart broke. He no longer trusted me. He didn't believe I was pregnant. "Our baby is still here. He's going being ok," I grabbed his hand and placed it on my stomach, but Billy pulled away. "I'm sorry, Billy," I said shaking my head sorrowful. "I really fucked things up but I did it for us. I will be back for you. I promise. Then we can leave and be free from all of this."

I opened the door and ran out. Billy chased behind me. "Tell Brock it was me. Tell him that I was a mole. Tell him anything to keep you alive."

"Dalla," Billy screamed to my back. I didn't turn around. I hopped on his bike and sped off.

I watched Billy chasing behind the bike. He only stopped when he was grabbed by one of the guards. He tussled with them but was quickly over powered. They discreetly shoved him into the back of a black Hummer like a prisoner. A few of them ran in the house like they were looking for me but by then, I was already gone.

23

MONA

Two Weeks After Bobby's Fake Death

I got to find Vinchi. This Ranch is big but ain't big enough for his lil ass to get lost unless he wanted to. He's avoiding me because he knows what I'm gon' ask for and he ain't prepared to tell me no yet. He also knows his mama. And that shit means I ain't taking no for an answer.

Shit is bad right now. We all at risk. The only two people I see as being safe around here is Bobby because he already at the morgue and Billy because Brock got him hidden somewhere no one can find him. But, that ain't stopping me from trying.

What's left of Bobby is laying in the morgue frozen solid. Mr. Badd hadn't started an autopsy and he ain't even mention a funeral or nothing. He don't want this to get out yet. He thinks we under attack and I think he's right, but the only difference is this attack is coming from the inside and he got to realize he part of the threat too.

I love Brock like my own skin. There ain't nothing I wouldn't do in the world for him. I'll proudly take a bullet for him. My respect for him goes even deeper than my love but lately, that's been dwindling. I try my best to be a team player. I put on a straight face around him but he starting to notice my change too. That makes me nervous. He looks at me like he regrets ever telling me the truth about killing his mother. To be honest with you, I regret it too. I guess we both were wrong. I'm not as strong as I thought I was because I can't get over him killing his mother. A Badd woman. The woman that gave birth to him. It ain't like I thought she was something special and to be honest with you, the bitch didn't think too much of me either, but still there are rules to this shit and he broke them. Him killing his mother not only put our lives in jeopardy but our entire legacy. There ain't no honor in what he did.

I sacrificed so much for this name and to have it all get shit on makes me grit my teeth. You think I wanted bitches fucking my husband? Dealing with their drama every day was enough to give me a stroke, but I did it for Brock. Then, it meant something. Now, I'm starting to think it ain't mean shit but him getting to nut in women raw dick without any consequences for me; I must be a big fucking joke. I always went along with his plan no matter what I thought about it. I told him he was right when he was wrong. I silenced my voice for years and that shit wasn't easy cause I got the kind of voice that can move mountains. But for Brock, I only spoke when I was spoken to and when he talked to me, I hung on to every word like it meant something. Even if he was just asking me for a glass of water. I wasn't just his wife but his loyal partner. The queen that sat on the throne right beside him. But now, I'm thinking I wasn't shit but a glorified groupie; less than a sidekick. A fucking minion that made him feel better about himself.

Shit, I got to shake these thoughts off. I can't be feeling like this. *Can I?* No, I can't. I can shake this shit off. I been fighting with my thoughts ever since he told me about Mama Badd and they only got worse after Bobby died. But, I'm gon' shake myself out of this funk and get my head back in the game. I got to do what I do best which is get shit back in control; I'm gon' take matters into my own hands because this Badd shit ain't his kingdom alone. It's got other Queens and Kings too. I been protecting this Ranch way before I said *I do* to Brock. And I'm gon' continue to do it too. It ain't going down like this. Not on my watch.

I must have been riding around on this golf cart for an hour now and there still ain't no sign of Vinchi. I checked the Casino, the Chapel, the gun range and even the morgue. I checked everywhere but Brock's prison. Vinchi avoiding me and I'm avoiding Brock. I turned off my two way because Brock been paging me for the last hour. I don't have to answer to know what he want. He called a mandatory family meeting. I'll be at the meeting but I just ain't in the mood to think about it right now. Not until I find Vinchi.

Security is tighter than it's ever been. Brock called in 15 extra guards. Security cameras are being watched around the clock and all business has been shut down. That means we ain't making no fucking money. The Casino is shut down and so is the hospital. He canceled two events that two of our best clients booked at the Chapel. If he was gon' do all that, why not just let everybody know about Bobby because if they smart enough they know something is going on. But what the fuck do I know? I'm just a Badd wife.

Pushing on this petal has got my damn foot hurting. I pull off the road and park the cart under a tree to give my foot a rest. I'm not even here 10 seconds before one of the new guards come rushing my way.

"Excuse me, Mrs. Badd," a young man says to me. I can hear the trembling in his voice.

"What is it?"

He swallowed hard. "You..." he hesitated. "You can't park here, mam." he blurted out then jump back like he was expecting me to swing at him.

Is that all people think of me? If they say something I don't like, they expect me to hit them. I certainly hope not because if that were true, then I'll be weak. Now, don't get me wrong. I'll put a nigga on his back real fast, but it's got to be for a reason. There is an order to this shit.

"Is that right?" I said and massaged my foot. This is the third time this has happened to me this week. Brock don't want nobody outside the camera zones. Not even me.

"Yes, mam," he said still looking at the ground. His eyes led up and he watched me massage my ankle. "would you like a ride back, mam?"

"No," I answered quick. He gave me a funny look and took a deep breath.

"But, mam I insist."

"Why?" I'm getting annoyed.

"Mr. Badd has been looking for you. Your presence has been requested at the big house." Then he held out his hand for me to grab. It was shaking.

I was so pissed I could have grabbed his hand with my mouth, but it wasn't nothing personal. It was Brock.

"You tell Mr. Badd I'm busy working!" I didn't even notice I was screaming until I seen the youngster jump back.

"I have strict orders, mam. I have to bring you back." He said in a sterner voice. Then he grabbed my forearm.

That's when I pushed his ass and he went flying onto the pavement. He jumped up and grabbed my other arm. I whopped upside his head with my fist. All he did was duck but he kept pulling me towards his truck.

"Get the fuck off of me!" I demanded as he tried his best to pull me away like a prisoner.

I clutched my fist and suckered him right in his jaw. That's when he let me go. While he was rubbing the right side of his face, stunned by how hard I hit, I caught him slipping and gave him another one even harder on the left side of his face. He fell to the ground and grunted. I was just going in to kick him in the rib cage when I saw somebody else's boot stomping him like an oversized cockroach. I looked up and it was, Brip.

"Brip, calm down." I tried to pull him off the guard. He was going to kill him and didn't even recognize it. "Brip, I yelled again. This time grabbing him by the shirt collar and then put both my hands on his face and made him look me directly in the eyes. "It's okay, Brip. It's okay."

When Brip nodded at me, I knew he was coming back to reality.

"What the fuck this nigga doing put his hands on you?" Brip hissed and tried to get back at the guard but I pulled him back.

"It's not his fault. It's Mr. Badd. He gave strict orders." "To touch you? Hell, naw. That shit ain't right. What the fuck has gotten into, Brock?"

"Nothing. He just trying to protect us?" I tried to play the peacemaker. Brip was the only Badd brother we had left on our team. We needed him. I needed him.

"Who all these fucking new folk walking around here anyway? I just had to bust another one's nose. Talking about I was parked in a restricted area. What the fuck!" Brip punched the air then rushed back towards the guard and started wailing on him again. I couldn't stop him this time.

"Brip, that's enough. Let's go. Mr. Badd has called a meeting."

Brip finally stopped kicking the guard. He wiped the sweat from his brow and exhaled, leaning back on his legs. The poor young man was lying on the ground; he wasn't moving. I finally turned back on my two-way and instructed the medic to come and get him. I followed Brip to his truck. He jumped in the truck like he didn't do what he done to the guard; he had no remorse. Brip rolled down the window and spit outside before wiping his nose and sniffing hard.

"You okay?" He turned to ask me. He was genuinely concerned.

"I'm good, Brip," I responded wondering to myself what type of monster we created in him.

———— ··●·· ————

Before I could even get one foot in the door, Brock started to go in on me.

"Where in the fuck have you been, Mona? I've been calling you all day!" He yelled so hard, spit flew out his mouth. I dodged his liquid bullets.

I kept my cool. "I'm sorry, Mr. Badd. My two-way ain't been acting right." I tried to walk past him, but he pulled me back only to give me a stern look in the eye like he was trying to see what I've been up to. He let me go and Brip and I followed him to the study. "Where's Vinchi?" I asked.

"Handling some other business? Why?" he said to me like I had no rights to my son.

"I ain't seen him in a few days and I want to make sure he's okay. You know how he felt about his uncle, Bobby."

"Vinci's fine," Brock said to me stern. "Every solider knows there's going to be causalities."

"Bobby wasn't no fucking causality," Brip interjected.

"Calm down," Brock said to Brip, quieting him up before he got started on an irate rampage.

"What the fuck is going with all this security? If another mutha-fucka stop me, I'm gon' kill his ass. This is my home. I don't need nigga's questioning me about where I'm going and why."

"He put one down near the Chapel, Brock." I gave Brock a telling look, warning him about Brip's temper. Brock didn't respond because he didn't care. The more guards Brip put out the more he'd hire to replace them.

"I tightened security up for a reason. Bobby's dead and I'm gon' make sure that shit doesn't happen to another Badd," Brock said.

"How?" Brip demanded to know. "You got any leads on who the fuck did this shit? I got to get at them, Brock. I got to."

I turned to look at Brock. I can read what he was thinking, and I knew he had no leads just paranoia. "When we gon' bury him, Brock? Bobby deserves a proper funeral. We can't keep him like that for much longer, it ain't right." I said as calm as I could.

"I'm working on it," Brock said to both of us with an even tone. "This shit takes patience."

"No, this shit takes, bullets," Brip said and pulled out his Glock. "Lots of them," he kicked back his gun then looked around the room for the first-time noticing Taffy wasn't here.

"Where the fuck is my wife? She need to be in on this meeting too," Brip demanded. "Aye, " he yelled to one of the guards, go get my damn wife."

Brock sighed heavy like something was bothering him. "She's gone, Brip."

"What?" Brip said to Brock like he was speaking another language.

"What do you mean Taffy's gone, Brock?" I said, standing to my feet. Brip jumped up too. He looked out the window like he was expecting to see Taffy walk up.

"I don't know how she managed to do it, but she left early this morning. One of my guards caught it on camera."

"WHAT THE FUCK!!!" Brip screamed so loud the roof shook.

"Calm, down brother," Brock said in a stern voice. "Taffy ain't go far. We got bigger fish to fry right now. I need you out looking for, Lera. That's our lead on Bobby's death."

"FUCK LERA!" Brip hissed.

"Brip, calm down." I walked over towards him and grabbed his face. Once

Brip really got going, it would take an entire army to stop him. "What happened? Why would she leave?" I could see that Brip was hurting. Bobby dying was one thing but with Taffy being gone, Brip was likely to blow us all to bits. I wish Brock was smart enough to see that.

"I don't know, man." He started to punch himself against the head. He tried to hold back his tears. "She hate me. She hate me, man."

"No, she doesn't, Brip. She loves you more than anybody. I know that for a fact. It's just a lot going on right now." I tried to calm him down. "She probably just needed a break. I guarantee she's at y'all house in the city." I hoped what I was saying was true. With all this shit going on, it wasn't safe for Taffy to be roaming the streets alone. The Ranch may have been Brocks business, but the wives were mine.

"No, Mona. I don't think so," Brip said in a loud whisper. His body fell back into the chair heavy. He buried his face in his hands. "I killed her brother and Lera told her."

"What do you mean you killed her brother?" I was confused. I looked over at Brock hoping he can provide some sort of assistance, but he could care less. He looked right through his brother, offering no sympathy. He was agitated by Brip's whining.

"It was way before I knew it was her brother. Before I even knew her. It was some guy I was casing. Lera said that Dalla told her the shit and when she confronted me with it, I couldn't lie. I just couldn't lie to her." Brip started to sob.

"Man up," Brock said, jumping to his feet. He marched over to Brip and pushed me out the way. He grabbed Brip by the shirt collar and yanked him to his feet. "You crying like a fucking bitch over a woman when we about to lose it all!" He shook Brip and Brip didn't try to resist. "What the fuck is wrong with you, man?" He pushed Brip and he fell back into his seat trying his best to swallow his tears. He wasn't going to challenge Brock no matter how hurt he was by Taffy.

"She's not just a woman, she's a Badd wife, Brock!" I defended all of us Badd wives. We meant something too. With the sacrifices we make daily, we had to.

"SHE'S A WOMAN!" he yelled to me letting me know where us wives ranked in this legacy. "You should know better than anybody that I'm not going to let a woman ruin a legacy that took years to build. A woman can be replaced, this legacy can't!" Brock shot me a look that caused me to shake. He was reminding me of what he did to his mother; a woman. Was he trying to threaten me?

My heart skipped a few beats and my body went numb. I was falling into an emotional shock. I felt tears filling my eyes, but I wouldn't dare allow them to drop. At this very moment I realized I wasn't who I thought I was, and neither was Brock.

24

LERA

"Where are we going now, Bobby?"

Bobby and I have been roaming around like nomads. We must have slept in every dead in motel this city has to offer, and we never stay longer than 24 hours. Sometimes, less than that. Everything we ate came out of a paper bag and my clothes feel like they are starting to wear out. Bobby's been wearing the same grease stained wife beater for two days now and he's in serious need of grooming but we both are. My tank top and jeans are so wrinkled even the hottest iron can't smooth them out. My eyebrows are growing back thick and I'm in desperate need of a mani-pedi. This 1980's box truck that we are in doesn't have a radio and my window won't roll down. I'm tired, weary and confused. If Bobby has a plan, I need to know about it.

Bobby ignored my question. That's what he did every time I asked him something he didn't want to answer. Now I'm starting to think he's not answering because he doesn't have an answer. Maybe there is no plan.

"Why don't we just leave the city and set up somewhere else," I suggest again for the hundredth time. I rubbed the back of his head, but he dodged my touch. He didn't like it when I made that suggestion.

"Look, how many times I have to tell you that ain't possible? I don't run from anybody and neither do you. I got to find my brother!"

"Then what are we doing now?" I tried to keep my voice in a respectful tone, but it was getting hard. I felt like we were running in circles.

Bobby ignored my question again. "You hungry?"

"Yes," I said I was hungry, but not for food, a solution. A means to an end.

"What do you want?"

"Sushi, or a steak. That will be nice."

Bobby chuckled. "I hope you eat gas station sushi," he said pulling into a Shell station.

The moment the car pulled into the lot, I spotted Jayson right away.

"Is that, Jayson?"

"It looks like it," Bobby said and opened the door. "Stay here."

I watch Bobby walk over to Jayson. Jayson looks over Bobby's shoulder and makes brief eye contact with me. Was Jayson apart of Bobby's unwritten plan? I sure hope not. Bobby turned around to make sure I was okay. I tried to hide the confusion and disgust on my face, but it was hard. It wouldn't matter one way or the other to Bobby. I wish I could read lips. That way I'll have an idea of what's going on. But I can't. I can read body language though. By the way Jayson is looking over his shoulder every minute, I could tell he was nervous. He barely looked at Bobby just as if he were talking to a ghost. I'm thinking Bobby didn't trust everything he was saying because he had his arms defensively folded against his chest. He stared hard at Jayson when he spoke. Jayson seemed to fidgety to me. One second, he was leaning against a coke machine and the next second fidgeting with his lighter and a cigarette. Bobby didn't change his posture. He faced Jayson with his chest out and with a firm stance.

As their conversation came to an end, they both turned and looked at me at the same time. What was that about? Bobby shook his head yes like he was agreeing to something then turned back towards the truck. Jayson went back to his car and drove to park alongside of us like he was waiting on us.

Before Bobby could open the door and get inside, I started questioning him.

"What's going on? Why is he here? Are you sure we can trust him?"

"I can trust him," Bobby said to me like that's all that mattered. Bobby looked at me. He knew I was upset but that didn't matter to him right now.

"Are we in this together or not?" I asked.

"Haven't we been in this together?"

I hated when he answered my question with a question.

"I feel like I'm just along for the ride. I need to know the plan, Bobby."

"We going somewhere safe. Getting off the streets. Somewhere where I can clear my head for a while. That way I'll be ahead of the game. I just need you to trust me."

"I do trust you," I said quick. I didn't want Bobby thinking for one second that I didn't trust him. That wasn't the problem.

"Well stop questioning every move I make. I got this." He said and attempted to crank up the engine. As usual, the truck didn't start right away. Bobby had to push on the gas a few times before he got the engine to turn over. Finally, the truck started clucking and we followed behind Jayson.

We trailed behind Jayson for over an hour when we finally made it to some hick town I've never heard of. There was nothing here but open fields of green grass with cows and horses grazing in it. The houses were miles away from each other. It was nothing too fancy either. Mainly ranches with white painted wood sidings and huge porches. Every house had a barn somewhere off in the distance and a tractor sitting idle in the grass. I would've asked Bobby where we were, but I didn't bother. I guess I would find out soon enough. Jayson slowed down. He put on his left turn signal and we followed him to a neatly paved road. The first thing I noticed was the mailbox. It was different. It was pink with green cats painted on it.

The long driveway led us to a red brick ranch style home. It was more modern than the other houses. It had circular driveway and a three-car garage. We pulled up around the back where I spotted the in-ground pool and a pool house behind it. There was also what looked like a green house. At least that's what I'm assuming it was. It was made of glass and I could see plants inside. I looked around the entire yard and noticed that it looked professionally landscaped. There were a multitude of colored flowers and plants all neatly and purposely placed around the house. I could smell lavender and jasmine coming from all directions.

Before Bobby opened the door, he gave me a look like he was concerned about something, but he didn't have to be. I felt relieved. Finally, we got to sleep in a real bed. I guess this was another one of Bobby's hide out houses. I was grateful for it. I really needed this. I opened the door and inhaled deeply. I prayed this house had a kitchen as nice as the yard. I was already thinking about the meals I could cook for Bobby. This was the perfect place for him to relax and catch his breath. Being here was going to be the most normal I felt in a while.

I continued to look around the yard. I explored the back yard, giving the pool a closer look. It was nice. There was even a hot tub attached to it. Perfect. Me and Bobby was defiantly christening this hot tub tonight. I looked past the green house and saw what looked like a horse stable. Horses? That's odd but interesting. Horses or not, this is just what we needed.

"Lera," Bobby called for me to follow him. I couldn't wait to shower. I caught up with Bobby. We walked to the front of the house towards the driveway. There was a big trash bin sitting in front of the three-car garage. Bobby grabbed the trash bin and rolled it towards the side of the house. That was odd. I'd never seen Bobby do anything that domestic before. I don't even think I ever seen him lift a trash bag before. Maybe being in the country would bring out a different side of Bobby. A side that I really needed to see right now.

I happened to look up and caught Jayson cutting a look at me out of the side of his eye. It almost was condescending. What the fuck was his problem? I can't stand the bastard. I wasn't wearing my B-necklace, but I had no problem reminding him that I was a Badd wife. Regardless if my husband was presumed dead.

When we got to the front door, Bobby went to turn the knob without bothering to use a key. Before he could open the door good enough, he started inspecting the latch. "This shit ain't safe. This latch is broke. The door won't lock if the latch is broke."

"You ain't got to worry about that out here man. This is the boonies. Nobody locks their doors."

There were plants hanging on the porch. Nailed to the brick sidings were inspirational plaques with words like *love*, *live* and *learn*. I looked down and the outside mat read, *home is where the heart is*. I don't know who Bobby hired to decorate this place, but it definitely wasn't our style. That didn't matter to me though.

"I don't give fuck where we at. I'm gon' have to fix that shit." Bobby said toying with the latch. What shocked me was that he said *he* was going to fix it. Hm... that would be a sight to see. Bobby finally left the latch alone and opened the door wide enough for us to walk inside. Right away, I was met with the aroma of home-cooked food. If I wasn't mistaken, it smelled like Italian; I smelled basil and oregano. I could hear feet shuffling back and forth. I guess Bobby had a personal chef flown in. Thank God. I really needed this.

The entrance of the house surprised me. I didn't expect it to be this nice. Thick and glossy hardwood floors covered the foyer and wrapped around the hallway. The walls were painted a cool mint green with yellow accents. I looked down and noticed one of those scented wall flowers plugged into an outlet. The smell was strong and pleasant. It smelled like a Japanese cherry blossom. As we walked further into the house, I noticed more inspirational plaques and other wall decor that wasn't my style. There were lots of pictures of horses hanging on the walls.

The furniture was traditional. The couch was big and fluffy with floral prints. And, the plush area rug and huge lamp shades all matched the pink and mint green throw pillows. The house had a warm homey feel about it. It was like Martha Steward meets June Clever. I roamed around the front area. I started to get lost in the feel of the house. So lost that I didn't notice Bobby wasn't beside me anymore. Where did he go?

"Aye, Tara? Where you at, girl?" Jayson yelled towards where I assumed the kitchen was. I heard more feet shuffling.

Tara? Who in the hell was Tara? A female chef? I was cool with it. We wouldn't need her after tonight though. I was planning on sending her away and sending Jayson to the grocery store with my list. That way me and Bobby could have a few moments alone to connect.

"I'm here," I heard a woman with the sweetest southern accent respond.

I looked up and saw an average looking petite woman wearing an apron and pink flip-flops. The second Jayson saw her, he picked her up and swung her around in an embrace.

"What's up, baby?" he said and politely kissed her on the cheek.

Oh, so Jayson was screwing the help. That was going to change today. With all this shit going on, we don't need his little girlfriend in the mix adding to the drama. Besides, I wasn't sure we could trust her. I wonder what Bobby thought about this?

Jayson put the woman who called herself, Tara down. She looked up at me and flashed me a hesitant smile. She had the most perfect teeth I'd ever seen. Her teeth were pretty much the best thing she had going for herself. They shaped her smile and made her appear to be prettier than she actually was. She wiped her hands against the apron and walked towards me, extending her hand for me to shake.

"Hi," she said sounding like a Southern belle, "I'm, Tara."

"I'm Lera Badd," I said with authority. I wasn't wearing my necklace, but I still had to let her know who was boss around her. I didn't smile back at her. To my surprise, she didn't smile back at me or try to kiss my ass.

"Where's Bobby?" I looked passed her and asked Jayson.

"Oh, Bobby done got that screwdriver and is trying to fix the broken latch on the front door," Tara answered for Jayson. She said my husband's name as if she knew him. As a Badd wife, I took that shit as disrespect. "I told him that he didn't have to worry about that all the way out here."

"I told him the same thing," Jayson agreed with Tara. They both shared a brief laugh.

"You know, Bobby," she said with a smile and waved her hand in the air.

Now the bitch was pissing me off. What did she know about my husband?

"Excuse me," I said and shot Tara an *I'll kick your ass look*.

Surprising me a second time, she challenged me giving me the *I dare you to touch me look*. Before I could fully welcome her challenge, Bobby walked up holding a screwdriver.

"Bobby," we both said at the same time. Tara and I had a brief stare-down that was interrupted by Bobby.

"I fixed that door," he told her.

"Okay," Tara said shaking her head like it wasn't necessary, but she appreciated it.

I glanced over at Jayson and he was smirking and kind of shaking his head. What the fuck was going on? If the bitch wasn't so homely, I would feel threatened by her. She definitely wasn't Bobby's type, but she still was disrespecting me.

"I see you met, Lera," Bobby said looking my way. Why didn't he say his wife?

"Yes," was all Tara said sounding like a southern bell fresh out of charm school.

"Lera, this Tara. Jayson's sister," Bobby said to me in a nonchalant way.

Go figure. I guess being a bitch ran in the family.

"Oh, yeah," was all I said through a smirk. Being a part of the help staff was a family business for them. I gave Tara a closer look and could totally see the resemblance in her and Jayson. She basically was the female version of him. She was skinny with bad skin. And very plain. She had her pulled back in a simple ponytail that barely dusted the bottom of her neck and she wore no make-up.

"Tara has agreed to let us stay in her home for a while," Bobby said to me like I should be grateful.

Here home? What the fuck? I didn't like this at all and Bobby saw my face drop. He didn't try to appease me either.

"You ready to eat?" She said to Bobby like she only cooked for him.

"You know I am a girl," Bobby said rubbing his stomach. "You got it smelling good in here. What you got going on in the kitchen?"

"I made your favorite," she said then jumped like she let a secret slip.

"I like your famous lasagna too, sis." Jayson teased his sister and followed her to the kitchen.

Uncomfortable wasn't the right word to describe how I felt right now. Bobby followed behind Jayson to the kitchen. He didn't even wait for me.

Like an idiot, I followed behind the crowd blindly.

I couldn't even hate. Tara's kitchen looked like something right out of a cooking magazine. It had a high ceiling with skylights and lots of big windows casing the walls; it was bright and open. All the appliances were stainless steel and the refrigerator was huge. It had to be custom. Forget a double oven, she had a triple oven and gas grill on the island. There was a beautiful wall range exhaust vent hovering over her gas stove. I was almost speechless. And to top it all off, the spread of food looked amazing. The lasagna was beautifully placed in all-white serving dish. The salad was displayed perfectly in a wooden bowl and the bread was wrapped up in a beautiful cloth and placed in a contemporary bread basket.

Tara had a dining room attached to her kitchen, but the kitchen was so big, we ate at the oversized glass table she had placed near the bay windows facing her beautiful garden. I took a seat near Bobby. Right away, Tara went into homemaker mode and commenced to making Bobby's plate. I could have screamed, and Bobby saw it all over my face.

"You good?" he had the nerve to ask me.

I sucked in my lips and shrugged my shoulders. That was good enough for him.

"This looks, good sis," Jayson bragged. "But where the wine at?" Jayson teased.

"Boy, you know better than that. You know I don't allow no alcoholic beverages in this house," Tara said with a prideful smile like her choice not to drink made her better than us but really her not having alcohol for her guest just made her damn rude. "All the herbs in this lasagna came from my garden, you know. And the veggies in the salad too so eat up," she bragged.

"Wine and basil go good together," Jayson continued to tease his sister. She playfully smacked him on the head and all three of them shared a laugh like they were in some sort of secret club.

Tara loaded Bobby's plate up with food. He looked anxious to dig in when she placed it in front of him. I waited for her to extend the same treatment to me and Jayson, but it never happened. Partially because Jayson was grabbing the food and piling it on his plate like he'd never eaten it before. I didn't budge.

A few bites in, Bobby noticed I wasn't eating. Tara noticed right away. She looked at me out the corner of her eye.

"Why you ain't eating?" Bobby asked.

"I'm not hungry. I'm tired. I think I just need to rest." I said cold. "I don't have a taste for lasagna." I looked up at, Tara. She rolled her eyes at me.

"More for us," Jayson said and Tara chuckled.

That fucking bitch! I can't believe they were taunting me, and Bobby was letting this happen.

"We've been on the road all day. You need to eat something, " Bobby said and held a fork full of lasagna to my mouth. I really didn't want to eat the bitch's food but allowed Bobby to feed me in front of her. I bit into that lasagna and instantly wanted to spit it out. Not because it was nasty but because it was so damn good. The flavors exploded on my tongue like a bomb on my taste buds went off. "That's good, right? Make yourself a little."

"I'm good," I said to Bobby. "Where am I sleeping tonight? I just want to shower."

"Come on, I'll show you." Bobby tried to get up, but Tara stopped him, placing her small and dainty hand on his shoulder.

"No, Bobby. Stay and eat your food." She gently demanded, and he listened. "I'll show her."

Bobby didn't try to argue with her. He continued to stuff food in his mouth. He even reached over and grabbed more lasagna out of the pan before he was finished with is first helping. I'd never seen him eat this much before. Not even when I cooked for him. I started to feel so sensitive about the situation, I could have cried. What was going on? Why wasn't I being treated like his wife? Like a Badd wife?

"Let's go, honey," Tara said, and I got up and followed behind her.

I followed Tara down a long hallway to our room. We didn't speak to each other. On the way, I spotted what looked like a child's room. There was an Xbox and a gaming chair in the room. It was painted blue. I noticed a football sitting on the dresser alongside what looked like a collection of baseball cards.

"This is where you will be staying," Tara said and opened the door. The room looked comfortable. There was a king-sized mattress covered with an all-white fluffy comforter. It was inviting. "You have access to your own bathroom. There are clean towels in the linen closet. I'll put a plate up for you just in case you get hungry, " Tara said without looking at me. Then she closed the door.

After I took a shower I laid on the bed and dozed off. The bed felt like a fucking feather. I went to sleep instantly. I don't know what woke me up but I when I opened my eyes I heard Bobby's voice. Him and Tara where whispering outside of the door. I jumped up and tiptoed closer to the door to hear what they were talking about.

"Thanks for doing this, T," Bobby said to her.

"Boy, you know you don't need to be thanking me."

"I do. Don't mind, Lera. She just been through a lot." Bobby made excuses for me. I didn't need him to do that. Tara didn't respond. I couldn't see her but I bet she was rolling those beady eyes of hers. "Where's Blake?" Bobby said. His voice was even more at a whisper now.

"Don't worry. He's fine. He's with my mother in South Carolina. You know he didn't want to go."

"I know but I think he should stay there for a little while."

"Okay," was all Tara said.

Who the fuck was Blake? When it sounded like Bobby was coming closer to the door, I jumped back in bed. But, I moved too soon because they were still talking. A few minutes later, Bobby opened the door. I pretended to be asleep. He must have only peeked his head in the door to check on me because I didn't hear footsteps leading my way. I assumed he would go take a shower and join me in bed but instead, he closed the door and walked back down the hall. He didn't come back that night.

What the fuck?

25

MONA

"**I** need you to talk to, Brip. With Taffy being gone, you the only one he really listens to," Brock said to me.

I could really care less about counseling Brip about Taffy just, so Brock can manipulate him into doing his dirty work. I'm getting tired of this shit. It ain't right. Besides, I still haven't seen Vinchi yet and I'm starting to get worried.

We are sitting in Papa Badd's study. I never liked coming in here after he died; it feels to fucking creepy. Especially considering that he died right where Brock is sitting. I don't see how he sits in his father's old seat so comfortably and I mean that in more than one way.

I try to keep a straight face while Brock is talking to me; I have to play it smart. That means I must continue to do what I've been doing for years in order to survive; and push my emotions to the side. But this time, I'm doing it for a different reason.

I had an epiphany the other day when Brock was yelling at me and Brip. He don't respect any of the shit I've done, and he will do anything to remain on top. If he killed his own mother, none of us have a chance. Not even me and the kids. Every move that I made for him and this family, I did it from my heart. Coming from a woman that didn't have a family that was worth a shit, I prided myself in being a part of a family so influential and powerful. I thought that mattered to Brock, but it doesn't.

I helped Brock build this place. He didn't do none of this shit on his own. Yet, he insinuates that I can be replaced. What about my fucking efforts? He thinks that he can put me out of here and I walk away with nothing. Shit! That ain't gon' happen. It's time for me to start looking out for myself and my investment in this Ranch. Now, I don't know what exactly looking out for myself means specifically but I'm planning on taking this shit one day at a time and today, that means controlling my emotions.

"What do you need me to speak to Brip about, Mr. Badd?" I say to Brock but really, I couldn't care less. Now that Brock is talking again, I can piece together the bits of information he's giving me and try to figure out what's going on because as usual, he ain't telling me shit. I plan on entertaining him as long as I can.

"I don't need him going after that *girl* right now. I need him searching for, Lera."

"You mean, Taffy?" I say reminding Brock that the girl he is referring to not only had a name but a title; she was a Badd wife. But, it went right over his head.

"Yes," he answered and leaned back in his chair. "She's going to be an unnecessary distraction."

"Brip loves his wife. He ain't gon' just let her go that easy, Brock."

"Yeah, but I already got somebody looking for her. They gon' find her, but I need Lera."

"Why?" I asked hoping he'd give a full answer.

"Because Lera can bring me, Dalla," Brock said like he was putting the pieces to a puzzle together. I knew he had a plan.

"Shouldn't we be searching for, Bobby's killer? I think that person is more important than Dalla and Lera put together," I said in a soft voice. I wanted to remind him about what was important. Bobby was dead and the longer we let his killer linger around out there, anyone of us could be next. Especially, Taffy now that she's on the outside.

"There's a connection."

"What?" I waited to hear him out. I wasn't sure Lera had anything to do with Bobby's death. Brock is forgetting that Bobby died the day of their wedding and Lera had been on the Ranch the entire time. If there was foul play, she would have fled the ranch before we had a chance to give her the bad news. She only fled afterward and now, I don't blame her.

"Brock, we can't wait for Bobby's killer to make his way onto the Ranch. If he was bold enough to kill Bobby in public, the Ranch may be his next target."

"I'm pretty sure I know who killed Bobby and yes, it's bigger than Dalla and Lera."

"Who?" I leaned in closer to Brock.

"It was Ace Lucky," Brock admitted.

"That's bullshit? Right?" I didn't understand how it could happen. "How did you come to this conclusion?"

"Billy," Brock answered and leaned back in his chair. "When I gave Billy the news of Bobby's death, he started telling me shit I ain't never heard him say."

"What?" I said in a low voice. Hearing that Billy was alive and so accessible that Brock could inform him about Bobby's death relieved me and gave me chills at the same time.

"Ace been plotting against us for years. Billy finally gave me a few leads and come to find out, they been planning an attack. And with Bobby being dead, you right Mona. They bold enough to attack us any day now."

"So, what are we gon' do about it, Brock?" I was anxious.

"Go after him first."

"How?" I asked.

"By giving him what he wants," Brock said like he had it all figured out. "A few Badd's."

I gasped and then covered my mouth to keep Brock from seeing how shocked I was but it didn't work. He almost seemed amused by my response. Like he wanted to scare me. My heart stopped for a few seconds. Was he saying what I think he's saying? Is he going to hand over his own family into the hands of the enemy? Was keeping control of the Ranch that important to him? It had to be if he killed his mother, but he still won't tell me why he did it. It doesn't make sense. Neither does his plan.

"You know I'm with you on anything Mr. Badd but I'm not sure I understand your plan?" I said in a careful voice. I had to put my emotions aside. "Forgive me for being a little confused but did you just say you was going to give Ace Lucky a Badd?"

"No, what I said was that I was going to give Ace Lucky a *few* Badds," Brock said in a matter-of-fact way. "Meaning more than one." An evil smile spread across his face. "Ever heard of the saying, *a necessary evil.*"

I was speechless. The man I was staring at wasn't my husband. He was so possessed with greed and power that he was turning into someone else. The man I married would die for his family; not kill them off one by one. It was hard to keep a straight face, but I managed. Brock was staring right through me trying to see what I was thinking but I wasn't letting him read my thoughts. If I showed any sign that I disagreed, he would consider me disloyal and wouldn't tell me anything else and I needed to know the plan. That way, I could stop it.

"Okay," was all I could bring myself to say at such short notice. I avoided eye contact with him and started shaking my head like I understood where he was going with his plan. "So, who..."I stuttered then hesitated. I wasn't sure I was ready to hear him name the sacrificial lambs. "Who is it going to be?" I managed to say. I had to know.

Brock sighed like making the decision bothered him, but I knew better. He leaned in closer to me and rested his elbows on the wood desk. He clasped his hands together, using them to balance his chin, and stared at me.

"Bobby already gone and I need Brip. So, I decided Lera, Billy, Taffy, and Vinchi."

What the fuck! Did he just say, Vinchi? I couldn't have heard him right. I know he didn't name our son. Our oldest boy. Keep calm Mona. This nigga is really tripping but that don't mean you got to.

"Vinchi!" I tried to say his name calmly, but a yell slipped out instead. "You would sacrifice your son, Brock?"

Brock leaned back in his chair again like he was making himself comfortable. He had prepared to let me vent. He just stared at me. But, I had no words for him. My heart was beating too fast to speak. I couldn't breathe. I got to find Vinchi and leave tonight. I have too.

"I knew you wouldn't understand my plan, Mona. That's why I thought hard before I told you."

"Well, why did you tell me?" I said through a gasp.

Brock came closer to me grabbed my trembling hand and gave it a supportive squeeze.

"You know I need you on my side. You my rock. Without your support, the plan won't go as smoothly as I hope."

I pulled away from Brock's touch. "I want to be on your side, baby but I can't agree with you sending our son out to get massacred."

"That ain't my plan, " Brock was getting frustrated. He was used to me agreeing with him right away. He didn't like to be challenged.

"Am I hearing you wrong or did you not just say you were sending Vinchi and other Badd family members to be murdered by Ace Lucky? A long-time enemy of our family. Do you think this is a decision Papa Badd would have made? What do you really think he would think of you doing this right now? Really, Brock?"

Brock shook off my questions. He waved his hand at me like he wanted me to leave. He didn't like when I compared him to his father. It was something that he struggled with every day and he didn't need me reminding him that no matter how hard he tried, they were two different men.

"I would like your support on this, Mona but I don't need it. However," Brock gave me a cold stare, "I do expect it," he warned me.

"Send me instead of Vinchi. I'll go," I pleaded with Brock.

"What the hell good would you be to Ace?" Brock said almost laughing. Fuck him. I wanted to tell the coward to go himself, but I wouldn't dare. "Besides, my plan ain't what you think it is. I don't plan on Vinchi or anyone else getting hurt. They just bait."

I tried my very best to feel relieved by the idea of Brock not intentionally wanting to hurt his family but the fact that he would be so recklessly by putting them in harm's way was all the same to me. Besides, he killed Mama

Badd when he felt like she got in his way. I wasn't buying any of it. Brock was dangerous.

"Bait?" I managed to say. "Bait for who?"

"Talking to Billy, I learned a lot about how that nigga's mind works. He likes to mind fuck niggas. It makes him feel that he's in control. So, I figured, if I send Vinchi to him. Ace knows that he ain't gon' ever succeed in killing all of us unless he has help from the inside. Vinchi will play like he plotting against us and one at a time, he'll bring him a Badd just to make it look serious. First Taffy, then Lera, then who he wants Billy and Dalla. Once he's ready to kill them, I'm gon' have Vinchi off him, and problem solved."

"But how do you know he won't kill them as they come?" I asked with an even tone.

"No, he ain't go do that. That nigga wants to make a scene. He trying to document this shit on camera and everything. He's not interested in seeing them bleed one by one. He wants all the blood at once."

"But we still..."

Brock cut me off. "NO BUT'S MONA!" he stood up. "This shit is going to work," Brock sounded as if he were trying to convince himself.

"Okay, I'm with you. But, Taffy is gone, Lera is MIA, and Dalla's been in the wind for a while now."

"I already got eyes on Taffy. Once Dalla gets word that her husband Ace has Lera, her ally, she gon' go running for her. Then, I'll release Billy."

"Where is Billy?" I said quickly with the hopes of him opening up and telling me. But he just gave me a funny look. Brock was too smart for that one. He ignored my question like I never asked it.

"I'm gon' need you to keep Brip under control. He can't know shit about this. As far as he knows, Taffy is gone for good. You understand me?"

I nodded hesitantly.

"When are you planning to send Vinchi?" I had to know. That way I could get him out of here.

Brock looked at me and smiled like he'd just read my mind.

"Vinchi's already gone," he said snide.

My heart dropped, and Brock saw it. Instead of trying to ensure that everything was going to be okay, he walked out the study and left me sitting there crying to myself. I let a few tears slip then I finished that crying shit. Now, it's time for me to get my son back.

26

LERA

I woke up this morning and reached for Bobby, but he wasn't there; I wasn't surprised. We've been at Tara's house for almost a week now and Bobby still hadn't touched me nevertheless, slept next to me. I still reach for him every morning hoping that he'd come to me in the night; hoping that he'd missed the feel of my body next to his the way I missed him, but he's been too busy with that bitch, Tara.

I still can't figure the two of them out and I would interrogate Bobby about their odd relationship but he's never around. It's almost as if he's avoiding me or have I become a thorn in his side. Whenever I try to kiss him around her, he moves away from me like I'm plagued. When he sees me come into a room, he gets up and leaves before I have a chance to embrace him or interact with him in any way. When I'm around, he's always watching Tara like he's trying to scope out her emotions. He seems way too concerned with her. I don't understand why.

It's a little after 10 a.m. Lately I've been waking up late and going to sleep early. Sleep is my only escape from this nightmare I feel stuck in. I love Bobby but he's trying my patience. I still don't know what the hell is going on or what his big plan to rescue his brother, Billy is. I try my best to understand how he feels but I'm starting to get the feeling that he doesn't give a fuck about how I feel. He's just jerking me around blindfolded; he's been like my seeing-eye dog but he's not very good at it because he keeps running me into brick walls and leading me into traffic. I don't know if I'm at the point yet where I can say I don't feel safe with him anymore, but it may be getting there.

I stumble out of bed and make my way to the kitchen. I don't smell the aroma of southern style bacon and grits in the air and the kitchen is spotless, but I know Tara left my plate in the microwave as she always does. She really is killing me with kindness in a shady kind of way. It annoys Tara that I sleep to ten in the morning. Whenever I see her for the first time in the morning, she gives me this judgmental look of contempt as if I'm nothing more than a slob. "Honey, if you want your breakfast fresh, you gon' have to get up at 7 like the rest of us," she told me once condescendingly. I try to avoid Tara and her snide comments just for the sake of Bobby and my ego. If I got into it with Tara the way I really wanted to, I'm not sure Bobby would have my back.

I open the microwave, but my plate isn't inside. So, I open the oven, and nothing is there either. Just as I was going to the refrigerator, that bitch appeared out of nowhere.

"Good morning. Well...good mid-morning," Tara threw her jabs. Tara was fully dressed, looking like a boring librarian with her knee length plaid skirt and simple buttoned up blouse; she wore a pearl necklace. And of course, her hair is pushed back in a simple little pony tail. How in the hell was somebody like her even affiliated with Bobby Badd?

"Where's my food?" I spoke to her like the help I knew she was. Although it was a little past ten, it was too early for me to deal with her shit.

"I didn't make any breakfast for you this morning. Bobby wasn't hungry so there was no need for me to cook," Tara shot me a fuck you look.

"Well...I'm hungry," I said insinuating that as far as she was concerned, I was just as important to her as Bobby.

Tara looked at me and chuckled like what I said amused her. She folded her arms around her chest and tilted her head to the side, before rolling her beady little eyes at me. "Honey, let's get something straight," she dismissed me with a wave of her index finger, "I'm not your mama," she counted with her fingers, "your maid or your bitch so if you're hungry, you're going have to figure something out and it will not involve *my* kitchen because its closed." She straightened up her shoulders, defensively folded her arms around her chest and waited for me to reply.

"Tara, I got something I need to get straight with you," I pull the B part of my necklace out of Bobby's oversized wife beater that I'm wearing as nightgown, "you either need to fall in line or fall back."

Tara looked at my necklace and shook her head like it was worthless, and I was silly for assuming its superpowers would work under her roof.

"I knew the moment I laid eyes on you that you were a simple little chick. Bobby could have done a lot better than you..." she said and turned to walk away.

Her words and blatant subordinates burnt me like fire. I was so pissed, I grabbed her shoulder and attempted to spin her around back in my direction, but Tara grabbed my wrist and twisted it like she was trying to sever it from my arm.

"Bitch, let go of me..." I screamed.

"Don't you ever put your hands on me," Tara whispered, looking over my shoulder like she didn't want Bobby to witness what was going on.

"Where's Bobby?" I demanded to know before pulling away from her grip.

"Please don't bother him right now," she pleaded. Tara was still whispering. "Do you know how much stress he's under? Or, do you even care?" She said constantly looking, over her shoulder for, Bobby. She didn't want me to bother him.

"Of course, I care," now I was whispering. She made me feel stupid not to. "Bobby's my husband and your disrespectful ass need to recognize that."

"I know, I see your "B" necklace. That's all you care about, isn't it? All this shit he got going on and you walking around barking orders like you some fucking queen and sleeping to damn ten like you don't got a care in the world. Do you understand how serious this shit is?"

"I was there. I know..." I defended myself, but Tara was starting to make me feel so small.

"You don't know shit because if you did, you wouldn't give a shit about that necklace or anything else but, Bobby."

"I'm not doing this with you, Tara. What's going on in me and my husband's life is not your concern. Hopefully, we'll both be out of your hair soon." I turned to walk away but stopped. I wasn't finished yet. "I see the way you look at him. You think I don't know you're in love with my man?" I waited for her to respond but she didn't and that told me everything. She grabbed her pearl necklace and rolled one of the beads around her fingers like it was helping her curb the urge to tell all. "You need to learn how to respect me. You and Bobby will never be together because he loves me. He chose me," I said, and picked up my necklace again. All I went through to get the necklace, it had to mean something. Tara just looked at me and shook her head.

"Where is my husband?"

"He's packing. He's leaving in about an hour," Tara revealed to me like she knew more about him than I did.

"Thank God we're out of here. See...I told you." I waved my hands in the air grateful. I turned to look for Bobby.

"He's not taking you with him," Tara said to me in a matter of fact way. She sounded just as disappointed as I felt.

"Excuse me..."

"You staying here with me," she said a little louder and more aggressive.

"Fuck that...where is he?" I said, ready to confront him about Tara's outrageous claims.

Tara gave me a look that I couldn't read. I didn't know if my question made her uncomfortable or excited; I think it was a little of both. Tara took a breath and stood up straight. She refolded her arms around her chest and smiled at me with her eyes. She looked me directly in the eyes and said, "he's in my bedroom," like she felt relieved to be revealing the secret she's been keeping.

"Your bedroom?" I said both confused and stunned. Tara didn't respond back. At least not verbally. Tara raised her brow and shrugged her shoulders. She let her eyes do all the talking. She gave me a look that if I wasn't mistaken said *yes, I'm fucking your husband.*

Tara wasn't getting the satisfaction of seeing the look of despair in my eyes. I turned around and stormed towards her bedroom. It was located on the opposite side of the house. Far enough from my room for me not to know what the fuck was going on. Bobby hadn't slept in the bed with me since we got here. I just assumed he'd fallen asleep on the couch or didn't sleep at all because he was too busy working. But, I never assumed he was with Tara; was he really that fucking bold? The more I thought about it, the more I assumed it was bullshit. Tara was just trying to get to me. Even if Bobby was in her room, he was there for specific reason and it wasn't to fuck her. Bobby wasn't that stupid. And Tara defiantly wasn't fucking material. At least not by Bobby's standards.

I calmed myself down before I got to her bedroom. Tara was trailing behind me calmly, walking slow and steady like she had it all together. I took a deep breath and mentally crossed my fingers before I got to the door. I swung it open without giving a warning knock. I barged through the door like an intruder and saw something that made me question if Tara was right after all.

Bobby was shirtless, laying down in her king-sized bed comfortably in his boxers. One leg stretched out and the other was bent upward. He was holding a small picture frame in his hand. When he looked up and recognized it was me standing in the doorway, he quickly opened the draw to Tara's night stand and dumped the picture inside. Then he used a pillow to cover up his boxer as if I never seen him before. What the fuck was going on? I was at a loss for words and so was Bobby. He just looked at me, saying nothing. He didn't look sorry or nervous either. He just gave me a look that said, *now what?* Almost as if my very presence annoyed him.

"I'm sorry to disturb you, Bobby. I told her you were leaving today, and she got upset," Tara said in a calm voice, surrendering her hands in the air like there was nothing she could do to stop me from barging in on him. She sounded more like his personal assistant than his presumed lover.

"It's okay, Tara," Bobby said calm. He straightened up his posture on the bed so that his back was pinned against the pink upholstered head board that hung against the wall.

I looked around the room and thought to myself how tacky everything was. This bitch actually had pink carpet covering the floors with floral print pillows and matching rugs and throws. It looked simple, just like Tara.

Everything was placed perfectly and in order. That annoyed me. I just wanted to sweep over the top of her dresser, knocking over all the candles and potpourri she had neatly placed on top. But, I kept my cool.

Tears filled my eyes, but I pushed them back. I couldn't dare let Tara see me cry. I turned to face her. "Could you give me and my husband some privacy please?" Tara looked at me and rolled her eyes as if I hadn't said a word to her. She didn't budge. I shot Bobby a look. So, did Tara.

He took a deep breath and massaged his temples like he couldn't handle the stress. "Tara, it's ok. Give us a minute." Bobby swung his legs over the bed and stood up into a stretch like he didn't have a care in the fucking world. He searched the thick plush carpeted floor like he was looking for his pants.

"I put some clean sweats in the drawer for you, Bobby." Tara said sounding like a Stepford wife."

"Thanks, T," Bobby said genuine.

"Bobby are you sure I can't fix you something to eat? You have a long day ahead of you and you need to eat," Tara demanded politely. I couldn't believe the causality that was going on before my eyes. It was a slap in the face.

"Okay, Tara," Bobby said without putting up a fight. He took her advice like he trusted every word she said.

Tara smiled at Bobby and clutched her pearls. Then she looked up at me like I was a fool before walking out her room and closing the door behind her giving us privacy as if she didn't care to hear what I had to say to him. It wasn't important to her.

Bobby barley looked at me. He walked over to the chest and pulled out a pair of neatly folded sweat pants and threw them on quick. He went to the bathroom and I heard water running. He treated me as if I wasn't in the room. When he came out, his face was wet. He looked around the room like he was searching for things. Just as if I wasn't standing there.

"Bobby..." He finally looked up at me. "What's going on?"

"I got a few leads I have to follow up on. You can't come, it's too dangerous."

"But you promised you wouldn't leave me alone," I tried not to whine.

"You won't be alone. Tara will be here," Bobby said like that was a plus.

"I'm going with you, Bobby. We in this, together right?" Bobby just looked at me. He didn't respond. He continued to search around the room. To my surprise, he was very familiar with it. He walked in and out of the walk-in closet and pulled out bags. He opened drawers and started dumping things in the bag. "Bobby, I asked you a question? Are we in this together or not?"

"Lera..." Bobby said like he was annoyed. He paused like he was trying to figure out the right words to use. "I wish I hadn't gotten you involved in all this. I'm sorry..."

What was he really saying to me? I rushed over to Bobby and grabbed his hand. "Do you love me?" Bobby looked me directly in the eyes and didn't speak. At least not right away.

"I love you..."

"Do you really?"

"Hey..." he cut me off before I went on, "you know I mean what I say."

"Well you told me you needed me. You told me you never would leave me alone again. Then we get here, and everything changes? What's going on? Tell me?" I squeezed his hand and begged him.

"I can't let nothing happen to you, Lera. Can you understand that? So many of my family members are in danger and I let that shit happen right under my own nose. I can't let that happen again. I have to protect you guys..." Bobby said desperate but what got me was that he said *you guys*. Who else was he talking about? Tara?

"I can help you."

"No, I can't let her see you. If Dalla see's you..." he let the name slip.

I cut him off right away. "Dalla? You're going to see Dalla?"

"Lera, I just need you to trust me right now, okay."

"I don't trust her, Bobby."

"Me either but I don't see no other way around this thing but her. She agreed to meet me."

I knew I couldn't convince Bobby not to see Dalla, so I didn't waste my time trying. My heart raced at thought of him being face to face with her. Dalla was dangerous but Bobby was convinced she was the only person that could help him get Billy back. Ideally, even if whatever plan he had worked, I didn't know what that meant for us. Something was different between us and if him lying in another woman's bed in boxer wasn't proof of that, then nothing would be. I had to know.

"Bobby, are we okay?"

"I hope we will be," Bobby said then looked at me like he was confused. He saw me gasp and hold back the tears but offered no compassion to comfort me.

"What's going on with you and Tara?" I asked quick. Bobby looked at me and said nothing. He took a deep breath and swept his hands over his face like he was trying to remove the secrets his eyes were revealing.

"Its complicated," was all he said through heavy sigh.

Then he turned and walked into the bathroom, shutting the door behind him, leaving me with nothing but my fearful thoughts and tears.

27

MONA

B rock got me fucked up.

That mutha-fucka really think that I'm going to sit back and watch him destroy everything we got, starting with our first-born son. Shit! Fuck him and this Ranch. All that shit don't mean nothing to me when it comes to my first-born son, Vinchi. My flesh and blood. An original Badd. Not one of the fucking knock off's I was helping him produce in the breeding quarters. I did some real fucking stupid shit in my life, but I'm gon' correct all that shit, starting today.

Brock need to realize that he can't do shit without me. He been hunting Dalla for a fucking year now, but it only took me a damn week to find the simple bitch. All these years I made him feel like he was the King. Like all the great ideas I gave him really came from him and not my own resourceful mind. If it wasn't for me, this Ranch wouldn't be shit. There would be no order. Truth be told, he could never fill his father's shoes. He knows it too, but I never made him feel that way.

The Ranch flourished after Papa Badd died because I become the voice for Brock. All those late-night conversations of my counseling and coaching made this place unbreakable. Did I ever get a fucking thank you? Hell no. He would recite all the shit I told him at the family meetings like the ideas was his alone. Now, he wants to look at me like I ain't shit but a Badd wife. No, I'm this Ranch's mutha-fucking future and it's past. Just as quick as I built this shit up, I can tear it down. Let him keep fucking with me and my son.

As the true architect of this game, I will take authority and redesign the entire plan. Then what the fuck he gon' do? Replace me? Yeah, right. With who? A simple know nothing bitch like Taffy or Lera? Bitches like me don't come a dime a dozen. I'm that mutha- fuckin needle in a haystack. He will never be able to replace me. Ever! This place wouldn't be shit without me. Everything would dry up like an Egyptian desert if I left. Starting with the cash flow. Brock needs me, and he knows it. The mutha-fucker better start showing his appreciation for me or I'm fucking this shit up. All of it. He lost his fucking mind if he thinks I'm gon' just sit back and let him put our son in harm's way. How could he do that? Then again, I am talking about somebody that killed their own mother.

Let me take a few deep breaths and try to calm down. Otherwise, I'm likely to knock the shit out of Dalla when she gets here and that wouldn't be good. As much as I hate to admit it, I need the bitch right now just as much as I need air. The bitch is already ten minutes late, but I'm gon' let that rude shit slide. Ain't like she ever been professional at anything besides being a conning whore.

Finding her was easy as pie. A few leads on that phony breeder, Lisa, lead me right to her. Lisa was the very bold woman Dalla planted on the Ranch as a mole to fake a pregnancy. I called a few of my connections from the projects I grew up in, flashed the whore's photo and few Benjamin's and boom, the bitch was found. Brock don't know they only loyal to him because of me. I'm their link to the Badds. I protect and support their community.

At first, she didn't want to meet me. Lisa thought I was having her set up to be killed and she was right for thinking that way but when I enticed her with enough money to put her into early retirement, she couldn't help but to take the risk and meet me. She gambled with her life by meeting with me. Show's me just how much she values herself, but she was playing with winning cards. Once she got me in touch with Dalla I gave her the money and let the bitch live. At least for now.

Dalla on the other hand wasn't a hard bitch to pull. She agreed to meet me so quick, I almost got nervous. Then I remembered I wasn't scared of shit especially when it came to my son's life. So, here I am.

I decided to meet her at one of the abandoned warehouses we own in the city. It's supposed to be the same warehouse that Bobby took Lera to test her before I agreed they could marry. But, knowing Bobby who knows if that ever really happened. Brock really kept me occupied with a bunch of bullshit. While he ran the empire I designed for him, I was running around doing dumb shit like making up test for simple ass women and interviewing women to fuck him. I'm one stupid bitch. Brock didn't give two fucks about any of the women his brother's married or who I brought to fuck him. He just wanted to keep me out of his way.

Anyway, I figured this place would be the most discreet. Usually we lease it out, so our clients can do whatever type of dirty business they do privately. But, since Bobby got killed, that end of the business has been on hold. We really losing money.

This dust smell in here is fucking with my sinuses. Now I'm getting a headache. I hop over a few puddles of brown water only to land on what I looks like rat shit. Fuck! I scrap the thick brown mash off my shoes against the cracked concrete. Where is this bitch? A few drops of cold water fall from the ceiling and land on my shoulder before rolling down my arm. I start to feel itchy and then I sneeze, and it echoes against the hollow walls. I look up and see a huge hole in the ceiling and now understand why puddles of water are covering the floor. We need to get this roof repaired. The building is supposed to look abandoned not condemned. I stop myself in my tracks. There I go again. Always working for the Ranch. I shake the thoughts of and keep focused. I'm not a Badd wife today but a mother. A desperate mother.

Getting off the Ranch wasn't easy. I spent days trying to come up with a good reason to leave but I knew there would be no reason good enough for Brock, so I just left. I had to wrestle three guards just to get through the gate. Then one of them had the nerve to chase behind me in a car like I was an escaped prisoner. Honestly, that's probably what I really was. I never left the Ranch without clearing it with Brock. It wasn't too often that I got out. I never felt the need to; at least that's what I told myself. The guard trailed behind me for about a mile when I slammed on the breaks remembering I didn't have to run from him. I watched him jump out the car from the rear-view mirror, and as he ran to the car, I opened the glove compartment and pulled out my taser. He yanked open my door and reached for me but before he could touch me, I lit his ass up. When he fell to the ground convulsing, I continued on my way.

I knew the Hummer I was driving had a tracking device in it. Brock tracked everybody. Hell, I gave him the idea. That's why I parked the car in the projects and took my sisters, Nicchi's car, a silver Lexus sedan. The hottest car in the projects. I took care of my family all though I didn't see them often. She looked at me strange when I showed up at her door, demanding her keys but she was smart enough not to ask me shit. Although she was my sister, she wasn't a Badd. The bitch actually had the nerve to pop an attitude about handing over her keys, acting like I was the fucking repo man or something. I just ignored her.

I look at my watch. Dalla was now 20 minutes late. I'm starting to think that either the bitch is setting me up or not showing. I hop over a few more puddles, avoiding rat shit, and make my way to the broken window. I attempt to peek outside to see if there is any strange activity going on in the parking lot. Before I had a chance to look good, I hear a familiar voice call my name. I spun around so quick, I almost lost my balance and fell butt first into a large puddle of dirty ass rain water. Dalla is not the kind of bitch you want to have your back turned too.

She looked just like did when I last saw her. She has the snide smirk on her face like my very presence amused her. She slowly walked towards me. She was holding a huge stick. She used it to swat at the spider webs. Instead of hopping over the puddles of water like I did, she walked straight through them. She was wearing what looked like steel-toe rain boots and was dressed in tight-fitting army fatigue pants. Her hair was pushed back in a tight ponytail and she wasn't wearing makeup. The knees on her pants were tore out and her black tank top looked dingy. Where was this bitch coming from? Combat?

"You're late," I said stern. "My time is valuable."

"Actually, I've been here all night," Dalla smiled at me like she had one up on me. " I had to be sure there was nothing shady going on," she wasn't smiling anymore. She gave me a serious stare with her thick lips pressed tightly together.

"What makes you think shit ain't bout to go down?"

"Nothing. I'm just tired of hiding," Dalla said, still staring me down like she wanted to shank me. "What do you want?"

"What do you want?" I asked back.

Dalla sighed and rolled her eyes. "I don't have time for this shit. You contacted me."

"Yeah, but you didn't show up ready to help me out. So, you start first."

"My husband" she said quick.

"You mean Ace?" I know neither of us had time to bullshit but I just had to say it. I had to let her know the little I did know about her. She winced at the sound of his name like it made her sick.

"Billy. Billy is my husband," she said in a sorrowful loud whisper. "What do you want, Mona?" Dalla stared at me without blinking.

"I want my son," I said trying to push back the tears.

"What are you talking about?" Dalla looked confused and very shocked by the tears I was trying to hold in.

"Vinchi," I said through a cracked voice. I sniffed hard and took a deep breath. I straightened out the slump that was forming in my shoulders and walked towards her. That was enough emotions. Now it was time for business.

"What? Did he finally run away from your circus act of a family?"

"No, Brock sent him to Ace," I said quick.

"What!" Dalla said stunned. Her reaction shocked me. I never knew her to give a fuck about my son or anyone else in the family. "Is genocide your husband's favorite pass time? First his mother and now his son," Dalla shook her head.

I chose not to respond to her comment. "Bobby's dead and we think Ace called the hit," I filled her in. Instead of responding she shifted her body and stared down at the puddles in the floor. She was avoiding eye contact with me. What was that about? Did she have something to do with his death?

"What do you want me to do? I hate to tell you this, Mona but if Ace has your son, he's probably dead already," Dalla said curt.

I gasped just as if she hit me in the gut with that stick she was holding.

"No! My son ain't dead."

"Maybe not yet but how long before you think, Ace kills him? You don't know him like I do?"

"I know. That's why I need your help," I never been so humble in my life.

"What are you going to do for me?" Dalla shamelessly bargained with my son's life.

"I can get you, Billy." Dalla's eyes lit up. It was like I said the magic words. She dropped the stick and moved in closer to me like she was surrendering. Now, we were nose to nose.

"What you got in mind?" Dalla asked calm. I told her Brock's plan. I told her about Taffy fleeing and Brock hunting her. Then I told her about Brock planning to deliver her, Lera and Billy to Ace. When I was done spilling every detail about Brocks plan, including all the loops holes I found in it, I gave her *my* plan to put an end to all this nonsense. She was all ears. I just pray it works.

--- ··●·· ---

The guards opened the gate to the Ranch like they were expecting me. I guess Brock was tracking my every movement and knew I was home. The guard that I shocked with my Taser gave me an evil but respectful stare as he cleared my car for entrance. I watched him watching my car from the rearview mirror. He spoke into the radio phone until I lost sight of him. I knew he was speaking to Brock. I slowly drove up the entrance road not knowing what to expect. I was cautious. I felt like an escaped convict secretly returning to prison. For the first time ever, the Ranch didn't feel like home.

I thought about parking at the Casino and hiding out on the Ranch for a day or two before I confronted Brock, but that plan got dismissed before I could even give it real thought. Brock was driving towards me in the golf cart, head on. If I didn't stop first, I swear he would have run right into me. I took a deep breath and played it cool. Although he coined me as being weak because I was a woman, his emotions were way crazier than mine could ever be. He hoped off the cart and stormed towards the driver side of the car. I opened the door for him.

"Where the fuck have you been?" He yelled and clutched his fist like he was resisting the urge to knock me out.

I got out the car almost holding up my hands like I was surrendering to him.

"I was..."

"You wasn't at your fucking sister's house so don't give me that shit!" Brock answered for me. He screamed so hard, a few drops of spit landed on the tip of my nose. I didn't wipe it away. Not because I didn't want to but because I didn't have time.

Brock slapped me across the face harder than I ever been hit in my life. I was stunned by the force of his slap I became dazed; So dazed that I thought I saw a falling star, but I didn't. The only thing that fell was my body; I hit the ground hard. The rays of the sun shining directly in my eyes.

He stood over my body waving his arms and cursing. I didn't even know what he was saying. I felt more moisture on my face. Was he still spitting on me? No, I was actually crying. I leaned up but was so dizzy I had to catch myself from falling back down. Brock and I have had plenty of physical disagreements in the past, but he's never hit me this hard before. There was the occasional push or slap but nothing like this. I didn't even know he was capable of it.

I put all my weight on one knee and prepared to push myself up from the ground, but Brock shoved me back down with his foot. "Stay down," he said and pointed at me. He started talking into his radio, demanding back up. For the first time ever, I was speechless.

A few seconds later, I was surrounded by guards. Their large bodies hoovered over me, blocking the sun. The guard that I tasered, yanked me up by the arm. I didn't try to fight. I never felt this weak before. Brock watched me through two evil slits in his eyes. His jaw was clutched tight and fist balled. The man that I was looking at was not my husband. Brock reached in his pocket and pulled out a black bandana. It's what he used to blindfold his prisoners. "Take her to the prison," Brock ordered, staring me down like he would shoot me if he had to. I was about to start sobbing but I sniffed hard and dried every tear I had. I looked at Brock and my look told him that this time he went too far. I saw just a hint of hesitance in his eyes, but it didn't last long. He quickly looked away from me.

The guard prepared to cover my eyes with a bandana. Before he tied it tightly around my head, I stared at Brock with a straight face until my eyes were covered. Even though I couldn't see him, I was staring his way and I know he felt it. The guard tied the knot tighter than necessary. I didn't flinch, nor did I resist arrest.

"The prison at Zone 6," he said to security. The guard hesitated a bit like he was stunned then nodded, *ok*. There was another prison? I thought it was odd that Brock was blindfolding me when he knows I've been to the prison a million times before. Where the fuck was he taking me? As far as I knew the Ranch was divided into four zones; now there was a 6? And what about Zone 5? I thought I'd been to every place on this Ranch, but I was wrong; for the first time ever, I didn't feel like a true Badd. What was he going to do to me once he got me to Zone 6? Kill me? Even with all the evil possibilities of what was going to happen to me, I wasn't nervous or scared. But, I am hurt.

"Yes, Sir Mr. Badd," the guard purposely yelled in my ear causing my ear drums to vibrate. "Fall back, " he said to the other guards. "This is a restricted area. Authorized personal only!" I guess he was the authorized personal because after he tied my hands together and blindfolded me, he shoved me into the golf cart.

———— ··●·· ————

Wherever Zone 6 was it was off the map. Although I couldn't see, I knew we were driving into a rural area. I could tell by the way the cart struggled to accelerate. We slowed downed and I felt the cart dip in and out of what I assumed to be pot holes in the ground. I got slapped in the face with a leafy tree branch. At one point, I almost fell out the cart. The guard didn't give a damn though.

I wonder how many other secrets Brock was keeping from me? If there was a second prison in Zone 6 then what was on Zone 5? How could I have lived here all these years and not have known. I knew that there was more land to develop so I never bothered going in the woods but apparently, I was wrong. Brocks been lying to me from day one. He did a good job making me feel that I was a part of this shit, but I wasn't. My title is nominal. It carried no real weight.

We came to a stop. I heard the tires screeching but the cart kept moving. *Shit*, the guard mumbled under his breath. Finally, the cart stopped, and my body jolted forward. "Mrs. Badd, I'm getting out the cart now," he yelled at me like he was the police and I was a prisoner. Actually, all of our guards were real cops at some point. Some got kicked off the force for doing something shady, so we put them on the payroll. The others just heard about how good the money was and quit to come work for us. "I'm going to walk around and escort you inside the prison. Please don't put up a fight. It will only make things worse for you," he warned me.

He didn't have to worry about me fighting anymore. I needed to save my energy in order to think my way out of this situation. Otherwise, my plan with Dalla is going to be screwed. I got to get out of here. Vinchi is somewhere out there with that maniac, Ace, and ain't no telling when Ace gon' decide to pull the trigger and murder my firstborn, son.

I allow the guard to pull me out the car. "Be nice," he says again. "Mr. Badd gave me strict orders to handle the situation as I see fit, just in case you decide to resist."

"What's your name again?" I asked.

He waited like he had to think about his response before answering. "Officer Daniels," he replied after a few moments of silence.

"Officer Daniels when all this blow over, you gon' be off this Ranch." I heard him chuckle a bit like what I said didn't matter anymore.

"Who knows, you might be gone before me," he said under his breath, yet loud enough for me to hear him.

Now, even the help was disrespecting me. Fuck, Brock and this fucking Ranch. He leads me down a rocky path. My feet dipped in and out of small sink holes in the ground.

"I hope you enjoyed your life, Mr. Daniels. I hoped you lived it to the fullest," I taunted him and what I said must have got his attention because he stopped walking for a moment. He didn't say anything though. He just inhaled a deep nervous breath and kept walking. I guess my bark still was loud after all. But, I meant what I said. This nigga is going to die but first things first.

He pushed a door open and I immediately was greeted with a rush of cool air. Air conditioner? This wasn't like the main prison; hot, stale air. If I wasn't mistaken, I smelled food. Steak? Officer Daniels addressed someone. I heard several other voices. One of them seemed nervous by my presence.

"Daniels, what the hell is going on? That's Mrs. Badd?"

"I have direct orders from Mr. Badd. Don't worry. Take her to cell C."

"Nah, man, " the nervous guard backed down. "I didn't get that order."

"Well, you getting it from me! Take her or you, fired."

"Fire, me man." The guard didn't back down. That's when I decided to say something.

"Officer, what is your name?"

"Who? " They both said at the same time.

"Not you Mr. Daniels. The other one,"

"I'm Officer Todd, Mam," his voice shook. I could tell by his voice that he was a young man.

"It' okay. No one is going to fire you. When all this is over, you gon' have Daniels, job." I said cold. "He's going into earlier retirement where he will be able to rest, the rest of his life...Rest in Peace," I taunted him.

Officer Daniels let go of my hand. "Where you going man?"

"I quit!" he yelled, back.

"Todd, take me to where I'm supposed to be." After a little hesitance, the young guard carefully grabbed my arm and lead me to what I assumed to be Cell C.

"Mam, please take off your shoes."

I thought that was an odd request, but I complied. That's when my sock landed on what felt like soft carpet. The door creaked open and the first thing Officer Todd did was untie my hands. Once I was free, I snatched off the blindfold and couldn't believe who my eyes landed on. It was Billy.

28

TAFFY

There is no other way around it. I have to do what needs to be done. I have to kill Brip to make right of, Keno's death. Right now, nothing satisfies me more than killing that barbaric mutha-fucker.

How sick can one person be? It wasn't enough that he killed my brother and wounded the other one so badly he don't know left from right, but he had to have me too. All these years I've been fucking the man that destroyed my family. Waiting on him hand and foot. Sacrificing everything I ever was for his fucked-up family. Brip has done some low things to me but this takes the cake. This I will not forgive but I will get even. He's going to pay me in blood.

If I'm going to kill Brip, there is only one person that I know that can help me; Tony. That's why I'm here in Vegas. I have to see my mother. The last time I seen Tony was weeks ago when he was outside of me and Brip's condo, but I don't know where my brother lays his head. That's so fucked up. My own brother. I had to disown him just to be a part of the Badd family. All that is going to change.

Momma is the only one that can help me find, Tony. I been in Vegas three days now following momma. I had to be sure that Brip hadn't gotten to her first. So far, there's no sign of him, but I know he's coming to find me.

I fled the Ranch as soon as I got a chance and now I feel free. Aimless but free. I start to feel nauseous and I remember why. I'm pregnant. If I knew for sure this was Brip's baby it would be the first Badd that I kill. I would flush this mutha-fucka down the toilet with the same empathy I flush shit from my ass. But there is a good chance this child could be Malcolm's. I barely know Malcom but if this baby was his, it will feel more like mine. I don't want to give birth to anything Badd.

All these years I blamed myself for losing our babies. But it wasn't me it was, Brip. My unborn children where committing suicide in my womb. They chose death over the Badd way of life that was waiting on them. They were braver than me. Brip doesn't deserve a child. He's done too much fucked up shit. Our child could turn out to be a worst monster than him.

When Brip admitted to killing Keno, it was like I was stuck in a time capsule. I was right back in that moment when momma told me he was dead. Weak in the knees, gasping for what felt like a never-ending breath and a tightness in my gut that felt like someone was wringing my intestines into a knot. But now, I didn't have to wonder who did it. I know. It was the man I called husband.

The man that I spent years loving. The grief fell over me like it never left. It felt like I had been shot in the chest. Brip had no compassion. When I asked him did he kill my brother, he thought about it for a few seconds, then shrugged his shoulders and said yeah just as if I asked him did he remember to take out the trash. It was at that moment that I knew there was no turning back. It was right then and there that I decided he was my enemy and my love for him seamlessly transferred into hate.

Before I had Brip, Keno took care of us all. He was more than a big brother to me but the father I never had. He taught me how to be independent, how to be strong and fearless. Everything that I wasn't as a Badd wife. When he trained me to defend myself, he would always say to me, "*Taffy, don't wait for some nigga to save you always save yourself. Besides, ain't shit for free. Pay for your life with your own cash card, not some niggas.*" I loved Keno. He was the head of our family. He stabilized us. If he was still alive, there's no telling who I would be. An actress, an entrepreneur, a fucking human being and not private property of the Badds. Brip knew what I was going through when he met me. It had only been a year or so since Keno died, and Tony was a mess. Momma and I were struggling and Brip came in and seemingly saved the day.

We were still mourning, Keno. I wasn't thinking straight so I gave in to Brip and everything he was offering. I didn't ask questions. Keno would be so disappointed if he seen how I turned out. If he knew that I gave up my voice. That I had a husband that unapologetically fucked other women. That I had no free reign in life. That's ok though. I'm going to make it all right. I'm going to kill that mutha-fucker in cold blood and get back to the me that I really am.

Momma isn't going to be ready for what I have to tell her, but she has to know the truth. She deserves to know that Brip killed, Keno. I have to protect her. When Brip gets here, he's not going to be the sweet son in-law that she's grown to love. He's going to be angry and I just pray he doesn't hurt momma in the process of trying to track me down and haul me back to the Ranch.

It's a good thing I know Momma's schedule. With it being Monday, I know she's inside the Spa; I'm waiting outside. Her appointment was over at least 20 minutes ago but if I know momma like I think I do, she's still in there throwing around money, buying the respect and friendship from people that don't give two shits about her.

Finally, I see the door swing open and half of Momma's body is hanging out. Momma's wearing one of the Spa's teal colored sweat suits. Her pants are too small but I'm sure she did that on purpose because she loves shaping her ass with tight pants. I can already tell from the side view that Momma got breast implants. She'd been talking about it for years and she finally did it. Her shirt is too small too but again, she did that on purpose too. She wants to show off her new tits. I hear her talking in her loud country voice. I know the people inside are laughing quietly but they really are annoyed by momma. She's holding a bag full of shit she's never going to use.

A stick figured shaped white woman, wearing black yoga pants and a matching top, walks past me towards the door. She stands behind momma appearing to be patient, but I can tell she's not. Momma's still blocking the door like she owns the place. She places her hand up towards the white girl's face, gesturing for her to wait a minute as if she was in her way and not the other way around. Then momma steps back inside and the woman gets the opportunity to walk in. She's inside for a few seconds and then she's back half in and half out. She's laughing a loud laugh. To loud for that spa.

Then finally she waves her hand in the air and steps outside. She drops the bag she's carrying on the ground like it's hurting her shoulder. She leans up slowly like her back is bothering her and turns toward the Spa door and looks at her reflection. I can tell by the way she's adjusting her sweat shirt, she's admiring her boobs. She adjust her short burgundy wig and turns back towards her bag. I guess she gets the feeling that someone is watching her because she looks my way.

"Taffy," she said, shielding the sun from her eyes with her hand even though she is wearing sunglasses. I look over my shoulder, making sure we aren't being watched and start to hurry towards her. "Girl…get this bag," she says rubbing her lower back, "you see I'm over hear struggling." She doesn't seem happy to see me. She knows that whenever I come around, it's always drama but this time, its deeper than that.

I rush to pick up the bag but when I lift it, I get stopped in my tracks. It is heavy. I throw it over my shoulder and start to walk ahead of her.

"Let's go," I say.

"What? Where are we going? And why are you here? Taffy I don' told you I'm getting too old to worry about you and, Brip."

"Momma please. I don't have time to explain but we have to get out of here," I give momma a serious look and she looks back at me like she knows I'm serious, but she still wants to ignore it.

I walk ahead of momma and she is behind me cursing at me to slow down the entire time. We went a few blocks around the corner, on the other side of the tracks, and I stop at this Chinese restaurant. It's a hole in the wall and it's perfect. I look over my shoulder and see momma limping my way, shaking her head. I hold the door open for her.

"What the hell we going in this place for? I'm not eating here. I only eat at places with 5-star reviews this place don't even look like it got 2 asterisks," Momma dismisses the place and turns to walk away like what she said was final. She's fidgeting with her phone. Looking for a better restaurant I assume.

"Momma," I scream. "I don't have time for this shit!" I say and turn to walk in the restaurant.

I wasn't sure if Momma was going to come in or not, but I took a seat at one of the tables without waiting for the hostess. The place was a dump. It smelled like burnt grease and mothballs. The floor was sticky and the worn

Formica tables were lopsided. I sat down and scratched myself on the torn vinyl from the chair. Yellow foam bursts out through the cracked chair cushion. The table had water stains and crumbs on it. I grabbed a handful of napkins and tried to clean it the best I could before Momma got inside. If she ever came. It was hot as hell in the restaurant. There was a box fan sitting on top of the bar blowing hot air my way. When the waitress came with two paper menus, I shooed her away with a flick of my wrist. Although it was a Chinese restaurant the entire staff was Mexican.

When I looked up, I saw momma coming my way. She had her hand covering her nose and mouth like she couldn't take the smell. She was giving me the evil eye. She pulled out the worn chair and looked at it carefully before slowly sitting down. Like the slower it took her to sit, the better the restaurant would become. The place was a dump, but I knew it wouldn't be anywhere Brip would look for me.

"I wouldn't even drink the bottled water here," Momma complained. She looked up at me and rolled her eyes like I was trying to punish her. She pulled a handful of napkins from the dispenser and covered the table with it. Then she carefully placed her cellphone on top of the napkins. "Give me my bag," she demanded, and I leaned over and handed her the bag.

Momma started pulling face creams and body washes out of the bag like she was seeing them for the first time. She didn't seem so tense anymore. "Here," she said and handed me an eye cream, "this will help with them bags under your eyes. You got to keep yourself up, Taffy if you want to keep a man like Brip."

I didn't respond to her annoying comment. I was use to momma criticizing my appearance but in a sick way, I knew it was all out of love. "Mama," I said to her in an even tone. I needed her attention, but she didn't look up at me. She just ignored me. "Momma," I said again.

"Get a marriage counselor, Taffy. You can afford the best in the business," was all she said. She didn't even look at me.

Momma placed the items she took out of her bag back inside. Then finally looked up at me. She still didn't notice the haunted look in my eyes. Or at least she didn't want too.

"So, you not gon' even say nothing?" Momma said pocking out her chest. She wanted me to compliment her new breast.

"I thought the doctor recommended you didn't have the surgery?" I'd been down this road before with momma, but she don't listen.

"These judgmental American doctors don't know shit. I been wanting titties all my life and it don't make no sense that I had to go all the way to Dominica to get them."

"Momma you left the country without telling me?" I yelled. For a split second, I forgot why I was here.

"I'm a Badd mother not a Badd wife, I go where I please. Besides, you should have just let me go to your Ranch for the surgery. Don't make no sense that I'm not allowed there. I am your mother. I'm family now. I'm a Badd too," Momma said pridefully. "I should tell Brip about that rude ass doctor that denied my surgery. Maybe he will pay him a little visit."

I took a deep breath and lowered my head sorrowful at the monster I created. Momma was serious. It was time she knew the truth.

"Momma, I'm not a Badd wife anymore," I said to her careful. She darted her eyes at me so sharp, it felt like her look cut right inside me.

"What the hell are you talking about, Taffy? Brip left you for another woman, didn't he? I told you just to be patient with him. So, what he fucking other women. Every husband out there fucking other women. You think you gon' escape that? At least he taking good care of us!"

"Momma, it's not that," I said and grabbed her waving hands, lowering them to the table. I looked her in the eyes, trying my best to prepare her for what I was about to say next. "Brip, killed Keno," I blurted out.

Momma pulled away from my touch like it was hot, but she kept her eyes fixed on me. She was giving me a blank stare like she was seeing a ghost. Me mentioning Keno put her right back in that horrible moment when we found out he was dead.

"What?" she said in a faint voice like she was talking more to herself than me.

"He killed Keno momma and he tried to kill, Tony."

"You sound crazy," she dismissed me. She acted as if Keno was somebody that she used to know. Not her first born son. "Just as crazy as your, brother. What's gotten into you?" momma said through tears. She pulled one of the napkins from the table wiped her eyes.

"It's true, momma. He told me himself."

"You don't know what you heard. Ask him again, Taffy. Just ask him again and I bet he will tell you something different. It ain't true."

"Momma I know you don't want to believe this, but you have to. I don't have much time. I have to find Tony. We going to kill him. We going to avenge Keno's death."

"You sound crazy," mommaMomma yelled at me. "You keep your brother out of this mess. I don't believe you. You gon' mess up the best thing that happened to us since, Keno. How could you be so selfish?"

It was then that I realized there was no convincing momma. At least not right now. She had to go home and process everything I said and then draw her own conclusion.

"Momma I know you're upset but it's not safe for you here anymore. I want you to come back with me."

"With you? What we gon' do? Where we gon' live? How we gon' live?" Momma said in one breath. She had no faith in me.

"We gon' have to start over but at least we will be safe. Brip is going to be here looking for me soon and he's not going to be nice, Momma," I warned her.

"Brip wouldn't hurt me," momma tried to convince herself.

"He will momma. Especially if he knows that you know the truth."

"No," momma said shaking her head. She jumped up so quick the wobbly table almost fell over. "No...," she said again like she was trying to wake herself from a bad dream. "I'm going home, Taffy. And when Brip come, I'm going to tell him that I know it's I lie and that I love him. And everything is going to be ok."

"Fine, momma," I said with tears in my eyes. It broke my heart to see how dependent momma had become on Brip and the Badds. Just like I was. "Just remember when you walk into that fancy condo, its covered in your oldest son's blood. When you look at those new tits, remember you bought them with your sons' blood. Keno paid for all this Badd shit with his life," I said.

Momma gasped and the hauled off and slapped me across the face. We both stared at each other for a while, stunned and heart broken. Then I remembered that it was something else I had to tell her. I had to tell her about the baby. Maybe she'd be more willing to listen to me. But then again, maybe not. Momma is stubborn.

"I'm pregnant," I said and sniffed up tears.

Momma just stared at me. I looked up at her. She spoke to me with looks. Her facial expression changed every few moments. She was saying so much with her looks. But, she wouldn't speak to me.

"I don't know if it's, Brips," I confessed.

Momma looked at me like I finally fucked it all up. The moment she'd been dreading since I married Brip. Her worst nightmare was here. Momma dropped her head heavy like she was about to faint. She didn't look back up at me. I cried. I disappointed her.

I watched my momma slowly walk away, holding her bag like it had gotten even heavier. I wanted to say something to her. I wanted to call to her, but I didn't. I just let her go. She'll see that in the end it will all work out.

In the meantime, I prayed that, Brip didn't hurt my mother. That meant I had to move even faster than I thought. I have to get this shit over with.

29

LERA

It's only been three days since Bobby left and I'm already feeling abandoned by him. But, then again, that feeling started way before he left to meet, Dalla.

Me and Tara here in this house alone is just plain awkward. I try my best to avoid her but somehow, I always end up bumping into her in the hallway while she's carrying a laundry basket or watering her plants. She doesn't even acknowledge my presence. She just walks past me like I'm not even here. She hasn't even looked at me since Bobby left, nevertheless spoken to me. She's treating me like I'm a ghost, but she's got it all wrong. She's the fucking ghost and I want answers about her and Bobby's past. That's why I've been snooping all morning.

Little did she know, I stopped sleeping in and got up early enough to learn her schedule. I've been casing that simple bitch. She wakes before the sun rises and makes herself a simple breakfast. Now that Bobby is gone, long gone is the gourmet eggs benedict and homemade butter pecan waffles. All she does now is boil two eggs, put a few pieces of toast in the oven and cut a piece of grapefruit. Right after breakfast, she cleans her already super clean kitchen and then heads out to her horse stables where she stays for several hours doing who knows what.

I hate that I have to even stoop this low, but I feel like Bobby is hiding something and after all this shit he got me involved in, I deserve answers one way or the other. The day he left, it was like he was trying his best to avoid me. Him and Tara were whispering in corners but whenever I appeared, they would both stop talking. I felt like a fool. I felt no different from a dog he rescued from the shelter and no longer wanted but didn't have the heart to give me away yet.

If I had not wondered out the front door, I would not have known he was about to leave. I caught him and Tara loading stuff in her Escalade. I guess he was too good to take the beat-up truck we arrived in. When I walked up to the car, they both looked at me like they wondered what I wanted. I just stood there like a fool and watched them load the truck, not saying a word. Bobby glimpsed at me every now and again, but he never said a word. I waited for him to make the first move. To acknowledge me. To treat me like I was his wife. Like the woman who risked everything to be with him, but he didn't.

When they loaded the last bag, he leaned down and embraced Tara. The hug seemed to last forever. When they finally pulled away from each other, he lifted Tara chin up towards his face and spoke to her with his eyes. A language that only they could understand. He winked at her and she smiled then wiped premature tears from her eyes. He kissed her on the forehead and she pulled him into another hug like she was afraid. He squeezed her even tighter the second time and whispered something in her ear that made her perk up. She sniffed real hard and then nodded at him, straightening her posture and raising her shoulders like a soldier. Then he made his way over to me, offering me his sloppy seconds.

Tara watched us with her arms folded against her chest but not in a defensive way. She didn't seem concerned about Bobby showing me affection. She just seemed concerned about him.

"Were you going to even tell me goodbye?" I said to him shaking my head.

"This isn't a goodbye," Bobby repeated. "Listen, I'll be back in a few days. When I get back, we'll talk," he said to me almost like he was warning me that the conversation wasn't going to go well.

His statement felt like the beginning stages of a break-up conversation. I looked over Bobby's shoulder and watched Tara watching us. I had a feeling that she already knew the conversation Bobby was going to have with me. Bobby leaned down and pecked me on the cheek no different than a father kissing his daughter then gave me a weak hug that lasted no more than a few seconds before he turned back around and headed towards, Tara. He looked at her and nodded his head and she nodded back. Then him and Jayson jumped in the truck and drove off. He didn't give me a second look.

I wanted to cry right then and there. Not just because of the way Bobby was treating me but the situation I put myself in. Trusting a man with my life wasn't the smartest move I ever made, and it wasn't like me. Tara stayed in the driveway watching the truck until it was out of sight. I left shortly after he gave me that weak ass hug. I went back in the house and buried my face in Tara's extra fluffy pillows preparing myself to cry but surprisingly, it never happened. That's when I got the idea to take matters into my own hands.

Initially, I was just going to search Tara's room for clues. I didn't have anything specifically to look for. But, when I passed by Tara's sons' room, I felt compelled to stop. Besides, it was directly across from my room. It took two days for me to mentally prepare for what I was going to find. I prepared myself for the worst. Whatever I found, I wasn't going to mope around like a woman scorned I was going to deal with it right then and there. At least that's what I told myself.

I opened Blake's door and flicked on his light. A ceiling fan shaped like a basketball started to spin. The metal cord made a ticking noise as it hit against the sharp wooden blades that sliced through the air. I didn't know how old Tara's son was but by the looks of his room, he couldn't be older than 12. The room was full of sports gear. Football posters, basketball gear, and baseball cards. I went straight for the night stand and opened the first drawer. Inside was a kid's bible with his first name engraved on the front. I picked the bible up and thumbed through the pages. I went through the remaining draws and found nothing but comic books and candy wrappers. I pulled the drawers from a small wooden chest. I moved the neatly folded clothes trying to find something hidden. I started to feel ridiculous and was just about to leave and make my way to Tara's room when something told me to check out the closet.

Blake had a large walk-in closet. Everything was neat and organized. His clothes were coordinated by color and style. Perfectly pressed jeans on one rack, khaki pants on the other rack. My eyes landed on another chest, I opened it and it was full of art supplies. Crayons, markers, and a colorful assortment of construction paper. I opened another drawer and there were pictures that I assumed were drawn by him. One of the pictures was of a family. A stick figure man, woman, and child. They were holding hands and there was a huge sun and rainbow behind them.

I pulled another piece of paper from the stack, but it wasn't a picture but a letter that Blake wrote to his dad. It said, *Dear Dad, I miss you all the time. I wish you can be with me and Mom every day. Every time you come to visit I wish you can stay longer. I like it when you kiss mom like the dads kiss the moms on TV. Mom told me that you have an important job to do and that your job will keep us safe. She says that you are our hero. Sometimes I wonder if you're really Superman. When I grow up, I want to be a hero just like you. I love you.* He signed the letter, BB.

I knew Tara's son's name was Blake but what was his last name? It was at that very moment that I no longer believed in coincidences. My intuition and common sense told me exactly what the B in Blake's last name stood for but my faithful heart, told me a lie just to comfort me. I told myself that Blake's last name was Bailey or Brown. Not Badd like me. I don't know why but I folded the letter up and stuffed it in my back pocket then headed to Tara's room.

Tara's bed was made up so perfectly it looked like no one slept in it last night. Her pink carpet had vacuum lines on it. This bitch was anal as hell. I wasted no time and walked over to the night stand on Bobby's side of the bed. I opened the drawer and the first thing I saw made my heart stop. It was the picture Bobby was staring at. It was a custom frame that had the words *Family Is Love* engraved in it. But what stood out to me the most was the picture. It was Bobby, Tara, and who I assume to be Blake. They were standing in front of a Christmas tree in her formal living room. I recognized the room because of the ugly cheap décor and the horse pictures. Blake was in the middle of them and Bobby was smiling like I never seen him smile before. Tara looked just like she did now, simple but happy; complete even.

I zoomed in on Blake and told myself that he looked nothing like Bobby. I saw no similarities. He had Tara's same eyes and nose, but his complexion was the exact match of Bobby's. If I wasn't mistaken, he had Bobby's lips and forehead too, but I could have been imagining that. Was Blake Bobby's son? He couldn't be. Tara and Bobby must just be close friends and he helps her out with Blake from time to time. Bobby is a good guy and I can see him doing that. I flipped the picture over and placed it back on the nightstand. I couldn't bear to look at it anymore. There is no way Bobby had a son and didn't tell me about it. No one in his family mentioned it. The Badds didn't operate like this. They took their bloodline too seriously. I shook it off. I'm sure there was an explanation for it.

I pulled the second drawer out so hard, I almost knocked it off its track. There was nothing in it but a bible. I picked it up and thumbed through it the same way I did Blakes and a folded post-it note fell out. I opened it and it was a number on it with Dalla's name written underneath it. I don't know why, but I stuffed in my bra. I walked over to Tara's side of the bed and pulled out her drawer. Another damn, bible. I decided not to go through it. Something else caught my eye. It was a small jewelry box. I opened it and was so thrown back by what was inside, I started to fume. It was my B necklace. I took mine off days ago just to see if Bobby would notice and he didn't. Tara must have found it. Was she snooping through my room? That bitch! Did that wanna-be Badd wife steal my necklace? She'd been going through my stuff? I grabbed the necklace and the picture frame and ran out the room. It was time to confront, Tara.

I bust through the back door with so much force, that the curtain rod fell from the wall when it slammed behind me. Tara jumped up defensively like she'd been waiting for this moment. She was bent over one of her flower beds, digging in the dirt. She took off her gloves and rubbed her hands on her apron then looked at me like I'd lost my mind. I came charging towards her and instead of backing up, she stepped towards me.

"You even more pathetic than I thought," I pointed at her.

Tara just rolled her eyes like she had no time for my juvenile rant. "What in the world are you getting on about, Lera? Don't forget you are in my home," she said like she was warning me of something, then took another step in my direction.

"You been going through my shit?" I held up the B necklace. "You wish you had this around your neck, don't you?"

Tara looked at me and the necklace confused. "Is that what you think? I want that?" she said and pointed to the necklace like it didn't mean shit to her. She sighed heavily and turned back around to tend to her plants, dismissing me.

"If you didn't want it, why did you take it from me?"

"What are you talking about?" Tara spun back around.

"I found this on your nightstand, along with this," I held up the picture frame and Tara looked at me like a bull ready to charge.

"You've been going through our things?" she said like she was disgusted.

What pissed me off more was the fact that she said *ours*. I knew she was including, Bobby. My fucking husband. This bitch has officially pushed all my buttons. I lifted the picture in the air and broke it against her brick pavers. She gasped and jumped back.

"You are so typical. Just as trifling as you want to be, and you got the nerve to fix your lips to claim a man like Bobby Badd." She sucked her teeth and shook her head.

"No, bitch. Bobby claims me," I held my wedding ring in her face.

"That's what you think, huh?" Tara laughed like she was genuinely amused.

"You really delusional enough to think he would want you?" I taunted her.

"Look at you," I laughed, spitefully.

Tara just shook her head at me all sophisticated like a disapproving school teacher. "You don't even know him. I may not look like a video vixen like you but if you knew Bobby the way I do, you would know that he don't give a shit about looks. He cares about what's up here," she pointed to her head, "and in here," she pointed to her chest. "You walk around my house with your breast and ass hanging out your pants and got the nerve to judge me? Do you think that's what makes you a woman? Your sex appeal? That's all you got to offer Bobby is a good fuck...good luck with that," she scoffed. "Do yourself a favor. If you gon' call yourself his wife," her tone was so sarcastic it made me feel smaller than the tiny pieces of glass I shattered, "then do yourself a favor and get to know him."

"What do you know about, Bobby?" I challenged her.

"More than you will ever know. Bobby and I go back so far, you'll never catch up," Tara shook her head at me like I was nothing more than Bobby's travel-size whore. "And that's not your necklace, it's mine," Tara said in a matter-of-fact tone.

I was confused. What was she trying to say to me? The necklace I'd been wearing all this time was hers or was it a totally different necklace? I didn't know which one was the worst.

"Why would this be yours?" I said but was scared for her to reply.

"For the same reason why, the necklace in your room is yours except my reason is more genuine. I told Bobby marrying you would be a mistake, but he insisted. Had I disapproved, you wouldn't be facing me to this day you cheap whore," she spat out.

On that note, I reached out to grab her, but she caught my hand and twisted it around my back in one quick move. It was like she was trained to defend herself. I felt like my elbow was going to rip from its socket.

"Get the fuck off of me," I yelled and tried to free myself from her painful tight grip.

"Make no mistakes, Lera," Tara whispered in my ear, "I tolerate you because of Bobby but you will not put your hands on me in my own house. You understand me?" she said and shoved me to the ground.

I jumped up and charged towards her, but she didn't flinch. She stood her ground like she was ready for round two. That's when I stopped. I massaged my wrist. I felt defeated by her in more than one way.

"Is Blake, Bobby's son?" I stopped bullshitting and went after the answers I needed.

"Yes, Blake is our son," Tara said in a calm tone.

"So our marriage is fake?" I said to her and sniffed. Tara didn't respond. She started to look at me like she felt sorry for me. "Are you and Bobby married?" Tara still didn't respond. I took a deep breath and looked up at the sky like the answers to my questions were written in the clouds. "I'm leaving," I told her.

Tara shrugged her shoulders. "Well, I can't make you stay."

She put back on her gloves like none of this ever happened and went back to her flower bed. I felt humiliated. I ran back into the house, put on my shoes, and grabbed the keys to Bobby's broken-down box truck. I left as quick as I could, and Tara didn't try to stop me.

30

TAFFY

Malcolm stared back at me like he was seeing a ghost. The paintbrush he held in his right hand, dripped charcoal-colored paint onto the concrete, adding even more hue to the colorful palate that was his floor. He stared at me as if he was afraid to blink. Like blinking would cause me to vanish back into the figment of his imagination, but this was no fantasy. I was here, and I know it was a bad idea, but I had nowhere else to go and I needed him. I know I caused enough damage in Malcolm's life but right now, he was bait. Before I left the Ranch, I stole one of Brip's guns; a nine-millimeter pistol. I've been carrying it around in my purse like it was my good luck charm and my get-out-of-jail-free card. But, I couldn't wait to unload it on Brip.

Finding Malcolm was easy. He relocated to another side of town. With the help of Google and a few of his former neighbors, I was able to locate his new studio. After what Brip did to him, I was expecting his new place to be more secure and private, but it wasn't. I walked right into the front door because it was unlocked. There were no security cameras that I could see. Either Malcolm was too laid back or not taking Brip as seriously as he should. Nonetheless, I was here.

I had to find a peaceful place to rest my head while I regrouped. I couldn't find Tony and I looked everywhere. That's the thing about Tony. He found you; you never found him. So that meant, I had to kill Brip myself. After Momma, Brip would search a few more places before he finally gave in and accepted the fact that I was with Malcolm. His pride wouldn't allow him to look here first and when he did come, he would be alone. It would be too embarrassing and damaging for his men to see me with Malcolm. That was going to make things easier for me.

Malcolm dropped the paintbrush out of his hand. Or maybe it fell out. I couldn't tell the difference. He squinted his eyes at me like he was trying to be sure it was me. "Sarah," he said my fake name so sweetly. I was hoping he would at least put up a fight. Try to put me out and curse my fake name for all that I put him through, but he looked at me with the same passion as he did the first day we met. Like nothing ever happened at all. When he called me Sarah, it reminded me of how being Sarah made me feel. It's been so long since I'd been Taffy that I could no longer identify with her. I wasn't Taffy, I was a Badd wife. Not someone's daughter, someone's sister, or an individual but a Badd wife. That was an entity on its own. It was a shame that I felt more connected to an alias than I did to my birth name. But, all that was going to change once I killed, Brip.

When Malcolm moved from behind the canvas, everything I put him through showed. He was wearing a cast on his left hand. As he walked towards me, he dragged his right leg like he no longer had control over it. His knee looked permanently bent. Brip was a monster. He did everything to Malcolm but kill him. When he found me here with him, the first thing he was going to do was try to kill him, but I wasn't going to let that happen. It was risky, but I had to do it. It was the only chance I was going to get to vindicate, Keno.

"I'm, so sorry," I said through a whisper. Seeing his maimed body caused me to cry. "I did this to you. I…" Malcolm stopped me by gently putting his hand over my mouth. He smelled like paint thinner and frankincense. I closed my eyes and remembered that smell. I remembered rushing to wash it off my body before Brip got home.

"The universe brought you both back to me," he said and touched my stomach.

I jumped back startled by his revelation only for him to move closer. How did he know? Did this mean this baby wasn't, Brips? I pray it wasn't. Then, I could start loving it again.

"I dreamed you'd be back," Malcolm said and then leaned down and kissed me so softly on the top of my head, that it eased my sorrows.

How could he forgive me so easily? Maybe he was never angry with me. This man was truly selfless. Every feeling he had for me was pure. I looked up and made eye contact with him. I couldn't look away. I felt more emotionally connected in the moment of our glance than I ever felt with Brip inside of me. Our connection surpassed sex. Malcolm cupped the side of my face with his good hand and kissed me on the mouth deep, slow, and soft. He kissed me like I was the cure to everything bad. Like I was special. I started to melt from the inside out. I closed my eyes and pretended this was my life. As if the kiss he was giving me, was something I got every day. Like it was something I deserved.

"We have to lock the door!" I said remembering why I was here in the first place. The last thing I needed was Brip to catch us both off guard. I had to protect Malcolm.

"No," Malcolm said calmly. He continued to gaze deeply at me. "If they are meant to come…let them come. I'm not afraid, Sarah. You shouldn't be either. The Universe will protect us both."

"But," I tried to talk some sense in him, but he didn't let me. He pulled me into another kiss.

Malcolm managed to lift me and slide my panties off at the same time. All with a bum leg and a cast on his hand. I dropped my purse on the floor along with all the anxiety I had ever since I found out that Brip killed Keno. Malcolm was a much-needed mental escape. With my legs wrapped tightly around his waist, Malcolm carried me to the wall and pinned me against it. He never took his eyes off me. He kissed my neck and buried his face in my cleavage. He caressed between my breasts with his nose, inhaling me like my scent alone held the cure for all the brutality Brip put him through. He continued to kiss me everywhere. My chin, the tip of my nose, the side of my neck, and my ear lobes. Then he gently inserted his two thick, masculine fingers inside of me, sliding them in and out of me while he massaged my clit with the tip of his wide thumb. I bared down onto his fingers, squeezing my pelvis, and twirled my hips to his motion. His touch was so explosive I had to breathe in real deep to keep from coming.

My body felt so weak I had to wrap my arms around his neck to keep from sliding down the brick wall. He lifted me back up and unzipped his pants and seamlessly replaced his fingers with his swollen penis. He filled up every corner of my insides with each thrust. Each thrust was deeper than the next. I moved with his motion; we were in sync and all the while, he never stopped kissing me. The passion was so intense, I had no choice but to come. I exploded from the inside out. Malcolm felt it and stopped but only for a moment. He pulled me off the wall and carried me around the corner back to his bedroom. He cradled me in his arms like I was delicate. Then, he gently placed my body down on a mattress that lay on the floor.

He pulled off the rest of my clothes. I was down to nothing but my bare skin. He looked down at my body like it was his canvas and every imperfection was perfectly imperfect. He traced his fingers around my body like he was carving a sculpture. Touching every part of me. Then he pulled off his shirt and walked away. I don't know where he went but when he came back, he was completely naked. His large nappy haired chest stood out. I rubbed against his coarse reddish-brown chest hairs with the tips of my fingers.

"You're beautiful," he whispered more to himself than me. Then he flipped me over on to my stomach and continued to feel around my body like he was making a stencil of me. He kissed his way from the top of my neck to the bottom of my spine. Each kissed felt different than the next. Like they meant different things. Then he flipped me back over, spread my legs, and began to kiss my insides. He kissed around my inner thighs before he started to lick inside of me like his taste buds had been craving me. Just when I was about to get the moment of complete, Nirvana, I heard the door crash open. I didn't have to wonder. I knew it was, Brip.

The aggression and entitlement behind that kick of the door was a dead giveaway. He kicked the door off the hinges like the fact that it was closed offended him. Brip thought he owned the world. All he had to do was turn the knob but that wasn't brutal enough for him. I jumped up and tried to dash to my purse for the gun, but Malcolm pulled me back.

"We aren't running from him, Sarah," Malcolm said surprisingly calm.

"Let go of me," I said and tried to free myself from Malcolm, but his grip was too tight.

"Sarah, calm down. It's going to be ok. I promise. Everything is going to be ok."

I tried to release myself from Malcolm's grip again but this time I realized how tight it actually was. It didn't feel like a hold of comfort but restraint. That's when I decided to stop being the sweet damsel Sarah he thought I was and elbowed him in the side and finished him with a quick jab across the cheek. A move Keno taught me. I ran straight for my purse. By the time I picked it up and grabbed the gun, I was already facing Brip.

He looked at my naked body with bulging eyes. You would think he caught me and Malcolm fucking. It would have been nice for him to witness me riding Malcolm, but he was a little too early for that. I pointed the gun at him. Brip didn't look armed but I knew him better than that. I don't know what stunned him more, seeing me standing in Malcolm's studio naked and dripping wet between the legs or the fact that I was aiming the gun at him, with a look in my eyes that said I was going to kill him.

Brip started to self-destruct. He could be so weak when he wanted to be. He closed his eyes and shook his head like he was trying to wake up from a bad nightmare.

"What are you doing, Taffy? What the fuck are you doing?" his hands flew in the air and he paced around in circles taking deep breathes.

"I'm going to kill you then go back to the bedroom and continue to fuck the father of my child right over you dead bleeding body!" I said in one cold breath.

He looked back at me like my words were all the bullets he needed. His mouth hung open; Brip was speechless. A tear fell from his eye. Then he closed his eyes tightly and reopened them quick as if he was trying to make all my hurt from what he was witnessing go away but obviously it didn't work.

"Taffy…" Brip said through a broken voice, "please," he said like he was about to faint. "I didn't murder your brother the way you think. It was a job. He was a job. It's my job!! You know what I do. You know how I take care of us!!! If I knew he was your brother, I wouldn't have killed him but that was before us. Look, I haven't touched your other crazy ass brother Tony and that nigga done tried to kill me at least once a year since we been married," Brip revealed.

What? I thought to myself. Brip never told me that before. I thought I was the first person to give him that information. Upon that revelation, I lowered the gun but only a little bit. "You have to believe me, baby. I know I'm fucked up and angry but I ain't that sick. I didn't know that was your brother until after I married you and met Tony for the first time but it was too late then. I couldn't say nothing. I didn't want to hurt you. That shit bothered me too. You know I felt whenever you would cry over your brother? Do you?"

I shook my head. I wasn't going to allow myself to believe him. At the end of the day, this wasn't about reason, but revenge and I owed it to Keno to kill him. I had to. I didn't know that I was crying until I swallowed a tear. I was hesitating. I didn't expect it to be this hard. No, I had to do this. I had to. Raising the gun back up, I straightened my aim. Brip looked at me sorrowful. He didn't flinch. When I decided I could no longer stand the pitiful look in his eyes, I pulled trigger three times. The gun clicked all three times, but no shots were fired and Brip was still standing. The look he gave me was one I never seen before. He was still breathing and obviously untouched by the unloaded gun but in a way, I still killed him.

I looked down at the gun and opened the barrel and realized the gun had no bullets. Brip stared at me like he didn't know who I was anymore. I couldn't bare the look he was giving me so I turned the other way to see Malcolm charging towards me. He grabbed me from behind and restrained me after snatching the gun from my hand. Brip was still giving me a lifeless look. That's when I started to wonder if I'd made a huge mistake.

"I got her, Mr. Badd," Malcolm said to Brip and I felt like someone punched me in the stomach. Now I know where he went before he undressed. He called Brip and he unloaded my gun. Malcolm had his good arm around my throat. He tightened it a bit when he spoke to, Brip. I felt less than nothing and defeated beyond measure.

"I knew you took the gun from the house, Taffy but I didn't actually think…" Brip chocked on his words. He looked away from me like he couldn't stand the sight of me and I started to sob. What had I done? "You know you changed everything right?" I couldn't respond. "I know I fucked up in the past but this shit, changes everything. All of it, "he said and looked up at Malcolm then down at the gun Malcolm tossed to the side.

"The father of your baby," he looked over my shoulder at Malcolm, "sold you out for a few grand and this new studio…actually I mean the studio that I'm letting him borrow for a while," Brip said cocky.

Brip took a deep breath and stepped back. He reached in towards the back of his pants and pull out his pistol and aimed it at me. This was it for me. Brip was going to kill me. I closed my eyes and dropped my head and waited for it. Then he fired the gun. The sound shattered my ear drums and the burnt smell of gun powder filled my nostrils. I felt the blood splatter everywhere before I fell to the ground. When my knees hit against the concrete and my hands fell into a puddle of blood, that's when I realized Brip didn't shoot me but Malcolm. He shot him in the head. I couldn't bear to look at his lifeless body.

I managed to get up. My ears were still ringing from the gun shot. When I looked up. Brip was turning to walk away. He was leaving me.

"Brip, wait!!" I screamed but he didn't stop. He kept walking. His gun was still smoking. "Brip, please. Please don't leave me," I pleaded. I chased behind him and he finally stopped walking, but it wasn't because of me. Someone else had walked in the door.

"Vinchi?" I heard Brip say.

"Hi, Uncle Brip," I heard Vinchi reply. Then I heard another round of gunfire.

I stopped walking. I was afraid to turn the corner. Did Brip shoot his nephew too? Had I really damaged him that badly? It was silent.

"Brip, what's going on?" I called out, but he didn't respond.

"It's ok, Aunt Taffy," Vinchi answered for him as he came casually strolling around the corner looking just as creepy as his father.

"Vinchi!" I screamed. I tried to wrap my mind around what was happening. If Brip didn't shoot, Vinchi, then who got shot? I didn't want to believe that it was, Brip. Then Vinchi aimed the gun at me.

"Get dressed, Aunt Taffy," he said in a serious tone.

"Where is your uncle? What did you do to, Brip?"

"Uncle Brip is taking a nap. Now do as I say and get dressed. We don't have much time," Vinchi gave me a blank stare. He kept a straight face looking past Malcolm's bloody dead body and my nakedness. He followed me around, aiming the gun at me as I shuffled to find my clothes. My heart raced. What the fuck was going on? Did he really kill, Brip? His own uncle.

"Vinchi, where is your mother? Where is Mona?"

"She is where she belongs. On the Ranch" he said calm.

"What about, Brock?"

Vinchi didn't respond. Once I was dressed he grabbed my arm and lead me towards the door. When we passed Brip, I screamed. He was lying face down and he wasn't moving. Blood was streaming from his body.

"Brip," I tried to run towards him but Vinchi yanked me back.

"Stay calm, Aunt Taffy," he said and pulled out a rope from his pocket. "Don't move," he said and pointed the gun at me."

I watched him as he leaned over and tied Brip's hands together.

"Vinchi, we have to get help. Brip's hurt," I tried to be as calm as I could, but he just ignored me. "Please Vinchi. This is your uncle. He's hurt."

"He'll be fine," Vinchi said as he leaned up. He reached into his other pocket and pulled out a bandana. "Ties this around your eyes."

"Vinchi...'"

"Just do it, Aunt Taffy!!" He screamed. I didn't want to test him. He already shot Brip.

I tied the bandana around my eyes as quick as possible. This past week I thought of nothing but killing Brip now I'm praying to God that he's still alive.

When we got outside. I heard people screaming. The sight of Vinchi escorting me to the car, bloody and blindfolded was terrorizing. He threw me in what I assume to be the back seat and slammed the door.

"I did like you said and tied up, Uncle Brip," I heard him say to someone.

Was it Brock? It had to be.

"Brock!! Brip is going to die. Please, help him."

There was a silence for a while as the car pulled off. Then the person responded, and it wasn't Brock like I assumed.

"Calm down, Taffy. Everything is going to be ok."

I knew that voice like I knew my own voice. I couldn't believe who it was. It was Dalla.

"Vinchi, call Lera…. tell her I'm ready for the pickup," I heard her say. Mona was right. Dalla and Lera are both rats. Now, not only am I caught up in this, I got Brip involved too. I'm pretty sure the 'pick up' Dalla was ready for was Brip's body. At least she wasn't leaving him there. I can understand Dalla and Lera being in cohorts but what the hell did Vinchi have to do with any of this? Was Mona involved? What the fuck is going on!

31

MONA

I've been in this so-called prison for three days now and Brock still hasn't come to get me out and Billy won't talk to me. It's like he's pissed that I'm here. Hell, I'm pissed too. I've been demanding Officer Todd to get me in contact with Brock, but he keeps saying that Brock is busy. That means, he ain't trying to see me. Fuck him.

I can't believe this place. It's nicer than some of the luxury overnight rooms we have at the Casino. With the plush carpets, hard wood floors and floor to ceiling windows, it feels more like a day Spa than a prison. There are about 8 rooms, or should I say prison cells divided off from the common area which consist of the living quarters, kitchen and gym. My room is on the other side of the hall away from Billy's. I bet Brock did that on purpose.

Billy's been avoiding me. I wonder if he upset with me too? I don't blame him. He probably thinking that me being here is just a set up. Maybe he thinks Brock is trying to get more information out of him. I got to get him to talk to me. When I met with Dalla, I planned to grant her safe entry to the Ranch. She claimed to have maps of the Ranch and second way in. She was coming to bust Billy out of this prison and then take me to my son but that obviously that ain't gon' work now. Not unless I can contact her. I wasn't expecting this shit. The simple bitch probably think I flaked on her. That's ok. I'm gon' get my son back if I got to blow this whole fuckin Ranch up to do it, it's going to happen.

I look down the hall towards Billy's room because I heard his door open. Two half dressed women walk out giggling like they on vacation. These mother fuckin Badd nigga's ain't shit. I wonder if Dalla know that while she's been risking her life, planning to set her husband free, he's been fucking a different woman, sometimes two at a time, every night. Or at least it's been every night since I been here. I see the chef walking down the hall holding a tray with Billy's lunch. He watches the women's jiggling bare asses as they trout down the hall like they at the Play Boy mansion or something. I'm starting to think that this ain't no prison for Billy but a fucking mental retreat.

I rush down the hall and catch the Chef while he's still distracted with his ass watching. I snatch the tray and the key card to Billy's room away from him and dare him to challenge me. We have a brief stare down but, in the end, I win.

"Tell Officer Todd no more visitors for the next hour," I order him and at first, he doesn't move. Then I give him that look, and he rushes off to do just as I say. I tap on the door two times, alerting Billy that I'm coming in just like the Chef does, then I use the key card and walk in.

I hear the shower running. "Leave the food on the table", he yells from the bathroom. "And lock my door behind you," he adds. I guess he wants to be sure to keep me out. Well, too late for that.

I walk further into the room. It's nicer than me and Brock's Master Suite at the big house. Almost twice the size. I put the food down on the table beside a few drawings that Billy is working on. I pick one up and notice they are preliminary sketches of structures. Is he still working for the Ranch? Does Brock know this? My head starts to swarm with confusion.

There's also paintings of babies everywhere. None of the paintings are complete though. Some are just of a baby's face but with no body, others are of little hands and feet but no face. What the hell has been on this man's mind?

I look up and notice a balcony for the first time. I slide it open and step outside. There is nothing in front of me, but an open field surrounded by large trees and bush. Now I'm really confused. Brock called this place a prison but there ain't no security here. At least not in Billy's room. If he wanted to leave, he could. My room is nothing like this. It's comfortable but there ain't no windows nevertheless a back porch leading outside. When Officer Todd puts me in it for the night, the door automatically locks, and I'm stuck until he lets me out for air the next morning. If this place is a prison, then Billy is not staying in a cell but an overseer's suite. He's not restricted.

I'm so distracted by the outside view that I don't notice Billy is standing behind me, with a towel around his waist, looking at me like I'm breaking and entering. I look at him and shake my head. He knows I have questions and he gives me a look that tells me he's not in the mood to be interrogated. One thing for sure, Billy may not have been in prison, but he definitely got a prisoner's body. He's put on at least 20 pounds of muscle mass since I last saw him, and his abs are ripped. Dalla's going to be happy to see him but I got a feeling he don't give a fuck about seeing his wife. Just like Brock don't give a fuck about me.

"What you doing in my room, Mona?"

"I need to talk to you. It's important."

Billy sighed and walked back inside. He grabbed some clothes from a chest and walked back in the bathroom to get dressed. I took a seat at his table and waited. When he came back, he was dressed in his gym clothes. When he noticed I was sitting in front of his drawings, he rushed to the table and grabbed them like he didn't want me to see.

"What you and Brock been working on?" I let him know that I already had a look.

"You got five minutes before I call officer, Todd in here," he warned me.

"What the fuck is going on?" I blurted out. "Brock told me he had you in this prison. But this ain't no fucking prison. He out there hunting for your wife and…"

"I ain't got no fucking wife," he said harsh.

"What! That ain't what Dalla think. I saw her the other day."

"What you say?" Billy started walking towards me.

"I met with the, bitch."

"Was she alone," Billy said under his breath.

"Yes, why?"

Billy looked disappointed as he stared off into blank space for a while and then shook his head.

"Forget it," he said.

"She's got a plan to get you out of here. I told her I would help her but now I'm thinking you don't want to leave."

"What you helping her for? Y'all cool all of a sudden?" Billy said to me sarcastically.

"No but we can help each other. She wants you and I want, Vinchi," I said and watched his face to see if he knew anything. He looked confused.

"What you talking about? What's going on with Vinchi?"

"Brock sent him to Ace," I said. My voiced cracked. "Dalla said that Ace is going to kill him if he ain't already dead and …"

"Wait a minute, what the fuck are you talking about, Mona? Brock wouldn't do that dumb shit."

"You and I both know what Brock is capable of," I said and looked him in the eyes. He knew what I was talking about. He immediately looked away like he didn't want to hear what I was about to say next. "I didn't know what he did. I promise, I just found out and I'm not in agreement with it. I pro…"

"Shut the fuck up," Billy cut me off and stormed towards the balcony like he was trying to escape a reality he's been avoiding. "I thought you was smarter than that, Mona. You been listening to that bitch," he said referring to Dalla.

I got up to follow him. Something is telling me that maybe he don't believe that Brock killed his mother anymore, but I wasn't here to convince him otherwise. Truthfully, I could care less about all that shit right, now. I'm here for my son.

"Bobby's dead you know," I said quick. Billy's entire spirit dropped. "Brock knows that it's Ace that called the hit. Vinchi gon' be next if we don't stop him." I looked at Billy. He was trying to shake off the emotions of Bobby's death. "Brock's plan is fucked up. He got Vinchi there as a mole, thinking Vinchi going to be able to pull off killing Ace. It's too risky. Vinchi is just a boy. He ain't even had no real training yet. You have to help me. If not for me, do it for Bobby."

Billy rubbed his head like he was trying to escape reality, but I wasn't going to let him do that. He's been gone long enough. It's time for him to carry his weight again.

"We got to trust, Brocks plan," Billy said like that was final. His easy way out.

I always knew his ass was just as weak as his momma.

"What about, Dalla? Ace is going to kill your wife too. I know you loved her once."

"That bitch killed my father and lied about being pregnant. You see a baby when you saw her?" He turned around and gave me a desperate look. I was stunned by his revelation.

Now I understood his question about her being alone. I shook my head no. Dalla was alone. She didn't mention having a baby but why would she.

"Brock thinks you killed Papa Badd," I confessed. I had to get him off Brock's team. He obviously is poisoning his mind.

"My brother knows the truth now, but I might as well have killed him and Bobby. I brought her into our lives. I let her fuck everything up. I started all this shit with my suspicions about my mother, but the truth is…she killed herself Mona. Plain and simple. She wasn't happy for a very long time and it took me being here to realize that."

My heart stopped. It was at the tip of my tongue to tell him that Brock confessed to me, but I couldn't do it. At least not now. I don't know how he did it, but Brock managed to brain wash Billy. Now it was my turn. I needed to get my son back even if I had to lie. I wasn't sure if Dalla had Billy's child or not and I didn't care but I was going to make him believe it. It was the only way he could help me.

"I lied," I said to Billy. He turned around to face me. I didn't have to tell him what I was lying about. It was almost like he spent all this time down here hopping that Dalla had his baby. "Dalla wasn't alone."

Billy reached and yanked me by the shirt collar. I pushed him off me and clutched my fist ready to strike if I had too. I wasn't that bitch, Dalla. No one touched me like that. Not even Brock.

"Get your fucking hands off me! You forgetting who the fuck I am?" I warned him. Billy backed down. He didn't want a fight.

"Don't lie to me, Mona. I don't trust shit that none of you so called Badd Wives have to say!"

"I don't give a fuck. She had a kid with her. I thought it was just a scam. A way for me not to kill her. She knows I wouldn't hurt pure Badd blood, but I wasn't there to kill her, so I didn't give a fuck either way. She told me that she didn't want you to know. I didn't believe her, so I didn't bother telling you."

Billy was silent for a second. He looked like his mind was reprocessing everything he decided to be a lie. His body fell into a seat at the corner of his bed. His shoulders slumped over with the recurring burden. This meant a lot to Billy. But Vinchi means more to me.

"Boy or girl," he asks under his breath.

His question caught me off guard. But, I had to be quick with my response, so he would believe me.

"A girl," I said without flinching and he believed me. I saw it in his eyes. Weak mutha-fucka.

"We got to let her help us, Billy and we can't let Brock know. If I don't get Vinchi back, then he's dead and so is your daughter. Our kids didn't ask for this life; it's what we gave them. We have to help them both. Do what you want with, Dalla afterwards but this is Badd blood we talking about. Hasn't enough been spilled?"

Billy looked up at me. He didn't say anything, but I didn't need him too. I knew he was in.

32

LERA

I got about four miles down the old country road Tara lived off before I realized I had nowhere to go. All of this was starting to feel like a dream that I prayed I would wake up from, giving myself a second chance to make better choices. I fell in love with a man that I left everything for. My career, my livelihood, it's all gone. Then he fakes his death and I experience hurt I couldn't imagine, at least hurt I thought I couldn't imagine. Now, I find out I was just a pawn in his scheme and my marriage to him was fake. His brother has a hit out on me, I'm broke and broken. I didn't know what the fuck to do, so I called Dalla.

I was surprised to hear that Bobby never showed up. Instantly I thought that something happened to him, but I stop giving a fuck right away. I needed her help, but I didn't know how she should could help me; she was busy protecting her own ass and I couldn't trust her, but unfortunately, she was the only person I knew to call. Turns out, she needed my help too. No big surprise to me. I'm nothing but a pawn for these people. I want nothing to do with any of them but getting out this shit isn't going to be easy. Not if I wanted to make it out alive. She promised me safety and enough cash to get out of town, but she told me that it wasn't going to be. I agreed. What else could I do?

I drove the beat-up pickup truck two hours and met Dalla at some sketchy place in the woods. We took a boat across the lake and too my surprise, there was a beautiful modern styled cabin nestled in the middle of nowhere. I showered, and she gave me clean clothes to wear. After I got dressed, she hugged me, and I fell into her arms and sobbed like a baby. I don't know if I was just desperate for affection but Dalla didn't seem too bad. She treated me like she understood what I had going on. She sat me down at this make shift dining table and turned on a pot of coffee. That's when I told her everything.

I told her about Bobby's marriage to Tara and his son Blake. I also told her that he didn't trust her. She didn't seem surprised by that. Bobby stood her up the day he was supposed to meet her. Tara had to be the reason why. He listened to everything she said. She told me everything she knew about Tara, but it wasn't much. Apparently, Tara was right. Her and Bobby had a long history together. It went back as far as grade school. Of course, Tara was excommunicated by the family for her defiance and some other conflicts they had with her family. That's why Bobby kept their relationship secret all these years. But, when I told her about Blake, she was surprised. She didn't know that Bobby had a son. She said that would explain why he married Tara.

I guess he was trying to make me feel better, but it wasn't working. She said that Bobby probably married Tara to make sure that their son received his inheritance if anything ever happened to him, but Tara made it seem deeper than that. And I was no fool. Bobby and Tara were in love. And they probably always will be. When I started to cry again, she told me to get some rest because we had long days ahead of us. I didn't know what that meant and at the time and I didn't care. I just needed a way out but once again, I fucked up and made a huge mistake trusting her. She really got me in some shit. Even bigger than Bobby. But, at this point, there is no turning back.

———— ··•·· ————

"Open the bed, quick!" Tony yelled. He needed quick access to the back of the truck. I jumped out the truck but hesitated. I couldn't believe what I was seeing. This is what Dalla needed me to do? Tony was carrying Brip's bloody body over his shoulder in broad daylight. Blood from Brip's chest rolled down Tony's arm and splattered on to the concrete. I would have thought Brip was dead, but he was moaning underneath duct tape Tony plastered to his mouth.

I did what I was told and jumped back in the truck before anyone could make me out. My heart was racing. What the fuck did I get myself into? Somebody shot Brip and me being in this situation made me an accomplice.

After a day of rest at Dalla's cabin, she set me up with this crazy looking man that called himself, Tony. Where in the hell did Dalla find this guy? Something told me that Tony wasn't his real name. He didn't look sane enough to know his name. Tony looked like he just escaped a POW camp and was out for revenge. He had thick scare at the temple of his head. Every so often he would massage it like it hurt. Then he would get angry and anxious. I wondered what happened to him? He had to be military because he was so well trained, and his body looked like it could break bullets. But, he talked to himself and there was something deranged about his eyes. That's why I just avoided eye contact with him. When she told me to be his driver and to just trust her, I did it because I had no choice. But, I had no idea this was the kind of shit she was going to get me into. If I wasn't on the Badd's hit list before, I probably was number one most wanted now. Brip Badd is bleeding in the back of a truck that I'm driving. What the fuck!!

"Drive, Tony said as he jumped into the passenger side, slamming the door so hard the glass almost shattered. He had a big smile on his face. Like all his dreams were finally coming true.

"No, no!!!" I was in a state of panic. "That's Brip Badd. That's my brother in law. We have to get him help."

"Would you like to die with the rest of them, Mrs. Badd?" Tony gave me a serious look. I answered his question by slamming on the gas and jolting the car off to a screeching halt. What the fuck was I doing.

"Where are we going? Are we taking him to a hospital?"

"I promise we are going to take him somewhere to get dealt with until then take that right and jump on I20 and ride until I say stop," Tony said before leaning back comfortable in his seat. He started to whistle. Every so often, he would look through the back window at Brip's bleeding body then turn around and smile even bigger. "Today's a good day," Tony said to himself.

———— ··•·· ————

I was in such a daze that I didn't know how long we've been driving. When we came to a stop, it could have been 10 minutes or 2 hours; I couldn't tell you. When I looked up, Dalla was walking towards the truck. When I saw her, I immediately jumped out to attack her.

"What the fuck did you get me into! You trying to kill, Brip?" I reached out to grab her but before I could, Tony grabbed me, effortlessly restraining my body with his arms. "Let me go you fucking psycho!"

"Calm down, Lera. This isn't what you think," Dalla said to me annoyed.

"Really!" I screamed trying to wiggle my way out of Tony's grip. "That's not Brip in the back of the truck? Is he not bleeding out?" I begin to sob. "How could you do this? You know how much he loved you. Him and Taffy both." When I said Taffy's name, Tony let go of me, shoving me to the concrete.

"Taffy!" he yelled. He started breathing hard and turning around in circles "Taffy?" he yelled again. He said her name like he was looking for her. Did he know Taffy?

Tony was three seconds before flipping all the way out when Dalla ran towards him and put her hands on his shoulders, trying to comfort him. She was whispering something that calmed him down. Tony straighten up his posture and marched back to the truck like he was returning to duty.

"I don't have time for this shit, Lera. If you want to be a fool and defend the very people that has hit out for your life, then you do that. But you will not fuck this up for me."

"I need to know what the fuck is going on?" I said through tears.

"And you will…just not right now," Dalla walked toward me and put her hand on my shoulder like she did Tony. I guess she was hypnotizing us because I felt calmer. "Take us to Tara's…don't ask questions," she added before I had a chance to interject.

I sniffed back up my tears and straightened out my shoulders. "Ok," was all I said. The fear I had was instantly replaced with vengeance. Tara was one bitch I wouldn't mind seeing bleeding in the back of a truck. She was the only person standing in the way of me and Bobby and it was time to get rid of her. Dalla got back in her truck and followed behind us.

———— ··●·· ————

I tapped on Tara's door alone. Just like Dalla instructed me. Tony was hiding in the corner and Dalla was still parked at the end of the driveway. I heard her behind the door. It was like she was debating if she should open it or not. I knocked again. Tara was smarter than she looked. When she didn't answer the second time, I got nervous. I was starting to think she was on to us. Just when I was about to turn to walk away, I heard the latch unlock. Tara slowly opened the door and then faced me with folded arms and an attitude. I hated her fucking guts.

"Why did you come back?" Tara said snide. "Bobby's actually out there putting himself and my brother in danger looking for your simple ass," Tara said giving me an evil glare.

Bobby was looking for me? What did that mean? It meant I fucked up that's what it meant. I was just about to tell her to run but it was too late. Tony bombarded her, bursting through the door and tackling her small framed body to the ground. It was a harsh sight to witness. I stood there frozen with fear and shame.

"Wait! No, Tony don't hurt her!" I yelled to him.

Tara was putting up a good fight. It was impressive. She kicked Tony three times in the nuts and got out of his grip by twisting her body and sliding underneath his leg. She almost was free but Tony, who obviously felt no pain, grabbed her leg, and yanked her back towards him and straddled her. He tied her up right in time for Dalla to pull up.

Tony restrained Tara to one of her dining chairs. Tara didn't cry. She didn't look at Tony. She didn't even look at Dalla when she strolled in the house. She just kept her eyes fixed on me. I couldn't face her.

"What do you people want from me?" Tara said like she was in control. She was fearless.

"Where's Bobby?" Dalla kneeled in front of her.

"Apparently on a dummy, mission." Tara kept her eyes fixed on me. "I told him not to trust you," Tara said to Dalla.

"I knew someone was talking in his ear. That was your biggest mistake. We were so close. So close to all this being over with and you go and fuck it up."

"I don't get you people with your selfish and greedy motives. Untie me! I have nothing for you!"

"Bobby is going to do what I ask him one way or the other."

"He's done with you!" she said to Dalla but looked to me. "After this, it's over for good."

I tried to turn to walk away but Tony yanked me back. "Stay put!" he whispered loudly to me.

Dalla pulled the cordless phone from the wall and kneeled back down in front of, Tara. "It's not over until I get what I want. What's his number? He's been avoiding my calls, but I know he'll answer you especially when he finds out I got Blake," Dalla confessed.

"What!" Tara and I both yelled at the same time.

"Dalla, what the fuck is going on? You leave Bobby's son out of this, bitch!" I charged towards Dalla only to be tackled by her body guard, Tony.

"Tony, restrain her. Get her ready to go," Dalla ordered Tony.

Ready to go? What the fuck did she mean by that? Was all this planned? Dalla never meant to help me. This was all another one of her set ups. How fucking dumb could I be!

"Will do!" Tony yelled and grabbed my hands, tying them together with the same rope he used to restrain Tara.

"Tara, I had nothing to do with this. You have to believe me!"

"You had everything to do with this!" Tara yelled chocking on tears. It was the first time I seen her emotional. She tried to wiggle her way out the restraints, but it was useless. "Leave Blake alone!! He's just a child!! Please have some compassion."

"Tara, I'm going to need you to calm down and give me Bobby's number. If you want Blake to stay safe, you'll do it."

While Tara was sobbing and giving Dalla Bobby's number, Tony was putting the final touches on me. He tightens the rope that's wrapped around my body and masked duct tape on my mouth, painfully clasping my lips together.

The phone barley rang once before Bobby answered. It was like he sensed something was wrong with, Tara. I guess their connection was special.

"Tara…what's going on?" Bobby sound concerned.

I started to cry at the sound of his voice. I felt like my life was ending right before my eyes. The compassion he had for Tara was undeniable. It didn't matter that he was out looking for me. That probably was more of his conscience. His heart was with Tara and their son Blake.

"Bobby," Tara's voice cracked.

After hearing the fear in Tara's voice, Bobby said "I'm coming home."

"No!" Tara warned him.

Then Dalla spoke.

"Bobby, I told Tara that Blake will be safe but I'm going to need you to do what I asked you too."

Bobby was silent for a while. It was like he was trying to regroup after being thrown off by hearing Dalla's voice and Tara crying. He sensed the danger his family was in.

"You dead, Dalla," was all Bobby said.

"Bobby," Tara yelled. "Lera's here," Tara blurted out. Bobby went silent again. I wonder what he was thinking? I tried to scream that I'd been set up, but I couldn't. My voice was muffled. Bobby couldn't hear me. For all he knew, I was just standing by being an accomplice. "She helped Dalla. She told her about Blake. She brought them here," Tara shot me evil stares in between tears.

"Tara calm down. They gon' pay for this. I promise…we going to get our son back."

Although I was already on the floor, I felt like I had fallen. Hearing Bobby speak about me the way he did, like I was nothing, was worse than taking a bullet.

"What's it going to be, Bobby? All you have to do is get Brock to Ace. I will handle Mona and Billy. Same plan as before." Dalla paused waiting for Bobby to reply. He was still silent. "I know you got a tracker on Tara's truck. You want to find her, follow the tracker but first, I'm going to need you to deliver Brock as planned."

"You gon' pay for this, Dalla. You both will…" Bobby said referring to me. "And you both know, I mean what I say." He hung up.

"Get them in the truck," Dalla ordered Tony. Things were finally going her way.

33

TAFFY

Brip's dead. I can feel it. And I'm next. How did I put myself in this situation? I was so stupid believing that I was invincible. I thought that I was beyond death because I was a Badd. We all did. I convinced myself that I had a good life. But what made it good? Money? Power? Now look how it's all ending. I did nothing **meaningful in life and now, I'm about to be murdered by this maniac.**

I heard stories about Ace Lucky but to the Badds he was nothing more than a joke. No real threat. Well, that's all bullshit. This nigga is a psychopath and he has me locked in some room in his basement tied to a chair. He keeps threatening to stick his dick in me. I don't know what's stopping him. He hasn't done it yet. But he has been slapping the shit out of me every chance he gets. He's been grabbing my titties out my bra and sticking his hand down my pants while he whispers the awful way I'm going to die in my ear. He said he's going to feed me to his gators. It became real when he showed them to me. I can't fight him anymore. For some reason, I think that annoys him but I'm too weak. I'm weak from the inside out.

When I hear the door crash open, I flinch and close my eyes. I know it's him. He's been terrorizing me every hour or so. I can't take much more. I'm just ready to die. I'm leaning down on all fours with my hands tied to the bottom leg of a wooden chair. I bury my face in the carpet and close my eyes as tight as I can. I don't want to see him. I don't want to smell his cologne. I just want to disappear. When I close my eyes even tighter, I see blood rushing from Malcolm's body and then I see Brip lying face down, blood pouring from his chest. Two lives gone and all because of me. Now it's my turn to die. I try to shake away the nightmare that I'm living but I can't. It's over for me. It's time for me to go meet my brother, Keno. I hope he won't be mad at me because of the way it all ended.

"Taffy," I hear a female voice whisper loudly. Still I don't move. I just keep my head low and my eyes shut. When I feel a hand touch me, I jump. It's him. I just know it's Ace.

"It's ok. I promise. I'm going to get you out of here," the voice says to me and massages my back. The person tries to untie me, but I won't let them. "I'm sorry, Taffy. I'm so sorry," I hear her say. I finally raise my head and look over my shoulder. It's Dalla. That bitch! She has her nerve to apologize to me. She had Brip shot and me hauled here to be a prisoner. What the fuck was wrong with her? I loved her once. I don't understand how people can claim to love you and then betray you so easily.

Just seeing her causes me to burst into tears. I don't know if my tears are fueled by anger or relief from seeing a familiar face trying to comfort me. She places her hand on the side of my face and gives me a sorrowful look. I jerk away from her touch. I try to speak but nothing comes out but a moan. I lost my voice from all the screaming. I'm so dehydrated my throat feels like it's full of rocks. So, I give her an evil stare instead. She hears everything I want to say through my look. I can tell by the way her face drops.

"Don't fight him," she tries to give me advise but it's too late for that. But, I'm smarter now. I know not to fight, Ace. "Please...just don't resist. It won't be long, and all this will be over," she says before jumping up and away from me like she didn't want to be seen with me. That's when I see Vinchi. He's leading two men in with a body. They drop the body on the floor. I look closer and its Brip. I start to struggle and try to free myself so that I can run to him. He's not moving. Then in comes Lera and another girl. Dalla takes the tape from their mouths and orders Vinchi to untie them. He does what she says and then they all leave us to die.

"Taffy," Lera runs to me but I kick her away. I try to curse at her. I want to tell her not to fucking touch me, but I can't. "Who did this to you?" I continue to kick at her and she steps away before crawling into a corner and crying uncontrollably.

"Do you betray everybody you once claim to love?" The woman says to Lera. Lera just covers her ears and tries to tune her out.

I try to free myself. The woman sees me struggling and runs to my aide. She tries her best to untie my knot but it's not working. She stops and searches the room. She grabs a mirror from the wall and breaks it. Then she cuts me free. She gently massages the welts on my wrist, but I pull away from her and crawl to Brip. I cup his face in my hands and lean down towards his chest, listening for a heartbeat. The woman comes over and checks, Brip's pulse.

"He's still alive. You must be, Taffy. Brip's wife?"

I nod. Who was this woman? "I'm Tara," she says calm. Her name sounds familiar. I used to hear Mona fussing about her, but I never paid it any attention. "Bobby's told me a lot about you." She says kindly. For some reason, hearing her voice comforts me. She wipes the side of my face with her hands. "It's ok. He's coming for us," she says confidently. Then I start to cry. She doesn't know that Bobby is dead. She doesn't know that we are in the house of the psycho that probably killed him. She doesn't know that Ace will be down soon to greet her and Lera and to probably finish off, Brip. I lean down and kiss the side of Brip's face.

"We got to try and stop the bleeding," Tara says. She pulls of her jacket and presses it against Brip's wound. I place my hand on top of hers for added pressure. It's the least I could do. I don't take my eyes off my husband.

"Where are we?" Tara says to me, but I don't speak. Then she looks up at Lera. "Do you know where we are?" she walks towards Lera who seems to be in a daze. She kicks her foot and Lera jumps. "You brought us here. You and that bitch! Tell me where the fuck we are?" she kicks at Lera's foot again but Lera just shakes her head confused. "Your pathetic, you know that?" Tara continues to taunt, Lera. "It's over for you and your little partner," she leans down and grabs Lera lifting her from the floor. To be so tiny, the girl has a lot of strength. "Where's my son? What did you do with him?" She shakes Lera but Lera just cries and cries. Tara slaps her across the face and Lera falls back to her corner. "You weak bitch! You gon' pay for this. I'll be sure of it."

I hear the lock on the door click and we all freeze. Tara looks at me as I scurry away to my own corner. I know it's him. I can smell him. The door creaks open and in walks, Ace. Everyone is quiet. Ace looks around the room and smiles big. When he sees Brip's body lying on the floor struggling to breath, his blood saturating the carpet, he smiles even bigger. He slowly walks towards, Brip.

"Taffy is this your husband?" he says and kneels alongside Brip looking him up and down like he was cattle to be slaughter. "Well...he's much smaller than what I imagined. Word on street is that he's like and urban Hercules or something. He don't to seem to be too big of a threat." Ace lifts up the jacket Tara placed over his wound and analyzes it. "Who did this?" Ace says like he's disappointed. "Who the fuck did this!!!" Ace yells so hard, spit flies from his mouth. He jumps up and takes a deep breath.

"Get him to the medic," he yells towards the door. "This nigga is going die when I say and by my hand alone!!"

A few seconds later, two men came rushing into the room and lift Brip's body. They struggle with his dead weight. One grabs his arms and the other grabs his legs. They lift him with the same regard you would dirty laundry. I start to scream and run towards Brip. Where were they taking him? *No!* I yell. Ace grabs me by the throat and lifts me up with one hand before pinning me against the wall. Lera starts to scream uncontrollably and Tara jumps on Ace's back. "You get your hands off of her," she yells. Big mistake. Ace drops me. I gag for air as my body slides down the wall. He grabs Tara by the back of the neck and holds her down. Tara is struggling to move.

"Who the fuck are you?"

"You get your hands off me you maniac," Tara says. She's not afraid of Ace and he can sense that. That's a big mistake on Tara's part. "You really think you're going to kill Brip and Taffy Badd and live to talk about it? Your pathetic, she says and breaks free long enough to spit in his face.

When I see that, I close my eyes. I couldn't watch what happens next. I hear Lera screaming and pleading and Tara gagging. I hear a lot of commotion. It sounds like he's throwing her body against the wall. Glass breaks and bodies thump.

"She's Bobby Badd's wife. His real wife," Lera says. What was she talking about? Bobby's real wife? Was that just a ploy or was she telling the truth?

When I open my eyes, Ace is standing over Tara's body holding a switch blade. Tara is on conscience. Ace is looking at Lera and then back at Tara like he's debating what to believe. He wants to kill, Tara but he decided to wait. Lera may have just saved Tara's life. At least for a few hours. Ace looks at me then turns to walk away. He's still holding the knife, breathing hard. Just when he was about to walk out the door, he turns back around slowly. He wipes the side of his face again like Tara's spit is still there. He rushes towards her with the knife. Lera pleads for her but he doesn't listen. He lifts her body up by her shirt collar and stabs her four times. Blood spills from Tara's mouth and her eyes bulge open, then he lets her go. Her body fell towards the ground in slow motion. When she hits the floor, she gasps for air then shuts her eyes. My whole body shudders. Lera stares at Tara with her mouth open. She's shaking uncontrollably. Ace looks at me and smiles.

"It all will soon be over," he says and winks his eye at me. Ace sets his sights on Lera. Her grabs her by the hair and drags her out the room. Lera is screaming but she doesn't fight. She's smart. He shuts the door behind him. I hear Lera screaming until her voice becomes a faint whisper off into the distance.

That's when I realize that this is really happening. We all are going to die soon.

34

DALLA

"Taffy gon' be there, right?" Tony asked me anxious for the third time. "We just gon' grab her and go, right?"

We were on our way to the Ranch. I never thought I would return. At least not under these circumstances. My plan changed so many times who knew one would finally work. I shouldn't be surprised though. I've been relentless. Finally, I was going to see Billy. So many thoughts were causing my emotions to swarm. I was just as anxious as Tony, but I was also afraid. I was afraid to face, Billy. I was afraid that Brock was going to catch and kill me. I was afraid because of all the things I've done that led up to this point and the thing that I still had to do. The last and final devious thing. Turn Billy over to, Ace. It was the only way to get our son back.

"She knows we coming, right?" Tony went on. I just shook my head yes to shut him up. I had to think. I had to clear my head so when I saw Billy I knew what to say and how to say it. I still love him, but I love our son more. Ace left me no choice but to choose and I chose my own flesh and blood. Being a real family was all I thought about up until the day I pushed him out. When he was still inside of me, I was living a fairy tale thinking that me Billy and the baby were going to be together. After Ace took my son, that fantasy ended quick.

"Tony, we going to get Taffy back, I promise. We just have to stick to the plan. Remember the plan?" I gave him a careful look. He shook his head yes, but I knew he didn't remember. It was sad what happened to him. A brilliant mind like he's lost. All he needed was the right person on his side and he still can be brilliant. Him helping me this far has proven that.

Tony and Bobby were the two areas I had one up on, Ace. He didn't know that Tony was related to Taffy and that Bobby was alive. They were my plan to make sure that everybody came out of this alive. I told Tony that Taffy was at the Ranch to get him to help me with Mona and Billy. When he gets there and finds that Taffy isn't there, I'm going to tell him something else and he going to believe me. He trusts me. Which is sad, but I need him to. He remembers when I use to work for him and Keno. He thinks I'm on his side and I kind of am. Sort of. But, who knows what the hell is going to happen. I lied and told Bobby I had his son. Bobby was full of secrets. He had a son and he had Tara. I finally had something I could use against him. I knew reconnecting with Lera would be a blessing.

As we get closer to the Ranch, I start to panic. My heart is racing, and beads of sweat are forming on my forehead. I told myself that this wasn't about Billy anymore, but I lied. I was shocked when I finally heard from Mona. This plan was supposed to transpire days ago but she never called. I thought that maybe she changed her mind or the whole thing was a set up. But, when I met with Ace and saw Vinchi, I knew she was telling the truth. Now I know better than anyone that a mother will do anything for their child. Even betray the ones they love. Ace lies seeped into Vinchi's childish mind like butter. Brock was stupid thinking that this would work. Vinchi was Ace's pet. When he shot Brip, I knew that Ace had brainwashed him. I didn't tell him to shoot, Brip. Neither did Ace.

Mona told me that she found, Billy. She said that he was doing as good as could be expected. I don't know what that was supposed to mean, and she didn't care to elaborate. This wasn't about me or Billy for her anymore. It was about Vinchi. She guaranteed us safe entry on the Ranch. It helped that we weren't coming in from the front gate. I had one of Billy's maps. I got it from the shoebox I found in his closet a year ago. I only grabbed what I needed and left the rest. There was more than one way on the Ranch and he knew them all because he designed them. Places that Brock didn't even know about. We were entering in through a side where there was nothing but bush and a narrow dirt road that would lead us straight to where I needed to be. At the private prison in Zone 6.

What was I going to say when I saw him? What was he going to say to me? Did he still love me? Did he ever really love me at all? I wasn't sure. These were question that I didn't need to focus on. Besides, the answer to these questions would only distract. This was all about our son, BJ. Billy Jr.

I had BJ at the lake house where Billy and I first made love. Right on the same bed. I hired a Spanish nurse to live with me at the lake during my last trimester. I used a stash of money I found in Billy's condo to pay her; the money also helped me move around after I gave birth. She gave me regularly exams and made sure that everything was ok with the baby. Being pregnant slowed everything down for me. More than I needed it to, but I couldn't be out making dangerous moves pregnant. I was too vulnerable, and I had to keep my child safe. The nurse had connections in Mexico. It was where I was going to send BJ until me and Billy came for him but that didn't work out. Ace found out. Apparently, that day I met with Angelo, the baby she was talking about her and Flo having was my BJ. They'd been watching me. Waiting for me to deliver. The day I went with the nurse to hand over my child to safety, he was takin from me. He's been with Angelo and Flo ever since. I had no choice but to meet with Ace after that. I was forced to be part of his *Badd take down* team. He knew that I would do anything for my son, including hand over his father, Billy.

"We here," Tony said looking down at the map and then back out the window.

He was right. I took a deep breath and stopped right in front of the tree that Mona marked for us and waited. A few minutes went buy and out pops one of their guards, driving a four-wheeler. He waved for us to follow him into the woods and we did. It was time for me to face, Billy Badd. My estranged husband.

———— ··●·· ————

"Wait here," Mona said. "Billy will be out in a few." She blocked the door while looking over my shoulder every few seconds. I never saw her so paranoid.

"Mona, I need to see him," I said to her calm as I could. "Please, let me in?" I asked humble.

"He don't want you here…he only doing this because…"

I pushed Mona out the way. I didn't wait this long and come this far to deal with her bullshit. "Billy," I yelled. I looked around the room. Where were we? "Billy," I yelled again.

Mona came behind me and yanked me by the shoulder.

"Shut the fuck up," she whispered still looking out the door. "You gon' alert the other guards and this whole thing is going to be a bust. We got to go now," she grabbed my hand and forcefully lead me back towards the door.

"Wait," I tried to tug away from her, but her grip was tight. "What about Billy?" I yelled.

"He ain't coming!" Mona said without slowing down. "Let's go…take me to my son. Take me to get Vinchi."

I stopped moving all together and Mona starts to drag my body out the door. I pulled away from her and ran back inside. Mona chased behind me. She grabbed me again and when I turned to fight her off, I heard Billy say, "let her go, Mona."

Mona did as he said. When I turned to face him, it felt like I was moving in slow motion. By the time I was facing him, I was already crying and didn't even know it. Without hesitating, I ran to him and reached to hug him but he grabbed my arms and pushed me back like I had a plague.

"Billy," I said. My voice cracked. Billy looked back at me like the mere sight of me disgusted him. He hated me. "Baby," I said and walked towards him. "I told you I would be back to get you," my voice dropped by the end of the sentence. Billy didn't budge. He just stared back at me like I was an intruder.

"You shouldn't have come back, Dalla."

"I came for you!" I started to panic. Everything I did, I did for him. He still didn't understand that.

"This ain't about me. It never was," Billy said and turned around to walk away.

"Wait," I called out. I rushed towards him and swung him back around to face me. Before he could fight me off, I wrapped my arms around his waist and buried my face in his chest. I hugged him tight. So tight, he had to pry me off. I closed my eyes and tried to savor the moment. I tried to make it just like the moment I seen in my dreams, but he wasn't making it easy. He finally pried my arms off from around him and pinned me against the wall.

"Calm down!" He said to me like I was a crazy person then pinned my hands above my head. "Look at me," he demanded. I was looking at him but the tears that were forming in my eyes blurred my vision. "Were you ever pregnant?" he asked me like he really didn't want to know that answer. It was if he didn't want the answer to be no just as much as he didn't want it to be yes. Regardless if I answered with a yes or no, both answers would mean something he wasn't ready for.

"Yes," I said through tears. "He has BJ...he's going to kill him. That's why I'm here," I said in one breath. That's when everything hit me like a ton of bricks. I slid down the wall burdened with suppressed emotions. Billy pulled me back up. He wasn't gentle.

"Don't lie to me," he said and punched a hole in the wall right by my head.

I reached in my pocket to grab the only picture I had of BJ. Billy jumped and tackled me to the floor like I had a knife. I fought him off and threw the picture at him.

"After all this...you still don't trust me?"

"You killed my father," Billy said to me through pierced lips. "Didn't you?"

I didn't speak. He knew I did but I never said it. He also knew why. I cleared my throat and tried to speak words, but nothing came out. I knew Billy's relationship with his father was rocky. After all, he blamed him for his mother's death. I convinced myself that I was doing him a favor by poisoning his father. I avenged his mother's death and protected him from Ace; killing two birds with one stone but I guess all this time away, he had time to think about it and now he was vengeful. He looked at me like he didn't know who I was. Like I was his enemy. Was I? I ignored his question and focused on what I knew to be important. BJ; our son.

"Ace is going to kill our son if I don't hand you over," I said quick. "All of you," I added letting him know just how far I would go to save our son. I hope Billy saw the sorrow in my eyes and believed me. "I gave birth to him alone. Without you…" I looked down and remembered the stressful and most joyful moment of my life. "I tried to keep him safe and rescue you, but I failed. I obviously failed you both. I don't care what happens to me anymore. I don't even care what happens to you…" Billy looked up at me. He knew I was being honest. I saw it in his eyes, but he still didn't want to believe me. "I just need our son to be safe."

Billy stared down at the picture frozen. BJ shared Billy's features. They had the same eyes and peanut butter complexion. Billy could deny that BJ was his if he wanted, but he would only be lying to himself.

"Mona said it was a girl…" he said under his breath. I was confused by what he was saying.

"Mona said what she had to protect her son. Just like I'm doing what I have to, to protect ours. With or without you! This is going to end tonight, Billy. It has too." I grabbed Billy's hand as one last plea for his help. I squeezed it, but he didn't squeeze back. He was too conflicted. He had been lied to by so many people, he didn't know what to believe anymore; he didn't even know right from wrong. "This may be the last time I see you, Billy Badd. Even through all this, it was all worth it," I said before leaning to kiss him on the lips. Billy closed his eyes as my lips touched his.

When I pulled away, his eyes were still closed. I didn't wait for him to reopen them. Billy was still asleep, and I had not time to wake him. I turned to walk out the door. I didn't bother looking back. I felt a hand grab my shoulder. It was, Billy. I turned to face him, and he just stared back at me. He either didn't know what to say or was too scared to say what he really wanted. So, I said it for him. After all, this may have been the last time I saw him again.

"I love you, Billy and I'm sorry…I'm truly, truly sorry. I just wanted us to be safe and happy. I'm going to make this right for, BJ."

"BJ," Billy said under his breath, looking down at the photo.

"Billy Junior," I repeated.

I walked out the door with Billy still staring down at the picture. Mona was waiting for me outside. She had this anxious look on her face. I never thought I would say this, but I related to her. "Let's go get, Vinchi," I said to her and she nodded.

35

MONA

What the fuck did he do to my son? He would never treat me this way. When we pulled up, Dalla and that crazy nut that was with us pulled me out the car like I was a prisoner. That's when Vinchi came running outside. I just knew my son was going to fight them off me, but he didn't. Instead, he grabbed me and lead me down in a basement.

"Vinchi!" I yelled to him, but he didn't respond. It was like he didn't even know me. "Baby, its Momma. You don't have to do this anymore. Your dad sent me to get you."

He ignored me. Vinchi either knew I was lying or didn't give a fuck. My son wouldn't even look me in the eyes. "Baby, whatever happened here can be forgiven. It can all be over, and I can take you home. Your dad won't be mad at you. I swear." Vinchi still ignored me.

Where did I fail my son? I spent years concerning myself with the Ranch and being there for Brocks every move, but I didn't take time for my own children. Vinchi was the oldest of six boys I had with Brock not to mention our children with the breeders. I neglected them all for the Ranch. What was it all for?

We got to a door and Vinchi pulled out keys to unlock it. Before he opened the door he finally looked at me and shook his head. "I wish you wouldn't have come here mother," he said before pushing me into the room and locking the door behind him. "Vinchi," I screamed and tried to open the door. I banged on it hoping to get his attention, but it didn't work. "Vinchi!" I screamed again.

I turned around and saw Taffy lying on the floor half naked and trembling. On the other side of the room was another body lying on the carpet bleeding. Blood was everywhere. Did Vinchi do this?

"Taffy," I ran to her. When she heard my voice, she jumped and leaped in my arms like I was her savior. "Get yourself together. I'm getting us the fuck out of here," I told her and tried to calm her down by squeezing her into a hug. I didn't want to know what had happened to her. This was all Brock's doing. This situation proved that he didn't give a fuck about us Badd wives.

"Where are we?" I tried to get Taffy to talk but she wouldn't. She was too out of it. "Is this Ace Lucky's place?" Taffy nodded yes. "Did he do this to you? Who is that laying there bleeding?" Taffy just shook her head uncontrollably and closed her eyes real tight like I was bringing up bad memories. I pulled her into another hug. Poor thing. I blame myself for this.

"Just be calm. I swear we gon' get out of this shit!" I let her go and walked over to the woman lying on the floor. Blood was everywhere. When I got closer, I notice that it was Tara. Bobby's old girlfriend. We banned him from seeing her. What was she doing here? And what the fuck happened to her? This was bad. I reached down and checked her pulse. She was still breathing but honestly, she wasn't my concern. She wasn't a Badd wife. I'm not sure how she got mixed up in all of this but I'm only concerned about Taffy and Vinchi.

I look around the room. Searching for everything all at once. A way out. A weapon. Anything but there was nothing. Lying next to Tara were pieces of glass from a broken mirror. I take the sharpest piece and carefully stick it in my pants. Then I start to pace the room to think. I have to keep my cool. I wasn't expecting this shit. I was expecting to come through this nigga's gate blasting and banging but apparently, Dalla had a different plan for me.

Dalla told me that Bobby was still alive. She said that he was going to get

Brock to bring him here to rescue us. I don't know how truthful that was but the idea of it was all I had to hope for. I'm not sure if Brock would care if I was here or not. And Billy letting Dalla walk out the door showed he didn't give a fuck about her. We need Brip. If only I had a way of getting in contact with him. I know that he wouldn't let none of this shit go down the way Dalla had it planned.

The door opened, and some man pushed Lera inside. She fell to the floor and grabbed her side. Her shirt had been ripped off. Half her bra was showing. Someone attacked her badly. I didn't trust Lera no more than I trusted Dalla, but she was here with us now. If we were going to get out of this, we all had to pull together. We had to woman up. Shit!

"Lera," I said standing over her body. "What the fuck are you doing here? What happened? Who did this to you?"

I tried to pull her up, but she screamed and grabbed her side.

"He's crazy, Mona," she said in between heavy breaths. "He...he assaulted me," she said and choked on her tears. "He's going to kill us all."

"That ain't gon' happen," I assured her.

Lera looked up at me like I was delusional. "It's over Mona. Can't you see that?"

"No, I can't!" I never see an ending. Just beginnings. "Where is Vinchi?"

"Your son is helping him. He shot, Brip," she said and moaned before gasping for breath. At this point, it was obvious that she had a broken rib. But I couldn't focus on that. What she was saying about Vinchi was crazy. He would never shoot his uncle.

"Vinchi would never hurt his own blood!"

"Believe what you want," Lera said and tried to crawl away into a corner.

"Wait," I had her talking. I needed to no more if I was going to get us out of   this   situation.   "Where   is   Ace?" "He knows you're here. He's coming for you next. He said he was going to kill us all. He's crazy, Mona. Even you can't fight him. We're dead," she said and gasped for air.

No! This wasn't it. After all these years, it wasn't going to end like this. It couldn't.

I decided that I wasn't going to wait for Ace to come for me. I demanded to see him. I started to bang and kick at the door. Demanding to see him. Taffy cried at the thought of seeing Ace sooner than she had to and Lera must have passed out in that corner because she wasn't moving or talking anymore. It took about 30 minutes but finally Vinchi unlocked the door.

"Uncle Ace will see you now. But don't worry...he won't hurt you."

Uncle Ace? What type of lies did that maniac feed to my son? I followed Vinchi up the stairs to the main house. We walked down a long hallway. There were pictures of Ace all over the house. This man was a board-certified sociopath.

"Did he hurt you?" I tried to get Vinchi to talk to me.

"No, he's family, mama. He wouldn't hurt me."

"Did you shoot your Uncle Brip?"

"I had to," was all Vinchi said.

I felt like I been stabbed in the chest. Vinchi had officially turned against his family. I blame Brock for this foolishness. I will never forgive him for this. As we continued to walk down the hall, we passed by a room. Dalla was inside with the oddest-looking couple. She was hugging a baby. I guess it was her and Billy's son. That's one thing the bitch didn't lie about. She looked up at me with tears in her eyes and now, I understood why she did everything she had done. She was trying to protect her child. All the while Billy is probably somewhere getting a fucking lap dance. I swear. I got a right mind to off all the Badd men. Everyone except Brip. That's my heart. He is loyal.

We got to the end of the hallway and stood in front of two double doors. Vinchi knocked twice and then pulled out the keys to open the door. Ace puts a lot of trust in Vinchi. Before he opened the door, Vinchi turned to me and said, "Everything is going to be okay Mother. No one will hurt you."

I walked into the room and faced this clown of a man, Ace Lucky. I wanted to knock his ass to the ground, but I wasn't foolish. I knew how to deal with a sociopath. I had to make him feel like he was in control. That was what he wanted. It's what he needed to function.

"Mr. Lucky," I said calmly.

"Mona Badd," he said with a big smile. "Who would have ever thought you would be here?" He stopped smiling and walked slowly towards me. I stood my ground. "I hear you are the heart of the Badd operation."

"I like to think that we all do our part," I responded calmly. "What's your plan for today? For us, women?" I said in a way to let him know he had the weakest links.

"You all are merely honey for the bees" he smiled at me.

"I see you took a liking to my son?" I kept a firm stance.

"You mean my nephew…he reminds me a lot of myself when I was his age."

"Nephew…Ace come on. What are you talking about?"

"Oh, your husband didn't tell you that we are brothers? Why else do you think he killed his mother? He wanted to keep that secret."

I gasped. Could Ace be telling the truth? Brock never told me why he killed his mother, but he did say he did it to protect us. I tried to control my emotions. I had to keep my guard up. I pretended like I knew what he was talking about. I looked at Ace like what he just told me didn't make sense, but it made all the sense in the world. I never believed the rumors before but now, I'm not sure what to believe. Is this what all this is about? Is Brock not a Badd? I took a deep breath and composed myself.

"Mr. Badd did what he had to do. He's the best person to run the Ranch."

Ace laughed. He saw right through me.

"You are one loyal woman, Mona Badd. Or should I say, Mona Lucky?" He stroked the side of my face and I wanted to sock his ass, but I didn't flinch. "You didn't know did you?" he smirked.

"Mr. Badd tells me everything," I lied the best I could. "We can talk about family history and all that other bullshit that means nothing right now or we can talk about what you really want. How can I help you get what you want?"

"I want the Badds and I want them dead," he said harshly.

"Let's be reasonable. You want the money and you want the power. You don't need us dead for that. You just need me."

Ace laughed again. "You? What can you do?"

"I have full access to all the money and our clients," I watched Ace watching me like he was considering my offer. "I can help you, Ace."

Ace leaned over and whispered in my ear, "It's not enough."

"Let's talk," I tried to convince him, but it wasn't working.

Ace turned his back to me.

"Vinchi, take your mother back to the basement."

"Wait, promise me you won't hurt the girls anymore. They are terrified."

"And you aren't?" he shot me an evil stare, warning me to be afraid.

That's when I saw that look in Vinchi's eyes. That look that told me he remembered who he was; a Badd. And I knew he meant what he said when he told me he wasn't going to let anything happen to me. Vinchi gently grabbed my arm and led me out of the room. Ace was staring at me with an evil smirk on his face. He didn't want money, he wanted blood.

Before Vinchi unlocked the door to the basement, I turned to him and said "Vinchi, remember what your father told you to do. Remember why you came here. You are our only hope of surviving. Otherwise, he's going to kill us all."

He stared back at me like he was confused and then he nodded. I don't know if he was agreeing with me or dismissing me but Vinchi was all we had now. I had to get him back on our side. He was the only one who could get close enough to Ace to kill him. I feared if he didn't kill Ace first, Ace was going to kill him.

36

DALLA

I watched Taffy close her eyes and prepare to die. At first, her eyes were closed so tight, her entire face squinched. But, then after a while, everything relaxed. I guess she was making peace with herself. I wonder what she was thinking about. I wonder if that squinched face was her regretting becoming a Badd wife. It wasn't until this very moment that I ever regretted meeting, Billy. Because of my love for him, everyone is going to die tonight; Me and my child included.

I knew Ace wasn't going to let us live. When I showed up without Billy and Brock, he got pissed and knocked me out. I woke up bleeding and lying beside the pool. The same spot where I'm lying helpless now. When I came too, he kicked me back unconscious. I tried to convince him that they would come and at first, he believed me, but he got impatient. Then, he stopped believing me. I don't believe it anymore either.

I bought myself a little more time with my son. Angelo and Flo were there with him. Flo didn't want to hand him over. She'd been his mother all this time. When she gave him to me, he cried for her. Angelo rubbed Flo's back, calming her down by whispering something in her ear that made her feel better. Flo just was as scared for BJ as I was. Before Ace came for me, Angelo told me she wasn't going to let our son die but when he snatched BJ from my arms and ordered one of his men to escort me to the basement, I saw the fear in both their eyes. They were just as hopeless as me. Angelo watched Ace with squinted eyes, but she knew not to make a move. At least not one that he seen coming. It would only hurt BJ. If I died, it gave me peace knowing that BJ would have someone that loves him. Regardless of how fucked up Angelo and Flo were.

Three hours later there is still no sign of anyone that can help us. I thought they would come. I thought at least Bobby would come just to save his son but by now, I'm pretty sure he knows that I lied when I said I took him. Before Ace came for me, I planted a seed in Tony's ear about Taffy being locked in the basement, but he didn't understand me. He trusted his partnership with Ace. If Ace could brainwash a sane person, brainwashing someone in Tony's condition must have been a breeze. He didn't understand why Taffy would be here and in any danger. The whole idea frustrated him. All he wanted was the Badds dead. Just like Ace. It was his only train of thought right now. Without my direction, Tony couldn't save us. I haven't seen him since.

Just as Ace is about to kick Taffy's battered body into the pool with his gators, he stops like he has a better idea. He looks over at me. BJ is screaming his lungs off. He can sense the danger we're in. I hear my son, but I can't see him. Too much blood and tears clouding my vision. I see Ace's shoes walking towards me. He's wearing his combat boots; he's appropriately dressed for this gruesome war he's winning. He's standing over my squirming body. I'm too weak to lift my head. He yanks me up by my hair.

"Killing you would be too easy," Ace whispers to me. I can't see him very well, but I know he's smiling. "You're going to watch them all die. Including that bastard son of yours and then you and I are going to celebrate our accomplishments."

I cringe at the thought of spending the rest of my miserable life with Ace. I would kill myself first. Ace pushes me towards a man and I fall into his chest. The man yanks me up. "Take her to the back and get her cleaned up and ready for me." Ace orders and I know just what he means... He wants to watch me die slowly.

"Ace, please don't hurt my son. Please don't kill, BJ..."

Ace slaps me with the back of his hand and blood flies out of my mouth.

I fall back onto the guard and the guard straightens my body back up, so I can walk.

"He's dead but don't worry. Tonight, we'll make another son. A stronger one," Ace said evilly, before stroking the side of my face.

"No!!" I screamed at the top of my lungs. My voice echoed throughout the basement and Ace laughed his evil laugh. The echo of his evil heckle overshadowed my scream.

The guard pushed me towards the door. I wiped my eyes, trying to clear my vision enough to see BJ one last time. That's when I noticed Lera and Mona. They both were on their knees with their hands tied behind their backs and tape around their mouth. They looked weak and helpless. Vinchi stood by Ace's side like he was the heir to his throne. He did nothing. I looked past them, and I caught a glimpse of Angelo holding, BJ. She gave me a reassuring nod and it gave me a little hope that everything was going to be ok. I needed that right now even though I knew it wasn't likely that BJ would live. Angelo wasn't going to let him die easily. He had someone to care enough to protect him with their life.

When the door slammed behind us, I had officially failed my son. I couldn't even die for him like I planned to do. I started to sob uncontrollably. The guard continued to push me down the hallway. I fell to the ground and he struggled to lift me. "Keep moving," he ordered. I just wanted to die. I shuffled my feet slowly. I wanted to be with my son. "Let's go," he said irritated. That's when he grabbed the back of my neck and guided me down the hall. His grip was tight but unfortunately, not tight enough to kill me.

He continued to push me down the hall like I was unwanted cargo then all of a sudden he stopped. He released my neck and naturally, I fell to the ground. Shortly after that, he falls beside me. Blood poured from somewhere on his body. It saturated the sides of my pants. What was happening? Did Ace kill him? When I looked up, Bobby had his hand out, reaching for me to grab. At that very moment, Bobby was like God to me. They came but Bobby was looking at me like he wanted me dead. He's pointing his gun at me, but he doesn't shoot.

"Where are they? Where is Tara?" he whispered loudly, and I pointed towards the pool area. Because he had the gun pointed at me, I thought it was best that I didn't tell him that Tara was in the other room, bleeding out.

It was all my fault. All of this happened because of me. Innocent people are hurt or dead. "How many guards he got?" Bobby asked quick.

"A dozen or so," I managed to say. He still has the gun pointed down at me. I looked over his shoulder for Billy, but I didn't see him. Instead, there was some man with dreads holding an assault rifle. He's looking at me like he wants me dead too.

"If it wasn't for my brother, you'd be dead already," Bobby says to me cold.

"Where's Billy?" I asked.

"He's getting *his* son," he said staring down at me with his finger on the trigger.

"Let's go," his man said and rushed off. Bobby followed behind him.

He came for us. Billy came. I thought to myself. I still heard Bobby's footsteps rushing towards the pool when I heard the first round of gun fire. Was Ace killing my child or were we being rescued?

I ran towards the gun shots. Blood was at the bottom of my shoes and I slid all over the hall, falling only to get back up. I wasn't taking cover until I knew my son was safe. I burst through the door, only seconds after Bobby. The powerful pop and vibrations of the gun shots burst through my ear drums. I fell to the floor, but I hopped back up quickly. I didn't try to dodge bullets. I just ran towards my son. I was using my body as his bullet proof vest.

It was a war zone. Bodies and bullets were dropping everywhere. Thick gun smoke fogged the room. It smelled like someone let off a stink bomb. I chocked and coughed up the debris. I saw Tony grab Taffy and run off. I guess he did understand me. Vinchi had a gun to Ace's head but he didn't shoot him. But, someone shot Ace in the leg. I had a feeling it was Tony because a gun dangled in his hand as he rushed off with his sister cradled

in his arms. Billy was standing on top of the balcony with Angelo and our son. Angelo stood behind him, shielding BJ. She was standing behind him while he fired a rifle, taking out all of Ace's men like it was a sport. When he spotted me, he stopped for a few seconds, considering my safety but then continued to shoot. Bobby backed him up. Between the sounds of the guns, the grunting of people getting shot and the blood squirting and pouring from every direction like rain showers, I fell to the ground and curled up in a ball. I covered my ears and closed my eyes until it all stopped.

37

MONA

Three Days Later…

We're all lucky to be alive but a part of me died a few days ago. So, did a good part of our Badd legacy. We never came this close to death and recovering from it ain't going to be easy. Nothing is going to be the same again.

Thank God Billy and Bobby came to our rescue. If it wasn't for them, all of us Badd wives would be dead and gone. Brip too. He's been at the clinic recovering. The doctor said that he lost a lot of blood, but he gon' be alright. He ain't talking though. At least not to me. He keeps this weird look on his face like all the bad things he's ever done and seen is starting to haunt him. With Taffy gone and all the trauma from thinking Bobby was dead and being shot by Vinchi, Brip ain't gon' be mentally stable enough to resume his position. The boy needs help.

Sometimes I wonder if they only came for him. It wouldn't surprise me if they had. I'm starting to think that us wives were nothing but casualties in all this. Somebody to take a bullet for them.

I'm glad that Bobby is alive. It makes us appear to be strong. Seeing him was like seeing a Badd guardian angel. It threw me completely off guard and in the chaos of it all, I really believed that Bobby had come back to life to save our legacy just like Christ saved the church. But he was always here. I wonder if Brock knew that he was alive? I'm sure it would make him feel better. If it wasn't for Bobby, none of us would be here. Ace was expecting Billy, but he wasn't expecting Bobby. He didn't plan for it and that's why shit went down the way it did.

Through all that gun fire, I looked up for Brock, but I didn't see him. I needed to see him fighting for us. I needed to see him willing to take a bullet to protect me the same way I would him; for me and Vinchi both. And, for the legacy we built but he never came. That broke my heart more than anything. When we got back to the Ranch, Brock took a little cash and packed up and left. No goodbye, no private message for me to wait for him; just gone like none of it meant nothing to him all these years. Or at least that's what they tell me.

With that nut Ace still being alive and no one out hunting for him, I fear for Brocks safety. Vinchi had a chance to pull the trigger but he couldn't do it. Ace ran off and by the time Vinchi finally got the nerve to shoot him, Ace was able to dodge his gun fire. That wasn't hard though because on his way out the door, he grabbed his sister or brother or whatever in the fuck she is and let her take the bullets for him. When he was close enough to the exit, he dropped his sister's body and literally stepped right over her to escape. That man is worse than a monster. He's a natural born demon. And, he's still alive!

Now they got Vinchi in the same prison Billy had been in. I demanded him to be released but they don't listen to me anymore. Nobody does. Not even the guards. It's embarrassing to see my subordinates giving me orders. They say they can't trust Vinchi. But I think they all waiting to fill Brocks shoes.

They are watching me like a hawk too; it's like they trying to figure out what to do with me. They don't trust me either. For the first time ever, I'm scared. I can't believe Brock left me like this. Who knows what's going to happen to me or what they will decide. I can't imagine being put off the Ranch. Joining regular society without my necklace but that just may be my fate. The thought of it makes me sick to my stomach.

Even through all of this, I got my head in the game. I'm an emotional wreck like the next person but we got to keep pushing. When I try to discuss our next move, they just dismiss me. They been having secret meetings without me. My voice is finally gone. Bobby and Billy too weak to run this Ranch. It's all finally going to tumble down.

Bobby got his secret son on the Ranch. Tara is here too. All these years he's been seeing that bitch. I ain't got nothing against her no more though. We all were in danger together. I hate to say it, and Bobby don't want to hear it but that girl ain't gon' survive. Bobby got the doctors trying to patch her back together like they got God like powers. He is threating the doctors, but they can't do nothing to help that girl. Ace sliced her like he was butchering a pig. I'm counting the days before she dies. And that's only going to make things worse for the Ranch. I haven't seen his son since he got here. He still hiding him from us like we wouldn't do nothing more than welcome pure Badd blood. Him thinking otherwise is just plain insulting.

And Billy got his own problems with that baby. That screaming baby. He ain't stop crying since that night. It's like he haunted. Poor thing. He needs his momma. Every child needs they momma. The child been long enough without parents. Billy don't know how to raise no baby and he ain't letting Dalla near him. She risked her life for that child, but he doesn't care. He wasn't going to bring Dalla back to the Ranch. Bobby was going to leave Lera too. If it wasn't for me, neither of them would be here. They both at the clinic recovering but after that, Billy told me they both got to go. Where the fuck they gon' go? Bobby was so pissed that Lera was here, he was going to throw her off the Ranch himself. I literally had to barricade myself in front of him to keep him from doing it. If he wasn't so preoccupied with Tara and his son, Lera wouldn't be here and Dalla wouldn't be alive.

Lera begged him to forgive her, but Bobby looked at her like he hated her. At that moment, I knew Lera had wished she died. Bobby treated that girl cold. But, he was carrying Tara's dying body in his arms. I guess he didn't have room to feel sorry for Lera never the less forgive her for whatever in the fuck she did to him. Billy still pissed at Dalla, but I know he still love her. I can see it in his eyes. But that ain't stopping him from trying to get rid of her. He been avoiding her. He won't let Bobby kill her though, but Bobby wants her locked away in Brock's dungeon. I ain't letting that shit happen though. They Badd Wives. That means something to me and when all this is said and done, I'm gon' make sure it means something to them too. Thank God Taffy is safe. Her brother scooped her up like he was her knight and shining armor, but she still gon' need us. I heard her brother ain't got the sense of a turnip and he can't be trusted to keep her safe. Besides, how long can Taffy survive on the streets with no cash?

I haven't seen Dalla and Lera since we been back. They had me in the prison with Vinchi for a while before they let me go. I'm not sure why they let me go. It kind of freaks me out. Like they planning to kick me off the Ranch too. But, after all we went through, I'm sure they ain't ready for that kind of fight yet. I ain't leaving here without taking what's mine. In the meantime, I'm gon' make right of the wives. But, I got to go see them. I need to speak to Dalla. I have to let her know what they planning to do, and I need her to look after Lera for me. Lera ain't like us. She weak as fuck. She ain't gon' be able to survive. Plus, Dalla is the only person that can help me find out what happened to Brock because Billy and Bobby don't seem to give a fuck.

They didn't seem surprised when I told them Brock was gone either. They said nothing. They didn't even try to look for him. That makes me wonder if they had something do with it. Did Brock leave on his own accord or did they make him disappear? Hell, he may even still be on the Ranch for all I know. With the way they are acting, I'm starting to think something funny is going on. If so, that means me, Vinchi and the rest of our kids are all in danger. But they all forgetting that I ain't no weak ass bitch that's gon' let some nigga discard me like I'm irrelevant. I'm an original Badd wife and even before that, I was not to be fucked with. I ain't letting no weak ass mutha-fuckers phase me out like I never existed. I'm gonna get what's owed to me. Me and my kids. With or without, Brock. This shit is ending but only to start again. If the Ranch belongs to anybody, it's me.

This family officially got bad blood between them, but I can assure you, I ain't going down without a fight!

38

DALLA

I'm watching Lera rock back in forth. She is sitting at the corner of the bed with her hands folded tightly against her chest. She's rubbing her arms like she trying to soothe her pain and staring into blank space. She stopped crying today and stopped talking two days ago. We've been here for three days now and I got a feeling that any moment now, the guards are going to storm in here and throw us out on the streets. She got to snap out of this shit if she plans to survive.

No one has come to see us but the doctor. The first day we got here, I watched the door, waiting for Billy to come in with our son but he never did. There ain't no sign of Mona either but, if it wasn't for her, neither of us would be here. I was alert enough to hear them tell the men to leave us, but Mona wouldn't let that happen. After everything that happened, they didn't have the energy to fight her so here we are. Fuck both of them. Fuck this whole place. If Billy thinks that I'm going to sit back and let him take my child from me, he's got me fucked up. I risked my life for my son and I'm not letting him, nor Ace try to keep him from me.

I get up to stretch my legs. I'm dying to feel the sunlight against my skin. We've been stuck in this stuffy room for too long. There is no window to let light in. I have no sense of day and night. A few more days of this and I'm going to be just as bat shit crazy as, Lera. It bothers me that Ace is still alive. I saw him get away. He always gets away and he never gives up. I don't know what that means for us but it ain't good. Ace came to close to glory to give up. If anything, he's more motivated now than ever to strike again. That means, once I'm off the Ranch, I'm back to running and hiding but I'm tired. I'm so fucking tired.

I stand up on my toes and arch my back into a stretch. It's what I do whenever I think about Ace and being back on the outside. Then I walk towards, Lera. I kneel in front of her, but she doesn't even notice me.

"Lera," I wave my hand in her face and snap my fingers, but she just keeps rocking. Ace raped her. She told me before she let her mind go wherever it is now. Then she told me it was because she killed, Tara. I tried to tell her that she didn't kill Tara, but she started to go crazy. So, I told her that Tara was still alive. I wasn't sure if that was true or not. I hoped I was right because that would mean I wasn't a murder and maybe Bobby would forgive me and hopefully change his mind about killing me. I didn't mean for Tara to get hurt when I took her to Ace.

I also told her that Bobby knew what happened to her and that he killed Ace because of it. I lied again and for a short second, she perked up a little but then started sobbing uncontrollably. The doctor gave her a sedative but when she finally came to, she wasn't coherent.

I wish I had the luxury of going slap crazy and forgetting it all. I know it's morbid but going crazy would be the first mental vacation I had in years, but I can't. I still have work to do. I know there ain't no chance that me and Billy would ever get back together and I'm not wasting my energy on trying but I need my son more than I need air right now. He's all I thought about since I pushed him out. He's all I have in this world and the only good thing that came out of me being a part of the Badds. He's my gift. My reparation.

When I hear the lock on the door click, my heart stops. Is it time for us to go yet? I stare at the door until it opens all the way. My heart is pounding against my chest. I'm not ready to leave yet. I can't be. I have no plan. I always have a plan, but my brain is too fried to think. Once I get back on my feet mentally, then they can let me go but not now.

One of the doctors walks in and I exhale so heavy that I fall back onto the edge of the bed in a slump.

"Good morning," The doctor says. It's morning. That's good to know. "How are you feeling?" He asks me, and I shrug.

"I'm doing better than her," I point to, Lera. At least I think I am but who knows? "She's totally out of it. "What did you give her?" The doctor looks down at Lera and examines her. He flashes a light in her eyes and checks in her ears then takes notes. None of what he's doing seems to be helping. "What's wrong with her? I ask.

The doctor leans up and looks over his notes. He pushes his glasses away from his face and rest them on the top of his head. After a deep sigh, he looks back at Lera and shakes his head like he feels sorry for her.

"PTSD," he says. "Post-traumatic stress disorder," he says to me slowly, so I can understand but I already knew what it meant. "She can snap out of this but she's going to need therapy."

"Did you tell them this?" I said referring to Bobby more than anybody. The doctor doesn't answer my question. He just looks up at me and back down at his clipboard. That's when I knew he did tell Bobby but obviously, Bobby doesn't care. "What about, Tara?" I ask him. He looks up at me again and says nothing.

"I'm going to give her another sedative. It's all I can do until they release her."

"Release her?" I repeat. "When do they plan to release us?" I add myself to the equation.

"It's not my decision and against my recommendation but they're releasing her tomorrow," he says and shakes his head like he doesn't approve. "I have to follow Mr. Badd's orders."

"What! No! He can't do that. She will die out there!" I yell. "What about me? When are they releasing me?"

"I don't know. Try to get some rest. I will be back in a minute with her sedative. I will bring you something to help you sleep" he says and walks out the room. He locks the door behind him.

I can't believe this shit. How could Bobby do this to her? In this condition, Lera isn't just a target for Ace but anyone. I guess this way Bobby can kill Lera without ever touching her. A guilt-free murder. What a fucking coward. I blame myself. I brought Lera into this. When she came to me she was scared and desperate and I took advantage of that. I can't let her get hurt anymore. I get up and try to wrap my arms around her, but she jumps like she's about to freak out, so I let her go.

"Lera, you got to snap out of this shit. You have to!" I start to shake her, but she doesn't even notice I'm there.

I hear the door click open again. The doctor is back quicker than I thought. At that moment, I got the idea to break out and confront Billy and Bobby. I can't let them do this. I can't let them kill this girl. When the door opens wide enough, I prepare myself to charge through the door but to my surprise, it's not the doctor but Mona.

She was the last person on this planet that I ever thought I would be happy to see.

Mona, I exhaled relieved. I didn't know how happy I was to see her until I reached out to hug her. She must have been happy to see me to because she hugged me back. It only lasted a split second before we both started to feel weak and decided to hide it by pulling away from each other. That let me know we still needed each other. I knew why I needed her but why did she need me?

"The doctor said they are releasing, Lera today…" I went right into my spill.

"I know," she said and leaned down to look at Lera. "It's fucked up!"

"How could Bobby do this to her?"

"Tara probably ain't gon' make it through the night," she says to me and my heart stops. "Bobby blames her for what happened to Tara. He blames you too…" she warned. "Bobby wants you dead, Dalla."

I sighed and struggled with my emotions. I wanted to cry. "I didn't know…"

Mona cut me off. "We ain't got time for all that," she didn't care to hear my excuses. "I know you was doing what you had to do, and you didn't mean no real harm. Don't go blaming yourself for none of this shit. That's gon' make you weak and Dalla you need to be strong right now if any of us wives gon' make it out this shit on top."

"What do you mean?" I was confused and burdened by thinking that I had a hand in killing, Tara.

"They letting Lera go which is just as good as killing her in this state but they taking you to prison. And, not the nice one but Brock Dungeon. They planning to keep you there until they find out all they can about Ace and his whereabouts after that…" Mona looked at me and swallowed hard. She didn't have to finish her sentence. I knew what was coming next.

"But, I don't know shit!" I yelled. I just wanted this to be over.

"Look, we ain't got much time but I got a truck outside waiting on you both."

"What?" I was confused.

"I'm getting you off this Ranch. Both of you. But you got to promise you will find Taffy and look after this girl," she said and looked at Lera.

The last time I saw Taffy, she was in Tony's arms. That meant she was safer than any of us. Tony loved Taffy more than life. He would die before he let anything happen to her. Taffy was blessed. But Lera and I were fucked. No one loved us but at least Mona cared.

"I can't," I fell back down into a slump. I was exhausted, but Mona yanked me up.

"You can! And you will!!" she yelled. "We ain't always seen eye to eye but you still a Badd and you strong. I know that now. This girl needs you and so do I," she revealed.

"Why?" I was confused. In my mind, Mona hadn't lost anything. She still had the Ranch and Brock.

"Brock is gone," she revealed and lowered her face to the floor. She looked hurt and embarrassed. She worshiped her husband and for him to abandon her and their family was more than a slap in theface, but a punch.

"What? How? When?" Brock was the Ranch. I couldn't imagine him not being here. "What the fuck are they up to?"

"I don't know. They ain't telling me shit but for some reason, they are keeping me around. That tells me that Brock is still giving orders. Otherwise, I would be out. I need you to help me find him. They got my son in that prison and who knows how long they gon' keep him there. I need to know what happened to Brock."

"He could still be on this Ranch," I told her.

"I know. Do you still have access to the rest of the maps that Billy drew?"

"Yeah, but it's going to be hard to get them."

"I need you to try," she told me.

"What's in it for me?" I had to think of myself. It's how I survived this long.

"Your son and financial security. I plan on giving all you wives enough alimony to start your Ranch if you wish. Just as soon as I can break into the safe. Then, I'm gon' find my husband Brock and exile him and his brothers and take this fucking Ranch!"

Mona had such intensity in her voice, I shook. If anybody could take this Ranch, it was going to be her. She knew all the ends and outs.

"Ok," I said shaking my head in agreement. She knew I believed in her and that made her feel better about everything she was going to have to do to take control over the Ranch.

"One of the guards is helping me pull this off. I need you to drive that truck to my sister Nicchi's house. Here is the address," she handed me an envelope. "I already talked to her, you'll know what to do once you get there."

I took a deep breath and sighed at the thought of being on the run again. Especially with Lera holding me back.

"Ok," I said hesitant.

"Don't worry, Dalla. We gon' come out on top and I put that on my life."

"Look after my son," I said to her trying to fight back tears. I wish I could see him but it's not time yet. It's disappointing but I will wait an eternity for him if I have to.

"You know Badd blood is my business. I'll guard him with my life if I have to," she looked at me sincerely. "Find Taffy. My plan won't work without her. Keep them both safe, Dalla. You all they got."

"And bad blood is all I got…" I said scorned.

"Fuck them niggas!" Mona said harshly. She looked at me and nodded.

After letting what she said to me sink in, I couldn't agree more. "Yea fuck them!" I repeated. We both shared a brief sinister smile.

The guard came and carefully tied tape around Lera's mouth to prevent her from screaming and carried her out of the clinic and to the truck. I cranked up the truck and left without a trace. I watched the Ranch in the rear-view mirror as I sped off.

Hopefully, the next time I see this place, Mona will have burned it to the ground and be holding my son, standing over the ashes finally at peace.

To Be Continued in *Badd Blood*

Badd Blood
Coming Soon

If you enjoyed this book, please leave a review and/or share this story. Author Zee. W can be followed on Facebook @ThisWritersLife and Instagram @AuthorZee.W. Or, by email at authorzee.w@gmail.com